ALSO BY D

THE INQUISITOR

DAVID PENNY

For Lucy

PLACE NAMES

After a number of requests from readers, I am now adding a short glossary of place names at the start of each book for those who would like to know where I am writing about. All locations can be found in modern day Andalucia, Spain.

Gharnatah: Granada
Ixbilya: Sevilla
Malaka: Malaga
Qurtuba: Cordoba

CHAPTER ONE

Thomas Berrington's horse reared as a cart came too fast from an alley and almost spilled him from its back. He was only saved the indignity when Martin de Alarcón grabbed his reins and brought the animal under control. Then the stink hit him like a physical blow and Thomas wrapped his long tagelmust across his mouth and nose.

"What is this?" He stared into a cart where bodies lay tangled together. Mottled dark buboes showed at neck and armpit on some, but not all. Thomas leaned forward, cursing a curiosity he did not welcome but was unable to resist. He had seen the marks often enough before, the first time in Lemster when he knew nothing of the world beyond England.

"This is not for you," said Martin, drawing his robe across his face in copy of Thomas, though the stench from the cart could pass through a stone wall. It was one more grain of chaos in an already chaotic approach to the great city of Ixbilya.

The journey from Gharnatah should have taken ten days, but they had covered the distance in three, a chain of replacement horses allowing them to ride fast and hard. Now, as they approached the sprawling city Thomas's body was sore, his eyes harsh with grit, and he knew he should not be here but had been offered no choice. No realistic choice.

Thomas jerked his reins free of Martin's grip and used his knees to steer the horse toward, not away from, the cart.

"Who are they?" He spoke not to Martin but the man who led the cart. He had fallen, as surprised by the encounter as Thomas, and leaned on the cart as he regained his feet. A tall hat that rose to a point had tipped from his head and he picked it up but did not replace it. A skeletal face with dark hair and shaved cheeks, he looked as if he belonged in the cart almost as much as his charges.

"What's it look like? Dead bodies. Or don't you recognise them?" A voice more cultured than the man's look suggested, but he had clearly fallen on hard times.

"Where are they going?"

"Some to heaven, but most to hell." The man smiled, a glint of insanity in dark eyes. Stained robes covered him to the neck. Thomas couldn't blame him for not replacing the tall pointed hat worn by plague carriers for the heat was fearsome.

He stared at the pile of bodies. The black swellings on most were familiar, but he had no fear of the disease, in the same way as this man showed none. Thomas had suffered a bout in childhood and somehow survived, and was now sure it could not lodge in him a second time. Perhaps this man was the same, or too witless to care, but Thomas sensed an intelligence he would not expect in one performing such a task.

"Where are the bodies to be buried? You know they should—"

"There are pits prepared." The man pulled at the donkey strapped to the cart.

Thomas leaned close, eyes narrowing. "This man did not die of the plague."

"I don't pick them, I only transport," said the man, still walking.

"Come away, Thomas." Martin de Alarcón remained at a distance, reluctant to approach the tainted bodies. Thomas knew Martin meant well but ignored him.

"Stop the cart."

"Who are you to disrupt the business of the city?" said the man.

"I am sent for by the Queen," Thomas said. "She is a friend. And you are?"

The man finally stopped tugging at the donkey. He looked up at Thomas, trying to decide whether to believe him or not. A tall man on a tall horse. At least the horse appeared to confirm his words, a sleek Arabian no doubt stolen during battle, but the man was obviously not impressed and tugged at the donkey again, which twisted its head in defiance but started to trudge on. Thomas pushed his horse ahead of the cart, making him stop once more. He dismounted and climbed on a wheel to see better, leaned across to examine what had first sparked his curiosity. The shirt of one of the dead had been torn, either before he died or as a result of being tossed on the cart with the others. The gash revealed damage to the left side of his chest. A deep incision which had bled profusely, indicating he had been alive when it was inflicted. Thomas pulled at the flesh and pushed a finger inside. The cut was not deep enough to kill, not caused by a knife or sword but something smaller, something with which Thomas was familiar. He had instruments in his own bag which were capable of inflicting such a wound.

"Where did this one come from?" Thomas lifted the head of the man by his dark hair. Brown eyes stared up at him, sightless.

"I draw the cart and people bring out their dead. Who they are isn't my concern. I don't keep records." Even so he glanced at the man's face before shaking his head. "He's on top of the others so he'll be recent. Where from I couldn't say. Dead and Godless is what he is." He turned away, forcing Thomas to jump clear, losing his footing as the cart started up once more. He landed awkwardly and almost stumbled before righting himself. When he looked up Martin was staring at him with an expression of distaste.

"You know you're going to have to wash before going anywhere near the Queen."

"I was planning just that after the journey we have suffered." Thomas remounted his horse and twisted in the saddle to watch the cart disappear around a turn. He tried to forget what he had seen. "How long has the plague been in the city?"

"A month, a little more. It came early in the year then disappeared to wherever it goes. It's worse this time, though. Summer heat, they say."

Thomas wasn't sure if the plague cared much about heat or cold. He didn't know that it cared much about anything other than killing men, women, and children in agonies. He had lost his mother and brother to the disease and almost died himself. The plague was the reason he had left England, the reason he had come to Spain. He could thank it for that, at least.

"Why do you do it?" asked Martin.

"Do what?" They approached an area of flat ground bounded on one side by the city wall, on the other by the river Guadalquivir. A line of charred wooden stakes was set in the ground, cold ashes gathered beneath. Three monks raked at the coals, drawing them into piles. A wooden bridge spanned the river. On the far bank lay two substantial buildings. To the left was a low stone edifice that ran almost two

4

hundred paces. On the right, a towered castle faced the river bank as if to repel invaders. On the near shore ships were drawn up along a stone dock, flying a cascade of flags from a dozen lands. Here and there men worked at loading or unloading cargo, the men too were from many lands, some as dark as the pitch that caulked the hulls, others pale skinned and blond-haired like Olaf Torvaldsson. The thought of the Sultan's general made Thomas think of the man's daughter. Not the blonde one he had once lain beside, but the dark haired one who now shared his bed and would have been his wife by now if Martin hadn't arrived to disrupt everything.

"Why do you always get involved in things that are none of your business?" said Martin de Alarcón.

"How do I know whether it's my business or not if I don't get involved? What are the stakes for?"

Martin frowned, puzzled, and Thomas pointed.

"Oh, those – for the burning of heretics." As if it was the most natural thing in the world.

"What heretics?"

"What heretics is none of your business," said Martin. "Again."

"What do they do with the dead? The ones we saw back there. If they bury them they know to use lime, don't they?"

Martin sighed. "Don't you ever stop?"

"No. Which means it's easier to answer me than not, then perhaps I will stop."

"I've seen little evidence of it so far." But it seemed he was willing to humour Thomas. "They are taken a mile beyond the walls and tossed into a long pit. And yes, as far as I know they use plenty of lime."

They had passed a quarry as they crossed the flat plain leading to Ixbilya, a sudden thrust of the hillside with a sharp wound dug in its side. The city walls were made of

5

stone cut from there. It would be a good source of lime as well.

"The Queen should not be in the city if there is disease," Thomas said.

"If she was not in need of your services she would already be gone. But she cannot travel as she is."

"Then we had best go see her," Thomas said, and saw Martin shake his head.

CHAPTER TWO

Martin de Alarcón led the way toward a small gate set in the city wall. Thomas followed, knowing Martin was aware he would rather not be here. He should instead be lying beside Lubna. Beside *his wife* Lubna. It had been so very close, their marriage, and he tried not to think what Jorge's reaction must have been after the weeks he had spent planning the event.

The cloying heat of the day was beginning to fade as a breeze picked up from the south. Thomas turned in his saddle and stared at the charred stakes, troubled. The wind plucked at cold ashes, lifting them to twist in the air like shadowed wraiths. He opened his mouth to speak then closed it again, for once restraining himself. He didn't consider Martin a friend, not quite, but he knew him better now after the three day journey. It should have taken a week at least for them to travel from Gharnatah, but no more than six days had passed since Martin first left Ixbilya to now return at his side. On the journey, the long journey even if Martin considered it short, they had spoken more than ever before. Unlike many at the Spanish court Martin was no sycophant. He had earned his place through intelligence and cunning. Both a soldier and statesman, he was close to those in power without losing touch with the common man. Thomas had grown to like and trust him even more than he had, yet remained aware he fought for Spain. Which begged the other question – exactly why was Thomas here at his side? But he had no answer, other than a surfeit of loyalty to a woman he had grown to consider a friend despite the difference in their stations.

"How many?"

"How many what?" Martin's voice was hoarse, and he sounded as tired as Thomas felt.

"How many have been burned?"

"It's none of your business." The same words as before.

"What if I want to make it my business?"

Martin coughed a laugh. "Make it what you want and see how far it gets you. It will still be none of your business."

A cry sounded and Thomas lifted from the saddle to look ahead as men, women and children streamed through a gate in the city wall. They spread across the field, making their way toward the killing ground. As the crowd thickened it made progress difficult and Thomas saw it would be impossible to use the gate Martin had planned.

"Is there another way?"

"Of course there is, but it will take longer." Martin looked around, dismounted. "It will be quicker to walk." Without waiting for Thomas he strode away, abandoning his horse where it stood.

Thomas stayed in the saddle, urging his mount forward. Shoulders pressed against his legs. Someone punched his thigh as the crowd grew ever denser, until he had no alternative but to follow Martin's example. He could not abandon his steed as Martin had, at least not abandon what was carried in the two saddle bags hanging across its back.

Thomas reached up and pulled them free, laid the bags across his own shoulders and settled the weight of them. They contained his instruments, medicines, herbs and lotions. He had brought only what he considered essential, hoping he could find whatever else he might need when he arrived. He recalled the packing of them, and the unexpected visit that had led to him doing so. Three days was all that had passed, but it seemed like half a lifetime.

"She's bleeding," Martin had said as he stood in the doorway to Thomas's courtyard as though he had every right to be there. "She fears she will lose another child."

Which was why Thomas had been sent for. Birthing was something he was familiar with. Birth and death, the book-ends of life. He knew that Isabel, Queen of Castile, had lost children before. It was not unusual. Carrying a child to full term could be difficult, and some women were more prone to losing them than others. Isabel, it seemed, was one such. Which is why Thomas had been sent for. A vote of trust, he supposed, even if it was one he would rather not have been cast.

"I am to tell you it is a matter of urgency," Martin had said. "A matter of great urgency." Morning light outlined the al-Hamra atop the hill across from the Albayzin where Thomas's extended house sat. Lubna would be over there with her sisters and her sister's friends, Jorge fussing over the proceedings like a mother hen. A tall mother hen. The planning of the wedding had been taken from Thomas – for which he was grateful – but he was beginning to believe Jorge wanted to steal control of his life as well.

The day before Lubna had been called for by half a dozen giggling women, her sister Helena among them, and taken across the Hadarro river to be bathed, oiled and shaved, to have her skin marked with henna in twisting, ornate patterns. The night of henna was tradition, and

9

Jorge had all of a sudden become a great believer in tradition.

"I'm getting married," Thomas had said, remaining seated. He nodded at another bench, but Martin stayed on his feet. "I'm getting married today."

Martin continued to stare at him. "Do you have water?"

"In the kitchen." When Martin entered the house Thomas returned his gaze to the palace, knowing what needed to be done but trying to put off the decision.

Martin returned with water dripping from his beard, his mouth outlined where the dust had been washed away.

Thomas stood. "I will need an hour."

"I was told to find and fetch you without delay."

"I expect you were, but I still need an hour." Thomas stared at Martin. He wondered, if it came to a fight, which of them would be the victor. Martin, he suspected, but he also knew the man could not be completely sure. Not that it would come to that. The Queen needed Thomas, which gave him some small, some very small, leeway.

"Try to make it less," said Martin at last, perhaps seeing a stalemate would do nothing but waste more time. "I have something I want to do in any case. Where does Boabdil's mother live?"

"He won't be there," Thomas said. "Gharnatah, even this side of it, is not safe for him. Last I heard he was somewhere in the east. Making trouble, no doubt."

"Then it won't take me as long as it might, so you had best hurry."

Now, surrounded by the throng of the city, Martin disappeared among the bodies ahead of him. Thomas tried to settle the saddle bags but failed to find any comfort. From within came the rattle of metal instruments. Instruments he had taken another half hour to select and pack while Martin climbed the steep slope of the Albayzin on some quest he had refused to explain. When they left the house four horses waited outside, two saddled, another tied behind each to be used when the first grew weary. The sound of their leaving had been loud through the cobbled alleys of the Albayzin but they drew little attention. Two more men on horseback, and if anyone recognised Thomas and wondered where he was headed they didn't say.

"How did you sneak into Gharnatah?" Thomas had asked, curious.

"I never sneak anywhere. I rode in. I asked someone where you lived and the first person I stopped told me."

Thomas grunted, admiring the man's bravery, or stupidity. At least Martin had taken the precaution of dressing in the long dark robes favoured by the Moors. Now, in his own city, he was dressed as a Spanish noble, albeit a bedraggled and filthy noble. Thomas pushed through the crowd, ignoring protests, until he caught up with Martin.

"How much farther?"

"Not far, but I would prefer to be without these crowds. They'll thin soon enough when the burnings are done."

Their path took them around the edge of the crowd, close to where fires had burned. As they reached the closest point Thomas turned to watch as fresh faggots of wood were stacked. Rumour had reached Gharnatah of what was happening in parts of Spain. The suspicion and persecution. The cleansing by fire.

"I thought you were a Christian country," Thomas said, knowing it was not his place to judge, but unable to say nothing.

"We are," said Martin. "And what is done here is done in the name of God." His voice was low, as though reluctant to speak in defence of this action. He crossed himself, touched two fingers to his lips.

They passed the bridge leading from the far bank, to be

confronted by a group of individuals tied together, wrist to wrist, ankle to ankle. Held here on the edge of the water out of sight.

"Do you need to make such a spectacle of it?" Thomas heard the disgust in his voice and hoped Martin did too.

"The citizens need to see we protect them."

Thomas spat on the ground. These people needed him, but he wasn't sure he could do what was being asked. Men and women stood with heads bowed, rough tunics thrown over them, each marked with a slash of red, no pattern to the marks other than what they indicated. These were the conversos Thomas had heard of. What made the sight worse was that each knew the fate awaiting them.

"At least we have the mercy to behead our enemies," Thomas said. "This is beyond cruelty."

"You have no understanding of what we do."

"Nor do I wish to."

Martin stopped so suddenly Thomas walked into him. "This is not your country, and these are not your people." Each phrase was punctuated by the thud of a closed fist against his chest. "It is none of your business what is done here. Do what you have come to do and look the other way. We are fighting a war. One that has come too close to home."

The two men stared at each other. Thomas felt an urge to strike out at Martin, but knew it would do no good other than as a release for his anger. He tucked that anger somewhere inside where it could smoulder like the ashes of the fires.

"Take me to the Queen then, away from the stink and these people." Thomas offered one last glance at the figures. Twelve of them, two women among their number, all with downturned faces. A melee of priests and hangers on jostled in preparation for the coming executions. At the rear stood a tall man dressed in black robes. Not a priest, nor executioner. For a moment his gaze caught Thomas's, hesitated, then moved on.

People continued to stream through the gates as Martin led the way to a smaller door set into the wall. He pounded hard and eventually a grill opened and the face of a man appeared.

"This is a private entrance."

"As well I know. I am Martin de Alarcón, on the Queen's business, and I demand entry."

"You could be anyone." The man's eyes scanned Martin from head to foot. "You don't look like you're on the Queen's business." His gaze shifted to Thomas, who stood patient, the saddle bags still across his shoulders like some pack animal.

"If you force us walk to the Macarena gate then I will make it my business to discover your name and be sure to report your assistance." Martin turned to look to where the fires were being re-laid, fresh wood being stacked to form a platform. "I am sure no man can be considered completely innocent these days."

By the time Martin turned back the door was already being unbolted. But whether the man had opened it to allow them entry was brought into question as it swung inward and a group of robed men emerged. Thomas stepped back, a chill of fear running through him. He wanted to run but knew it was too late. The lead figure stopped at the sight of Martin, then his head turned.

Thomas had been aware Abbot Mandana, the rogue priest who had almost killed him and Jorge three years earlier, had been taken back into the fold. He had seen him in the ranks of soldiers scattered across the plain below Ronda before it fell, but he had not been close to the man since hunting him down for the kidnapping of a royal prince. The man's gaze, when it fell on Thomas, was as cold as ever. He looked older, and held his left hand across his chest. Except there was no hand anymore – a wolf had torn it from him.

"What are you doing here?" Mandana's voice was rough, his clothes reeking of smoke.

"He has come to attend the Queen," said Martin.

"She needs no heathen near her."

"Thomas is an Englishman, Abbot. As good a Catholic as you or I."

Mandana made a sound in his throat, half cough, half laugh. His companions moved on, leaving the three of them in a loose triangle. The guard made to close the door but a glance from Martin stayed his hand. Mandana's gaze remained on Thomas, his eyes tracking his face. It was as though spiders crawled across his skin. Mandana smiled to reveal long, yellow teeth. "The sacks suit you, Don Berrington. You always were stubborn as a mule. Try to make no trouble, sir, for troublemakers are not welcome in Sevilla these days."

Thomas pushed past him. It was either that or strike the man. He cursed at the thickness of the crowd that made progress near impossible. He turned to ask Martin if there really was no better way when all at once the pressure eased. More than eased as men, women and children stopped dead in their tracks and a murmur ran through the crowd, the same word repeated. *The Ghost. It is the Ghost.*

Thomas craned, trying to see what had caused the commotion but too many bodies lay between him and whatever had caused them to stop. And then they began to run. Slowly at first and then with a growing clamour, climbing over each other, trampling the weak underfoot in a haste to escape.

"Leave," said Martin, his voice sharp. "Leave here now."

But Thomas had never been a man to turn away from unpleasant sights and pushed forward, progress suddenly easier as the crowd fled. So it was he saw the source of their fear. A man had been hung against the wall. Ropes at his wrists and neck were tied to spikes and the body swung from side to side as if only recently placed there.

Thomas took a step closer, then more, staring up at a figure whose chest was bared and cut in the same way as he had seen the body in the plague cart less than an hour before.

"What is this?" he said. "More of your damned torture?"

But Martin only grabbed his arm and dragged him away, not needing to repeat his words again. *Not your business.*

CHAPTER THREE

By the time Thomas left the Queen's inner chambers he had almost forgotten his encounter with Abbot Mandana and the strange sight of the hanging man. They would come to mind later, once he was alone, but for the moment there were more pressing matters. From behind he heard footsteps and the closing of a door. He didn't turn, not yet, but made his way to a window that spilled late sunlight across the wooden floor, staining it blood red. Which, he considered, was appropriate.

"Do you have the cloth?" He turned, his attention on what the nurse held in her hand. Only when he took it did he raise his eyes to see who had attended Isabel. "You," he said.

A brief smile touched Theresa's lips. "Did you not recognise my voice, Thomas Berrington?"

"It has been some time." But something of her tone had been familiar, and had he not been so distracted by Isabel he might have realised who the voice belonged to.

It would have been inappropriate for him to lay his own hands on the Queen, or even to be afforded sight of her body. Instead he had stood behind a screen and issued instructions to the women beyond. This woman amongst them. This woman who he had almost laid hands on three years before when they shared the duty of attending to Prince Juan, Isabel's only male heir.

Thomas turned his attention back to the cloth, reaching for it. White linen, stained red with royal blood. "She still bleeds, then."

"Not so much, but yes, she still bleeds."

"And the child moves? You are sure?"

"I am as good at my job, Thomas, as you are at yours. Yes, the child moves. Another boy, I am sure."

Theresa appeared not to have aged. If anything she looked younger, a little slimmer, her auburn-red hair bright with the sheen of health.

"I need to go in search of supplies," Thomas said. "Marjoram, fennel, valerian root. Lavender, of course, but that is everywhere. Feverfew and black cohosh if I can find them. Do you know of somewhere?" Thomas's gaze rose to meet Theresa's and he felt a jolt of arousal at the hunger he saw in hers. He suppressed it, knowing he would have to work with this woman over the next weeks until the Queen recovered. Or lost her child, the supposed boy.

"I am meant not to, but yes, I know. I will provide directions. You will find most in the narrow alleys east of the palace, where the Jews live. There is a woman there who is much prized for her skill in such matters." Theresa shook her head. "Some people continue to believe in magic rather than place their trust in God's mercy."

Thomas held her gaze. "And you?"

"I believe in you. If you say these herbs are needed then I will tell you where to find them." She tilted her head to one side so thick hair covered one eye. The move made Thomas uneasy. "Can you cure her?"

"I would prefer to have examined her myself, but–"

Thomas held a hand up as Theresa started to speak. "No, I trust your abilities. It is only that I would have liked to see for myself. I know such is not possible, but even so..." He glanced down at himself. He had scrubbed his hands and face but beneath the robe his body was coarse with grit. "I need to bathe. Send me those directions and I will do my best."

"Then she will recover," said Theresa. "The child too. Shall I ask for a bath to be sent to your rooms?"

"If you can."

Another smile. "And wash you as well, if that is your wish. You turned me down once, remember, but the offer remains. You know it does, do you not?"

"I was to be married less than a week ago."

Theresa laughed. "Is that meant to be a polite refusal? What has being married to do with anything? Particularly for one such as you. Is it true that in Granada a man may take many wives? I have heard rich men there have concubines. Do you have a concubine, Thomas?" She placed a hand against his chest. "Would you like one?"

"What I want is to wash the stink of travel off me, to dress in clean clothes, and in the morning I will go in search of the herbs I need. Nothing else concerns me."

Theresa left her hand in place a moment longer, the pressure of it having no effect now as Thomas thought of Lubna, who would be nursing her disappointment alone in Gharnatah. And of the news she had broken to him the morning before she left for the palace. Isabel was not the only woman in his life to carry a child.

"Then I will send a note for you." Her hand slid away and she began to turn.

"Wait. Do you travel with the Queen now? The last time I saw you we were in Qurtuba and now you are here in Ixbilya—"

Theresa offered a laugh. "Where?"

"Sevilla, then." Though Thomas believed the word sounded almost the same. He would have to remember to use the Spanish pronunciation, as he would the Spanish names for the herbs he sought. "Are you close to her?"

"She trusts me," said Theresa, starting to turn away again

"One thing more," Thomas said, and she turned back, a look of impatience on her face that surprised him. She was not the same Theresa he had once known. Something had changed in her, she carried some sadness that had not been a part of the woman he had known.

"Have you changed your mind about my offer?" But it was not said to tease, she was merely playing the part expected of her.

"When I came into the city there was a man hanging from the wall," Thomas said. "And the crowd were calling out a name. The Ghost. Over and over."

He watched Theresa's expression stiffen.

"Ignore them, it is superstition, nothing more."

"The body wasn't superstition. And I saw another with the same wounds in a plague cart. What is going on in the city?"

"Pestilence, nothing more. Some fool finds it amusing to occasionally display the bodies and the mob have given him a name. Ignore it, Thomas. You are here to care for the Queen and nothing more."

He watched as she finally made her escape, watched until she disappeared. He wiped a hand across his face, and wondered if he could save the life of the child Isabel carried. He would do his best, but sometimes his best was not good enough. And he knew she had lost other children early. It was said she had difficulty carrying to full term. Which would be... Thomas shook his head. He should have asked. Not seeing Isabel himself he had no idea how far along she was in her pregnancy. Long enough for the child to move, which would make it three months, more likely four. But what if it was seven months? That would make a difference to his treatment. Thomas knew he had distracted himself with his questions about what he had seen. It had been a mistake and he went to the door Theresa had used, wanting to ask the more important questions he had neglected.

He passed through a series of rooms without paying them heed. They were each there to offer protection to the inner sanctum where Isabel, the Queen of Castile, lay nursing her pain and fear. The first room was empty, and Thomas walked faster, passing through two more before he heard voices, recognising Theresa's, plus that of a man. The words were muffled until he used a final door, and then they cut off abruptly.

Both people turned toward him, only Theresa familiar at first. The man was tall and thin. He was dressed as a priest in a long dark robe, the hood thrown back to reveal luxuriant hair that would more suit a noble than a man of God. His face was clean shaven. Thomas frowned, trying to place where he had seen him before.

"You are the other doctor?" the man said.

"Are you Isabel's priest?" Thomas had heard tell of her confessor, but if this was he then he was not what he had expected.

The man smiled. "A confessor of sorts, but I am like you, Don Berrington. Before you were sent for I was the Queen's physician." The voice was cultured, with only a slight accent. Thomas listened hard for a note of hostility but found none.

"For how long?" Thomas asked.

"Since she came to Sevilla, so two months." The man glanced at Theresa, a brief flicker of his eyes, but it was enough. Theresa made a curtsey and moved away. "Come, you must be tired and hungry, let us sit together and discuss the Queen and what treatment you intend for her." Still nothing there, nothing at all.

Thomas followed the man, hanging back to observe him, a sense of confusion about their encounter. He recalled the last physician to the Queen, the one he had met in Qurtuba, and the enmity shown him then. They moved along corridors, any servants they encountered standing with downcast eyes until they passed. Thomas saw this man was treated with the same deference as a noble, yet he was not, which told something of the honour afforded him.

They came to a small chamber set with a table, food and wine already laid. The man indicated a chair.

"This was to be my supper, but there is enough for us both, I am sure. Sit, Don Berrington, and forgive me in advance. I have a thousand and one questions for you and fear I will inundate you with them, so let us eat first." The man poured dark red wine into fine crystal goblets before taking his own seat. Despite wanting to bathe Thomas took the offered chair, the food sparking his own hunger. They had eaten little and badly on the journey, and the meal laid before him sweetened the air with the aroma of familiar spices. He waited for the other man to start, but when he sat without speaking Thomas reached out and pulled the leg from a fine capon and bit into it, wiping grease from his beard.

"You have the advantage of me, sir."

A smile. "I doubt that. My name is Samuel Ibrahim. Like you I trained at the infirmary in Malaka. A fine city, and cooler than Sevilla."

"You are a Jew?" There was no judgement in Thomas's words. Jewish physicians were renowned throughout Spain for their skills, and he was pleased Isabel had seen fit to appoint one.

"I was, but now I am a good Catholic."

Thomas wondered if this change was a means of furthering Samuel's career or a genuine conversion. He tore a chunk of soft bread free and dipped it into a spiced sauce, used his fingers to take one of the pieces of marinated pork. He noticed that Samuel helped himself to small strips of capon, bread and beef, but ignored the pork.

"Have you been treating the Queen?" Thomas asked.

Samuel nodded. "I believe I have stemmed the worst of her bleeding, and Theresa tells me the baby still moves, so there is hope."

"How long until her time?"

"The child will be born before the turn of the year. A month either way. You know how it is, Don Berrington, short of asking a man and women when last they laid together it is impossible to be more accurate. And particularly when that couple are King and Queen of Spain."

Thomas worked the timings, aware that when he had last met with the Queen on the plain below Ronda she must have been carrying the child, possibly not even aware of it herself. Ronda had fallen at the beginning of May, so Isabel may not have noticed the lack of her monthly bleeding. Which raised a thought.

"This problem she has," Thomas said, "is it the first time she has bled?"

"The first time this pregnancy. She has done so before and lost the infant as a result, which is why you were sent for."

Thomas listened for any hint of resentment but heard none, unless it was because they spoke Spanish and he missed it, but he thought not. He found he was growing to like this Samuel Ibrahim, even if he wasn't being entirely honest.

"How have you treated her?" He expected Samuel to say he had bled Isabel. It is what most Spanish physicians would do, a universal panacea that frequently caused more harm than good. Thomas bled the occasional patient, but only for a specific reason such as a surfeit of blood.

Samuel glanced across the food arrayed on the table. He reached out and speared a chunk of the pork with his knife and popped it into his mouth. His eyes stayed on Thomas as he chewed, as if aware of what had been on his mind. The scene that afternoon beside the river was testament enough to how dangerous being a Jewish converso could be in this new Spain, and Samuel was making a point: he had left his old life behind. The thought sparked a connection. Samuel had been the man at the burnings, standing back from the others. Thomas was sure it had been him, but did not know the significance of it.

"I have raised her feet, at times uncomfortably so, but the Queen does not complain." Samuel continued, unaware of what Thomas was thinking. "She never complains. I have made potions containing fennel and lavender, and I believe they have slowed the loss of blood. I have also had the nurses manipulate her both externally and internally."

"And she has not objected?"

"She is an excellent patient. What would you do, Thomas? What am I missing?"

"There are other herbs I would use. I plan to search them out in the morning." He offered Samuel a look. "Theresa tells me there are places to the north, in the Jewish quarter. Perhaps you would like to accompany me? I intend to leave early so I can make up my liquors by noon."

"And you will teach me about them and their uses?" said Samuel.

"It is unusual to find a physician in Spain willing to learn. It will be a pleasure. Come find me soon after dawn. My rooms are–"

Samuel held up the hand holding his knife. "I know

where your rooms are. Better accommodation by far than I am offered, but that is as it should be."

Thomas stood. "I saw you earlier today," he said, "on the river bank where the burnings take place."

Samuel smiled. "I wondered if you would mention that. I saw you too, though I could not be sure it was you then."

"What were you doing there?"

A shake of the head. "Nothing that concerns the palace or our working together. I… assist at times. But I would rather not talk of such things, not here."

Thomas was reluctant to drop the matter without discovering more, but knew it could wait until tomorrow. For now, he needed to clean himself, and to sleep.

Samuel rose and offered his hand, which Thomas took.

"There is someone else you will have to meet soon," he said. "The Queen's spiritual advisor. He objected to your being summoned, but she was adamant and, for once, overrode his wishes. He will want to talk with you." Samuel smiled. "You may need to convince him that as an Englishman you are a good Catholic despite living among heathens."

CHAPTER FOUR

Thomas woke to the touch of a hand on his shoulder. He sat up fast, grasping the wrist of the man who leaned over him. He had been dreaming of another hand, that of Theresa on him, except she and Lubna, Helena too, had been mixed together so he could not be sure who he dreamed of. It took a moment to shake off the lingering sensations that flooded his body.

"I was asked to wake you at dawn, sir." The man pulled his wrist free of Thomas's grip and stepped out of reach. "I have brought hot water and food. Both are on the table in the other room."

Thomas waited until the man had withdrawn then slipped from the high bed and found a linen robe to cover himself. He ate quickly then washed himself thoroughly, despite having bathed the evening before. Satisfied he was as clean as he could make himself he returned to the bed chamber and dressed as he would have at home, linen pants and shirt, a loose cotton robe and leather sandals. Already the heat of the day had invaded the room and he knew he would need to keep himself covered if he was to be effective.

As he passed through the palace door nearest the Cathedral and entered the wide cobbled yard Samuel pushed himself from the wall where he had been waiting and fell into step beside Thomas.

"Theresa sent me a list of who can help," Thomas said, reaching into a pocket and withdrawing a slip of paper he passed to Samuel. "Do you know these streets?"

Samuel glanced at the paper, scanning it while they continued to walk. The early sun threw long shafts of light and shadow across the square fronting the massive Cathedral. Thomas recalled being told it had been designed to be the most wondrous place of worship in the whole of Christendom, a message to the defeated Moors who once ruled the city. He had heard a tale about the original chapter members, who were said to have stated: *Let us build a church so beautiful, so grand, that those who see it finished will think us mad.* Well, if that was their intent it certainly met the brief, he thought. Men worked high on wooden platforms as they laid tiles on the domed roof. Sometimes Thomas questioned the wealth spent on such shows of power, but doubted the gold would be spent any wiser if used on some other pointless show of vanity.

"Yes, I know these places," said Samuel. He handed the slip of paper back to Thomas, who returned it to the inner pocket from which it had come. "They are not the safest in the city, but I am known, and you do not look like a man of influence, so we should be able to complete your task without being accosted."

Samuel touched Thomas's arm, turning him toward a maze of narrow alleys that led away north into a jumble of buildings. Almost as soon as they entered the sun was lost. Walls rose three or more stories high, only a narrow sliver of pale blue showing there was a world beyond.

The temperature dropped, but still remained warmer

than Thomas was comfortable with. He could only imagine how hot the city might become as the day progressed. Within the palace it was cool at all times, and was the best place for the Queen to lie. Thomas wondered if she would hold the growing child within her or not. He knew that, despite what few skills he possessed, there was little he could do to influence the outcome. Give him a man with a sword wound, a broken leg, or clouding of the eyes, and he was sure of his abilities. The interior of the body, at least while it remained alive, was a darker science to him. He had delivered children using the knife – had saved the life of the old Sultan's youngest son that way, but in that instance Safya was already dead. Most of the women he worked on in such a manner did not survive. It was brutal, bloody work, only carried out when not to do so meant the loss of both mother and child. It reminded him of what some in al-Andalus named him: *qassab*, butcher. A reputation earned due to his apparent coldness to the suffering of others. So be it, Thomas thought. Pain was fleeting, even his own, and he had suffered much pain and lived through it. If a life could be saved he considered pain a price worth paying, even though he knew others disagreed.

The alleys Samuel led them through turned and twisted. Occasionally they passed through small squares where some remnant of the city's lost Moorish past remained as fountains splashed water and rills cut through limestone tiles. The people of this area moved slowly, their voices low. Thomas was sure those they passed must reside here, for it was not a place a casual intruder would be welcome. He was aware of glances cast in his direction, but Samuel was obviously known.

"These streets have not changed in centuries, have they?" Thomas said, his own voice as low as those he passed, something about the place both calming and disturbing.

"Should the Moors ever return, which they will not, there is much they would recognise. Less so in other parts. Why pull down beauty only to replace it with ugliness?"

"They did that with the Cathedral."

"Of course, because they had to, and the Cathedral is also a thing of beauty. But here... well, few Spaniards enter far into the barrio." The alley widened into a square, larger than some they had passed. Here stalls had been set up and a crowd was gathered to purchase fruit, vegetables and meat, although unlike the rest of Spain outside al-Andalus no pork was on display, reminding Thomas of Samuel's deliberate show the evening before, confirming the conversion from his former faith.

They passed a closed doorway where a rough slash had been daubed across in red. It was not the first Thomas had seen – at home in England they had used the same mark to identify a plague house. Except here the daubing was rushed, as if whoever made it wanted gone from the place. Or had many other houses yet to mark.

"Plague," said Samuel, unable to know Thomas's thoughts. "All who lived here have been taken by the pestilence, the house marked as unclean."

"Don't the homeless seek shelter in such places?"

"Some, yes. But of those who do many die. Few are willing to take up the offer of a new house so readily anymore."

"Is what I seek much further?" Thomas asked, aware the Queen remained in her bed, feet elevated, waiting for something he may not be able to offer.

"We will find Belia Orovita here," Samuel said. "She sells herbs and potions in that corner." He pointed, but other stalls hid whatever he was trying to indicate. "She is the best herbalist in Sevilla, possibly in the whole of Spain."

"I have a little knowledge," Thomas said.

"Not like Belia does." Samuel pushed between a group selecting the best fish, which to Thomas appeared suspiciously fresh until he remembered the small fleet of ships pulled up at the dock.

The stalls thinned as they approached the far corner. Here the goods were clothing, bolts of cloth, carved boxes and ornaments. One small table had a rack on which stringed instruments hung. The owner sat at a stool plucking on gut strings, the sound both strange and redolent of the surrounding city.

Beyond, in the corner beside an open doorway sat a single straight-backed chair next to a small table. A woman sat with her back to them but turned when Samuel called her name, a smile already on her face at recognition of his voice. Thomas stopped, surprised. He had expected someone older, and far less beautiful. Previous sellers of the herbs he now sought had always been crones, their knowledge etched into every line of their face. It seemed to him the kind of expertise they possessed was dying with each of them, the raw materials becoming more and more difficult to obtain. This woman was not one of that kind. She was tall, with dark hair falling along her back. Her skin was dusted the colour of honey, her eyes dark pools. She was not Spanish, but neither was she Moor. He suspected she came from a place far from Spain.

"Belia, this is the famous surgeon Thomas Berrington. He needs some of your products."

The woman cast a glance toward Thomas that made it clear whatever Samuel might say she reserved judgement on just how famous he might be. Or how skilled.

"What is it you wish, sir?" Her voice was soft, with an accent he couldn't place. The name identified her as a Jew, but her features reminded him more of North Africa. Her clothing too resembled that worn by Berber women, long and flowing, but on her fashioned of fine cotton rather than hemp or linen. A long scarf hung at her neck, but her head was uncovered.

"I will leave you with Belia," said Samuel before Thomas could answer. "I have people I must visit while I am here."

Thomas caught Samuel's sleeve as he turned away. "Come back for me when you are done. I have no hope of finding my way to the palace on my own."

Samuel smiled. "I will return in an hour. More than enough time for both of us to attend to our business. And if you finish sooner I am sure Belia will recommend a place you can get something to eat and drink."

When he had gone Thomas reached into his robe and pulled out a clutch of papers, each torn from a larger sheet the night before as he had searched his memory for anything that might help the Queen. He had started writing them in Arabic, then remembered where he was and rewrote them using Spanish. But looking at Belia he suspected she might have understood them in either language. He laid the pages on the table, running a hand across them to smooth the creases.

Belia looked at the papers then turned to disappear through an open doorway. Thomas thought she had abandoned him, but after a short wait she reappeared with a second chair and set it down for him. She took her own and looked up, waiting until Thomas sat.

Belia leaned close and turned some of the slips of paper. The faintest smile crossed her lips. "Do you always carry paper and something to write with?"

"Not always, but mostly if I can, yes. Why, is it so strange? A man cannot hold all the knowledge he acquires in his head." Thomas arranged the papers into some kind of order of importance. He doubted he would obtain everything he needed, but even a little would prove useful. "Udara leaves," he said, turning to his task. "And feverfew, black cohosh…" He read out the herbs and tinctures he sought, pushing each piece of paper aside when finished with. When he looked up Belia was staring at him without expression, all amusement gone from her eyes.

"You know of these?" she said. "And you know of their uses? Who is it you treat?"

"That I cannot say."

"You are a friend of Samuel, so perhaps I can guess. But do not worry, the Queen's secret will be safe with me. Is there much bleeding?"

Thomas returned her stare. He had told her nothing, but she knew who Samuel worked for, and it seemed she knew of the Queen's condition, too. In turn he knew he needed this strange woman who, despite her attitude, he was warming to. It was her knowledge. Belia was skilled. She had seen immediately why he needed the herbs. Thomas was aware of his own nature, and how he was drawn to those who sought and nurtured knowledge, as Lubna did. Though sometimes he wondered what it was that drew him to Jorge.

"Do you have them? Not all, perhaps, but some, and the Udara most of all. I know it is difficult to obtain, but–"

Belia held up a hand and he stopped talking.

"I have Udara. Only a little, but enough for your needs. It is expensive, though."

"Money is not an issue."

"No, I suppose it is not. Some of what you ask I do not have here but may be able to obtain if you need it." She leaned forward, hands resting on the table. Thomas noticed her fingers, the length of them, and saw henna patterned on her skin, twisting away along her arms. "Some of these are useless, others dangerous. I will tell you exactly what you need, but you must exchange information with me first."

"I cannot tell you who–"

Once again her raised hand stopped him.

"You have no need to. I know who, though neither of us will ever mention the name or position of this individual again. You treat a woman in her mid-thirties, a woman who has birthed several healthy children already but has also lost others before their time. A woman who bleeds." Her eyes lifted from an examination of the scraps of paper to capture Thomas's. "How long before her confinement?"

"The end of the year."

Belia nodded. One of those long fingers reached out, hesitated, then pushed some of the papers to one side. The others she gathered together.

"I will fetch what you need. I have all of these, and one or two other items that will be of use." She rose, tall and slim, waiting. "I can put together what you need, and then you can pay me, but only when the – when your patient has recovered." She tilted her head to one side. "Unless you wish me to show you where to get that food and drink Samuel mentioned, while I prepare the mixtures for you?"

"I would rather wait here, if I can," Thomas said.

A flicker of a smile.

"I wish to learn from you," he said, which was the truth, and this time the smile Belia offered carried a hint of pride.

CHAPTER FIVE

The bag of mixtures Belia had sold him knocked together in his bag as Thomas walked through alleys which grew narrower and narrower, until at last a square ahead opened out and he stepped into sunlight. Heat wrapped around him and he raised his tagelmust, aware he must appear an odd sight in Ixbilya, but perhaps less so here. He saw no-one in the square, but heard voices emerging from a shaded court-yard from which also came the splash of water. He made his way to the house he believed to be the right one and rapped on an open door. The voices stilled, then came a slow slap of sandals on marble and Thomas stepped back, an involuntary gasp coming from him.

The man that caused the reaction stopped in the door-way, as surprised as Thomas, but it was he who spoke first, in fluent Arabic.

"Have you pursued me here deliberately? Do you wish to dash me down even lower, or have you come to kill me this time?"

"I – I was looking for someone else." Even as he spoke Thomas knew the words made no sense. Abraham al-

Haquim, ex-governor of the now defeated city of Ronda, supposedly impregnable until this man's actions had at least in part caused its fall, had no doubt made his way to someplace he and his skills might be welcome. And no city in the whole of Spain had a larger population of Jews than Ixbilya, not even Gharnatah itself.

Al-Haquim remained silent, waiting for Thomas.

"I am not looking for you, Malik. I seek a colleague, a physician by the name of Samuel Ibrahim. I was told I could find him at this house." He watched al-Haquim, aware this meeting could prove dangerous. The man at least partially blamed Thomas for his disgrace and exile from Ronda. The truth was different, but Thomas had no intention of telling him he had pleaded for his life with Fernando, who had wanted the Governor executed in the most brutal manner for what he had done. Fernando was a fierce general, but continued to hold to the old ways of chivalrous combat. Al-Haquim's panicked response of hurling live Spanish prisoners from the three hundred foot cliffs of Ronda had set him beyond such mercy until Thomas intervened. Not because he felt anything for the man, but because he knew that to create more martyrs would only extend the fighting. So it was that Abraham al-Haquim had ridden from Ronda astride a fine stallion.

"Well, you have found him, it seems." Al-Haquim said. Someone moved behind him and Thomas peered into the shade, trying to make out who it was, fearing a soldier, aware he had come to this place unarmed. "I always considered you a lost soul," said al-Haquim, "but this is too much a coincidence. Tell me, why are you really here? Have you come to inflict yet more suffering on me?"

"I speak the truth, Malik." Thomas continued to use the honorific not due the man in hope of winning him over.

Two figures sat in the shadows, neither recognisable

against the fierce light of the sun. One rose and came forward. "It is my fault, Abraham, I was meant to return for him. I left him with Belia and have been gone too long."

Al-Haquim half turned. "Is it true you know this man, Samuel?"

"The Queen sent for him, so of course I know him."

"He is allowed access to the palace, yet still you deny such to me?"

Samuel made a sound, not quite a sigh of exasperation, but Thomas heard such in the exhalation of breath. "It is not mine to gift, as well you know. And I do what I can. Thomas is known to both King and Queen. Some even say he is friend to both. Perhaps you should direct your request to him, he may have more success than me."

"I doubt you have even asked," said Abraham, and Thomas heard the same whine of privilege in his voice that had been present in Ronda – a man risen beyond his abilities, a man of thwarted ambition without the skill to further it. If Thomas thought he had even the slightest chance of finding his way back here he swore he would avoid this house in future.

"Perhaps I will get Thomas to ask the Queen," said Samuel. He slid past al-Haquim and came into the small plaza. The sun was almost overhead, only narrow patches of shade clinging to the base of buildings.

Samuel touched Thomas on the arm. "Come, I have something else to show you before we return to the palace."

As they reached the alley on the far side of the plaza Thomas hesitated once he hoped he was obscured by shade and glanced back. Abraham al-Haquim remained in the doorway watching them, an incongruous figure still dressed in the finery of a Governor of Ronda, a town no longer ruled by al-Andalus. In the moment before he turned away the third figure who had remained hidden approached and stood beside al-Haquim's shoulder and a sound escaped Thomas.

"Are you unwell?" Samuel stopped and placed a hand on Thomas's arm. "Is it the heat?"

"You know that other man as well, do you?"

Samuel raised his gaze. "The Abbot? He and Abraham work together."

"Odd bedfellows," Thomas said.

"We live in odd times."

"Was he part of the business you came here to attend to?"

"Al-Haquim is an influential man."

"Is, or has made himself? He cannot have been here long, four months at most. How has be grown influential in so short a time?"

Samuel offered an impatient glance and started away. "Does it matter? Accept that he is. The Jews of Spain support each other. You don't see us fighting amongst ourselves, do you? We serve our masters and keep to ourselves. Even a converso such as myself is subject to suspicion. Abraham seeks to protect us all, whichever God we follow."

When they entered the Cathedral plaza Thomas stopped in surprise, for they had been walking less than a quarter hour. He cursed himself for becoming distracted by his own thoughts, knowing he could never find al-Haquim's house again. It was lucky he would never want to.

The heat of the day was untempered here by any shade. It beat against his head with a relentless pressure.

"Does the Queen know who you visit?"

"What the Queen knows is none of your business. Do what you were brought here to do and go home." An angry glance. "And if you mention this matter to her I will hear of it and make it my job to have you disgraced."

So you may slip once more into your position as her physician, Thomas thought? But he did not speak the words aloud. He wished he had not angered Samuel, for he had started to like the man. Except he had lied to him, even if only a lie of omission, and the reason for that was something to be thought on.

"What do you do for them? For him, Mandana?"

"Protect our people," said Samuel.

"Your people? Mandana isn't your people. And I've never known him to protect anyone."

"You are a stranger here and do not understand what goes on. I do."

"I am willing to listen," Thomas said, still annoyed at Martin de Alarcon's dismissal of his questions when they arrived. "Explain to me what happens here, and what concern it is of yours."

Thomas wondered if he would receive another rebuttal, or the start of some answers. He knew he shouldn't care what happened here. It was not his city. But he had never been able to quell his curiosity.

Samuel was staring ahead as they passed the last buttress of the Cathedral, the palace lying beyond the wide square, when a scream halted them both in their tracks.

Thomas turned, searching for the source of the sound, a wild cry that augured no good. He looked up, wondering if one of the workmen clinging like spiders to the Cathedral roof had fallen, but they appeared not to have heard. And then a man came running fast from within a wide door and almost knocked Thomas from his feet. He grabbed him, holding tight as he tried to pull free.

"What has happened?"

"Let me go, damn you. Let me go."

"Not until you tell me, is someone injured?"

The man realised only a reply would allow him to escape. "It is the Ghost. He has taken another."

That name again. Thomas looked beyond to the open

doorway, and the moment he was distracted the man pulled away and ran hard across the square.

"Come away," Samuel said, tugging at Thomas's sleeve.

Thomas pushed him away and started across the cobbled stones. He heard Samuel follow, still urging him to ignore the disturbance, but he did not look around. As he came closer to the door he heard a woman sobbing. The same woman whose scream had stopped them?

Inside his eyes saw only darkness, slowly adjusting to glimpse burning candles, an altar, and arranged on it – for that was the only way he could interpret what he saw – the body of a man, his torso uncovered to reveal a bloody gash in his chest, the same wound he had witnessed not a day before. The woman who had screamed sat on a side bench, head in her hands, and Thomas went to her.

"Do you know him? Is it your husband?"

She glanced up, face wet with tears, and shook her head. "I came... I came to light a candle for my husband, but that is not him. My... no, it matters not. Only this man matters now." She rose to her feet, swaying, then sat again and put her head down.

Thomas glanced at Samuel, who had entered behind him. He nodded at the woman, then went to examine the dead man. For dead he had to be. Nobody could survive the wound inflicted on him.

The body lay across the steps leading to the altar. Feet on the stone floor, head on the top step. Arms flung wide as if to better reveal the damage to his flesh. Thomas knelt, leaning close to observe, not yet ready to touch but knowing he would soon. Blood ran fresh from the wound, marking it as recent. He angled his head, then stood and brought a candle to shed more light.

The wound was deep. It had opened the chest cavity wide enough for a hand to slip inside. Thomas placed the candle near the body and only now did he allow his hands to test how recent death had come.

There was no sign of rigor, and a warmth continued to cling to the flesh. Thomas rolled up his sleeve and slipped his fingers into the wound. Yes, still warm. The man had been dead less than an hour, perhaps much less. Curious, Thomas explored deeper, stopped short when he discovered an absence within the chest. The man's heart was missing. He probed deeper, hand sliding past wet organs in search of that which kept a man alive, but the heart was gone. Taken. He stood, wiping the gore from his hand on his robe as he turned. The wound reminded him of those he had seen the day before, in the cart, and the man hanging on the city wall, but this time slightly different. Unless he did not remember right. He had more chance to study this body than the others. Three deaths in less than twenty-hour hours? Why was the city not in uproar? Or perhaps it was and he had not been here long enough to recognise such.

The woman had gone and Samuel now sat on the bench, his head to one side as if he had been watching Thomas's examination with curiosity.

"This is not who the man meant, is it?" Thomas said. "A dead body? A ghost?"

Samuel glanced up to meet Thomas's eyes. He shook his head, little more than a shudder.

"This man must have died in unspeakable pain, and not long since. Someone would have heard his screams." He looked beyond Samuel. "Who was the woman? You should have kept her here, I might have wanted to question her."

"She is no-one," said Samuel. "A poor soul lighting a candle for another lost soul, nothing more. She would know nothing." He glanced at Thomas's right hand where blood-stains still showed. "Why did you do that?"

"Do what?"

"Thrust your hand into him. He is obviously dead. What did you learn beyond that?"

"I learned his heart has been taken."

"And that tells you what?"

"It tells me a great deal."

Samuel coughed a laugh. "When I heard you were coming to attend the Queen I made enquiries. I needed to be sure you were the right man."

"I am."

"Yes, it is what everyone told me. You are the best physician in the whole of Spain." The statement only served to increase the frown on Samuel's brow. "But they also told me you meddle in matters that are none of your business. That death is attracted to you. Almost as if you encourage it."

"I save lives, I do not take them unless there is no alternative."

"Not you, perhaps, but some men carry bad luck with them. Are you one such, Thomas Berrington? A harbinger of death?"

Thomas shook his head. "We need to know who this man is. Only then might we discover who took his life."

Samuel stood and echoed Martin de Alarcón's words. "It is none of your business. Leave this for the Hermandos." He turned away, stopped half way to the doorway. "It is not the first such death but hopefully it will be the last discovered."

Thomas watched him walk away, called out before he reached the door. "Who is this ghost?"

Samuel stopped. His shoulders hunched, and then he turned, his face obscured by the brightness beyond.

"It is a name given by the mob, by thoughtless men and women, a name not worthy even of children."

"The Ghost," Thomas said, giving the word the same emphasis he had heard when the man had spoken it. "How long has be plied his trade?"

But Samuel only turned away and was gone.

Thomas glanced behind. He had gathered all the information he could, and Samuel was no doubt right. The local Hermandos would seek out this man's killer. And it truly was not his business. His business lay in the palace waiting on him to heal her, and *that* was what mattered most.

CHAPTER SIX

The facilities were not as Thomas would have wished, but they would suffice. His assistant was not the one he would have liked either, but he too would suffice. Thomas thought of Lubna and wondered what she was doing, imagined how angry she must be with him. He wanted to think of her more, longer and deeper, but the Queen waited for the lotions and liquors he was producing so he set his own needs aside for hers.

"Tell me what you are doing, and what this is for." Samuel stood close, too close had Thomas not been focused on his work. He had not wanted the man here, not after where he had found him, who his companions were. And then there was the matter of the dead man in the Cathedral. Thomas had more questions but knew they would have to wait until later. Samuel was not without skill or knowledge, and the fact he asked questions of his own showed he wished to acquire more – a trait Thomas approved of.

"This mixture contains the leaves and bark of the Uduru plant native to the forests of Africa. It is difficult to find, but your friend Belia has great knowledge and a long reach."

"Not a friend," said Samuel. "But it is true she has knowledge. Sometimes I think too much knowledge, which can be a dangerous thing in these times."

"Do you use her for your own potions?"

There was a hesitation. "Sometimes, if conventional medicine fails. What will you do with the mixture?"

"Uduru can be used in two ways, as a potion to be drunk, and as a salve applied to the body. In this instance I will use both. I will make a pill the Queen must take three times a day until the bleeding stops, and then for two days afterward. The salve is to be applied to... a certain part of her body."

Samuel laughed, less affected by what they had witnessed in the Cathedral. "A certain part of her body? Come, Thomas, we are both men of science."

"Then you do not need me to state the name, do you."

"Will you explain to me how you know about these mixtures, and what they are used for? I know only the little Belia chooses to pass on when I go to her, but she holds her knowledge close."

Thomas let eight drops of raw alcohol run into the dry mixture in his mortar bowl and worked it in, adding four more when he saw the mix was still too dry.

"Perhaps when we are done. There is wine on the table, fetch it if you will."

Samuel crossed the room, returned a moment later with the bottle. After an hour with Thomas he had removed his dark robe as the air in the room grew warmer. Now he stood, more comfortable in a loose cotton shirt embroidered with abstract patterns, and linen pants. He had removed his shoes. Dressed this way served to accentuate both his height and thinness.

Thomas poured a little of the dark wine into the mortar, mixed it and nodded, satisfied. He scooped the thick mixture into a prepared tray he had brought with him. It had been

43

fashioned for him by a smith and was in itself, despite an apparent roughness, a work of art. A single sheet of sword steel rolled and rolled again until it could be flexed in the fingers, then heated and an iron rod pressed hard to form indentations. Thomas filled each of the four rows and four columns with the mixture and used a length of wood to remove the excess.

He handed the tray to Samuel. "Put it on the window sill for now. It must be baked afterward, once it has started to harden. You know where the kitchens are, I take it?"

"Oddly enough I do not, but I am sure I can find out. Theresa will know."

"Is she with the Queen?"

"Most likely. She has little life outside these walls."

Thomas began to clean the table, once again wishing for the smooth marble of his workshop at home, allowing himself to think of Lubna now he was involved in nothing more than repetitive tasks she would normally carry out. It was easier to think of her than other things that picked at his mind. He pictured her, short and lithe, washing down the marble surface, tendons in her arms standing out. Stronger than she appeared, stronger in more ways than he could count.

"Here, help me. Take any dirty tools or jars I have used and wash them. Wash them well. Have you not been tempted yourself, Samuel? Theresa is a fine looking woman, and from what I can tell willing for the right man."

"I have heard an occasional rumour, but perhaps I am not the right kind of man," said Samuel.

Thomas wet the table before using another cloth to dry it. He looked around, his mind already moving on to the preparation of the salve. They would be here until late afternoon, and then he would send for Theresa and give her instructions.

It was full dark by the time they were finished and Theresa had come and gone, yet still Samuel showed no inclination to leave. Thomas might have been annoyed had he not been so tired. He still ached from the journey and had slept little since he arrived, but when there came a knock on the door and a servant put his head through to tell them food had been laid out he asked Samuel if he would to stay. There were still questions he wanted answered.

The scent of the food arrayed before them sparked a pain in Thomas's stomach and he tried to recall the last time he had eaten. The day before, with Samuel, the hospitality now reversed.

When he spooned a portion of capon in sauce onto a plate he discovered it strongly spiced and knew it had been the Queen herself had ordered the meal. He had eaten with her before, the last time after the fall of Ronda, and knew she favoured the stronger flavours of Moorish cuisine to that of her own country, which tended to thick stews and even thicker meats, none of which tasted different to the other.

"You said you enquired about me," Thomas said as he selected food for his plate. "Who did you ask? There are few here that know me other than the Queen, and I am sure you would not question her."

"Theresa said she and you spent a great deal of time together when you were in Cordoba to attend Prince Juan." Samuel poured wine for them both, picked at a sliver of meat before glancing up. "Did you bed her? She is, as you say, a fine-looking woman."

"We worked together, nothing more." Thomas recalled a time when he had almost weakened, if weakness it would have been and not two consenting adults thrown together under extraordinary circumstances. "So what was it Theresa told you about me? Is it she who believes me too curious?"

Samuel laughed. "No. She has nothing but praise for you, and, I suspect, an admiration that verges on love. It was another physician I consulted. He had heard of you by reputation, studied in the same infirmary in Malaga as you. As I did myself."

"Would I know him?"

"He was after your time. He is the best physician I have ever met." He stared at Thomas, waiting to be challenged.

"He must possess rare skills indeed. I would like to meet him."

"Perhaps. I will ask next time I see him, but he has taken a different path now."

"What kind of path?" Thomas asked, but when Samuel answered it was only to return to an earlier subject.

"Yes, Theresa is a handsome woman. I understand her husband is older by some measure, and chose to remain in Cordoba."

"Is that so? Her domestic arrangements do not concern me so long as she is good at her job, and I know she is that."

Samuel chuckled. "And there was me believing what people say."

"What do people say?"

"That you are a cold fish."

Thomas smiled, more than half tempted to tell him of the concubine who once shared his bed, tales that would make most men envious. Except Samuel appeared uninterested in either man or woman. Thomas wished for Jorge's presence, for he was a better judge of humanity than him.

"It is of no matter to me what people think."

"See? That is exactly what I mean. You should care more." Samuel picked up a piece of meat, sniffed and returned it to the plate before choosing something else. "It is no business of mine if you mounted her. Good for you if you did. Some say it is a man's duty to spread his seed as widely as he can."

Thomas smiled. "But not you." He was aware they had slipped into small talk when there were more serious matters to discuss, but the lethargy that flooded his limbs, the spiced food, the darkness against the windows all conspired to push other concerns from his mind.

A lift of the shoulder. "I have little opinion on the matter."

No, Thomas thought, I don't suppose you do. He poured himself more of the excellent wine and surveyed the remains of the meal. He decided he was no longer hungry and rose from the table. He stretched, the bones in his spine cracking and popping. He was still tired from the journey but knew true rest was impossible until the Queen was restored. Or not.

"For a man to be given a name, this Ghost, it tells me it is not the first time he has killed."

Samuel remained at the table sipping at his wine. He said nothing, as if he had not heard.

"When I came from the Cathedral it was clear word had spread. The crowd talked of nothing else. I have seen the same before. Those attracted to the mystery of death yet repelled by the act itself. Even here where death is sanctioned."

"Your concern is for the Queen, nothing else. This Ghost is none of your business."

Thomas looked to the west where a faint sliver of purple light remained on the far horizon.

"I have more questions to ask, about Mandana and al-Haquim. About the Inquisition. An exchange, perhaps – I will teach you my techniques in return for answers to those questions."

"What if I have no answers?"

"You are involved with the two in that house, you cannot

deny it. I would know what Mandana is planning, not what he pretends."

"I will consider your request, but it is difficult for a man in my position. When will you know if your magic works?"

"Science, not magic. This time tomorrow, perhaps sooner if, as you say, she is already mending. The human body is a thing of wonder, so frail and yet so strong." Thomas slapped at his neck as he heard the whine of a mosquito. "It was Mandana I saw in that house, wasn't it? Is he still a man of God or not?"

"He is still a priest, still an Abbot," said Samuel, "or claims the title whether it is his due or not." An expression of distaste crossed his face. "Ask me about him if you will, but not tonight. It has been a long day and I am fatigued. There is much you need to know when I can make sense, for he has spoken of you even before you were sent for."

CHAPTER SEVEN

When Thomas returned from an early visit to Belia to collect the promised herbs she had not had the day before he discovered Theresa sitting on the edge of his ornate bed. She did not see him at first because he had removed his boots on entering the outer room. She was staring through the window to the gardens beyond, her face in repose, body relaxed, one hand in her lap, the other spread on the bedcover. Thomas watched her until an unease crept through him and he coughed to attract her attention.

"Where have you been?" She was on her feet in an instant.

"I had business elsewhere."

"The Queen is your business."

"And it is on her behalf I have been working. I take it you are here for some purpose other than to question me? Has Isabel's condition worsened?"

"The opposite. She is better. Much better, and asking for you. She ate a good breakfast, bathed, and now is waiting on you. She has been waiting almost an hour and is sure to want to know what is so important it caused you to ignore her summons."

"Let me change. Tell her I am on my way, I will be right behind you."

Theresa smiled and offered a curtsey so ornate it came close to insubordination.

As soon as he was alone Thomas stripped and washed quickly before dressing in something more appropriate for greeting a Queen. He had noticed that new clothes had been brought to the room and wondered if they were Theresa's doing.

Thomas had only just finished dressing when Theresa returned and called out, asking if he was ready. He tied his shirt as he went out and accompanied her to the Queen's chambers. Isabel sat in the outer room on a solid oak chair padded with stuffed velvet. Thomas stopped and did as he had with Theresa, studying this woman while she was distracted. She was pale, but he expected such. The swelling of her belly was barely discernible beneath an ornately patterned robe.

Isabel turned her head and offered a tired smile. "Send someone for a chair, Theresa, then leave us. We have matters to discuss, my cousin and I."

Thomas felt the skeins of loyalty twisting inside. This was the soft Isabel, the Queen who called him cousin not in reference to family but to honour him and his friendship. When a servant carried in a second chair, far lighter than the Queen's, Thomas sat. Of Theresa there was no sign.

Isabel patted her knee. "Come closer, Thomas." She stared at him, her gaze flickering across his face, and Thomas had to force himself not to turn away. "You look tired."

Thomas smiled. "As do you, your grace. My journey was long, but nothing in comparison to your difficulties."

"Do not call me that when we are alone. You, who has saved the child I carry. Are we not friends, Thomas?"

"As you say." But still he could not bring himself to use

50

her name. Not yet. Later, perhaps. He had always found informality easier with Fernando because they had fought side by side. "Are you well enough to be out of bed, your grace?"

She made a moue of distaste but allowed the formality. "Come, feel my neck, or whatever it is you do. Samuel is a big one for the feeling of the neck. I do not recall you ever having the need of it."

"I have never had a call to treat you before, your grace." Thomas rose and crossed the space between them. She looked up as he came, a small figure with red-blonde hair. Not a pretty woman like Theresa, but handsome, with a sense of assurance that spoke to him far more than the shallowness of looks. Thomas laid his fingers against her pale throat to find the pulse. It was steady, strong, a little fast but not abnormally so.

"Your medicines are powerful, are they not? I feel myself recovering by the hour."

"The body is a wonderful creation, able to heal itself with only a little help. Would you show me your tongue, your grace?"

"Only if you ask correctly." She pressed her lips together, struggling to suppress a smile.

"Can I see your tongue, please… Isabel." He stressed the name, making her smile.

"Much better, yes?" She opened her mouth and Thomas leaned close. Her breath was stale, with a hint of the rigours her body had been through, but he could tell she was mending and returned to his seat.

"You will stay at my side," said Isabel, no hint of a question. "As my physician."

It was the same statement she had issued on several occasions before, and though Thomas had not deliberately said no he always went away in the end. However much he admired the woman sitting near him he left her because his life lay elsewhere.

"For as long as I can."

Once more that moue, and then a sly smile. "I have dismissed the other, so you must stay."

Thomas leaned forward. "Samuel? You dismissed Samuel? Why?"

"Because I have you now."

"But I am not here all the time. I have other–"

"Then you *should* be here all the time." Isabel's eyes remained on the view, avoiding Thomas.

"Am I not to sleep? Not to have a life of my own?"

She sighed, still avoiding his gaze. "He is not as good as you. You said as much yourself."

"And meant it. But he is as good a physician as I have seen in Spain, and more than good enough to attend you when I am elsewhere. I will tell him to return."

At last her gaze fixed on his. "It is not your place to do so. It was my doing he is gone."

"And you will accept him when I ask him to return." Thomas refused to look away, the moment stretching out as a silent battle of wills took place. Finally, Isabel made a sound and shifted in her seat, the gardens once more offering an appeal.

"Do what you must. I expect I have to do as you say, do I not?"

"Where is Fernando?" Thomas wanted to change the subject, aware of how close he had come to insubordination, unsure how Isabel would have reacted if she had been more stubborn.

"If I tell you then you will have to stay. I do not want you running off and telling your friends of his plans."

Thomas smiled. "I believe you may already have."

Isabel laughed, the previous matter forgotten, the sound

cut off abruptly as some remnant of pain troubled her. Thomas rose at once but she held up a hand. "No, I am fine. Just a foolish woman who forgets she has been unwell. If you ask of my husband then I must return the query. Your wife is well?"

Thomas had always been vague in the past when Isabel talked of Lubna as his wife, but now he wanted her to know the truth, his response edged with a hint of resentment.

"We are not married. We were about to be when Martin came for me."

"Martin de Alarcón? Yes, I sent him for you, but what has that to do with a marriage?"

Thomas hesitated, but he had gone too far now. "Lubna and I were to be married the day he came. All was prepared, but I considered your need more important."

"You came here rather than marry?" Isabel leaned forward.

"I made a decision. The right one, I believe. A marriage can wait, a Queen cannot."

Isabel stared at Thomas for a long while before before she sat back in the chair. Her body relaxed as though suddenly tired and she closed her eyes. Thomas waited, knowing she did not sleep. When she spoke, her eyes still closed, the words surprised him.

"My spies tell me you are looking into things of no concern to you."

Thomas wasn't entirely sure what she referred to. His visit to al-Haquim's house, or the body in the Cathedral? In both cases there was only one person he could think of who knew of both.

"Your spies?"

A lift of the lips, but the eyes remained closed. "Yes. Did you think I would not have spies? How innocent of you." Now her lids rose, her gaze once more capturing him, but the subject changed yet again, though he knew it would return soon enough to what he did not want her to know. "Tell me, in your opinion is Samuel Ibrahim a good doctor? If I do as you ask and return him to his position in the palace can I place my trust in him?"

So was Samuel one of her spies? Is that what she was telling him? But if so why dismiss him in the first place?

"He is curious, which I always consider a good sign. Yes, he is a good doctor. You can trust him." Though he wondered if he spoke the truth. Hadn't al-Haquim called Samuel his spy? Was the man walking a dangerous tightrope between two masters?

"I would rather put my trust in you. Is he as good as you?"

Thomas stared into her eyes. Finally he shook his head. "No, of course not."

Another smile. "One of the things I most admire about you is your lack of modesty. In other men it would seem boastful, but in you it is not, because you always speak the truth. So why were you visiting that man?"

Oh, but she is a clever woman, Thomas thought, and whoever her spies are they see everything.

"Samuel told me it was where I would find him. Surely you have been told of his visits?"

"You have a surfeit of curiosity, Thomas. And the Cathedral? Was that any of your business?"

"Was I meant to ignore it? Besides, being curious makes me good at what I do," Thomas said. "Samuel has a little of it too, but not so much as myself."

"Why the interest?"

Thomas looked down at his hands, the fingers long and slim. The index finger on his left hand had a deep scar running almost the whole length of it, but he could not recall the reason why. Some fight in the last thirty years, he supposed. He had fought a great deal once, often for no reason at all. The anger of youth needed little reason.

"You must know there have been deaths in the city, Isabel?" He looked up, deliberately using her name, for were they not close friends, and close friends could talk of anything?

"There is pestilence," she said. "Of course there is death."

"The death I talk of is deliberate. They call him the Ghost."

She waved a hand, a dismissive gesture. "The crowd talks of everything and nothing. I have not been long in Sevilla and my mind has been elsewhere. I carry a son, another heir to the throne of Spain, perhaps." She studied Thomas, her eyes tracking his face, and he tried not to look away. She was silent a long while, then she drew a breath deep into her body. "You tracked another killer in Cordoba."

"A killer who remains unpunished."

"He claims it was not him."

"Of course he does, but we both know different."

"Will you chase down this Ghost as well?"

"Are you asking it of me?"

"I am not, but will it make any difference if I do or not? It appears to me you always do what you want regardless of my wishes." The faintest of smiles. "In other men, I would consider it a weakness. In you... perhaps not. You have been of service to my people in the past."

Thomas tried to determine if she was giving him permission to investigate or not, aware she would never directly make the request, and he dare not ask in case she refused. Her gaze had gone to the darkened window once more, losing focus, and as he watched he saw how tired she was.

"I will let you rest, Isabel," he said, his voice so low it barely disturbed her.

She nodded, the slightest movement. "Yes. I need sleep. Do they not say sleep is a great healer?"

"People say many things that have no basis in fact, but this may be one that does." Thomas experienced an urge to cross to the small woman and kiss her cheek, even as he knew such a thing impossible. The warmth of the room, the night pressing against the windows, the almost near silence of the palace triggered a sense of closeness that encouraged dangerous thoughts.

He stood abruptly. "I will see you in the morning, your grace. Sleep well."

She glanced at him, something in her eyes matching what he had been feeling, and Thomas turned away quickly and strode for the door.

In the rooms beyond he found Theresa next to a window, looking into the city where lamps illuminated the streets and people gathered and broke like smoke in a breeze. She heard Thomas's boots on the wooden floor and turned.

"Isabel tells me she has dismissed Samuel. Why did you say nothing to me? Where will I find him?"

Theresa shook her head. "He has friends over there somewhere." She waved a hand but whether in the right direction neither he nor she could be certain. "So, it will be you tonight." She smiled. "If you need company to keep you awake you only have to ask." But even as she spoke the words Thomas sensed some underlying sadness and wondered if she missed her husband.

"Have you been waiting for me? Did you want something?"

"Always," said Theresa, still no joy in her voice, as if the teasing had grown stale. She glanced away. "I wanted to know if you thought the Queen improved."

"What is your opinion?"

"I am the nurse, you are the physician."

"Humour me."

"I believe whatever was broken is mended, and that it is your doing. All your doing." She turned suddenly and laid a hand on his chest, a mannerism that threatened to become a habit. "Now tell me, do you agree she is better?"

"Yes, she appears to be. Do you know who told her of my interest in the death in the Cathedral?"

Theresa shook her head. "Has there been a death?"

CHAPTER EIGHT

Thomas gave in to the midday heat and threw his hood back, believing he had finally reached his destination. He wiped a hand across his face to clear the sweat but almost immediately it returned. The small square he had entered looked familiar, but so had others he had passed through in search of the house he sought. He had visions of wandering these alleys for weeks until he expired for want of food and water. Perhaps even lack of company. He had seen no-one. Heat assaulted the city like some ravening beast, driving its population indoors. And then, as he crossed the square to enter yet another alley, on the far side he caught a glimpse of water and knew he was close.

Thomas had spared little notice to where Abraham al-Haquim's house lay when he first came here, but now he stopped to study it from a distance, gauging, judging. It was wide, two stories high with a further level behind outer walls that hinted at a courtyard. It was the house of a man with both money and power. In this place where most dwellings were tumbled cheek by jowl such lavishness stood out. It told him al-Haquim had found a position he no doubt believed matched his importance. Even if it was the importance of defeat.

There was no closed door here. Instead a man stood to one side as though interested in no more than the view of the small square, but his eyes tracked Thomas's approach.

"You were here the other day." His hand rested on the hilt of a workmanlike sword, but for the moment it remained undrawn.

"I seek Samuel Ibrahim. Do you know if he is within?"

"If he is I didn't see him enter, but he comes and goes at all times so it is possible."

Thomas tried to cool an ember of impatience. "Do you think you could ask? Or I will go myself if it's too much trouble." He took a pace forward and the man moved to block the door. Thomas judged him and found what he saw wanting. He could knock him down with a single blow, take his sword and walk in. But he would prefer not to.

"A message it is, then," Thomas said, rewarded when the man frowned as though they had tussled and he had lost, though what the contest had been remained a mystery to him.

He half turned and called out a name. A young man, still shy of eighteen years, came running and the guard, for that was what he was, whispered into the youth's ear. Once they were alone Thomas deliberately turned his back and tried to judge what lay in the square to amuse someone such as him all day. Not much, he concluded. A water trough to one side might provide a little entertainment when women came to wash clothes and fill buckets. The houses surrounding the four sides were well appointed with waxed shutters on the windows.

Thomas turned when he heard the slap of bare feet on marble.

"The master says send him in."

The guard offered a puzzled look before stepping aside, and Thomas moved past into a shaded courtyard almost half as big as the square outside. The architecture would not look out of place in the royal palace, even down to splashing water and tall palms amongst which parakeets nested. The tower Thomas had seen from outside sat on the edge of the courtyard, an arched entrance open to the cooling air. Sitting on stone benches were Abraham al-Haquim and Samuel. The third figure should not have caused Thomas surprise because he had glimpsed him at the house before, but his return to power still puzzled him.

Abbot Mandana smiled at the discomfort he had caused.

"Which of us do you seek, Don Berrington?"

"I would speak with Samuel. I believe I owe him an apology."

Mandana smiled to display long yellow teeth. "He was only now saying the same to us. That he is owed an apology, if not more." He patted the bench beside him. "Come, sit, we are all friends here, you can speak in confidence."

Thomas didn't believe a word of it, but he made his way to one of the benches set cross-ways to the others. Al-Haquim clapped his hands together, and when the youth came instructed him to bring coffee and cakes.

The three men stared at Thomas, waiting.

"I would speak with you alone if I may." Thomas looked only at Samuel.

"As the Abbot says, we are all friends here."

Thomas took a breath, trying to gather his thoughts from where they had been scattered by Mandana's presence. He leaned forward, resting his arms across his knees. "Is that true? If so I'm not sure I believe any of you." His eyes rested on Mandana, who he considered the notional leader, also the most deadly.

"I heard you discovered a body in the Cathedral yesterday," said Mandana, his gaze sharp, examining Thomas.

"Not discovered, but yes, I saw a body." He glanced at Samuel. It was obvious how the news had reached Mandana. "Another of your pieces of handiwork?"

"I am a changed man. A penitent who recognised he has strayed from the path of righteousness and asked forgiveness. Which has been granted me."

"So you have no interest," Thomas said.

"I have an interest. Am I not a man of God, and did this atrocity not take place in God's house? So of course I have an interest, and we may discuss the matter further before long. But you want to talk with Samuel. As I said, there are no secrets here."

Thomas looked toward Samuel once more. It was clear he had found time to tell them about the body, but had he neglected to tell them of his own dismissal?

"Have you said nothing?"

"You talk in riddles," said al-Haquim. "What does he mean, Samuel?"

"I am dismissed." Still without meeting anyone's gaze. "It seems I am no longer needed now *he* is here."

Mandana turned his entire attention to Samuel. "Is this true?"

"I am no longer in the employ of the palace."

"God's teeth, man, can't you do the simplest of tasks? How are we to know what goes on now?"

So, Thomas thought, Mandana might be Fernando's man but he was not the Queen's. Interesting.

"You could always ask Thomas," said Samuel, and Mandana laughed.

"Yes, of course." He turned. "Will you become my spy, Berrington?"

"You know my answer, Abbot."

"I can guess it, yes." His gaze locked on Thomas's. "You need not fear me, Berrington. I am not the man I was. I have learned the lessons of humility and duty. And I make a good friend to have in this city... in these times."

"Are you for or against what is being done?" Thomas asked. "The questioning, the torture, the burnings? I would consider they are something you might relish."

"I am a changed man. That is what this did to me." He held up his arm to show the mottled stump that now terminated it.

"I could have returned that at one time," Thomas said. "Not that it would have done you much good. The wolves had made a meal of it by then. But your rings are, I believe, in the possession of the King now."

"I have grown accustomed to the loss," Mandana said. "Two hands might be considered superfluous to need. And better than the loss of my life."

"How did you survive? The gorge was deep and the wolves many." Despite his hatred of the man, Thomas was curious.

"Oh, I am a hard man to kill. Yes, the gorge was deep, but there was water at the bottom and a pool to break my fall. As you can see, I survived."

"And wormed your way back into favour."

"Quality of mind and loyalty are rewarded in Spain."

Thomas glanced away for a moment. "And these men?"

"We share common interests," said Mandana. It was only the two of them now, the others ignored.

"You didn't answer my question. Are you for or against the burnings?"

"I have nothing against executing those disloyal to the crown, but we three share doubts about their purpose."

"Why you? Him I can understand." Thomas nodded toward al-Haquim. "Samuel too in some ways, he is caught between two masters, and such is a dangerous place to be. But you? The last I heard you were Fernando's weapon, doing work no-one else would."

Mandana leaned forward. "It is because of that, Berrington. What is happening here is a distraction from our true work." A smile. "Which is the utter defeat of your friends in Granada. We will drive them into the sea. We will hunt them down, every last one, until their filthy presence is scoured from this land." He stared again into Thomas's eyes. "And then you will have to decide on which side your loyalties lie. You and that dark skinned wife of yours. And the gelded fool you call friend."

Mandana sat up as coffee arrived, accompanied by a tray of tiny sugared cakes. "I must leave, Abraham," he said as he rose to his full height, his long hair hanging grey across his shoulders. "Walk with me a while and let these fools discuss what secrets they will."

Thomas was sure the move was a ploy and someone would be nearby listening, but the servant had come and gone and Mandana and al-Haquim left through the gateway to walk across the small square.

When the sound of their voices had faded Thomas waited a moment longer then leaned forward. "I did not know you had been dismissed until this morning, but I have spoken with the Queen. She was hasty and has been made aware you are needed. Your position is restored, so you can return to spy for Mandana once more." He narrowed his eyes. "Is that what he asks of you? What power does he hold to bend you to his will this way?"

"I will not be needed while you are here."

"You know full well that is untrue. And before many

months pass I will leave again and she will need you more than ever. So return. Do not allow pride to make a fool of you."

"Why would you leave?"

"I don't belong here. My life lies elsewhere."

"A life that is drawing to a close," said Samuel.

"As may be. But it's my life and I choose to live it as I see fit for as long as I can." He leaned closer, his body tense. "Now tell me what you do in this house with these men. Do you know what they are?"

"Important is what they are," said Samuel. "I need the friendship of such men in these times. I might have converted but that is no protection, not these days."

"What is it you do, the three of you?"

"We try to save people."

Thomas shook his head, sat up. "I don't understand. You and al-Haquim perhaps, but Mandana is a different beast and has little in common with either of you."

"Yet he is against the persecution that taints this city. We do what we can, exert what influence we might, and save some from the fires."

"You know what he did? Mandana?"

"Some falling out is what I heard. I haven't asked because it is of no relevance to what we do here."

"Why did you tell him about the body?"

"He has an interest."

"Yes, I expect he does. But what kind of interest, I wonder?"

"An interest is all I know. You should ask him yourself. You are old friends, are you not? That is how he refers to you."

"Is his interest in this one death only? Or have there been others?"

Samuel reached for one of the small cakes and popped it into his mouth, a moment's surfeit of sweetness.

"Yes, there have been more. You heard the name the mob spoke. The Ghost. The Ghost. They must name everything, good or bad, but a name takes time to grow in the imagination, and the deaths have been going on for a year or more."

CHAPTER NINE

Thomas pushed at the hand shaking his shoulder and muttered, "No!" But the hand remained, shaking harder. He rolled over to find not Theresa, as he expected, but a guard he had not seen before. The man brought a lamp which he set on the table.

"Is the Queen unwell?"

"Not as far as I know. Has she been?"

"Um, no, she hasn't. What do you want? It's the middle of the night."

"There's someone at the gate asking for you."

"Then send them away."

"The man is insistent."

Samuel, Thomas suspected, or even Abbot Mandana. Except Mandana would be granted admittance – or would he, without Fernando present?

Thomas tossed the thin bed sheet aside and dropped his feet to the floor, barely aware of his nakedness. The guard turned away in any case while Thomas dressed quickly, not bothering with a robe.

"Let's get this done with, then," he said. The guard led the way through the palace, the lamp held high. All around other lamps had been extinguished. Closer to the royal chambers they would no doubt burn all night.

"Did he give a name?" Thomas asked. Sleep still clung to him. He had been deep below the surface when he was woken, strands of unreality continuing to cling to his mind.

"Lomos."

"Lomos?"

"That's what he said."

Thomas shook his head, confused. What was Jorge's brother Daniel doing here? The last time they had met was in Qurtuba three years before. He knew the smith now fashioned weapons for the King, so was that why he had come? But if so, why ask for Thomas?

They reached the parade ground outside the palace walls, other walls protecting the long, wide space. The air here was barely any fresher than inside the palace, the heat of late summer hanging like a veil across the city even late into the night. Heavy oak doors reinforced with iron stood barred, a small door set into them also shut.

The guard led the way across the cobbles, boot heels loud.

He hesitated before throwing the bolt on the small door. "He can't come in if that's what he wants, not unless he has business."

"Open the door," Thomas said. He stepped through into the night and heard the bolt being shot behind.

The man standing outside looking across the outer square toward the cathedral wasn't Daniel Olmos, but the other one Thomas didn't associate with that name even though it had been his at birth. A cart sat on the cobbles beyond.

"What in the name of God are you doing here?"

Jorge turned slowly. "It's good to see you too, Thomas. I see your humour hasn't improved. Neither has mine, but we will come to that later. Lubna's with me, and she's sick."

Thomas pushed past him to the small cart and climbed on the bed. Lubna lay wrapped in a blanket. Thomas knelt and felt her face. She was hot, burning up. He pulled the blanket clear and touched her belly, which barely showed any swelling.

"What are you doing here?" he said, his voice soft.

Lubna opened her eyes and smiled once before closing them again.

"How long has she been this way?"

"Two days. She started throwing up, then complained of a bad head. She got worse so I pushed the mules faster."

"Why did you bring her at all in her condition?" Thomas said.

"She wasn't like this when we left. Do you consider me stupid?"

"Not this. The child she is carrying, idiot."

Jorge stared. "She said nothing about a child. She is…" He shook his head, emotions playing across his face without filter. "You and she…?"

"I think I can be sure this time, yes." Thomas put his arms beneath Lubna and lifted. The heat of her came through the layers of clothing. He had to get her inside and find out what was wrong, but feared he might already know. He slid from the bed of the cart and started across to the barred gate.

"Wait, I'll bring Will," said Jorge.

Thomas stopped, turned back. Lubna stirred in his arms, barely any weight at all.

"You brought Will too? Damn, but you truly are a fool, aren't you?"

"Thank you, Jorge, for bringing my loved ones across miles of dangerous country."

"Exactly," Thomas said, turning away again. "And yes, bring him. Does he have any symptoms?"

"None, other than looking forward to seeing you. Which I consider suspicious enough."

Thomas kicked at the door with his foot, waiting for it to open.

"They'll have to open the whole thing to get the cart inside," said Jorge.

"The door will be a start." Thomas kicked again. The guard should have been waiting on the other side. What was the man doing? And then a small panel opened and a face peered out.

"Open the door, damn you!" Thomas said.

"What's wrong with her?"

"She's ill. I need to get her inside before I can find out why. Now open the damn door!"

The face withdrew and the panel closed. Thomas took a step back ready for the door to open. Minutes passed and nothing happened.

"He's gone," said Jorge. "Probably needs someone more important to make the decision."

Lubna stirred in Thomas's arms, eyes opening again. Her hand came up and cupped his face, the touch hot. "I ache," she said. "I ache everywhere."

"Your belly?"

A flicker of a smile, soon extinguished. "Still healthy, I think. He was kicking this morning, anyway. I wasn't as ill as this then."

"Why did you come? The journey is too much for you in your condition."

"I am with child, not sick," said Lubna, a flash of her usual spirit showing.

"And now you are sick," Thomas said.

"And no better for your welcome. Did you expect me to

remain at home, an abandoned woman? Do you know how long I waited for you to come to the palace?"

"I sent a message," Thomas said.

"Yes. A message. You sent a *message*. Did you not think to come yourself?"

"Martin was insistent."

Lubna made a sound and turned her head away.

"He's not coming," said Jorge. "They've abandoned us."

"I'll remember his face," Thomas said, turning away. Jorge was right. They would not gain admittance now, not until morning, and perhaps not then. "I know someone who might be able to help. You'll have to leave the cart though, it's too wide to take where we're going."

"Our belongings are in it," said Jorge. "And I brought money."

They each of them had more gold and jewels than a man could spend in a hundred lifetimes since liberating three chests from the abandoned house of a dead man two years before, but Thomas kept his hidden. Jorge, who had never had funds of his own because his every need was catered for by the harem, found the idea of spending gold a novelty. He had even purchased a house near Thomas's for the four Nubian slaves he had somehow acquired while they were in Ronda.

"How many bags?" Thomas asked, walking toward the cart.

"Three."

"Including the money chest?"

"No chest. It's hidden among my things."

Thomas stopped at the cart. The three bags were laid on the bed of the cart, one larger than the others. He dragged it to the edge, tested the weight, then heaved it off onto the ground.

"You take this one. Will is lighter than Lubna, and you are bigger than me."

Thomas expected an objection, but Jorge laid Will on the cart while he tugged at the bag, pulling a pair of trousers from within and fashioning a strap from them. Thomas nodded, admiring the ingenuity, and did the same with the other two bags.

On the cart Will stirred, perhaps disturbed by Lubna when she was laid beside him. He groaned, then said, "Pa!"

Thomas leaned across and kissed his face, welcoming the short arms that clung around his neck.

"Jorge will carry you, my sweet," he said, and Will nodded. He loved Jorge almost as much as he loved Thomas and Lubna. But then Will loved everyone. He had turned three earlier in the year, had some words now, and a curiosity that Thomas encouraged. He wondered what his son would turn into with so many fathers in his life. And Will was his son, he was in no doubt of that, even if there was doubt over who the true father might be. Helena, who was undoubtedly his mother, continued to remain silent on the matter.

Now Will held his arms out to Jorge, who picked him up and held him to his chest, kissed the top of his blonde hair, straight like his mother's and almost as long.

Thomas settled the two bags around his shoulders and lifted Lubna. Walking wasn't easy, but he knew the way now and it wasn't far. As they passed one of the doors daubed with a slash of paint Jorge asked the same question Thomas had a few days earlier, and Thomas passed the same information on that Samuel had given him. A plague house.

"Is that what is wrong with Lubna?" asked Jorge, all the softness leached from his face.

"I don't know."

Belia peered from an upper window when Thomas

rapped on the door then disappeared without a word. A moment later bolts were thrown and she ushered them inside.

"What do you need?" No hint of reluctance from this woman he had met on only two occasions.

"Somewhere to lay her, and willow bark to start with. She has a fever and I want to bring it down."

"I have other herbs if you need them." Belia led him through to a room at the back, larger than he would have guessed from the outside. A door gave on to a small court-yard where the slabs had been lifted and replaced with soil. The space there was packed with a surfeit of plants.

"She is with child, so I want to take things slowly until we know what's wrong." Thomas laid Lubna on a long table once Belia had cleared it of the tools of her trade. The space reminded him of his own workshop, smaller but with the same bowls and jars of herbs and spices.

Belia leaned close and felt under Lubna's arm and Thomas realised he should have done so himself, cursing his own stupidity.

"It's not plague," said Belia. "Hopefully no more than a fever." She went to a shelf, scanned her finger along its contents then plucked a jar down. With swift movements she ground the contents into a fine powder and mixed them with water.

Thomas sat Lubna up and Belia made her drink the entire contents of a small cup. Only then did she turn to see who else had come into her house. Thomas saw her gaze take Jorge in from head to toe. She gave a sharp nod, as if in approval.

"And who is the boy?"

"My son," Thomas said, no hesitation. "Will."

"Is he ill too?"

"Not as far as I can tell."

Another nod, trusting his judgement.

"I cannot thank you enough for this," he said. "I didn't know where else to go. I have no friends in the city."

"You have one friend," she said. "I will make tea. Is anyone hungry?"

"There is no need."

"I'm hungry," said Jorge.

Belia smiled. "You look like you might always be hungry, for one thing or another."

Thomas tried not to groan. Jorge was doing it again. And what made matters worse, however hard Thomas studied him he could never see what it was he did.

Belia waved a hand. "There are chairs in the room through there. Out that door and turn right. Go sit, I'll be through in a moment."

"I'll stay with Lubna," Thomas said.

"Then I will fetch your tea here."

There was a hard wooden chair and Thomas pulled it close to the bench. He reached across and felt Lubna's neck. Her heart raced but not dangerously so. He thought the fever had abated a little but feared this might only be wishful thinking. He leaned forward and rested his forehead against her shoulder, stroked the skin of her arm. From the other room he heard muffled voices, Jorge's unmistakeable tone, Belia's lighter, but coloured like his with strangeness. The pair of them strangers in a foreign land. Thomas wondered what Jorge would do when the Moors were defeated, what would happen when there was no harem to care for, no scented ladies to amuse. He knew Jorge would survive. The boy he had turned into a eunuch all those years ago had become his most trusted friend. They had fought side by side, and sometimes Jorge even proved himself useful. He had come a long way from the effete palace plaything he had once been. Jorge was now the possessor of both muscle and skill, as well as a keen sense of people that Thomas envied.

He jerked awake at a touch on his arm. Belia stood beside him, a cup of steaming liquid in her hand. She placed it on the table then leaned across to touch Lubna's chest.

"She improves," she said.

Thomas did the same. Belia was right, Lubna was cooler, her temperature almost normal.

"Perhaps no more than a fever, then," Thomas said, relief in his voice.

Belia touched his arm. "Let us hope so. Are you sure you don't want some food?"

"It's the middle of the night, you should go back to bed. You do not have to cook for me or my companions."

"I like your friend, the big one. The little one, too. He looks like you, a little."

Thomas smiled, said nothing.

"Besides," said Belia, "it is not the middle of the night anymore." She inclined her head to the window where grey light filled the small courtyard.

"I see you grow your own poppy and hemp," Thomas said.

"It is not the best place, but I have more plants along the river bank west of the city, and in other places I keep secret. The ones I grow here are herbs that don't object to shade and which are useful to keep on hand."

"I have a garden at home," Thomas said. "It is south facing. My poppy and hemp does well, but other things less so."

"Such is the way of the world," said Belia. "Come through, she sleeps the sleep of recovery now. Please, come tell me of your garden, and Granada. I would visit one day perhaps, when it becomes part of Spain."

And with that she broke the fragile bond that had been growing between them. At least that was how it felt to Thomas.

"I will stay with Lubna," he said. "I am sure Jorge is more than capable of amusing you."

CHAPTER TEN

As Thomas walked toward the palace from Belia's house the first hint of dawn was painting the streets with grey light, and the last person he expected to call out to him when he reached the Cathedral square was Abbot Mandana. The man stood partly hidden within an entrance, waving the one hand that remained to him.

"Berrington, here." A tone of voice that expected no refusal.

Thomas stopped and looked around. There were few people on the street yet for the day was barely begun. The only others he had passed were those who drew carts to collect the plague dead.

He tried to decide if ignoring Mandana would be the wisest course of action, was on the point of doing so when the man called out again.

"There is something you must see!"

Which was all it took, that damned curiosity taking control again. And Thomas still wanted to know what Mandana was up to. He wouldn't put it past the man to be pursuing his own interests while the city degenerated into chaos. It was exactly what Thomas expected. So he turned and trotted across the cobbled square, determined it was better to know all be could if he wanted to stop the man.

"This had better be good."

"Not good, no," said Mandana, "but I believe it will interest you. I would welcome your opinion. You saw the body on the altar yesterday – did you examine it in detail?"

"Enough to determine cause of death, and that it was in no way natural."

Mandana offered a curt nod. "Then tell me about this one, too." He turned and strode to where a shaded courtyard held half a hundred orange trees, their scent sharp in the pre-dawn air. Pulled to one side was one of the plague carts, so common on the streets that Thomas barely noticed them anymore, unlike the population who fled at their sight. This one was empty, but its bed showed stains where previous residents had lain.

"Here," said Mandana, and turned into a small alcove.

Thomas stopped, staring at the figure of a man naked to the waist. Two orange trees grew close together here and his wrists were tied one to each. The nails hammered into his palms were redundant and would not have supported his weight without the ropes.

"Is it the same as yesterday?" asked Mandana.

"I will need to examine him," Thomas said.

"Then do so, and quickly before someone comes this way."

Thomas looked around. The body had been hidden to him when he entered the courtyard, but now he saw that anyone crossing it, should they look in this direction, would have a clear view of the man. As if the body was being displayed. He glanced at the sky, judging where east lay, and saw that as soon as the sun rose high enough its light would spill into this space to highlight the gruesome scene. The body had been deliberately posed, left here where sunrise would make its presence clear to anyone who passed.

He leaned close, not yet touching, his eyes taking in the cuts to the chest wall, the exposed ribs, six of them sheared through. It would have taken a specific instrument and some strength to open the chest in such a way.

"Is he–"

"Be quiet," Thomas said. "My work will go faster if you say nothing." He didn't glance behind, his entire vision peeling the layers from the body. He rolled up a sleeve and slipped his hand into the wound, searching for what had been missing in the first body. Except here the heart had been left in place, and was apparently undamaged, but Thomas could not be sure without removing it, which was something he had no intention of doing. He tested the body for rigor and found the limbs stiff, but not as stiff as they would have been six hours ago. Thomas estimated the man had died no more than two days before, no less than one. He pulled the sleeve of his robe down to cover the smear of blood and turned to Mandana.

"The wound is similar, but his heart has been left in place. I judge this man and the other could have died at the same time, or near enough. Their wounds would indicate the same. Samuel tells me there have been other deaths going back some time."

Mandana nodded. "A number, yes. They began near a year ago. Long enough for whoever is doing this to be given a name by the mob."

"Are all displayed this way? In public view?"

"No, the displaying is recent. The last six bodies only. Before then... well, some were found discarded amongst the plague dead, others partially burned. Whoever is doing this didn't want his work recognised at first. Now... well, now it seems he does."

"Why the change?"

"Perhaps you should ask when you find him, Berrington."

Thomas took a pace away from the body. "Can you find someone to remove this man and dispose of him, before he becomes another source of gossip and fear? And you and I need to talk."

"I know little that can help."

"I would rather be the judge of that. Where were you going when you saw me?"

"Going? No, I was coming. One of the Cathedral workers sent word."

"To you?"

Mandana nodded.

"Why? Is your interest known? Surely the Hermandos are a more natural choice."

"The man recognised him," said Mandana. "He is known to Abraham, and I was there when the message came."

"So it was not sent to you directly."

Mandana made an impatient sound. "Does it matter who the message was for? I was there when it was delivered and came at once."

"Why the interest?"

"You said we needed to talk," said Mandana, "and you are right, we do, but now is not the time. I know of another killing site and would welcome your opinion on it. When can you make the time?"

"Not today."

"But soon," said Mandana. "Come and find me soon."

CHAPTER ELEVEN

As soon as Thomas walked through the gate that marked the border between city and palace he knew he was in trouble, but did not regret the delay. He had walked from the Cathedral without noticing his surroundings, trying to puzzle out exactly what was happening in the city, unable to understand Mandana's interest. He cursed his own curiosity which was already scratching away at his resistance. He recognised the reason, knew himself well enough to acknowledge it was the following of skeins of mystery that attracted him, and wondered when that need had first sparked inside. Perhaps in childhood when he had been forced to prove his own innocence of murder. It was the first time he had used the mental muscles since honed. It was also, he recalled, his first experience of the sickness that now ravaged the city. The sickness that took his brother and mother, and almost Thomas himself.

Guards stood to either side of the entrance to the palace and as soon as they saw him one started across the yard. "You are to come with me," he said, "by order of the Queen."

Thomas followed, believing a storm was about to engulf

him, but knowing it would pass. What he did not expect was to be led not to the Queen's chambers but into a wing of the palace he had never seen before. A long corridor led to a stone-walled room where a grey-haired man sat working on some papers spread across a table. He must have heard their footsteps from far off but only now did he turn his head. His eyes tracked Thomas up and down, showing nothing.

"You are Thomas Berrington?"

Thomas nodded. "You have the advantage of me, sir. I thought I was being taken to the Queen."

"Soon. After we have talked." The man indicated a second chair on the far side of the table, gathered his papers together and slid them into a drawer. When he laid his hands on the table Thomas saw his fingers were marked with ink stains.

"I don't talk to people without a name," Thomas said, half expecting some kind of smile, a twitch at the corner of the mouth at least, but nothing. Instead the man leaned closer, his gaze sharp, probing.

"You are close to the Queen. She has talked of you." Now an expression came but it held no trace of amusement. "In my opinion she talks of you too much." He tapped a finger on the table, over and over, a habit, perhaps even a nervous habit. "I am Friar Hernando de Talavera, advisor to her grace in all matters of religion." His eyes met Thomas's, held them with an unexpected ferocity. "You are from England, I understand?"

Thomas nodded, unwilling to say more until he knew what the conversation was about.

"And England is a Catholic country?"

Another nod.

"So, can I assume you are also a Catholic, even if you choose to live amongst the infidel?"

"What do you want of me?" Thomas said.

"Of you? I want nothing *of* you, only to investigate your

heart and mind. For someone as close to the Queen as you are it is my duty to ensure she is not subject to the wrong kind of ideas. Heathen ideas."

"I am her physician, not her confidant. I leave matters of her soul to you, Friar."

"She speaks of you as a friend. A close friend. She claims you are one of her closest friends." A pained look crossed the man's face.

"Then you are privy to information I am not."

Talavera sat more upright, his fingertips continuing their constant tap-tapping, barely audible, but the movement annoyed Thomas and he had to restrain himself from reaching out and stilling the hand.

"I am the Queen's confessor, so I am privy to all things. She holds nothing back from me. Nothing at all. Make no excuse, Thomas Berrington, for I see into your soul just as I see into the soul of the Queen."

Thomas spread his hands. "You are still talking of matters I know nothing about."

Talavera made a sound. "You are an intelligent man. The Queen claims so, as do others I have questioned about you. Do not pretend ignorance with me."

"You have questioned others about me? Who?"

"I am not at liberty to say. What I can tell you is that in most instances you are well liked, and respected."

Thomas smiled. "In most instances?"

"As I say."

"Tell me what you want of me." Thomas leaned forward himself, closing the space between them.

"I want you to cure our Queen and then to leave. I want you gone as soon as she is well enough to travel."

"She is well enough now," Thomas said.

"That is not the opinion of all."

"Who is her physician, these others or me? Is my word not to be trusted?"

"That is why we are having this conversation. I do not have to like you, Thomas Berrington, but I must respect your skills. What I hear is you are loyal but headstrong, not subject to following orders you disagree with, and the purpose of an order is for it to be followed, agreement or no. As the word of God must be followed. I also hear your loyalty is unbending, which is something of which I approve, as long as it does not warp into something more than loyalty."

Thomas wondered when the man might say something he understood, so remained silent in hope of a point being made he could sensibly respond to.

"Why do you live with the infidel?"

"Because I choose knowledge over superstition."

Talavera scowled. "There is no greater knowledge than the knowledge of our Lord Almighty and his son Jesus Christ. As a Christian you know that, yet you do not embrace it."

"I embrace logic, beauty, and science."

Talavera's scowl grew, revealing stained teeth. "Science and religion are poor bedfellows."

"Which is why I choose the path I do."

"The world is changing. If you are as intelligent as people say you must know your way of life is coming to an end. God will prevail in this land and all will be swept aside, your science included."

"Tell me what you want of me." Thomas's hands had curled into fists and it was only through an effort of will he did not close them around Talavera's neck.

"I told you what I want. You will cure the Queen and you will leave this land."

"And what if she does not want me to leave?"

"She is a loyal servant of the church. She will do what is right. She always does."

"A church that burns people for following their own God? Are there to be yet more fires tomorrow? That church?"

"Yes, that church. So it may protect itself from the evil within."

"You approve?"

"It is not my place to approve or not. There are others concerned with such matters. My concern is the Queen's inviolable soul, and I will do anything to protect her."

"As will I," Thomas said.

"Tell me," said Talavera, "do you believe it was you or God who cured her grace?" The priest crossed himself at mention of his master.

"I believe the Queen's devotion helped her to recover, but it was my hand that mixed the potions, Theresa's hand that administered them, and another woman who supplied the herbs. She may have recovered on her own through faith alone, but I believe God works through those who walk this earth. He does not bother making an appearance himself. Not even for a Queen."

"Sir, your words are close to blasphemy."

"I speak the truth."

"Whose truth? God's truth? There is only one truth, and it is not yours."

"Are the burnings God's truth?" Thomas's anger sparked him to utter words he might come to regret. This man was close to Isabel, in some ways even closer than her husband, and certainly far closer than Thomas himself. The torture, the executions, were done in the name of their God, which was why Thomas had turned his back on all religion.

"The burnings cleanse." Talavera glanced aside, his first sign of weakness. "Spain faces greater threats than ever before, and there are times we must perform acts beyond what we wish."

Thomas waited for the man to say more. Instead he firmed his shoulders and washed a hand across his face, the moment gone. Whatever Talavera's opinion of the Inquisition it was one he held close. It might be voiced to those he trusted, but it was clear he did not trust Thomas. There was still something he might reveal if it was asked, and Thomas rested his arms on the table in mirror of Talavera.

"Tell me what you know of Abbot Mandana, Friar."

"I know you were involved in his pursuit a number of years ago," said Talavera. "After he took Prince Juan."

"I rode alongside King Fernando, and when it was done we all assumed Mandana dead, yet here he is, once more at the heart of events. How did such a thing come about?"

"His being alive, or his being involved?"

"I understand a pool of water is responsible for his being alive."

"It was God's will," said Talavera, crossing himself again. "And his involvement is because the man possesses skills few others do. I will say no more on the matter." Talavera stood and walked to the window, though there was nothing to see other than a corner of the stone wall that surrounded the palace gardens. Thomas wondered if the turning of his back was in dismissal or to hide his true thoughts.

"Tell me one thing. Do you trust Abbot Mandana to do what is best for Spain? For King and Queen?"

"He is the King's man," said Talavera, which was no answer, but all he was going to offer.

"And the Queen?" Thomas said. He watched as Talavera's shoulders stiffened, but he refused to turn around.

Thomas rose, uncertain of what to do. An edge of anger still ran through him, and he was aware he needed to set it aside and use logic. He stood with his fists on the table, trying to decide whether there was anything more to be learned. This man was close to Isabel, privy to her deepest thoughts, to the fears she carried unaided. Oh to be a spider on the wall when the two of them talked, that would be something to wish for. He steeled himself to walk away, a harder thing to do than confront Talavera, but also wiser. Thomas turned, a sense of failure settling through him, just as a servant appeared, flushed as if he had been running.

"You are Thomas Berrington?" the man asked, and when Thomas nodded, "The Queen needs you. She needs you now!"

When Thomas saw Theresa with the Queen a moment of fear ran through him.

"Are you unwell, your grace?"

Isabel smiled. "Theresa was only keeping me company until you arrived. She will leave now."

"Is it seemly, your grace?" said Theresa.

Another smile. "I believe I am safe with Thomas. Besides, we are not alone." She inclined her head toward the three paiges that stood against the walls, staring at the ceiling to ensure they did not meet the Queen's eyes.

A second chair had been placed crossways to where Isabel sat, and as soon as Theresa left the room she indicated it, waiting for Thomas to sit.

"I have sent for food and coffee. It is coffee you prefer, is it not? And water for me. I am being good, you see." She was far too amenable, and Thomas watched her closely, wary. The message brought by the servant had sounded urgent, but now the Queen was relaxed, almost flirtatious. "Tell me, what is more important than the Queen of Spain?"

Steel encased in velvet. She shifted in her chair as if some inner pain troubled her.

"Do you have some discomfort, your grace?"

"Do not try to distract me, Thomas. Where have you been?"

"You know where I have been. Your advisor Friar Talavera wanted to ensure I am not about to corrupt you." Pleased when he saw a twitch of her lips.

"And who called on you in the middle of the night?" The trace of a smile gone now. "Were you so desperate you had to drag some woman in from the street? I have seen the way Theresa looks at you. Could you not have slaked your lust on her? I am sure she would be more than willing."

"The woman is my–" Thomas stopped. No, he would pretend no longer. "She was to be my wife. Our wedding was interrupted by Martin when he came for me. I told you this when I came."

Isabel stared at him for what felt like an age, her face without expression. Finally she leaned forward, her finger-tips touching.

"Yes, you said something. I am curious why you would do such a thing, interrupt your wedding and come to me instead?"

"The wedding had not started, and I considered your wellbeing more important. So did Martin. He was insistent."

"He is a good servant, but had I known…"

"How could you have known?"

A shake of the head, as if it was a failure on her part. "Is she the one who ate with us in Ronda? Small, dark haired? She is beautiful. You have chosen well."

"Sometimes we have no choice," Thomas said, knowing it might sound wrong. "I mean, love has no reasoning, it just is. Jorge says that all the time."

"Jorge is the tall one. I remember him. Handsome. He was

there in Ronda, too, wasn't he? Have they all followed you to Sevilla?"

"And my son."

"Your son? He is here, in the palace?"

"They came last night but were not admitted."

"Why not?" A wave of the hand. "It does not matter. They must join you. Your wife and son must be with you. But perhaps not the handsome one. He was the cause of trouble last time he lived in the palace."

"Jorge remains with a friend."

"I would meet with them. Your wi–your woman follows the cult of Islam, does she not? I recall us talking of it. She surprised me."

"She has a habit of doing that."

"And we must talk of your wedding. Send her to me when she arrives. I have matters of state to attend to, but later this afternoon send her to me so we can talk of weddings, woman to woman. And send your son, too. Juan and he shall be friends." As if life could be organised so simply, but perhaps for one such as her it could.

"He is younger than Juan," Thomas said.

"Then Maria." A smile touched with mischief. "Perhaps we can make a match between them."

"He is no prince."

"No. Not yet."

CHAPTER TWELVE

It was almost noon and another building stood in front of Thomas. Lubna remained in Belia's house, asleep beside Jorge. When she woke Thomas would take her to the palace, but he did not want to rely on Isabel's hospitality, knowing it could be withdrawn as swiftly as it had been offered. Hence the house they stood in front of.

Will clutched Thomas's hand, patient, quiet. There had been a change in the boy over recent months. He had never been silent, even though the words he spoke were often garbled, one phrase in Arabic, the next Swedish, another Spanish. Then he had changed, saying less and watching more. Thomas worried the boy spent too much time with Olaf Torvaldsson, a man who said little and watched everything. Olaf had been training Will, Thomas unsure whether that was for the good or not, but he did know they were living in dangerous times. An ability to fight would be useful, but was the age of three old enough? Olaf claimed so, claimed it was the perfect age to begin learning how to use the shield and axe. He intended to turn Will into a miniature berserker. "When the Spanish come," he had said. "everyone must be ready." It had been a long speech for Olaf. Long but true.

"It's certainly big enough," Thomas said to Belia, who stood the other side of Will, his other hand in hers. "And you are sure nobody lives here?"

"It is a plague house," she said. "It was a rich merchant's. The entire family were swept away and now it lies empty, for no-one will risk entering. There are a hundred such houses throughout the city. They will stand empty for years unless someone takes ownership. There is a man who uses my services sometimes who works with those living in shacks outside the city walls. I suggested they could make use of the houses, but even they refuse, though they barely have a canvas roof over their heads."

"So are more rational, or more stupid?" Thomas examined the two story facade that fronted the street. "Jorge likes big houses, but Lubna will be in the palace with me soon. Even Jorge, big as he is, will have enough room where you are."

"If the Queen lets Lubna stay," said Belia. "I hear she is jealous of your other women."

"Then you hear more than me."

"I thought your son was Jorge's when you brought them to me, and Lubna his wife. Why did you not correct me?"

"Had I known I would have. You know Jorge is incapable of becoming a father, don't you?"

Belia laughed. "Do you think I want to bring children into a world such as this? But it is a pity, for he would make a good father. It is why I thought him Will's. It is clear the boy loves him, so I thought... well, you know what I thought. Jorge is unattached?"

Standing in the fierce heat of midday, Thomas said, "Yes, unattached for the moment." He glanced at Belia, beautiful in her own right, something otherworldly about her. "You know he does not understand the concept of fidelity?"

"I think he may have mentioned it to me at some time during the night, but I was otherwise occupied and paid little heed. Besides, you assume I am looking for permanence. We may all be dead tomorrow. No-one can predict where this pestilence might strike, or when there will come a knock on the door from those red-robed priests."

"How many has it taken?"

"The sickness? Thousands in this city alone. You have it in Gharnatah, but not as bad as here. Did you have it where you come from, Thomas, this England?"

"I came close to death as a boy. My mother and brother were taken. My sister was spared, as was my father."

"I am sorry you lost those close to you."

Thomas glanced at her. A tall woman, dark hair covered in the Moorish manner, except she was not a Moor. He suspected Belia's race to be far more ancient. "I was not the only one, and at least I survived."

"How old were you?"

"I had twelve years, almost thirteen. It was the summer before I sailed to France." Thomas started forward, jerking Will with him, and Will in turn pulling Belia. "I suppose we had better look at this house, then."

The door stood closed but unlocked, a white mark across the dark wood sufficient to keep out interlopers, left this way when the last of the dead were taken out. Thomas stopped on the threshold, holding Will back, who was curious to see inside. He took a breath through his nose, let it out from his mouth, moving his tongue around. There was a faint hint of what had happened here, but soap, water, and effort would clear it. A wide staircase rose from a spacious hall, splitting into two galleries from which rooms led. To the left a large room acted as both kitchen and dining room, a windowed balcony looking over the river.

"This is indeed a fine house," he said. "You are sure no-one will object to us using it?"

"Not immediately. People have long memories where the plague is concerned, but eventually questions will be asked, by the city authorities if not its population. As you say, it is a fine house, and fine houses are worth money. How long will you stay in Sevilla?"

"Likely no more than a month. I hear the Queen is already planning to travel north while she still can."

"Will you go with her?"

"If she hasn't dismissed me by then." Thomas stepped into the hallway. Limestone flags provided a smooth floor. Thomas felt like an intruder but knew it was his own emotion being projected. The house was neutral, as houses are. "I don't suppose I can employ someone to scrub every surface with lime, can I?"

"Superstition."

"Or not," Thomas said, thinking of the work that was needed to clean and make the house habitable. Did he want to bring Lubna here? "Is there not somewhere smaller? Somewhere people have not died in?"

"I did not expect you to be superstitious." Belia released Will's hand and walked deeper into the house, opening doors that had not been opened in a month or more. "Look, there is a good larder here, and the balcony is wide. It is a fine house indeed. We could all live here and never see each other if we did not want to."

"Try telling that to Jorge. You would come with us, to live here too? You could move your business here where the neighbours are richer."

"I do not do what I do for money. You only ask because you want someone to help clean." Belia softened her words with a smile. She walked to the cold fire and knelt to examine shelves near the floor. Thomas watched her, uneasy.

"Jorge," said Will, beside him.

"What about Jorge?"

"Jorge like here." Will waved a hand at the wide room that took up almost the entire ground floor, and Thomas smiled.

"Yes, Jorge would like it here. What about you, Will? Do you like?"

Will tugged at his hand, drawing him to the tall windows that looked across the river. Castillo de Triana, the home of the Inquisition, was not visible from the house, for which Thomas was grateful. A narrow door stood open and Will pulled free of Thomas's hand and ran outside onto the deep balcony. There was a railing, but even if there had not been the balcony was only four feet above ground level. Thomas looked up and saw another, set out from the rooms above. Yes, Belia was right, it was indeed a fine house. When he returned Belia had found soap and buckets and was scrubbing the surface of the abandoned table. Thomas took another bucket and started at the other side of the room.

When they were finished Will was nowhere in sight. Thomas had grown used to leaving the boy to wander freely at home, both in his own house and at the palace, where he knew he could come to no harm. He checked the front door but it was still shut, a bolt thrown across. He climbed the stairs, calling out, but could not find his son in any of the four rooms on the second floor. He searched for a ladder to an attic but found none. He ran down the stairs, taking three treads at a time.

"He's out there," said Belia, who had already started work on the chairs and walls.

Thomas went to the balcony. Will was standing on the bank of the river, the water wide and deep, the current strong. A man stood beside him, one Thomas recognised, and he leapt the balcony railings and ran toward the water, calling his son's name.

Will looked up and grinned, his hand clasped in that of the other man.

"Mananana," said Will.

"You are a lucky man, Berrington," said Abbot Mandana. "If I had a son I would like one such as this. He is curious, like his father. He wanted to know what I was doing here, but of course I could not tell him the truth, so I said I was coming to see you, which is also the truth, just not the whole truth."

"Is there any more news about what happened this morning?" Thomas held his hand out and Will, taking a last look at Mandana, released his hold and came to him. Thomas wondered if the house Belia had brought them to was not a poor choice after all. He looked along the river bank, relieved to find the killing ground out of sight. Would the smoke and the smell of burning flesh be, too?

"Nothing. I am here for trade on behalf of al-Haquim. A corsair is to dock this afternoon with a cargo of slaves. They will be useful, for much work is going undone with so many dead." He glanced down at Will, up at Thomas. "You are willing to help me still, are you?"

"You said there was something else you wanted to show me." Thomas made no attempt to hide his disdain.

Mandana smiled and nodded toward the house. "Do you intend to live here?" He nodded at the house. Belia was visible through the glass, bending to scrub at something on the floor. "Is that your wife?"

"A friend."

"Ah. A friend. You are a fortunate man to have so many friends. Take care of them, for we live in dangerous times. Speaking of which, yes, if you are ready to help we should talk."

"Where and when?"

"If you can make it tonight that would be good. And then I will show you another sight tomorrow."

Mandana dropped to his knees and held his an arm. Will, always far too willing to trust everyone, ran across and flung his arms around the man's neck. Mandana hugged him, whispering into his ear, but his gaze stayed on Thomas the whole time.

CHAPTER THIRTEEN

"What did that man say to you?" Thomas carried a tired Will as he followed Belia through streets grown busy.

"Something," said Will, his words soft with coming sleep.

"I know he said something, but what?"

"No, Pa!" Will roused, upset at not being believed. "Said something bad."

"He said something bad to you? What bad?"

"Pa… no… said *something*… something *is* bad. Tell your Pa something is bad." The words were jumbled, slurred, but the effort at conjuring them up exhausted Will and he laid his head against Thomas's chest and closed his eyes. Within moments his small body stilled. Thomas wrapped him safe within his robe as men and women jostled past. It was late afternoon, the heat of the day finally slackening, and the populace were about in search of food, drink and entertainment. Word had spread there may be more burnings, but Thomas knew different. Let them stream to the waterside in search of their measure of horror. For himself he had seen too much of the real thing, at too close quarters, to ever want to see more. Now and again as he passed knots of people he overheard the word Ghost, always uttered softly, as if you say it too loud might conjure the spirit itself.

Belia turned from the main thoroughfare into an alleyway, quieter here and shaded. Thomas followed, staring at her back until he realised he stared too hard, a flush of guilt running through him.

Lubna was awake when they arrived at Belia's small house, but told them Jorge continued to sleep. "He has barely closed his eyes since we left Gharnatah."

Thomas took her hand while Belia went through to the small kitchen.

"He should not have brought you, it wasn't safe."

"After you had abandoned me on our wedding day?" said Lubna, her voice cool. She withdrew her hand and laid it in her lap beneath a belly showing little sign of the child she carried.

"You know that was not my doing."

"Is that so? You could have said no. You could have said you needed another day, even half a day. Half a day and we would have been man and wife."

"As we will be." Thomas reached again for her hand, but Lubna burrowed both between her thighs. "We can marry here."

"In Spain? A Catholic country? Next you'll tell me the Queen has arranged for us to wed in the Cathedral."

Thomas looked away.

"She has, hasn't she?"

"No. But I told her what happened," Thomas said. "She was angry with me, but she knows I had to come. Samuel said she was recovering before I arrived, but I am not so sure. The child she carries is important to her, to Spain."

"Who is Samuel? Another of your Catholic friends? You are becoming a good friend to Spain, Thomas. Do you forget they want every Moor expelled from this country?"

"Isabel says not, she says—"

"*Isabel* says not? Are you sure it is me you want to marry, Thomas Berrington? She is pretty, I hear. They say power attracts, and she is the most powerful woman in Spain."

Thomas sat back, mouth open. He shook his head. "Listen to yourself. This isn't you. Isabel is Queen of Spain, not just some woman. And yes I consider her a friend, and she me I think, but it is you I love." He leaned forward. "It is *you* I want to marry, you I *will* marry. Tomorrow if you wish it, today even."

"It is too late today."

Thomas gave a soft laugh. "Yes, it most likely is. Tomorrow then. I am too tired to do our wedding night justice in any case."

Lubna shook her head. "You could ask Jorge to substitute, I don't think he ever has problems in that area."

"No. And he should, considering what I did to him." Thomas stared at Lubna. "You and he…"

It was Lubna's turn to laugh, the tension between them set aside for the moment, but Thomas knew it would return. He had not treated this woman as well as she deserved. And now she carried his child. Another son? Or a girl? A girl would be welcome. A sister for Will.

"Jorge and I have slept side by side since leaving Gharnatah, even today because Belia has only one bed in her house, and we have kept her from it long enough. But Jorge loves me in a different way to you." Lubna pulled a face that made Thomas laugh. "He does not force himself on me."

"Force? I'm trying to recall when force has ever been required." This time when he reached for her hand it emerged like a butterfly from a chrysalis and he took it. "It appears you are feeling a little better."

"All I needed was sleep. And Belia's potions. And of course the care of the best physician in the whole of Spain."

"If he's touched you I will kill him!"

"Oh… he has touched me," said Lubna. "He has touched me in all my private places, but most of all he has touched me here." She placed her free hand between her breasts. "In my heart." A shake of the head. "Now if only the idiot would get his priorities right we might be wed before I make him a father."

Yes, Thomas thought, there is that.

A sound came from upstairs and he glanced at the door. Lubna raised her hand from her chest to smother a giggle.

"Are they doing what I think they are?" Thomas said. "Already?"

"He is rather charming. And I think Belia likes him."

A cry sounded, a rattling of wood against a wall.

"I should hope she does. But so soon?"

Lubna's expression melted into seriousness and she leaned close, cupping her hand to Thomas's face. "Who knows what calamity might strike us? Disease or violence or any number of other perils? We must all make the most of every moment of every day, should we not?" She waited for him to nod before saying, "As should we."

Thomas smiled. "But you already said there is only one bed. Unless you intend all four of us to tumble together?"

She slapped his cheek lightly and glanced at Will, who continued to sleep in the makeshift cot fashioned from two chairs and a cushion.

"I have found us a fine house, in any case," Thomas said. "I will take you there in the morning, or tonight if you wish."

"Like you intend to marry me tonight or tomorrow?"

"Yes, exactly like that. You will like the house. It is even better than the one in Gharnatah. And we will marry, I promise you. Here or Gharnatah, whichever is your wish, whenever is your wish. Now, this instant, if it what you want."

But it seemed a kiss was sufficient, and more than enough to make Thomas forget the troubles that gathered around him.

This time the guard barely glanced at Lubna when she accompanied Thomas through the gate. Light had leached from the sky to leave a faint line far to the north-west. Thomas carried Will, who had woken full of questions about the city, the people, the streets, the big building with a funny spire, the palace walls, the gate, the guard, the cobblestones, the soldiers, until Thomas said he would answer all his questions, but not now because he had something to do, and Will pulled a face but fell silent, his eyes wide as he took in the splendour of the palace. Not as splendid as that in Gharnatah, Thomas thought, but different, with tapestries on the walls, tables and chairs instead of cushions, and guards wearing the uniform of Spain.

"He thought me your whore," said Lubna, when they arrived at Thomas's rooms.

"Who did?" Thomas set Will down and he ran off to look through the dark window where scattered lights pricked the dark.

"The man at the gate. He thought I was a street girl you were bringing back. I saw him look away and then I saw him look again when he thought I wasn't." She smiled. "Will you treat me like a street girl?"

"My, you have recovered, haven't you?"

"I have missed you, Thomas Berrington." She came close, her arms snaking around his waist, and he enclosed her inside his. She moved softly against him, the swelling of her belly more obvious now she was so close.

"I'm not sure Will is going to sleep again so soon." He

kissed the top of her head, the scent of the journey still on her, and he wondered if Theresa could arrange for another bathtub to be brought.

"The wait will make it all the sweeter." She twisted out of his arms and went to join Will, kneeling so she was on the same level before looking back. "Besides, didn't you say your day was not yet finished?"

The air had taken on a chill as Thomas returned through streets only occasionally illuminated, and he drew his robe tighter, wrapped his tagelmust to cover his head. A stillness as deep as the night had settled into him, a stillness brought on by his conversation with Mandana. The man had not told him the truth, barely even a small part of it, but it had been enough. Even more importantly he had asked for Thomas's help in tracking this Ghost that he claimed terrorised the city. Thomas had seen little evidence so far, but there were so many terrors in Sevilla he wondered how one more could make a difference. Except those overheard conversations were enough to tell him the deaths concerned the population even more than the plague.

Ahead one of the plague carts crossed the roadway, wheels creaking. The hooded man leading the mule drawing it turned his head to study Thomas then moved on. He had passed half a dozen the same as he returned, assuming their work was conducted while others slept so as to keep the sight hidden.

"This is work for the Hermandos, is it not?" Thomas had said to Mandana, only the two of them in the dim courtyard, wine and food between them on a low table fashioned in Moorish style. Al-Haquim had been present but left with the boy who brought the food, his hand resting against his back.

"They have other demands made of them. The Inquisition uses them to gather their suspects."

"Have you asked them?"

"Of course I have." Mandana was sharp, then Thomas saw him make an effort to control himself. Only then did he recognise how much the man was asking of him, how much he was needed. "They do not care. What are a handful of bodies amongst the hundreds? People talk of this Ghost on corners and at inns, in their houses and places of work. It is why I need your help."

"You want me to investigate?"

"As you have before. Do not pretend you are not intrigued."

"My first duty is to the Queen," Thomas said.

"Samuel told me she is healed, that he can perform most of the duties required now. Or do you offer her some other service I do not know of?"

"She trusts me more than Samuel. Besides, I have other responsibilities, too."

"Your wife, your son, that pretence for a man. Yes, I know. You will refuse me?"

Thomas knew he would not, could not, refuse. Not because Mandana asked, in fact despite it being Mandana who asked, but because he had grown addicted to the process, the uncovering of layers of details until a suspect lay exposed. And, if he was honest with himself, his pride did not want someone else to take the credit. It was a weakness, but he knew he was a man of many weaknesses, and in this case it was a very small one.

Which is why as he entered the palace his mind was at rest.

CHAPTER FOURTEEN

When Thomas woke the silk of Lubna's skin lay against his and he believed it was the first night he had slept undisturbed since arriving in Ixbilya. He rolled to his back and pushed hair from his face, stared up at the ceiling where light from the undraped window cast knife-sharp shadows.

"Pa."

Will knelt at the foot of the bed, eyes bright, expression eager.

"What is it, my sweet?" He held a finger to his lips. "And speak soft, Ma is sleeping."

"Ma is not sleeping," came a muffled voice.

"Go there." Will pointed through the window to where the ornate gardens stretched to a distant wall.

Thomas sat up. "I don't know. I expect you can if I ask. Do you want to?"

Will nodded enthusiastically. "Birds, Pa." He held his arms as wide as he could. "*Big* birds."

Thomas had heard them, far too soon before dawn, cursing their noise. Peacocks, exotic creatures imported from the east. There were peacocks in Gharnatah and now the birds were here too. Thomas had still not decided if he approved of keeping such large birds if they were not to be eaten, but had to admit an admiration of their beauty, if not their cries.

"Let me see if I can find someone. You wait here with Ma." He rolled from the bed, wide and comfortable, fit for a Duque, perhaps even a King, and wondered who these rooms were reserved for here in the heart of the royal palace. Thomas wrapped a sheet around himself and padded through the outer rooms to the hallway. A man stood at the far end, waiting, and Thomas beckoned him over.

"My son wants to run in the gardens. Do you know if it is allowed?"

The man stared at Thomas as if he had lost his wits. "The gardens?"

"Yes."

"Why?"

"It is not your place to question why." Thomas suppressed a flare of anger. The day had started too well to be angry at fools. "If you cannot make a decision go ask someone who can. You know where I am. And I assume you know who I am."

The man turned, hesitated, then trotted away. Thomas sighed, deciding he might as well dress and go to see how the Queen was faring this morning. When he returned to the room for his clothes Lubna was leaning over Will, tickling him, the boy's face bright red. Hearing him Lubna turned, grinning, and Thomas felt his heart might stop. At one time he had lived with one of the most beautiful women in Spain, but Helena never touched his heart in the way this woman did. None had, not since another long ago, now lost to him for good, and he knew the raw love of youth was nothing compared to what he felt for Lubna.

"Can Will go?" his son asked. He had started to refer to

himself this way of late as his speech grew better. Thomas wondered if it was because he spent too much time with Olaf, who often referred to himself in the third person.

"I've sent someone to ask." Thomas dropped the sheet and went in search of clean clothes. Already he had grown used to the silent care that went into making his life comfortable. Dropped clothes were secretly folded or, if dirty, cleaned. He found pants and a shirt of fine linen and pulled them on. When he turned to look for shoes Lubna was staring at him, a hunger in her eyes. Thomas smiled and shook his head. "Will and I are going for a walk with the peacocks."

Lubna pulled a face and slid back beneath the covers.

There was a knock on the outer door and Will sprinted toward it. Thomas grabbed him, swinging him through the air. "Better get dressed first, boy, this is a palace remember. You're not at home now." He deposited Will on the floor and helped him dress, then went to say goodbye to Lubna. She was still in bed and he knelt beside her, allowed his hand to snake beneath the cover to find her warmth.

"Stop it," she said, "or I will not be responsible for my actions."

"Were you responsible last night?"

"I have still not forgiven you," she said.

"Then I would like you to not forgive me again, as soon if it can be arranged."

"I thought you were going for a walk with Will."

"I am."

Lubna sat up and winced. "I'm not fully recovered yet," she said. "I will stay here and sleep longer if it is allowed?"

Thomas felt her brow, but the fever had not returned. "It is probably the last of whatever ails you. At least we have our own privy here so you can make a dash there if need be."

Lubna pulled a face and Thomas laughed, leaned in to kiss her brow. "Yes, sleep, it will do you good." He rose as another knock sounded. When he went through Will had already opened the door and was staring up at the tall figure of Martin de Alarcón, his mouth open in admiration.

"The Queen?" Thomas said, fearing he had come on another errand.

"The Queen is occupied with matters of state, which we must thank you for, Thomas. No, I heard someone wanted to see the gardens. I assume it is not you?" Martin made a show of staring around, keeping his gaze raised. "But I see nobody else here."

Will tugged at Martin's pants' leg.

"Ah…" He knelt. "You cannot be Thomas's son, can you? You are far too handsome a boy."

For a second Thomas felt a flash of doubt he had not experienced in more than a year, but pushed it away. Whoever Will's true father was, he was Thomas's son, there was no doubt on that, no doubt at all.

"Pa han-nom too. Ma says all time," Will said.

"Does she? Well, in that case it must be true." Martin hesitated. "She can see all right, can she?" He held a hand out and Will, ever trusting, slid his own inside its grasp. Martin glanced at Thomas. "Are you coming? You can return to your woman if you want, I think I can take care of this one on my own."

"I will come. Lubna needs the rest."

———

The peacocks rose into the air with squawks of protest as Will ran full tilt toward them, convinced he could capture one despite the growing evidence against.

"He's as stubborn as someone else I know," said Martin. "You're a lucky man, Thomas."

They had seen no-one else in the gardens and Will was

more than able to amuse himself. Once or twice Thomas had to intervene when he saw him trying to reach a plant that was toxic. On each occasion, he knelt and showed his son how to identify the plant and explained it was not to be touched. Will nodded as if he understood, and Thomas knew he would need to repeat the lesson, but already the boy could recognise a number of plants and herbs. In a few places Thomas slowed to examine the ground, wondering if he could persuade Isabel it would be a good idea to plant her own herb garden. He could ask Belia to select medicinal plants and tend it for her. The more knowledge was spread the better for the world.

"I need to ask you something," Thomas said as Martin walked beside him.

"Sounds serious."

"It is."

Martin stopped. In the distance a peacock called out, its wings beating a pattern through the air as Will chased it.

"I want to ask about Mandana. Has he changed?"

"In what way? He lacks a hand now, but you already know that. In other ways, yes, he has changed from the man you once knew."

"Explain it to me," Thomas said.

Martin started to walk again. "It would help if you told me what you want to know. I have little to do with the man these days, but he has managed to worm his way back into a position of, if not power, then influence."

"I hear he is close to Fernando."

"As am I," said Martin. "He is not close in the way you might think. The King has a need for a man loyal to him who lacks a conscience, a man who has soldiers who share his distorted view of the world."

"You don't approve."

"Mandana can be useful, I understand that. But if it was

me? He would have been dead years since. He has no place in a civilised land."

"You have told Fernando your opinion?"

"I have, but although he listens he tells me sometimes the decisions a king must make are hard."

"Does Mandana know how you feel about him?"

"I have told him to his face, but he only laughs. He laughs more than he used to, as if he finds the entire world amusing."

"Do you fear what he might do? What he might instruct his men to do? Mandana does not suffer enemies to live, particularly enemies who have the King's ear."

"I would like him to try," said Martin, and Thomas knew he would be a hard man to kill.

"He has a position in the castle over the river, as well as some strange friends."

"You can say its name," said Martin. "Castillo de Triana, home of the Inquisition."

"What is your opinion of that organisation?"

Martin stopped. "Do not ask me that. Do not ever ask me that again. I consider us friends, but no friend would ask such a question, not in this city."

"Then I will ask you something you can answer. Is Mandana involved?"

"He sits on the panel of judges."

"Yet I hear he is not in complete agreement with the methods used or the victims chosen."

"Not victims. Heretics. There is a difference. And if he has doubts he does not express them and would be wise to keep it that way. As you would be wise to not get involved in matters that are nothing to do with you."

"He showed me the body of a man that had been cut into."

"So? There are many dead in this city. Too many. And people still fight and get themselves killed."

"This was not the first, I understand," Thomas said.

They started to walk again just as Will appeared at the end of a long avenue of neatly tended bushes. He was hand in hand with a girl his own age, while an older boy walked behind. A tall man and two women brought up the rear. Will saw Thomas and waved, called out. The older boy looked up. For a moment his face remained blank, then broke into a grin as he launched himself along the avenue, neatly avoiding the lunge of his protector.

Thomas knelt as Prince Juan, heir to the thrones of Castile and Aragon, threw himself into his arms. The boy clutched tight around Thomas's neck.

"I will not tell your mother that you ran so fast, Juan. You remember what happened last time, don't you?"

Juan extricated himself and straightened his jacket as if embarrassed at his sudden show of affection. Then he thrust out the leg which had been broken, the leg Thomas had repaired.

"See, I can run even faster now, all thanks to you." He turned as Will and the girl approached, the girl's features familiar even though Thomas was sure he had never seen her before. "He claims to be your son," said Juan, sounding now like the young Prince he was.

"Then he claims right. And the girl, she is your sister?" He searched his memory, trying to place Isabel's children in order. "She is Maria, is she not?"

"Juana did not want to play today." Juan leaned closer. "She is too serious. So I had to bring Maria, but she is too young for me. I have eight years now."

"Then you are almost a man," Thomas said, pleased when Juan suppressed a smile. "And a man must accept his responsibilities and play with his sisters even if they are young."

"Can your son fight? What is his name, Thomas?"

"Will. Short for William."

"Juan is not short for anything," said Juan, as if that made him better, which well it might.

"People do not shorten the names of princes." Thomas glanced at the two women and lone guard who shadowed the royal children. "It seems each has made a new friend. Can my son accompany them for a while? It will do them good to learn how others live."

The guard looked uncertain, as did one of the women, but the other nodded, a smile on her face, and Thomas tried to recall if he knew her or not.

"It is time they had a drink and something to eat. He can come with us, if you will allow it, sir?"

Thomas knew Will would be safe, and there was something he needed to do. Nothing would befall his son inside the palace. Not unless he ran too fast down a stair, and he suspected Juan would prevent him doing that.

"I have rooms in the eastern part of–"

Thomas was interrupted by the woman. "I know who you are, Thomas Berrington, and I know where your rooms are. I will ensure your son is safely returned and arrange for someone to be with him until your business is complete."

Thomas tried again to remember if he knew the woman or not. There were so many who attended the Queen, and so many who tended to similar looks. Whether he knew her or not she knew him.

"My wife will be awake by then, you can leave him with her." Once more it was easier to avoid any explanation, and perhaps soon it would no longer be necessary.

CHAPTER FIFTEEN

Thomas was pleased to find Jorge and Belia downstairs when he arrived at her house in the square, and made no mention of their sleeping arrangements. Jorge's actions were no surprise, but Thomas had not thought Belia so ready to tumble into bed with him so soon after their meeting. But knowing Jorge as he did it might have been expected.

"Belia tells me you have bought us a new house." Jorge sat at the table, picking at slices of fruit. The aroma of coffee laced the air, together with the scent of fresh bread. "I would as soon stay here." He glanced at Belia. "If I am welcome, that is."

Belia reached out and stroked Jorge's head, the stubble of hair beginning to appear.

"Liberated rather than bought," Thomas said.

"Is it a fine house?"

"It is indeed. Belia might like to move there as well, though it will be no permanent home."

"How long?" asked Jorge. He wiped his fingers in a cloth and stood, stretching. "And I hope I need to do no work on it." After his bones had clicked he slid his arms around Belia and pulled her against him.

"Until Isabel releases me," Thomas said.

"If she releases you. Ah well, there is little to keep me in Gharnatah these days, and Ixbilya has its charms."

Thomas shook his head and avoided looking at them. "You will need furniture, food, and wood for the stove, and fresh bedding and beds too, most like."

"And clothes?" said Jorge. "Do they have fine clothes for sale in this city, silks and the like?"

"If you are willing to pay."

"I am always willing to pay," said Jorge.

"I know of someone who can furnish the house," said Belia, slipping from Jorge's arms and tidying the table. "I will ask them to arrange it. We can all sleep there tonight if you wish."

"Lubna is with me in the palace now," Thomas said. "Tomorrow will be soon enough if we need to. I would accompany you but I have an appointment. I would take Jorge with me if you can spare him."

"You are welcome to him. I suspect my task will be easier if he is otherwise occupied. Does your patient need any more medicines prepared?" Belia had no need to mention a name.

"She is recovering, thanks to you. But Lubna has a belly ache. If you have something for that I will take it."

Belia smiled as she moved away.

"She complained on the journey," said Jorge. "We took food where we could, and I was ill too. She's tough, and Bel will find her something to help."

"Bel?"

Jorge raised a shoulder and examined his nails, finely filed and perfect. "What is this other matter? You haven't gotten involved in something that is none of your business again, have you?"

"What makes you say that?"

Jorge made a show of innocence. "I said nothing."

"You have no need to. But yes, possibly."

Jorge shook his head. "Then I had best come in case you get into trouble. I'm sure Bel can spare me until this evening."

"This business might also involve a pair of old friends."

"Who?"

"You will meet one this morning. The other not, but I will try to explain everything when our business is done." Thomas was reluctant to tell Jorge too much. Their morning would prove difficult enough, and if he tried to explain how difficult Jorge might not come, and Thomas wanted him there.

Jorge maintained a constant commentary on the city, the people, and particularly the women as Thomas led him through fine thoroughfares toward the river. He grew more quiet when they reached the start of the Barcas bridge and caught sight of the charred posts, holding back as Thomas stepped onto swaying planks.

"Is that thing safe?"

Thomas rocked, sending wavelets dancing away from the pontoons on which the bridge rested. "I've seen forty men cross it. I am sure even someone as big as you will be safe."

"I am not big", said Jorge.

Thomas knew it was true, though the new slimmer Jorge could do nothing to reduce his height, and it marked him out in this place where even Thomas was regarded as tall.

"Just come on," he said, turning away.

"Where are we going?" The bridge dipped as Jorge stepped onto it. He gripped a rail, but after a moment fell into step.

"There." Thomas nodded to where Castillo de Triana loomed from the edge of the river.

"And what is there?"

"It is the home of the Inquisition."

Jorge stopped. After a moment Thomas did too and turned back to him.

"Why are we going to the home of the Inquisition?" said Jorge. "Should we not be running as fast as we can in the other direction?"

"It is not us they want," Thomas said.

"I did not assume they did, but still I would rather not go there."

"We are to meet someone."

"An Inquisitor?"

"No." Then Thomas reconsidered. "Perhaps. But not like the others." He was still confused at the change in Mandana. "You will see when we get there."

"So mysterious," said Jorge. "Always so mysterious."

As they started up again Thomas wondered if Jorge's good mood would survive the meeting.

There was a single soldier guarding the entrance, a heavy double door thrown open on one side. Likely no more than one man was ever needed, for most people avoided this place rather than sought it out. Thomas gave his name and said he was expected. The guard disappeared for a moment, no doubt to pass on the message. When he returned he took up his stance, standing a little straighter, staring at Jorge as if he had never seen his like before, which was no doubt true. The man would be unable to tell Jorge was a eunuch, but he could tell he was different.

"When do you plan to tell me who we are meeting?" said Jorge.

Thomas sighed, knowing he had drawn this out too long. "An old friend. One you believed dead."

Jorge shook his head, opened his mouth to speak then snapped it shut as he stared beyond Thomas to where Abbot

Mandana had appeared at the gate. When he managed to tear his gaze away it locked on Thomas.

"Him? How?"

"A deep pool of water, apparently."

"Why did you bring your pet, Berrington?" Mandana's voice was hoarse, as if he had stood too close to the flames of the Inquisition. Thomas could imagine the man there, near enough to hear the screams that turned to whimpers and to smell the stink of burning flesh. Unless he truly had changed.

"My friend has skills I value. Are you going to keep us standing here in the sun all day or show me what you brought me here for?"

Mandana turned abruptly and walked inside. Thomas glanced at the guard, but it seemed they were now granted admittance and he walked into the shadows of Triana, hoping Jorge would follow but knowing he would continue even if his friend remained outside.

Inside the castle the air was cool and carried a dampness which rose from the river, together with the taint of corruption, as if something foul rotted beneath the flagstones. As he followed Mandana deeper he was aware of the weight of stone above, of the array of corridors leading ever deeper into the interior, and the further they penetrated noises came, faint at first, then louder until they could not be ignored. Voices calling out in fear and pain, screams, sobs. And other sounds. As they passed a cell where the door stood open Thomas peered inside to see a naked man laid across a wooden instrument. A guard stood at one end, his hand on a ratchet. Two red-robed priests were at the man's feet, which were blood-caked from some earlier torture.

"Tell me the names of your friends," said one, and the other nodded as if it was the most incisive question ever.

"There are no names! I have told you again and again, I am innocent."

The priest nodded and the guard heaved on the handle of the rack. Fresh screams filled the air.

"Berrington!" Mandana's voice was impatient. "Do you want to see this place or not? I judged you strong enough to take these sights, but perhaps I was wrong."

Thomas cast a final glance, not wanting to but drawn to the scene, then started away. "Show me then, and let me leave." He glanced at Mandana. "I can leave, can't I?"

"Of course. I need your skills."

Thomas wondered what might happen when Mandana no longer had that need. He led the way through a series of turns as Thomas tried to make note of the direction they went, not that he was likely to ever want to return here. At last Mandana's steps slowed. The cries and stink of torture had been left behind. To the right a wide corridor led away to a series of dungeons. Ahead another door was half open.

"Is this the place?" Thomas asked.

Mandana nodded. "You can enter alone, I have no wish to see it again."

Thomas took three paces, pushed the door wider, then stopped and glanced down at the latch. There was a heavy iron bolt, but it lay on the inner side only.

Mandana smiled. "What, did you think I was going to take you captive?"

"The thought had crossed my mind."

Mandana held his arms out, a picture of innocence. His missing hand marred the effect.

"Go in, tell me what you see."

Thomas took a step, still hesitant. "Will you be waiting here?"

"I have other business to attend to. Besides, this is not for me but you, to provide more information to help you catch this killer."

"What if I have questions?"

"Find me later. Ask and someone will bring you to me. But if you have questions I will be disappointed in you." Mandana began to turn away but Thomas had not yet finished with him.

"How long since the chamber was used?" He had no need to mention what it had been used for.

"Two months."

"And how often?"

"I don't understand."

"How many times did he kill here?"

"Once. Do you think we would allow the man to kill at will inside the castle?"

"I don't know, would you? Or would someone else? Are you sure it was only the once?"

"That I have been told of."

"And who were the victims? Was one of them displayed?"

"He was."

"Where?"

"In the courtroom where the guilty are tried. He had been sat in one of the chairs used by the priests. His head was on the table in front of him."

"Who?"

"The new Bishop of Ronda, visiting the Cathedral here. Now really, I must go, already I am late for the court."

Another man of God, Thomas thought. There had to be some significance. Did the killer hate all religion, or only Catholics?

"Wait. One final request. I want to know what you said to my son."

"I whispered a message for him to pass to you."

"Would it not have been simpler to tell it to my face?"

Mandana smiled. "It amused me to do it the way I did."

"And the message was?"

A sigh. "I expected you to have worked it out by now. "I said to him, 'Tell your father Samuel is a bad man'.

Not *something*, as Will had said, but Samuel. And why was he bad? Thomas started to say something, but when he looked up Mandana was striding down the corridor, and the room behind was calling.

The chamber was small and empty. There had no doubt been a table here but it had been taken away, though Thomas wondered why because he doubted any blood stains would have concerned anyone within these walls.

Thomas walked the perimeter but nothing remained. He went to the door and shut it, threw the bolt then pulled on the ring set in the wood. The door was solid, secure. He leaned his ear against it, heard nothing. Would the screams that had filled this room be heard from outside? However thick the wood of the door the noise must have passed through. Except what were more screams in a place such as this?

He walked the floor, his gaze hard against the stone. A stain here, another there, but whether they were from the killings or nothing more than business as usual here he could not tell. He wondered why Mandana had bothered to bring him here. There was nothing of any use.

Or was there? Thomas wondered if he was here not to uncover evidence but to experience the place.

He walked to where he believed a table would have stood and lay flat on the floor, crossing his arms across his chest and staring upward. The ceiling was high and made of stone, no doubt the underside of the floor of whatever rooms lay above. He glanced around, saw nooks where candles or lamps would have sat. There were hooks on the ceiling where more light could be hung from. Or instruments of torture.

Thomas wondered why this room had not been used again.

Then he thought about the Bishop of Ronda. It would have been a recent appointment, someone plucked from obscurity to instil Christianity in a town which until earlier that year had belonged to the Moors. Thomas did not think Ronda significant in the choice of victim, only the man's faith. And faith was the common factor so far in the instances he was aware of.

When the cold penetrated his body he rose, glancing around for a final time and seeing nothing that offered even the slightest hint of being evidence. It was the place itself that carried significance. Its selection deliberate, here in the heart of the Inquisition.

<hr />

Jorge had not waited at the castle gate but Thomas found him wandering along the straight road that led away from the river.

"Why are you working with that man?"

"He claims to have changed." Thomas said.

"And you believe him?" Jorge shook his head. "Can we go back to the city now? I have been searching for an inn but there is nothing I would want to go into this side of the river." He nodded as the rumble of cart wheels came from the bridge. "And those carts keep coming. How many dead are there?"

"Too many." Thomas stepped into an alley as the cart approached, the stink like a punch to the chest. "But not as many as there will be before the end of the year."

"So why are we here?"

"Because I believe I cannot catch it again, and that if we keep ourselves clean we have some protection. Besides, there is plague in Gharnatah, too. It is a year for plague throughout Spain." He watched as the cart turned into a dirt track, then was hidden behind a stone wall. "Let us see if we can find you an establishment worthy of your sensibilities."

"Did Mandana show you anything useful?"

"I am not sure."

Jorge laughed. "Well, there's a first. Thomas Berrington is not sure."

CHAPTER SIXTEEN

The rooms allocated to him in the palace lay empty when Thomas returned. There was no sign of Lubna or Will. Someone had been to clean and there was fresh bedding even though the previous was barely slept in, but this was a different world he had been invited into and it would be best to accept the small luxuries of life within its walls. He went in search of information.

Theresa was where he expected. He had worked out she lived and slept in a small room near the royal chambers, always on call, always available. She was reading when he arrived and looked up sharply, surprised until she saw who it was. She put down the papers she had been studying and stood, coming across to him.

"How is she?" Thomas asked, having no need to explain who.

"Improved yet again. All the better for having something to take her mind off herself."

"Matters of state?"

"Matters of friendship."

"Fernando is back?"

Theresa laughed, taking another step to close the distance between them. Thomas had become accustomed to her ways and could ignore the teasing, sure that was all it was. Or would be until he made some response, which he was determined would never happen.

"Not the King. Your wife and son. Juan brought your son to meet his mother and she in turn sent for… Lubna, is it?"

Thomas nodded. "Where are they?"

"In the courtyard. It is cooler there, and she is weary of being locked indoors. I made sure she was strong enough, do not fear."

Thomas knew Theresa took her duty of care seriously, and her diligence pleased him. He glanced beyond her. "What were you reading?"

She put a hand to her mouth, surprising him. "Do not reveal me, Thomas, please." Two more steps, closing the space between them to a foot and her palm touched his chest. She had bathed, and the clean scent of her came to him.

"Why would I do so? What is it?" He brushed past her and picked up the pages, unbound and written by a rough hand in Spanish. He read the words slowly, his lips moving at the unfamiliarity, and then smiled as he recognised them. "This is a translation of an Arabic text, one I know well." He dropped the papers. "There is no sin in knowledge, Theresa, none at all."

"They are not of Spain," she said, eyes downcast. "If some in the palace knew I was reading them I would be expelled. The Queen's spiritual mentor would not allow it. And if Samuel were to discover them he would betray me."

"Why would he? He told me himself he studied in Malaka. The texts there would almost all be in Arabic."

"He does not like me. I think I make him afraid."

"Afraid? I can think of no-one less likely to do so than you."

She lifted her gaze, smiled. "Ah... but you and I almost have a past, do we not?"

"Perhaps." The memory of it still troubled him, a reminder of his weakness as a man. "Now how do I reach this courtyard?"

"I will take you, but you must enter on your own." Her smile broadened. "Then I will return to continue my illicit reading."

"Do you know how Lubna is? She complained of feeling unwell this morning."

"In what way?" Suddenly Theresa was all seriousness.

"Nothing more than a bellyache, most likely something she ate. The food here is different to what she is used to."

"She seemed well enough when I saw her, but I was not close to them." The smile returned. "Your son is handsome, like his father."

Thomas scowled and turned away before she could inflict more of her teasing.

When he found them the Queen was almost dozing. Sitting beside her in an ornate chair Lubna seemed hardly less awake. Thomas hesitated a moment, watching both, loving both but in different ways. Isabel touched him as few others had, with her friendship and her discipline both, but Lubna touched him as only one other ever had, and that other was long lost. He saw their future together, stretching into the years ahead, more children running around, growing, having children of their own while Thomas's hair greyed and his skin began to wrinkle but somehow, in these visions of his, Lubna remained unchanged, as beautiful as he saw her now, forever preserved.

"Pa!" Will saw him and came running. He skipped onto the raised edge of a pool, his feet a blur. Thomas caught him as he launched himself and swung him around. Close behind came Juan and Thomas lifted him too, one in each arm, Juan too heavy if he was honest but the boy clung to him as if he was father to both.

"I like Will," said Juan, "but he talks so oddly."

"He is young," Thomas said, "and has too many languages. He makes sense to me, but not to many others, not even those close to him. But you speak at least three tongues that I know of."

"Yes, but not all at the same time! Can he play with me again?"

"Is he not too young for you, my prince?"

"Do not call me that, Thomas. You know my name. Are we not friends?"

"I like to believe so, and yes he can play, for as long as we are here, and I will fetch him when I visit your mother."

"He showed me how he is learning to fight," said Juan. "Not with a sword, he says, but a shield and axe. I am good with a sword now. I have a man who trains me every day. Will can come too and we will see which is better, a sword or a shield and axe."

Knowing who had been teaching Will, Thomas knew the answer but chose not to share it with the youngster. "A wooden sword and axe, I hope. And you must remember he is half your age."

"But tall and strong. He will be fearless when he is grown. I do so hope this war is over by then. I do not want to fight your son in battle, Thomas."

"I would not wish that either, Juan." He kissed the boy on the cheek and put him down, his arm beginning to ache. When he straightened it was to find Isabel staring at him, an indulgent smile on her face.

"He has not forgotten you," she said when Thomas approached. "He does not talk of you when you are gone, but look at him now, you are a hero to my son. A renegade

English hero to a prince of Spain. What are we to do about such a thing? Shall I take your head to teach him a lesson?"

"It would be hard lesson on him, your grace, and an even harder one on me."

"If you continue to forget my name I will be most tempted."

Thomas looked around, saw a chair set against the wall and fetched it. "How are you?" He reached to touch her neck, her forehead, satisfied with what he found. When he glanced up he saw Lubna watching without expression.

"Your medicines are a wonder of the world."

"They are not all mine. A woman in the city helped."

"Then she must be employed here."

"I will ask, but expect she will refuse."

"Is she another Moor?"

"She is…" Thomas paused, thinking. "She is not a Moor, nor a Jew, but she is closer to Jew than Moor."

"We have many Jews employed here, the palace could not operate without their skills."

"I will ask, as I say." But Thomas knew Belia would not work in the palace. There was something otherworldly about her, something alien to anything he had ever encountered before. It was no doubt what drew Jorge to her. "I see you have met Lubna." He smiled. "My almost wife."

Isabel tried to look stern but the effect was marred by the turning up of one side of her mouth. "And she has been telling me what a terrible man you are."

"Of course she has."

"How could you abandon her at the altar?"

"In Gharnatah we do not marry at an altar."

Isabel reached out and slapped him lightly across the cheek. "You know what I mean. You abandoned her on your wedding day."

"For good cause," Thomas said. "You called me and I came."

"I could have waited another day."

"I did not know that, and Martin offered me little choice in the matter. We will marry another day, but if something had happened to you or your child I would never have forgiven myself."

Isabel gave a snort of derision. "And Lubna will never forgive you." She sat back as if suddenly tired.

Thomas glanced at Lubna, who continued to watch them with a blank expression. It was not like her. She could be short with him, angry at times, but always there was emotion in her eyes. Isabel, who knew her less well, had not seen it.

"I have made it my business to correct the situation." She held up a palm as Thomas began to protest. "No, there is no need to thank me. You will marry here, in the Cathedral."

"Lubna is not–"

"It is all taken care of. There is a side chapel that remains as it was before the rebuilding, part of the original mosque. The service will be there. We have spoken of it and Lubna has agreed. She says you will have two weddings, one here and one when you return home. If you return home." Isabel leaned close and lowered her voice. "I will not have your child born illegitimate."

Thomas pushed hair back from his face, knowing he had no say in the matter, no say at all. When he glanced at Lubna the faintest of smiles showed.

CHAPTER SEVENTEEN

Jorge and Belia had managed to obtain a bed from somewhere and insisted on showing it to Thomas before they would allow him to leave. It was a dark, ugly piece of furniture, too small for comfort. When Jorge lay on it his feet stuck over the end and they had placed a wooden box there to support them, but he did not appear to mind.

"Was this the best you could find?" Thomas said.

"I told you, furniture is in short supply. But your idea was sound. This is the bed of a ship's captain." Belia glanced at Jorge's oversized frame. "Hence the size. But it is untainted and will do until we get something better made."

Thomas did not want to point out they were unlikely to remain long enough for a bed to be commissioned, but he did mention it to Jorge as they made their way through streets starting to cool as the sun set. There were less people about, many staying indoors to avoid the plague, but Thomas knew they would emerge in their thousand to witness the next burning.

"Belia knows I will leave," said Jorge. "We have discussed it, and she is content for us to have what we do for as long as we can. I told her she can return with me but she says her place is here." He shook his head. "I have no idea why. This city stinks and is tainted by death."

"All Spanish cities stink," Thomas said. "I forget that when I am in Gharnatah so it always comes as a surprise."

"What do you want with Mandana again so soon?" asked Jorge. They were approaching the square where al-Haquim's house sat. Thomas had explained their destination, but not the reason.

"I have questions, and I want to probe harder to see if he has truly changed."

"You will want me to do what I usually do, observe?"

Thomas nodded. "It is what you are good at."

"Of course. That and other things, but the others are of no interest to you, I know. Why do we come to this house? Has Mandana no place of his own?"

"I asked, and was told he has rooms in Castello de Triana, but how often he uses them is open to question. This is not his city. At least it wasn't, but that may have changed." Thomas slowed as they approached a new guard at the open doorway. Light remained in the sky but already lamps had been lit in expectation of the coming night. "Let me do the talking."

"As if I could stop you."

The guard had been told they were expected because he nodded them admittance without comment. Thomas led the way through to the inner courtyard, half expecting to find it empty, or for al-Haquim to be alone and unwelcoming, but three men sat at a table laid with food: lamb, chicken, pork, sauces and rice and lentils. The smell of the food scented the air and made Thomas's stomach grumble.

Mandana kicked at a spare chair with his foot. There was only the one, so Jorge moved to a sit on the low wall edging a pool of water. Thomas knew he would watch from there, silent, missing nothing. He took the offered chair, also a cup of wine when passed to him by Samuel, who he had not expected to see, particularly in light of what Mandana had said to his son.

"Eat if you wish," said Mandana, but despite his hunger Thomas did not reach out.

"You have sent no word about those I can question, so I have come to question you." He glanced toward Samuel, who sat without expression. "That includes you, too."

"Then ask them while we eat."

"You said the deaths have been going on for a while. A year, did you say?"

"Near enough. And–" Mandana cut himself off, about to say more but thinking better of it.

Thomas waited, glancing between Mandana and Samuel. He ignored al-Haquim as nothing more than a convenience to the others, a place of safety.

"You may as well tell him everything," said Samuel. "There is no point asking for his help then withholding information." Samuel turned from Mandana to Thomas. "Yes, the first killing we know of was near a year since, but what we do not know is how many may have come before."

"Why would you say that?" Thomas asked.

A glance at Mandana, but the man was content to allow Samuel to take over the tale, such as it was. "I was asked to look at the bodies."

"Were they cut like the ones I saw?"

Samuel nodded. "With skill. Great skill, I would judge. The kind of skill that only comes with practice."

"So are we looking for a physician, like you and I?"

"Or someone who has killed elsewhere, who has honed his evil craft."

Thomas studied Samuel but saw no deceit, but he knew

Jorge would also be watching and report to him later if anything was amiss.

"How many?"

Samuel shook his head. "It is impossible to tell. So many dead in the city this last year how could anyone know?"

"You said the method changed. The bodies used to be hidden but recently they are displayed. So when did that happen, and how many since?"

"Two months, perhaps a little longer. And ten bodies."

"Ten! A death every five or six days? Why is Sevilla not in uproar this man be caught?"

"You have seen how it is," said Samuel. "The pestilence, the Inquisition. But there is fear. You have heard what they call him, and a name only comes when the mob fears something, but the killings are simply more death among death. And not every five or six days. The bodies always come in pairs. As far as we can tell they have always come in pairs. At first a month, two months might pass. More recently the interval has grown shorter. This last pair come within days."

"Why a pair?" Thomas said.

"When you catch the killer you can ask him, for I do not know the answer."

"You said a medical man, like you and me. How many physicians reside in Sevilla with that level of skill? It is something you would know, I am sure."

"And physicians who came here around a year ago," said Samuel, smiling when Thomas nodded. "There are more than before, come to treat the pestilence, for the little good they do, that any of us can do, but they ease the pain of some and offer a form of comfort to others. There must be half a thousand who call themselves physician within the city walls, but I can think of only a score who might be capable of what you have seen."

"And those who have been killed – you said they died in pairs. Side by side, or separately?"

"It cannot be determined." Mandana took up the conversation, as if now medical matters were decided he could make a contribution. "But I suspect so."

"And names? You know the names of the victims and their backgrounds?"

"Some. Not the early ones, for many came from among those who sleep outside the city walls, who reside outside of society. But more recently, yes. Which is why my interest, Berrington." Mandana leaned forward, a single arm across his knee. "More than a few were men of God. Priests, workers on the Cathedral, monks. Not all, but more than makes sense if they were picked at random. And Abraham's interest is because many of his people have also been chosen."

"Let's start with the two most recent victims," Thomas said. "Do you know who they are?"

"Both of them," said Mandana. "One worked as an administrator for the Cathedral. The other was a tailor, a Jew known to both Abraham and Samuel."

"They have family?"

Mandana looked toward Samuel. "The administrator, none. The other man?"

"A wife and three children," said Samuel. "They should be taken care of."

Mandana gave a brief shake of the head. "Abraham might be able to do something, it is no concern of the city." He returned his gaze to Thomas. "Samuel can provide you the details if they are of interest to you."

Thomas looked toward al-Haquim. "Did you see the bodies, Malik?"

"Of course not, but the Abbot and Samuel have explained

everything." His tone was dismissive, the same as it had been of all criticism when he ruled in Ronda

Thomas turned back to Mandana. "What business are the killings to the three of you? You have not yet told me what you are plotting, but it is not the chasing down of a murderer. My guess would be something more dangerous."

"Which is why I am trusting you," said Mandana. "What we three do is of more importance than the death of strangers."

"But they were not all strangers, were they?"

"God's teeth, man, we are fighting for men's souls here while hundreds die every day of the pestilence." Mandana leaned forward, all hint of amity draining from his face. "You tracked me down years ago, and you have tracked others since. It is what you do, what you are good at." A wave of the hand. "Oh, Samuel tells me you have other skills, but this," Mandana stabbed his finger onto the table, "this is what you do that others cannot." A glance toward where Jorge sat, examining his fingernails and looking as if he found them wanting. "The pair of you. Even that heathen wife of yours. Do you think I do not know everything you do? You are watched, Thomas Berrington, on behalf of the Queen, but she in turn is watched, and I have sources everywhere. Everywhere."

Thomas returned the Abbot's stare, unwilling to be intimidated. "Once more, why? You have admitted you have other priorities. Why ask me at all? I too have other matters to attend to. Important matters."

"I told you, some of the victims are known to us."

"I need a name," Thomas said. "It will be a starting point, at least."

"He was the head of an important family."

"I still need a name if you want me to help. I can play politics too, if needs must."

Samuel glanced toward Jorge.

"And he revels in them." Thomas waited as looks were exchanged.

After a moment Mandana said, "Leave us, we will send for you when we have made a decision. This is not a name we can reveal without discussion."

Thomas was tempted to walk away from the table and keep going. He got as far as the main entrance when Jorge caught his arm.

"They will tell us," he said.

"I'm not sure I care anymore. Mandana will have something planned behind whatever he reveals, and I trust none of those men. You saw what al-Haquim was like in Ronda." He strode into the square, came to a halt in the middle, turning around, taking in the facades of the houses. There was money here, and with money came influence.

"What did you hear said?" Thomas asked. It was not the words he wanted to hear about but what lay beneath them, the tides of shifting influence between the trio.

"I don't know Samuel, but it's clear you do, and that he respects you. If it is left to him he will tell you everything. Mandana is Mandana. Changed, as you say, but underneath? He is older, wiser perhaps, but also more wily. If he is planning something he will be hard to catch. Even harder than the last time."

"I don't think he is," Thomas said. "I see no advantage in any of this for him, but there must be some or he wouldn't be involved. You're right, he's not changed much."

Jorge laughed. "Perhaps he has and you and I are too cynical to see it. But there is another reason which you will see yourself, given time."

"Save me the time," Thomas said.

"Many of the victims are men of God. Some in important positions. And this killer, whoever he is, has been working undiscovered and unmolested for a year. A year, Thomas. How can such a thing happen?"

"You heard them. Pestilence, the Inquisition. I understand it."

"As do I. But a killer who takes men of God... I think Mandana fears for his own life. Perhaps al-Haquim too. Two men taken at a time. Two men killed side by side. In most cases a Christian and a Jew. Do you see why they fear?"

"Do you think Mandana has changed or not?" Thomas looked beyond Jorge to where a tall figure had appeared at the gate of al-Haquim's house.

Samuel walked across to them, his steps slow.

"It is time for me to return to the palace." He glanced at Thomas. "Thanks to you. I sleep there in case I am needed in the night. You will walk with me?" He ignored Jorge. When he saw Thomas frown his lips thinned in a tight smile. "No, the Queen would call on you, Thomas, but there are the children, and others who might need a physician." He gave a short laugh. "Perhaps even you at some time." He started across the square toward a shadowed alley.

Thomas glanced at Jorge, who shrugged, and they both followed.

"Do you have a name for us?" Thomas said when they caught up with Samuel.

"I do. The Abbot was unsure, but I persuaded him you are an honest man and will not spread this name beyond our circle. It is important the details of his death are not known."

"Do his family know? I will need to speak with them."

"They know he died at another's hand, but not how. That must be kept from them."

"I will do what I can, if I ever find out who the man is." Thomas was beginning to lose patience. "Was his one of the bodies I saw?"

"No. He died a month ago."

"So why reveal his name now? It would be more use to know who the most recent victims are."

"Their names are still being determined. This man is the most recent we have all the details for." Samuel cast a glance at Jorge. "I hope he can he be trusted. The man is – was – Felipe Tabado." He hesitated, as if expecting some recognition, but the name meant nothing to Thomas. "The Archdeacon of Sevilla," said Samuel.

"Are we allowed to talk with the Archbishop?" Thomas might not follow his old religion anymore but was familiar with the hierarchy of Catholicism.

"The Archbishop is no longer in the city. He was moved to Jaén after Tabado's death."

"Is there a connection?"

"None that I can discern. I believe it was considered wise he be moved. And the current Archbishop had been pressing for the position for some time. He is from an influential family, and considered the position his by right."

They emerged into the Cathedral square, a gibbous moon hanging above the dome.

"Is he under suspicion for the death of Tabado?"

"No. And you are not to go digging anywhere near him. Archbishop Mendoza is untouchable."

"Even if he killed someone?"

Samuel's voice was sharp. "Mendoza killed nobody. Do not let your imagination run away with you."

"It often does," said Jorge, looking away as if he had not been listening at all. "I will need to leave you now if you are going to the palace. Belia is waiting for me."

"I want to talk to you," Thomas said. "Tonight if I can."

"Then come find me, but don't leave it too late."

"Where will you be?"

"The new house, of course." Jorge started across the

square, drawing stares. Even dressed in ordinary clothing his difference made him stand out from everyone else.

Samuel started to walk away but Thomas stayed where he was and after a moment the other man stopped and turned back. "Are you coming?"

Thomas started walking. "Is there anything else you can tell me?"

"Are he and Belia together?"

"You might call it such. What they call it I don't know."

"So long as he treats her well."

Thomas smiled. "Jorge always treats his women well. What else do I need to know about this Tabado, Samuel?"

"One thing, perhaps. Whether it is relevant or not I do not know, but you might. He was married and lived in a fine house near the river, not far from the one your friend is in now. A rich man often takes lovers. It is expected."

"Who?"

"Theresa," said Samuel. "His lover was Theresa.

CHAPTER EIGHTEEN

Thomas went first to his rooms only to find Lubna and Will absent once more. He could scarce believe they were still with the Queen, but did not know where else they might be.

The wing of the palace housing Isabel's quarters was a hive of activity, servants coming and going, some carrying food, others staggering beneath the weight of wooden chests etched with the royal seal. The door to the royal quarters stood open, two soldiers guarding it. As Thomas approached he saw a few words pass between them before they nodded and stepped aside to allow him entry. Theresa's small room was set near the entrance and he turned in that direction even as he doubted he would find her there, but was surprised when she opened the door to his knock.

"Your wife is with the Queen," she said, blocking the door.

"It is not the Queen I came to see." Thomas took a step closer, but for once Theresa held her ground. She had let her hair loose and it fell in red waves to her shoulders. The air drifting from the room smelled of her. "It is you I want to speak with."

"There is nothing we have to speak of, not anymore. Once, perhaps, but not now."

Thomas put his hands on her shoulders and pushed her into the room, kicked the door shut with his heel.

"If you force yourself on me I will scream," Theresa said, but there was little strength to her words or resistance in her body. Thomas pushed until she had no option but to sit on the narrow bed. One other chair was set beneath a small table and he pulled it close.

"I want to know about Felipe Tabado." Watching as her expression changed. "There is no point in pretending you don't recognise the name. I know you were his lover."

"He is dead." A tear gathered in the corner of her eye, clung there for a moment before trailing along her cheek. Theresa wiped it away as if angered at her own weakness.

"I know he is dead, which is why we must talk. Others have died, and their deaths are linked to his. Did you see his body afterward?"

"I was his mistress," said Theresa. "A mistress has no rights. A mistress does not even exist."

"Did you try?"

"How could I? I did not even know where he was taken, or how he died, only that he was. I went to the house as usual. There was a small door to the cellar always left open for me. We would meet there, in the cool and the dark, but when I tried the door it was locked, even though it was a Wednesday."

"You went to him every week?"

"More. Monday, Wednesday and Friday. Saturday too if he sent for me. He was a vigorous man, with strong appetites."

"A churchman with strong appetites," Thomas said. "Now there is a surprise." And Theresa laughed, though there was no humour to it.

"Churchmen are the worst. Some of the things they ask you to do... but no, that has nothing to do with the matter you want to speak of." Theresa squared her shoulders and straightened her back. "Ask me what you will, Thomas. You have captured evil men before and if you unmask whoever killed Felipe then I will be in your debt."

"Did you love him?" It had nothing to do with his investigation, but he was curious.

"I liked him well enough, but I knew what I was to him."

"Did he give you things? Money?"

"What do you think I am? Not money, but he had influence, and as I say he had vigour. I am far from home and, well, I think you know I am a woman who has strong desires."

"There has to be more than that."

"Why? Oh, for a man it is all well and good, he can use whores if he wants and nobody casts any blame, even if he is a man of the church. But a woman? Do we not also want? Is it only men who wish for someone to lie beside? Felipe was kind."

"Did his wife know?"

"And had no objection. I suspect she was pleased he had someone else to direct his passion toward."

"So she would not have wanted him killed out of jealousy?"

Theresa shook her head. "If she had wanted anyone killed it would have been me."

"When you went to him, what, on Monday, did he seem different?"

"He sent a note I was not to go that day, not until I heard from him. I had not seen him for a week so was looking forward to our assignation. I imagined he would be too."

"When did you hear he was dead?"

"The following day, Tuesday, but not directly. I went to

the house and watched for some sign. I wanted to see if he was there, to see what had changed between us. I thought he had grown tired of me and found someone else, though I know I would not see her there. I suppose it was him I wanted to see, even if only at a distance."

"What happened?"

"A man came, a priest. He knocked at the door and was granted admittance, and then I heard a scream, his wife wailing. The priest must have brought the news."

"And this was Tuesday morning?"

"In the afternoon. The streets were quiet, so the priest was unusual."

"And you had not seen Tabado since the Wednesday before."

Theresa gave a nod.

Thomas stared at the stone wall behind her. The room had a single small window, additional light coming from a candle burning on the table and a second in a small ledge above the bed. It was a sparse place to live, and Thomas could not blame Theresa for seeking comfort elsewhere. She was right that women were judged by different rules to men, but not by him. For a moment he recalled what had almost occurred between them in Qurtuba and regretted his own stupidity. He had no longer been living with Helena, and at that time Lubna was nothing to him but a vain longing. Jorge had the right idea. Women were to be loved in all their variety, loved without regret or recrimination. Thomas knew Jorge had recognised the same in Belia, which is why he had tumbled into her bed immediately. As he himself should have done with Theresa.

He reached out and took her hands, cradling them between his, feeling something for this woman even if it confused him.

"Did he ever say anything to you about enemies?"

Theresa laughed, her fingers clutching at his. "Oddly enough we rarely spoke of such things."

"What did you speak of?"

This time the laugh was stronger. "Do you need me to tell you? Even you, Thomas Berrington, must know of what lovers speak, and enemies are rarely mentioned."

"Anything unusual, then. Did he seem distracted when last you saw him?"

A shake of the head.

"Do you know who was his mistress before yourself?"

"No."

"Would his wife?"

"Most likely, but is it relevant?"

"I don't know what is relevant and what is not, so I have to ask all the questions and winnow out good answer from bad." He released her hands and stood, towering over her slight frame, which seemed even more shrunken after he had brought back memories of what she had lost. "I am sorry, truly sorry, to have caused you pain. But…" He hesitated, wondering if he should simply walk away, knowing he could not. "Give some thought to his final weeks and see if anything seems odd to you, anything strange or different."

Thomas turned and left the room, closing the door behind him, leaving Theresa to nurse her misery in her lonely cell.

As he reached the end of the corridor he heard laughter, two women together, and he stopped. His mood was soured after talking with Theresa and he did not want to impose himself on Isabel or Lubna, so instead turned and walked to his own rooms and lay on the bed, staring at the ceiling as he shuffled the pebbles of reason around in his mind, trying to make sense of them. From beyond the windows a peacock shattered the night. A little while later came the sound of many feet, the changing of the watch on the parade ground, the chatter and laughter as the old guard returned to their barracks. Thomas wondered why Lubna had not yet returned.

He laid what he knew out in a scatter of knowledge with many missing parts, trying not to make connections yet because he knew to do so might lead him wrong. Here, here and here were nuggets of information that wanted to be drawn together and he deliberately kept them apart.

There were gaps, but he could fill them with a little imagination.

Two killings at a time. The evidence was scant, but the latest death backed the idea and he would question Samuel in the morning to see if he could fill in any of the gaps. He must know more about the earlier deaths. And if they were connected, the taking of two individuals, why were both needed? Thomas made a mental note, a picture in his mind of paper and ink, to ask if the victims had all been men. It was another factor if true.

Why were the bodies being displayed now, when before they had not? What had changed in the killer's mind? Did he want recognition now? And if so, why not before? Because he had not perfected his technique, but now had?

Thomas needed to know who the victims were. Ixbilya was a sprawling city, dwellings extending well beyond the city walls as they did in many Spanish cities where fear of attack was a distant memory. It was impossible to go door to door asking if someone was missing. Particularly when disease had taken one in twenty of the population. The plague carts continued to trundle through the streets. Every day more houses were marked with a red scrawl. But the disease was a distraction, one Thomas set aside as irrelevant.

And then, the most tangled skein of all, Mandana, Samuel and al-Haquim. Exactly what was it they were up to? Perhaps Samuel would let something slip if pressed hard enough, otherwise Thomas planned to return to that house and demand answers. He was working in the dark. Whoever was doing the killing, whatever their motive, he believed it was connected to what the three men were plotting.

The more he lay still the faster his mind worked, and Thomas knew he could not let matters lie until morning. He had just decided to approach Samuel now when a door opened and closed and a moment later Lubna entered the room.

"Where's Will?" Thomas said, sitting up.

"Next door in bed, already asleep. He's a happy, exhausted little boy. He has spent the entire day playing with Isabel's children. They will all sleep until late tomorrow."

Lubna let her robe drop to the floor and poured water into a bowl. She exposed her upper body and washed beneath her arms, around her neck, her face. Thomas stared, aroused at the lustrous glow of her skin, at the soft swell of her belly. When she was clean Lubna removed the rest of her clothes and padded to the bed. She pushed Thomas back and sat across him.

"You are over-dressed, my love."

"I take it you are feeling better."

"Much better." She pulled at Thomas's shirt.

"You called her Isabel," Thomas said, running his hands along Lubna's flanks, smiling when her flesh stippled to his touch. They knew each other so well now. There were no secrets, but still a few surprises. He gripped Lubna's hips and tried to lay her on her side but she fought him.

"Stay as you are, my sweet. Tonight I am in command. Speak no more of her, for I am your Queen tonight." She kissed his eyes shut and whispered words that made no sense other than to the two of them.

CHAPTER NINETEEN

By the time they reached the cathedral square Jorge had started to mutter under his breath again. When Thomas stopped abruptly Jorge continued on, his lips moving. Only when he noticed his audience had disappeared did he slow and turn.

"I woke you from sleep," Thomas said, "so there's no use complaining I interrupted some wondrous act of love."

"As if you would recognise such a thing."

Thomas smiled, secretly pleased when Jorge frowned at his expression. "Now is the best time for doing this, when Samuel is woken from a deep sleep."

"And not the only one," said Jorge. He kicked at the cobbles, staring down at his foot like a petulant twelve year old.

"No, but you are awake now so let's get it done." Thomas glanced at the sky but there was no sign of dawn. It was the deep of night, only an occasional lamp burning on a corner, and they had seen only one other man as they crossed the city, a priest on an errand, papers clutched in his hand, his back to them as he bustled away to the north.

Thomas had fetched Jorge because he valued his insight, and now was a good time to wake a man if you wanted answers.

The guards at the palace gate were half asleep but still Thomas had to explain who Jorge was and what he was doing here. Whether his story of Jorge coming to offer a second opinion on a sick child was believed was debatable, but the guard waved them both through.

Samuel's room was barely larger than the one Theresa had, but at least there were two windows. Thomas listened to Samuel's breathing change almost as soon as the door opened, even though he took care to enter silently.

"Is it the Queen?" Samuel swung his long legs from the narrow bed and reached for a robe. His eyes widened as Jorge came in behind Thomas, tall and broad shouldered, for once his face showing no hint of its usual softness.

"Sit down," Thomas said. "I have questions."

"I wondered when you would come," said Samuel. "Could it not have waited until a more civilised hour?" He looked between the pair before shaking his head. "No, of course not. Now is the hour, is it not? The hour men come calling with their questions." He washed a hand across his face and shuffled to the corner of the bed, which allowed him to lean against the wall. He drew the covers up to hide his nakedness. "Ask then. I will answer if I can."

"And if you can't?" said Jorge.

"Then make of it what you will." Samuel glanced toward Jorge. "Who is the big one?"

"A friend," Thomas said.

"Yours or mine?"

"I don't know you, do I?" said Jorge. He looked around before leaning against the wall.

Thomas stood at the foot of the bed, quickly shuffling his questions into order in his mind, but he knew there were only two of real importance, two he needed truthful answers to. He started with the less insulting.

"I cannot work out why you are involved with those two men," he said, folding his arms across his chest. "What does it gain you to be associated with such as them?"

"That might be one of the questions I am unable to answer," said Samuel.

"That is a shame, because it is the one I most want an answer to. Neither of us will pass on anything you choose to tell us."

"If Mandana discovers I have talked to you here, in the night, my life will be worth nothing. He has a long reach, and his men will stop at nothing. But you already know that, don't you."

"What if I tell you what I think they are doing? You need say nothing unless you wish, but my friend here will know what you are thinking."

Samuel offered a brief smile. "He reads minds, does he?"

"Yes, sometimes I think he does. Al-Haquim is easy – he is trying to protect his own people. Not because of any love for them, I know the man of old and he does nothing unless it benefits him. So what he does offers him something. Position. Power. Money. Any of those three would be enough."

"Or all three," said Samuel, his intention to keep his silence not lasting long. "He is a man ever in need of a position. He came here hungry to create one for himself whether it existed or not."

"Mandana's friendship would be worth a lot to someone such as him," Thomas said.

"What it is al-Haquim does?" said Jorge.

"Spirit suspects out of the city," said Samuel. "Offers places to hide for those who cannot leave."

"What places? In the city?"

"And outside," said Samuel. "There are townships beyond the walls."

"And those he helps leave, where do they go?" asked Jorge. "Qurtuba would be no good. Does he have friends in al-Andalus? He was Governor of Ronda, after all, so no doubt he still has connections."

Samuel said nothing, but his eyes remained on Jorge, and that tiny smile once more touched his lips. "Your friend is good."

"So he claims," Thomas said. "What benefit does Mandana get from the arrangement?"

"It is not just bodies," said Samuel, and Thomas could see the man wanted to tell him more, to unburden himself of secrets held too long. Once started it might be impossible for him to stop. Which was good. Because the most important question would come later.

"Influence," Thomas said. "Money. Slipping people to safety in exchange for gold and property."

"And people," said Samuel. "Mandana brings the names of those under suspicion. Al-Haquim chooses those with money and property and offers them an escape. Once they leave Mandana has the pick of their servants and guards. He chooses the best, the most corrupt, for his own purposes."

"Which is?"

"He has not revealed it to me, but I have my own ideas. As far as he is concerned Abraham and myself are doing work for our people, and I believe in his own mind he is trying to help his people."

"Your people? Have you not converted?"

"I have, but my religion does not cut me off from my race. They are still my people. This is a hard time for them and will get harder still." Samuel leaned forward, resting his arms across raised knees. "Telling you this puts me in your power. If word of what I do becomes common knowledge, reaches the ear of the Queen, I will be exiled at best, burned at worst. She is already uncertain about me. I am trusting you to keep my secret."

Thomas offered a nod. "Tell me what you know of Mandana."

"Abraham is a convenience to him. Their ambitions are not so far apart, but Mandana has a different end game in mind. He is trusted by the King but not the Queen. I know what he did, and I know your part in it. For taking her son she will never forgive him."

"And Fernando has?"

"The King needs men willing to do things others would shrink from. Mandana has a black soul, despite claiming to be a man of God." Samuel looked around the room until his gaze rested on Jorge, who he seemed to find less threatening. "Mandana does not agree with the Inquisition."

"I suspect there are many who do not," Thomas said.

"You are right. But it is the instrument of the Queen, one she believes important. I like to think she does not truly understand what is done in her name, but know she must. The stink of the fires reach even here inside the palace. Mandana believes the Inquisition chooses the wrong subjects."

"Explain," Thomas said.

"The Queen has a fine mind but a soft heart," said Samuel. "She is sore angered at those who profess to have taken up her faith only to continue their old ways."

"Unlike you."

"Yes, unlike me. She is content to employ Jews and Arabs and Moors, as evidenced by my own position. You can change religion but not who you are, not in here." Samuel patted his chest. "The Inquisition seeks out those who live a lie. You must know know what happens there. If a man confesses he will most times be pardoned as long as he does not stray again. If a person continues to insist on their innocence then they must be interrogated to uncover where the truth lies. If they still persist then there is but only one result, though all are offered a final chance to repent."

"I saw you, remember," Thomas said. "Instead of the agony of fire, do you offer them a more merciful end? And why, if they have repented, are they not released?"

"Because it is too late by then. But God is merciful, it is said, so they do not suffer the flames."

"And Mandana?"

"I told you, he believes it wrong."

"The burning, the Inquisition, what does he think is wrong? He can't have changed that much since I knew him."

"He believes it does not go far enough. He works toward the day *all* unbelievers are rooted out. Left to him they would all burn. The air above Spain would be black with smoke for years to come. He would see all non-believers killed. Not exiled, but killed, with him as the head of a holy army. At least the Inquisition only seeks out those who profess to a false faith." Samuel shook his head. "The man is mad."

"You will find no argument from me on that," said Jorge.

"You were there too, weren't you?" said Samuel. "When Mandana took Juan?"

Jorge nodded, a small inclination of the head.

"They talk of you both still, the servants, even the soldiers. They are impressed by little but they are impressed by you both. You recovered the Queen's son, which is why she loves you, Thomas." Samuel glanced at Jorge. "You too, even if you do not know it."

"The killings are nothing to do with Mandana, are they?" Thomas said.

"The killings?"

"The bodies I was shown. You have seen them too, haven't

you? Mandana must have called on you before I came. Did he ask you to investigate as well?"

"He knows I lack your skills. All of your skills. But yes, he called me to the bodies. The first was at the turn of the year but he told me there were others before."

"The first, you say. Yet he showed me two bodies. A pair. Were they different at the start?"

"It is impossible to know. Sometimes one body was found, sometimes two, but whether that was simply because we missed the other I don't know. Remember, they were not displayed until recently, and it is easy in this city to dispose of a body."

"Have there been only men?"

"Women too."

"Pairs of women?"

Samuel shook his head. "I know of two cases where there was one man and one woman, but not two women together."

"And the commonality between them?"

Another shake of the head. "Other than being dead I see none. Christian or Jew, male or female, good or evil, they all shared the same fate. Only the man who took them knows the reason why they were chosen."

"Why do you think the most recent bodies have been left on display?"

"It is something new, as you know. They used to be found in secret places or, as you tell me you saw, tossed amongst the dead. This pestilence offers more than enough opportunity to dispose of a body that might otherwise prove awkward. I am sure others have been killed and hidden the same way, in plain sight."

"And the cutting," Thomas said. "Is it always the same?"

"I have not seen every one, but no, it is not."

"But the same on bodies taken at the same time?"

Thomas saw Samuel consider the question, his gaze turned inward.

"Possibly. As I said, I have not seen all the bodies."

"The marks I saw would indicate the killer has knowledge of surgical technique, is able to dissect a chest without killing the subject. Skills that are rare in the general populace."

Samuel half rose to his knees. "Are you accusing me? Why would I do such a thing? I am trying to protect my people, not murder them."

Thomas's eyes tracked Samuel's face, sure the man was hiding something. For a moment, he had seen a recognition, perhaps an acknowledgement of something he knew only now.

"You must know many of the physicians in Sevilla, I am sure. How is it you have not come to the same conclusion yourself? Can you think of anyone both skilled enough and capable of doing what you have seen?"

"Who says I have not?" Samuel offered a glance toward Jorge, back to Thomas. "But I am not you, the famous Thomas Berrington, unmasker of killers. The perfect Thomas Berrington the Queen would raise up to glory if she could." Samuel hollowed his cheeks as if about to spit but restrained himself, and Thomas knew whatever friendship that might have sparked between them was now destroyed, if it had ever been. The man was jealous of his relationship with the Queen, but it was a relationship that still tore at his own loyalties. Some things were hard won and even harder refused.

"I will leave this place and you will not," Thomas said. "Your position will be restored in full once I am gone."

"And the damage will have been done. Do you have anything more to accuse me of or can I go back to sleep?"

Thomas looked toward Jorge, who offered a shake of the head.

"I may come again if something else occurs to me, and in the meantime I would ask you to think of who in this city is capable of what we have witnessed."

Back in his rooms Thomas closed the inner doors so their conversation would not disturb Lubna or Will, knowing even hearing a hint of Jorge's voice would wake his son in an instant.

"So?" he asked, standing at the window, watching as the first hint of dawn greyed the horizon. He knew it would come all of a sudden, a new day breaking too fast for a man who had managed little sleep.

"He told the truth about almost everything. I like the man."

"You like everybody."

"Not everybody, but him, yes. You know he is a friend to Belia? But she tells me it could never be anything more."

"I leave such analysis to you," Thomas said.

"Good, because you would be poor at it. Most of what he said was the truth, but he is lying about something. I don't know exactly what yet, but I will."

"When?"

"At the end."

"Could he be the killer?"

"The lie came after you asked him that. It came when you asked who in the city was capable of the crimes. I saw something in his eyes, some note of calculation. I think..." Jorge shook his head. He strode to the window and stood beside Thomas, too close as always but it would not be Jorge if he did otherwise. Now the dawn was coming hard, a horse in full gallop.

"He thinks he knows who it is." Thomas said.

"Yes," said Jorge. "When you asked him for names there was someone stood out for him immediately. Why did he not tell you at once?"

"Because I know who he thought of," Thomas said. "And so do you."

Jorge laughed. "You overestimate my abilities to read minds."

"Perhaps you do not see it because you share her bed."

CHAPTER TWENTY

Thomas held a muslin cloth to his eye. It contained ice chipped from a block used to cool the Queen's chambers. Melting water dripping down his face.

"I cannot believe Jorge hit you," said Lubna, leaning over him. "Take it away, let me see." She peered at the damage, shook her head. "You'll live."

"I am so pleased." Thomas looked across the room to where Jorge stood on the terrace, Will beside him, a small hand encased in a larger one. Thomas wondered if Jorge regretted his inability to father a child. He was so good with Will. Better than Thomas himself, he sometimes thought. Jorge had more patience, and a sense of fun that appealed to children as well as women. Thomas thought he should have prepared Jorge a little more before voicing his suspicions, but suspected the result would have been the same. After the blow was struck he had expected Jorge to flee. Instead he had stayed, pacing the room, eyes avoiding Thomas who, when he saw Jorge was not intending to leave, went in search of the ice. On his return Jorge opened his mouth as if about to apologise but nothing came out. It was then their pacing had woken Will, and Will in turn woken Lubna. Jorge took Will to the balcony and had stayed there since, watching morning flood the gardens. Each time a peacock screamed Will laughed.

"What made him hit you?" said Lubna.

Thomas explained.

"Oh, Thomas, you are a fool sometimes," she said when the short tale was finished. "Could you not have found some other way to satisfy your suspicion?"

"Do you not think she could have done it?" Thomas asked, his voice low for fear Jorge might overhear.

"She has the skill, certainly, but the motive? Think it through. Why would she?"

"If I knew why people were being killed it might help. You remember Eva two years ago, she was taking on the sins of evil men, she almost took Helena's. That was a motive. This… it is a mystery to me as yet."

"Then that is where you need to start looking before accusing your friends."

"I still want to talk with her," Thomas said.

"But not accuse. Please tell me you will not accuse her, not yet, not unless you are sure. I consider it impossible, but I have trusted in the past only to be disappointed. Jorge knows people better than anyone. He would have seen it in her, would he not?"

"Unless love has blinded him, as he nearly blinded me."

"Don't exaggerate. Jorge held back his blow otherwise he would have knocked you to the ground. He is strong now."

"He has always been strong, but managed to hide it well. The times we live in now are more dangerous."

"Or you attract danger, to both of you, to all of us."

"You would have me stop? To turn away from this riddle?" Thomas stared into Lubna's eyes. "Say the word and I will. For you, and for Will, and for this one you grow within you." He touched the swell of her belly and Lubna smiled.

"And what if I did? You would prowl these rooms like a sulking bear. I know I cannot change you, but all I ask is that you be careful. You have other responsibilities now."

"I am always careful," Thomas said.

"Of course you are." Lubna patted his cheek and he winced.

"When you two have finished with your foreplay can we get this over with?" Jorge came to stand near. His anger appeared to have burned low.

"Not yet," said Thomas. "I have been thinking."

"Not again. Are you sure that is wise? Look what happened the last time."

"We should question the household of the victim we know about to discover what connections there are, if any."

"Connections with Belia, do you mean?"

"With *any*one," Thomas said. "Can you not see why I suspect her as I do?"

"No, I cannot." Jorge's body tightened and Thomas readied to stop a second attack, prepared this time. "We must talk with her first before we do anything else, so I can see your crazy notions dashed to pieces. Only then will I be ready to help."

Thomas knew he needed Jorge. The man was an essential part of what allowed them to track down the guilty. He saw things others did not, things Thomas would miss alone.

"Let's make it quick then. With luck she will prove her innocence and we can move on."

"Or she holds up her hands and confesses," said Jorge.

Where to start, that was the thing, and a knack Thomas

knew he did not possess. This was what Jorge was good at, but he stood leaning against a wall, arms crossed over his chest, staring at Thomas.

"What is it," said Belia, "is Lubna unwell?"

"Lubna is recovered," Thomas said. He steeled himself, wanting this done, pushing on against internal resistance. "I have been thinking on these killings, the ones we are working on, Jorge and I. Something came to me, about the perpetrator."

"Yes? Do you need my advice on something?"

"Whoever is doing this knows the city and is known in it."

Belia nodded, and it pained Thomas to see the trust on her face.

"They may know herbs to still their subjects, and they will know the art of cutting a body cleanly, in exactly the right place to open it without killing. It is a small pool of individuals who meet such standards."

"You," said Belia, "and Samuel, of course, but you cannot suspect him, can you? I could name others, but no more than the fingers on both hands, myself included." She had looked at her own hands as she spoke. Now she raised her gaze and her face changed. "I see." She looked toward Jorge. "Are you here to arrest me?"

"I told him he is an idiot," said Jorge. "And I hit him."

"I can see someone has. Did you hit him hard?"

Jorge nodded.

"As hard as he deserved?"

"I am not strong enough to have done so, but hard enough."

This is the attitude I would expect, Thomas thought, if Belia is guilty of what I accuse her: dismissal and derision. So far nothing was proven or disproven. He wanted gone from here but knew he was trapped until there was a resolution.

"You have surgical instruments," Thomas said, "I have seen them. Do you know how to use them?"

"They were my husband's," said Belia, but it was not an answer.

"Were? What happened to him?"

"He died of the pestilence, not that it is any business of yours."

"When?" It was Jorge asked the question.

"Four years."

"He was a surgeon?" Thomas asked.

Belia nodded. "A good one, maybe even as good as you are claimed to be, maybe even better."

"You worked alongside him?"

Another nod, telling him much, but it was not proof, and as time passed Thomas was coming to the conclusion his suspicions were unfounded.

"You must have been a formidable team," he said. "His skill with the blade and yours with herbs. Formidable indeed. Is that why you are close to Samuel?"

"If you mean am I looking for a replacement husband, no. Besides, Samuel is not the marrying kind. If you mean am I looking for another surgeon to work with, my answer again is no. I am content with my lot. I have no ambition, it has been scoured from me." She glanced at Jorge. "You know this to be true."

Jorge inclined his head but said nothing, his expression unchanged.

Thomas tried to work through his own thoughts. Did he believe Belia or not? He still did not know. Could he make further progress until he was sure? He thought not. Better to do what he could and leave her to consider his accusation. If there was any truth to it she might begin to worry, might even flee, which would be all the proof needed. Even as the thought came to him he saw the truth behind it. Had he continued to suspect Belia he would not leave her in the house alone to continue killing. No, she had convinced him with her lack of any show of guilt. And then there was Jorge – Thomas could not believe he would lie beside a woman capable of murder. Jorge saw through everyone, saw direct to the truth at their core.

CHAPTER TWENTY-ONE

"Is this the place?" said Jorge. They stood on a wide street not far from the north side of the Cathedral. Fine houses lined both sides but the one opposite was the finest by far. It rose three stories from the roadway with a wide balcony extending out at the top. A further floor below ground would be where the scurrying work was carried out, and Thomas saw a thin woman emerge, bent over by the weight of a basket of washing. She turned left and hurried as fast as her burden would allow toward the end of the street.

"Should I?" asked Jorge.

Thomas shook his head. "There will be time later, and others down there."

"Do we take the usual course? You with the owners, me with the servants?" Jorge smiled. "I know my place, you see."

Thomas lifted a hand to his cheek but did not touch it. "Perhaps this time we should reverse our roles. The wife will not speak to a man with a black eye."

"Whereas you will scare the servants. Good idea." Jorge looked down at himself. "And I am dressed rather well today, so it might work."

"And your Spanish is better than mine," Thomas said.

"So it should be. I spoke nothing else until you unmanned me at twelve years of age."

"Not again," Thomas said. "I saved your life, remember."

"Once more, my thanks. So, is that your plan?" Jorge's tone indicated what he thought of the plan, and Thomas knew he should have come better prepared.

"We need to find out how much the wife knew, and whether her husband had enemies."

"Do I ask about Theresa?"

"Can you find out without being explicit?" Thomas said. "Ask about lovers in general. It's possible he had others before Theresa, or even as well as."

"But not on Monday, Wednesday or Friday, unless he was extremely virile, which men of God tend not to be."

"You know all about men of God, do you?"

"I know they are sour faced hypocrites," said Jorge. He smoothed his clothes, brushed fingers through the hair which had been growing out for several weeks now. It had little effect but somehow Jorge always managed to look freshly emerged from the bathhouse.

"It might be better not to mention that to his wife." Thomas started across the street, heading for the small door that offered access to the basement, while Jorge climbed marble steps and rapped on an oak door reinforced with scrolled metalwork. Thomas descended the steps without waiting to see if he was offered admittance, knowing Jorge could charm his way anywhere.

Thomas didn't knock but pushed the door open and ducked inside. The narrow corridor he entered was only a little higher and he stooped as he made his way to where light, noise and scent told him the kitchen must lie. He rapped on the frame of an opening and a girl of little more than twelve turned, her mouth dropping open as her eyes widened. Thomas knew his eye would be nicely blackened by now. He didn't think his appearance warranted such a reaction, but then he was an uninvited stranger.

"Tell him to put the fish in the larder next to the ice." The woman who spoke was obviously in charge but did not turn.

"It's not the fish man," said the girl.

The woman turned, wiping her hands on skirts already heavily stained. "What is it you want if you've got no fish?" She made no move to come forward, so Thomas took a few paces into the room. It was a little higher but his hair still brushed rough-cut beams. Fresh bread stood on a rack to cool, its scent making his mouth water.

"My name is Thomas Berrington, physician to Queen Isabel. I am tasked with investigating the untimely death of your master." He didn't know if it would work or not. His name almost surely not, but the Queen's more likely.

"About time," said the cook. She glanced at the girl. "Go and wait for the fish man."

The girl needed no more encouragement, pressing against the wall to avoid approaching Thomas any closer.

"What happened to your face, did someone object to your questions?" The cook smiled, no malice there.

"Your master was well respected, was he?" Thomas said. "Down here as well as up there?" He nodded at the low ceiling.

"He was good enough as masters go," said the cook. "There are plenty worse." She pulled up a stool and sat, offering that she had been on her feet since before dawn.

"And the lady of the house?"

"What of her?"

"Is she also respected?"

"For what? She was his wife so gets her respect by connection."

"Is this house owned by the church?"

"We used to have one of those, a church house, but master bought this soon after coming to the city. He said Sevilla would grow to be the heart of Spain and good houses never go out of fashion."

"So your positions are all safe, both here and above?" Thomas said.

The cook touched one of the loaves, misshapen where the last of the dough had been used. "As safe as anyone can be with this Ghost taking innocent folk, let alone the pestilence stalking the city. Are you hungry?" she said. "You look hungry to me." It was an invitation of a kind, and Thomas nodded. He would have done so whether he was hungry or not.

"Wash yourself and your clothes often," Thomas said. "I believe it discourages whatever brings the death." He saw the cook didn't believe him, but at least he had tried. "What do you know of your master?"

The cook cut a chunk of still warm bread and pushed it across the table. "There's wine in the pantry and cheese if you want to fetch it. I know everything that goes on in this house. Servants always do. We are invisible to those who keep us, and when you are invisible nothing is hidden."

Thomas brought the jug of wine and a round of hard cheese. He looked around, found rough cups fashioned from yellow clay and placed two on the table. The cook filled hers and drained it before filling it once more, the network of broken veins in her cheeks testament to her love of wine. Thomas sipped at his, surprised how good it was. He cut a piece of cheese and chewed on it, finding that also good. This household did not want for the best.

"You knew he took lovers?" Thomas said, when the pact between them appeared to be sealed.

"Don't all men? Even men of God are no different. And he was always discreet."

"Except amongst the servants."

"I already told you, we don't matter, do we. He was a handsome man. Handsome boy, too."

"You were with him as long ago as that?"

"His father employed my mother, her mother before that. He was a good master when he took over the household so I saw no reason to look elsewhere. He only took one lover at a time. He was thoughtful that way. And a good lover, too."

Thomas smiled at the cook's confession, but suspected any liaison would be long in the past now. But memories could warm, too.

"Did he have enemies? Someone who might want him dead?"

A shake of the head. "Oh, enemies, I am sure. He was a man of substance, held a position in the church others thought should be theirs, but to kill him in the manner done? Nobody could hate someone that much."

"So you know what was done to him?"

"I was sent to prepare the body. Took some work I can tell you, the way he was cut."

Thomas leaned forward. "Cut how? Is it painful for you to describe?"

"I've seen worse, but never done to someone I was close to. It was bad for me, I admit, but if you can catch whoever did it I will tell you anything you want to know. Do you speak true, you are a physician?"

Thomas nodded.

"Then you'll have seen some sights too. They'd taken his eyes. Both of them. But not rough, whoever did it possessed skill. They had drawn them out and cut clean where they join behind. The eyes lay beside him where he lay." She drank more wine, wiped her mouth.

"Taking his eyes would not kill your master," Thomas said.

"No. But what they did behind them would. Something had been used to gouge into his brain and scoop some of it out."

"Where was he on the table?"

"On his back," said the cook.

"I meant was he in the middle of the table or–"

"To one side. He lay to one side."

"Was there space for a second body beside him?"

The cook frowned, shook her head. "There was no other body, only the master."

"But was there space for another?"

Her gaze sought the corner of the room. "Possible, I suppose, yes. But there *was* nobody else."

"What did you do?"

"Do? I put his eyes back in their sockets. Once that was done it was only the slashes to his cheeks needed some stitching, which was easy enough. I didn't want the mistress to see him that way."

"Who did?"

"See him? I don't know. He was taken away by monks and buried the next morning. Everything was arranged. It was no big ceremony, not like it would be if it had been the Archbishop. The mistress went but the children stayed away."

"How old are they?" It didn't matter, but Thomas was curious.

"They have ten and eight years. Both girls, which is a shame."

"Why?"

"Do you need to ask, you being a man?"

"When you went to him it was to the place where he died?"

"Must have been." The cook filled her cup again but did not drink yet. From the floor above footsteps sounded, those of a man and woman, one set heavier than the other, slower.

"And where was this place?"

"It was a house, nothing more."

"A house where?"

The cook closed her eyes, thinking. Her fingertip moved on the table top as she walked the streets in her mind.

"Not near, but not too far," she said. "An ordinary house."

"Belonging to whom?" It was like extracting thorns from a dog's fur, one by one by one, except the dog would be snapping at your hand while this woman was passive.

"It belongs to no-one," said the cook. She reached for her cup but Thomas grasped her wrist before she could drink. She looked at his hand, at him, a first touch of fear showing. Thomas kept his expression cold, wanting this finished. Jorge's footsteps sounded across the floor above the kitchen. They could belong to no-one else. He would be waiting outside with whatever had been found out.

"Tell me why it belongs to no-one," Thomas said, though he knew the answer already.

"It is a plague house," she said, "with a mark on the door."

"And you went inside despite that?"

"Superstition, that is all it is. The plague comes on the mist, everyone knows that."

"Tell me, how do I find this house?"

CHAPTER TWENTY-TWO

"The wife knew everything," said Jorge as they walked across the city toward where the cook claimed she had found her master. "And she didn't care. I suspect she is someone who finds sex inconvenient, or is simply not interested."

"Not so inconvenient she hasn't managed to give birth to two girls," Thomas said.

"They are pretty things, too. The woman as well."

"So other than her knowing he took a mistress, did you discover anything useful?"

"A list of those who might want him dead," said Jorge. "Is that useful enough?"

"Is it a long list?" Thomas slowed, ignoring the people who crowded around him, their conversation muted and excited in turn. There were rumours the Ghost had taken another victim, but also of more burnings.

Jorge laughed. "Long enough. Twelve names."

"Do you remember them all? I will have to write them down."

"No need, I asked for that to be done. Her manservant did it as she brought them to mind. Most are churchmen, some of them important." Jorge reached into his robe and withdrew a folded sheet of paper, handed it to Thomas.

Thomas scanned the list. "Did she think any of these might have killed him?"

"I don't think so. I suspect there is some measure of revenge in the drawing up of the names. Do we question them all?"

Thomas refolded the paper and put it into his own pocket. "Some of them are in senior positions, I don't think we will be allowed to."

"Would Mandana help?"

"Mandana?" Thomas shook his head. "You want us to recruit him now? We could never trust anything he told us. Besides, his name is on this list too, is it not? Should he question himself?"

"I dislike the man as much as you," said Jorge, "but he is not behind these killings, not this time. He is up to something, we both know he is, but of this he is innocent."

"Then it is probably the only thing he is innocent of." Thomas started off again, pushing against men and women who knocked into him. "Damn these crowds."

A red mark still adorned the thin wood of the door, as if the symbol might protect those not yet touched. Thomas pushed open the unlocked door, for who would want to enter here, and called out. He expected no response and received none.

"Did she say where it happened?" asked Jorge.

Thomas pointed along the dark corridor to where another door stood closed. "At the end, through there." He led the way, knowing Jorge would be looking around, taking in the mean furnishings, the smell of something foul that clung to the air.

"I trust there will be no sign remaining," said Jorge.

"With luck there will. But stay out here if you wish, this shouldn't take long." He pushed the door and entered a room that spanned the width of the house and half the depth. Despite that it was a small room. A window showed a yard, bordered by the rear of another house which allowed neither sunlight nor breeze to penetrate. Another door offered access to the yard, but for what reason Thomas could not see. Nothing would grow there and any clothes hung to dry would remain damp two days later.

The table where Tabado's body had lain stood square in the middle of the room. A blackened hearth showed where cooking would have been done, but all sign of cooking pots were gone, as were any chairs. It was a depressing place to have died, and Thomas wondered how much of it Tabado had been aware of. Had he been conscious when his eyes were drawn clear of their sockets and cut loose? What would that be like, to have your sight suddenly stolen away? Thomas shivered at the thought and leaned over the table to distract himself. The cook had told him the body was on the left hand side as she came through the door, so that was where he started. He saw no sign to indicate anything abhorrent had taken place. There were no blood stains, but he would expect to see none so long after the act. He moved to the other side of the table and examined every part of it, with no better result. Finally Thomas knelt and crouched beneath the table itself, examining the legs until he found what he was looking for.

The marks were faint, but to someone who expected them they showed as bright beacons. Pale lines ran across three of the legs. The fourth was unmarked, but that might only mean the rope had not been tied so tightly there. Thomas lay on his back and stared at the underside of the table, his mind projecting backward to when two men might have lain side by side on it, their bodies immobilised by hemp rope. Was it hemp, he wondered, reaching out to where a fragment of something was caught in a splinter. Yes, hemp, and he tossed it aside to stare once more at the underside of the table, but nothing more revealed itself and he slid from beneath.

Did they die together or was it one first and then the other? There would always be one to die first, of course, but had the agony been drawn out for the second victim? Was he made to listen to the other's screams, knowing the same fate awaited him?

Thomas wished he knew who the other person had been. A man most likely. Samuel had said there had only been a few women chosen. A name might offer more information, a clue to the motive. He touched his pocket, feeling the crackle of paper. He doubted the list would tell him anything. If he drew one up of those who hated him it would be three times as long, but there were few who would want him dead. He smiled. Well, perhaps a few, but most who had wanted to take his life were dead themselves now, several at his hand.

He heard Jorge moving around upstairs and started to turn away. He had gleaned all he could from the house. It was inanimate, closed to him, and he knew the answer lay not in objects but people, and for that he would need Jorge even more.

On a whim Thomas looked around until he found a chair leg which had broken in half and discarded in one corner, a dozen rounded stones scattered there as well. A rag lay across two of the stones and without knowing why Thomas picked it up and turned it over in his hands. A piece of linen, nothing more. He examined it more closely for marks of blood, but there was nothing. He lifted the cloth to his face and breathed deep, not sure what he was expecting to find, but any residual scent, if there had ever been one, was gone. All the cloth offered up was dust and damp.

"What have you got there?" Jorge stood in the door, his examination of the rest of the house finished.

"Smell this," Thomas said, holding the cloth out and Jorge stepped away.

"What? Keep that dirty rag away from me."

Shaking his head Thomas prowled the single room again, not exactly sure what he was searching for that he had not already found. He stirred the ashes in the fire but nothing unexpected showed. He was about to give up when Jorge, being the taller of them, reached up to a shelf Thomas had missed before and took down a clay bottle stoppered with a rag. He held it out, a smile on his face at how clever he had been.

Thomas scowled and took the bottle. Shook it, but if it had ever held anything it was now empty. Even so he worked the rag loose from the neck, which was harder than he thought. When it finally came free he was rewarded with the faintest scent. He lifted the bottle to his face and breathed it hard.

"Smell this," he said, offering the bottle to Jorge.

"We have already done this. No."

Thomas shook his head. "This is how he manages to subdue his victims. Perhaps even keeps them subdued while he does his work."

Jorge stepped closer and reached out. He sniffed tentatively.

"What am I meant to smell? There has been something sweet stored here, sweet and acrid at the same time. Oil and lemon, perhaps, though there is something there I do not recognise at all."

"When I went to Qurtuba to heal Juan I brought liquor Lubna and I had prepared. Do you recall it?"

"Only the bottles you told me not to touch. Why, is that what I can smell?"

Thomas nodded, taking the bottle back. "It is. But why is it here? No – I know the why. *How* is it here? There are only a handful of people even know of its existence, and even fewer who could distill it."

"Theresa knew of it, did she not?" said Jorge.

"Yes. I taught her how to administer the liquor. But Theresa is not our killer."

"I'm glad to hear you say it. Or surprised. I wonder is there anyone you do not suspect?"

"I told you I was mistaken in suspecting Belia," Thomas said. "Is that not enough?"

"We should question the neighbours to find out if they saw or heard anything."

"It is a while since, and there would have been little noise if this rag truly was used to hold my liquor."

"People don't forget strange occurrences," said Jorge, turning to start the task.

But by the time they came to the end of the street nobody claimed to know anything, other than one old man who said there had been a plague cart pulled up. Thomas dismissed his tale, knowing people had died in the house before the murders. Of course there would be a plague cart.

At the end of the street he looked both ways. "Doesn't Belia live not far from here?"

"You never stop, do you," said Jorge. "Or do you want me to punch you again?"

"If you feel the urge can you try for the other side, this one is sore. She does though, doesn't she?"

"Four or five streets in…" Jorge frowned, turned a full circle before pointing, "that direction, I think. And Samuel two streets beyond that." Another frown, "Or two streets this way. When do we go back to Gharnatah, Thomas, this place depresses me and the women are ugly."

"Then you have found one who is not, as you always do. Al-Haquim's house is no more than five hundred paces from Belia's, isn't it? How far are any of those houses from Tabado's? Damn, but I wish I knew who the other man was."

"It would be good to have fewer suspects, not more," said Jorge.

"I already told you I am discounting Belia."

"So am I. Do you think one of these others are involved?"

"Samuel has the skill," Thomas said, "and I'm sure Mandana has access to those who could provide it."

"Or they are working together," said Jorge. "If you suspect them that would make more sense."

"There is that. But we don't know enough to make accusations, not yet. We need proof of some kind."

"And how exactly do we get your proof?" Jorge started along the alley, heading to where a splash of sunlight lit a cross street like a welcome beacon. Thomas did not know the answer to his question, but knew eventually he would.

CHAPTER TWENTY-THREE

Thomas and Jorge were not the only ones busy that day. By the time they had gone to the palace to fetch Lubna and Will night was falling, and Belia had spent her time acquiring more furniture. The house had lost its air of abandonment, and the scent of a richly spiced meal greeted them. Will ran through to hug Belia's legs and she bent to kiss the top of his head. Thomas watched, wondering what had possessed him to suspect her. Jorge's instincts were good, and Thomas had relied on them in the past. He vowed he would not make the same mistake again.

A table big enough to seat ten stood in the middle of the wide room that acted as both a place to cook and for relaxation – or that was how Belia had chosen to interpret it. Plates and fine glassware were laid, as well as jars of heavy red wine. Jorge poured a glass and handed it to Thomas.

"Boats, Pa," Will said, tugging at Thomas's shirt. He ruffled his son's hair and opened the windows so the boy could go onto the terrace.

"But no wandering off again," he said, and Will nodded, but whether he meant it or not was an unknown. All it would take was something interesting and he'd be gone. Thomas stood beside him for a while, understanding Will's curiosity. Lamps were set on tall poles, others hanging from ship's rigging as men worked to unload cargo from a caravelle docked almost directly opposite. Figures swarmed across both dock and deck, the ship's master watching from a position on the foredeck, and Thomas narrowed his eyes, leaning across the railing in an attempt to see better. He laughed, making Will look up and Jorge to appear at his side.

"Did Will say something funny?" asked Jorge.

Thomas pointed. "See the man on the foredeck?"

"The well-dressed one?" Jorge said.

"Do you not recognise him? It's that madman Columb, the one who wants to sail across the western sea to discover China."

"China is already discovered," said Jorge.

"I told you, he is a madman."

Will tugged at Thomas. "Is madman bad, Pa?"

"What? Yes, a madman is someone who's mind doesn't work right, Will."

"Bad?"

"Not bad, no, just misguided."

Will tried the word on his tongue, failing to manage it but taking the failure in good spirit. "Morfar say mad good."

"Olaf told you that?"

Will nodded, suddenly serious.

"When?" But Thomas knew when, knew he would have to talk to Will's grandfather about his idea of training a boy for the world.

"Fight," Will said, taking a stance as if he held a shield and sword. "Morfar say mad good in fight."

"Yes, he would. But so are brains."

"Brains?" Will held his palm in front of his face and

smacked it against his forehead. He grinned. "Yes, Morfar say brain good too."

"Are you going to talk to him?" asked Jorge.

"Columb? Why would I want to do that?"

"What are they unloading?"

"I don't know that either. Does it matter?"

Will stood on the railing, half hanging over, and Thomas picked him up by the back of his trousers and set him on his feet.

"He's not a slaver, is he?"

"Not as far as I know." Thomas glanced inside to where Lubna and Belia sat at the table, heads together like the oldest of friends. "Come on, let's go and eat." He picked Will up again and carried him swinging inside, the boy laughing all the way.

Later, when Will was asleep, curled on a settle beside the fire, Thomas pulled out the now crumpled sheet of paper Jorge had obtained and smoothed it on the table top. He had drunk too much wine and his belly was tight with good food, but he wanted to discuss his findings with the others while he still could.

Lubna came to stand behind him, wrapped her arms around his chest and rested her chin on his shoulder. The house was quiet, but the calls of the sailors and workers continued to come from beyond the open window, as well as flies and moths that batted against the lamps, causing their light to shimmer.

Lubna reached around and put a finger on the list of names, most now crossed through, including that of Mandana, but that had been Thomas's decision and not a result of their enquiries. It had been a hard day, with many difficult conversations. As he had said when the list was handed to him, many of the names were of men important in the city. His initial fear was they would be unable to question them or their households. Jorge had stilled that fear when he suggested they pretend they were on the Queen's business. He had made up a story that she wanted to appoint a new Bishop in Cadiz, and sought their advice. Now only four names remained and Thomas held little hope they could tell him anything more than he already knew. He hoped those they had spoken to would keep the conversation confidential, as asked. He might have doubted it, but the way each had subtly dismissed their rivals while putting themselves forward made him think self-interest would keep them silent. At least until they discovered there was no such post available in Cadiz.

Belia stacked plates to clear the table, set them aside and returned to her place beside Jorge.

"So," she said, "exactly what do you know so far? Other than I am your main suspect?" But she smiled when she said it.

"I apologise," Thomas said.

"You are not forgiven, but I am working on it. Tell us what you know so far, and let us see if we can help."

"Jorge knows it all."

"And Lubna and I do not, unless you think women cannot cope with such ideas."

Thomas shook his head. "Lubna has helped before."

"But you do not know me," said Belia.

Thomas almost asked Jorge if she was always this spiky but stopped himself in time. Belia had a point. Keeping the information to themselves meant something might be missed.

Jorge refilled their glasses as Thomas started. He laid out what they knew, what they could guess, and tried to explain what they did not yet know. They remained silent while he went through the explanation and when he was finished he picked up his glass, drained it and held it out for more.

Lubna had come to sit beside him, her hand in his resting in his lap. Belia and Jorge sat opposite, their shoulders touching, and Thomas had a sense of contentment he wasn't sure he had ever experienced so deeply before. The four of them here in the scented night, the sound of workmen outside, in a place they might call their own, if only for a time. It felt right. Only one thing spoiled the effect – this was Spain, not al-Andalus. But was that such a bad thing? Al-Andalus was doomed, Thomas knew, and in Spain he was a trusted friend to both King and Queen. A blessed individual.

"You need another list," said Lubna. "Of the victims."

"We don't know enough about them," Thomas said, "or even who most of them are."

"But you know some things. Here." She turned the paper over, got up to search for something to write with. When she came back she said, "Tell me what you know. Who is the one you are sure of? You mentioned a name before."

"Tabado," Thomas said. "Filipe Tabado, Deacon to the Archbishop."

Lubna wrote the name down in Arabic, right to left. Thomas reached out and stopped her.

"Let me, otherwise Belia will be unable to read it."

Lubna gave up the quill.

"I can read it," said Belia, "let her continue."

"He was married, wasn't he?" said Lubna.

Thomas gave her the details.

"Do you know who her father is?"

He shook his head, glanced at Jorge.

"I didn't ask. I could try going back but doubt she will talk to me again. She didn't like being questioned the first time."

"Even you? I thought you could charm any woman," Thomas said.

"It would be a dull world if such were so," said Jorge, and

Thomas saw both Lubna and Belia smile, knowing he had long since captured both their hearts.

Lubna rapped a knuckle on the table. "When, when, when."

"Two weeks before I arrived, as near as I can judge, so the middle of August."

"And the body you saw when you arrived?"

"Ten days, something like that." He tried to remember how much time had passed since Martin led him into the city. Ten days was near enough.

"And now it's the middle of September." Lubna drew a line and marked the days off, then extended it to the other side of the paper. "Now we need to find out when the others were taken." She ticked tiny marks, each representing a day.

"To what purpose?" Belia leaned across to look at what Lubna was doing.

"Thomas knows there is usually a pattern," said Lubna. "He has taught me that much over the years whether he meant to or not, and I am nothing if not a good student."

Thomas had no recollection of teaching her anything about this thing he did that he wished he did not, but knew Lubna missed nothing and remembered almost everything. Whether he approved of her interest or not it was too late now to change it.

"We need to know why, too," he said, and Lubna nodded. Jorge appeared to have fallen asleep, but Belia's eyes sparked with the excitement of the chase.

"There will be the usual reasons," said Lubna. "Jealousy, greed, hatred." She wrote them beneath the line of times.

"And sometimes there is no reason at all," Thomas said. "Nothing but bad luck. It was like that with Mandana, no reason for the choice of his victims."

"Except you told me it was not him did the choosing," said Lubna. "Didn't he have a monk who went prowling for the vulnerable? It would be that man's motives we would need to know."

"He took pretty girls," Thomas said. "And we all know the reason for that."

"Tabado was a man of God," said Lubna. "Do we know what any of the others were?"

"We do not even know how many, let alone their names or professions, though I am sure Mandana said several were priests or men of God. But we cannot base a theory on a single victim."

"We could consider it, why someone would take men of God. I agree we do not have enough information yet, but if we throw our net wide who knows what might be caught?"

"It is not just men of God though, is it? If the victims are taken in pairs only one of them is Christian. The others have been Jews and Moors. Unless we have not been told everything."

"Mandana will not have revealed everything he knows," said Jorge.

"He is a changed man, I hear," said Lubna.

"Pretending to be." Jorge wriggled his shoulders, getting himself comfortable.

"Go to bed," Thomas said.

"I am waiting for Belia," said Jorge. "I no longer sleep alone."

Belia slapped the back of his head and Jorge smiled, but remained with his cheek turned to the table.

"Supposing they were all men of God," Thomas said, "and I'm not saying they were or that I accept such as a connection, why kill them?"

"What if it was someone who hated their God. Someone like al-Haquim, or me, a Muslim. Someone who hated what their God is doing with these burnings?"

The Inquisition was a strong argument, Thomas knew.

The crowds who came to witness the burnings, who came to dance and jeer and take a perverse pleasure in the pain of others, were large, but still only a small proportion of the city. There would be others afraid, and fear could lead to hate and retribution.

"There is another reason for murder," Thomas said. "Jealousy. Sex, infidelity and jealousy." He tapped the paper. "Put Theresa's name down."

"You don't suspect her, do you?"

"Of course not. But she was Tabado's lover. How do we know she did not have others before him? What if she has an admirer who is killing her lovers one by one?"

Without raising his head Jorge chuckled. "Don't you mean two by two? And doesn't that challenge your argument? God's teeth, how many lovers do you think she has taken?"

"No, but suppose—" he started, only to be interrupted by a loud knock at the door. He sat up, as did Jorge, both men startled.

"Are you expecting another delivery?" Thomas asked. "More furniture?"

"Nothing," said Belia.

Another hammering at the door, louder this time, and Jorge rose to his full height, instantly awake. Thomas was first to the door. He nodded to Jorge, who took a position out of sight.

When Thomas flung the door wide just as a third set of knocks sounded, the man with a hand raised took a sudden step back.

"Are you Don Olmos?" The man frowned in recognition of Thomas, but knew he was not the one he sought.

"Who wants him?" Thomas blocked the entrance, making himself wide.

"I have a message." The man held a sealed letter out, and

when Thomas took it the red wax still held a hint of warmth. "It is important, he must read it at once."

"Is an answer needed?" Thomas asked.

"None I know of." The man turned and ran into the dark, the sound of his boots echoing from the houses on either side.

Thomas broke the seal and unfolded the letter.

"That is for me," said Jorge, coming out of hiding.

Thomas shook his head and handed it across. "Then read it."

Jorge went so far as to take the letter and pretend to look it over before handing it back.

"It's in Spanish," he said, as if that explained his lack of understanding.

Thomas smiled, the smile fading as he read the contents. He shook his head. "It's from the Queen," he said. "She wants to see you in the morning. You and Lubna. She wants you both to visit her." Thomas gave the letter to Jorge, who studied it once more.

"Is this her hand?"

Thomas glanced at the letter. "No, she has scribes to write her words. Her hand is finer than that."

"What does she want with me?" said Jorge.

Thomas looked at him, shook his head. "How am I supposed to know that?"

"She is your friend."

"Who has decided not to tell me what interest she has in you."

"And Lubna. Don't forget Lubna."

"I'm not likely to. I think she likes Lubna. And her children like Will." Thomas shook his head again, baffled at the way of the world. "Remember not to be late, Isabel rises early."

CHAPTER TWENTY-FOUR

In the moment of slipping from sleep to awake Thomas had no concept of where he was. The splash of sunlight on the wall was wrong, as were the sounds coming through the open window. But the shape beside him was the same, and he remembered they had stayed in the house by the river, and that so long as Lubna lay beside him he needed little else.

He swung his feet to the wooden floor and stood, stretching, a crack coming from the bones in his neck. A small hand clutched at his leg and he stepped away.

"Come back to bed," said Lubna, throwing the covers aside to show him what awaited if he did.

He looked, smiled, and found his clothes. Will would be awake, and he didn't want him annoying Belia or Jorge.

"Don't forget you have an appointment with the Queen."

Lubna made a noise and slipped from the bed as Thomas went barefoot down the wide stairs. The ground floor room came into view as he descended, Belia at the stove where water boiled in a pot. Segments of fruit were on a plate on the table, together with nuts and soft cheese. The perfume of baking bread brought saliva to his mouth.

"Is he still in bed?"

Belia turned, her face without expression, and Thomas wondered whether she had forgiven him or not. Most likely not, and he could not blame her for it.

"I tried to wake him but he complained so much I thought coffee and warm bread might have more luck than I did."

"Has he forgotten the Queen wants to see him?" Thomas said.

"No, he remembers, but he is lazy." At last a small smile was offered. "He claims to be a great warrior but I am not sure I believe him. A great lover, perhaps, but a fighter?"

Thomas picked up a fresh roll, tossing it from hand to hand, too hot yet to handle or eat. "Jorge claims many things, some of which have a basis in fact, most of which do not."

"Which should I believe?" said Belia. "I am not sure I have heard one that stands the light of examination."

"I am sure you have," Thomas said, uneasy at the conversation. Despite knowing Belia the longest of them, he did not know her well or deeply, not like Jorge would by now.

"Ah," she said, "that one. Yes, perhaps so. Will you continue your investigation today?" She brought a steaming pot of coffee and set it on the table before pulling a chair out for herself. She too reached for a roll, her fingers more used to the heat than his. She tore it into pieces and dipped one into a pot of oil.

"I want to see if I can discover the names of more victims."

"It will be hard," said Belia, one arm on the table, the other selecting a choice of foods with which to break her fast. "Scores a day die here, people go missing for a surfeit of reasons. Whole families take their goods and set out to escape the pestilence, others in fear of the Inquisition or the Ghost."

"You are still here," Thomas said.

"It is my home. And I am like you, I think, immune to the disease."

"I am not immune. I fell ill when I was young but lived. It is that which has made me safe, I think. If we could only infect everyone with a tiny piece of the disease perhaps it would work for all as it has for me."

Belia smiled, indulging his flight of fancy. "I never caught it, but still it avoids me. Perhaps I frighten it. I am not beautiful like Lubna or the Queen."

Thomas laughed. "If you were not beautiful Jorge would not be sharing your bed."

"Does he only sleep with beautiful women?"

Thomas saw she was not seeking a compliment, she was genuinely curious. "No, but if he has a choice he will choose the one he can lavish the most love on. It is not how a woman looks to him but how much he can please her. He says… well, as we've already spoken of, Jorge says a lot."

"What does he say of love?" Belia bit into a ripe fig, wiped at her chin. Her dark eyes captured Thomas like a moth to a lamp, and he wondered how she could not consider herself beautiful.

"Jorge claims to be able to release the full potential of a woman to her own pleasure."

A hint of a flush touched Belia's cheeks. "Well, yes, as we have agreed, he does spout a lot of nonsense. I will help you today if you will have me. Or trust me."

"I apologise for my suspicions," Thomas said, wondering how many more times he would have to say it.

Belia's expression remained unchanged, but when she spoke her voice was softer. "I understand your reasoning. I would have followed the same logic, no doubt, but I considered us friends, Thomas, and friends do not suspect each other of murder."

"I can say no more. I am sorry to the core of my being."

"It is because I know herbs and my husband was a surgeon, isn't it?"

"I saw the instruments at your house, clean as if used only the day before."

"They are kept that way to honour his memory." She smiled. "And the occasional client who trusts me, a women, more than the butchers of this city. Do you want my assistance or not? There is enough to keep me busy here, but I believe I can help."

"In what way?" Thomas realised the words sounded harsher than he meant, but Belia held a hand up as he started to compose something softer.

"I know everyone in this city who needs herbs. My husband knew even more. Men of science and medicine. Harridans who will scoop the child from a woman's womb when it is unwelcome. Women who create potions of dubious purpose. Everyone. You say your killer is skilled with a blade?"

Thomas nodded. Footsteps sounded on the stairs and Jorge appeared, dressed only in a pair of linen pants.

"Then I probably know who they are. Not *who*," Belia said, "but I judge there are no more than thirty men in the city capable of what you claim has been done."

"And women?"

"Only one." She stared at Thomas, eyes black and deep.

"How do we judge who might be guilty?"

"I have a plan of great subtlety. You ask them if they are the killer. Hold them to the wall if you must, but the asking will be enough. You ask and I will watch. If anyone is guilty they will show it in some way."

Thomas smiled, then laughed. Yes, it was a plan – but subtle? He thought not. However, it might work, and he nodded as he reached across the table to offer his hand. Belia took it, her own a moth trapped inside his palm. She smiled, more forgiveness in the gesture than a thousand words.

"Put her down," said Jorge as he sat. "She's mine."

Belia slapped him across the cheek and Jorge grinned. "Take care, the Queen will not be pleased if I come to her with a bruise to match Thomas's."

"What does she want with them?" Belia walked beside him, not a foot behind as most other women who accompanied their menfolk on the streets. Her back was straight, head held high, black hair catching every zephyr of breeze to caress her face.

"Lubna I can understand, Jorge not," Thomas said. "Perhaps she means to question them about me. She wants me to live in Spain, to become her personal physician."

"I did not know, but it makes sense. You should accept. There will be riches and honours. Jorge tells me she loves you."

"But I am not of this place."

"You are not of al-Andalus either, but you live there. Though not for much longer, I judge."

"You are right in that. And maybe when that day comes I will return to her if she will still have me."

"She will have you. She would be a fool not to, and from what I hear she is no fool."

"No." Thomas looked around. They had come to the north, almost to the city wall, and the houses here sat close together with only a few rising above a single storey. "What is your plan, Belia?"

"We are almost at the first name, then we will work our way back to the south. It will be a long day and require much walking, if you are able."

Thomas did not consider an answer necessary.

"What if we find no-one?" asked Belia.

"Then we think again, but I am confident. Your idea is sound. Whoever is doing this possesses skills known to you and few others."

"What if they are not known to me?" said Belia. "People come and go all the time. These days it is mostly go, but you have seen the ships that come to the dock. Sevilla is the gateway of Spain. All goods land here, and all exports are carried from them. But if these deaths go back some time, which you claim, then the person responsible lives in Sevilla. And if as you also say he has specific skills, then we may catch him before nightfall."

"That would be good. Then I can find out what Jorge and Lubna are up to."

Belia smiled. "Forget them for now, we are here." She stopped in front of a single story house with a sun-bleached door, some of the planks curling under the onslaught of the sun. She waited for Thomas to knock, so he stepped around her and rapped on the wood.

Neither Jorge or Lubna were at the house by the river when they returned. Thomas could scarce believe they were still at the palace, but the rooms had an air of abandonment, too newly populated to hold the sense of a person for long. He would go to the palace, but first he wanted to write down what they had discovered, even what they had failed to discover.

When he fetched a sheet of paper and sat at the table Belia said, "I have everything here," tapping her forehead.

"I am used to writing things down. It helps me think, to organise the information. Give me the names again, and remind me of who was not at home and who was, and those two who are possible suspects."

"No wonder you have to write things down if you cannot recall what we have done so recently." But Belia sat across from him and spoke the names.

Thomas wrote in two columns, one containing most of the names, men they had spoken to and dismissed. Some were drunkards incapable of the skill shown. Others too old. Others too soft – Jorge would have recognised the capability of each, but Thomas was learning, and Belia knew these men best of all.

In the second column he ruled a line half way down. Below he wrote the names of those who had not been home, and Belia offered a judgement on their character which ruled them out, but Thomas knew he would still want to talk to them. Above the line were the names of the two who were both skilled enough and, in both their opinion, of a mind that might encompass murder.

The first was a Moor by the name of Quys al-Amrhan, exiled from his homeland, the other of Jewish descent, named Ezera Salman.

"Tell me about this one, al-Amrhan." Thomas tapped the paper, careful not to smear the wet ink. The pot he had mixed sat in the middle of the table where it was safe from being tipped over. "You told me he was an exile, do you know why?"

"Only rumour, and I don't give credence to rumour."

"Neither do I, unless it is all we have."

Belia sighed. "Some say he killed an important man and had to flee for his life, others that he owed money. There are other tales, but none worth giving consideration."

"Who did he kill?" Thomas made a mark against the name, his writing small and precise.

"It was not murder was the tale I was told. He was trying to excise a tumour and the patient died."

"That is not so unusual," Thomas said. "I have lost patients myself the same way, more than I would wish, but it happens."

"I agree. The way it was told to me the man was important and his family blamed Quys."

"Where did this happen?" It made no difference, but Thomas was curious.

"Malaka." Belia used the Moorish pronunciation. "A fine city, other than for the flies."

Thomas smiled. "I studied there many years ago. I'm of a mind to take Lubna there to complete her training. But you are right about the flies."

"A female surgeon? She would not be accepted."

"Likely not, but trained she will be even more useful to me than she already is. Tell me about the other man, this Salman."

"Jewish and, as far as I know, still a follower of the old ways. A good surgeon, born in Sevilla."

"So why is he here," Thomas tapped the side containing two names, "and not here?" the other side.

Belia studied the table top, a short nail scratching at the surface. Thomas stared at the henna patterns that curled across her skin to snake into the folds of her robe, recalling the patterns Lubna had worn when she arrived but had since faded, those that had been applied for their wedding. It seemed a year ago, not a few short weeks.

"There is something about him, something cold. His patients have complained to me that he cares nothing for them, only for the displaying of his skill."

Thomas smiled, but resisted saying the same accusation had been made against him more than once. There were times being cold to a patient meant they received the best treatment.

"What is your opinion?" asked Belia.

"I didn't like Salman, but neither did he strike me as someone capable of cold-blooded murder. Al-Amrhan must wait until we find him at home, so tell me what you think."

"Is this cold-blooded murder?" said Belia.

"I don't know." Thomas scattered fine sand on the paper to dry the ink, blew the excess away. "If I knew why the man was killed, what his killer was looking for, I might have a better idea."

"Is he looking for something, do you think? I have not seen any bodies, so I must take your word for it."

"The cutting is clean, not like the strike of an angry man. They remind me of the incisions a surgeon would make to save a person rather than take a life, but taken lives have been, and for a reason we do not yet know. That is what we are missing. The man's motive."

"Does there always need to be one?" Belia rose and smoothed her robe. "Are you going to the palace?"

"If they are still there. And yes, there is always a motive even if it is not one we might understand, but it will mean something to the killer."

"I will walk with you as far as the market. When you see Jorge tell him not to be late for dinner. Are you and Lubna coming again?"

"I don't know, but best assume not. Whatever was so important to have them scurrying to the Queen will probably have consequences."

Belia offered an enigmatic smile but said nothing as she led the way from the room. Thomas folded the notes he had made and slipped them into a pocket of his robe.

CHAPTER TWENTY-FIVE

"What did you say?" Thomas stared at Lubna, wondering whether she had lost leave of her senses.

"We are to be married in the Cathedral."

"That's what I thought you said. But you told me you didn't want to be married here, it wouldn't be an Islamic wedding."

"It will not, but I know you do not follow Allah, so this wedding is for you. Besides, there is a place which may satisfy us both. She sent Jorge and I with a man who showed us a side chapel. It is a part of the old Mosque, and it feels right, Thomas. It feels like Gharnatah, not Spain. Unless you have changed your mind and do not want to marry me anymore?"

"No, I haven't changed my mind. I had thought you wanted to wait until we returned home, but if you want to marry here then we will. When?"

"As soon as we like. Unless you wish to invite someone. Isabel said she would grant safe passage to anyone we wanted to come from Gharnatah, other than the Sultan, Aixa and Muhammed."

"Anyone? Even your father?"

Lubna smiled. "Do you think he would come? I would like him to be here. And what about Helena, and my other sisters? Would they come too, do you think? We could invite Da'ud al Baitar, Britto even, he is a friend now, is he not?"

Thomas shook his head. "Why not everyone we know? I can't imagine Olaf coming, not here into the heart of the enemy. Besides, it would take a fast horse and rider four days to make the journey, likely ten days to come back if it was Helena. She likes to travel in comfort. Are you willing to wait two weeks?"

"I have waited two years, what difference will two more weeks make?"

"Then write to her. Write to your father – no, write to Helena and ask her to talk to Olaf. He might come, he's bloody minded enough. Where would they stay? You will have to warn them there is disease here. No, it won't work."

"Sit down," said Lubna, "and try to breathe. I will write and wait for a reply. Let us set a date twenty days hence, that should be enough time. Now tell me, how did you get on today? You started to tell me but I think my news knocked it out of your head." She wrapped her arms around him where he sat and kissed the top of his head.

"Where is Will?"

"With the princesses. They like to dress him up like one of their own."

"So long as he doesn't get used to it."

"Isabel said… no, I told her it was impossible."

"If it's what she spoke of to me I agree. We are not nobles and never will be."

"Particularly me. Are we to stay here tonight or go to Jorge's house?"

"Whichever you prefer."

"Then let us stay here," said Lubna. "I am becoming used

to the trappings of nobility even if I do not have the right colour of skin for it. But you do. Isabel said she would make you a Duque. She has a spare title or two lying around, she told me. One of them thanks to you and Jorge."

"Carmona," Thomas said.

"Yes, I think that was the name. Would you like to be the Duque of Carmona?"

"I want to go home," Thomas said. "With you. Married or not, though we would marry once we get there, I promise."

"Isabel still needs you. Until the baby comes, at least. And now I am also here I can help when her time comes. I met the nurse, Theresa, and we talked. I like her, she is good at her job. She talked about you. I think she is a little bit in love with you." Lubna shook her head. "Goodness knows why, you are no great catch."

"You know she was Tabado's lover?"

"That does not stop her gazing doe-eyed at you. But tell me, for I have distracted you, have you identified the killer you seek?"

"We have some names, but nothing is certain yet." Thomas reached into his robe and withdrew the list he had made, smoothed it out. Lubna leaned across him to read it and he allowed his hands to wander until she slapped them away.

"These two are your suspects?"

"So Belia says. The only pair both capable and of the right mind."

"And what do you think?"

"I think I need to know more about why the victims were killed, and to be sure if it truly is a pair who are taken each time, a pair who are killed side by side. But why does he only display one of them?"

Lubna came around and took a seat. Beyond the window the wall was painted ochre by a setting sun and a paige walked the walls putting a spill to lamps. It was a long way around the palace walls and he would not complete his circuit inside the hour.

"Can you be so sure it is always two?"

"The most recent have been. It is near impossible to tell with the first deaths, they were too long ago and the method had changed since. This displaying of the bodies. But since that began Mandana assures me it has always been two, and a killer like this will not change his ways."

"Why two, then? Are they the same or different? Are they always men, or are women taken as well?"

"I heard tell of a man and woman being killed together, but it may not have been related. Nobody thought to check them for injuries, so if they were cut in the same way I will never know."

"What was the theory, and have you written all this down?"

"I did so the night we were at Jorge's house," Thomas said. "You were part of it."

"But you know more now. Do it again, Thomas, put down everything you know and everything you suspect. Add what you learned today. And take a guess at what might be the logic of a twisted mind. You are good at that."

"Thank you." Thomas was unsure whether it was a compliment or not.

"And while you do so I will see if I can rescue our son from the hands of those princesses."

After she had gone Thomas stared at the wall, thinking of her words. *Our son*. Was that how she saw Will, as theirs? As good as if she had birthed him herself? The boy might not even be the fruit of Thomas's loins but he did not even think of that now, so perhaps Lubna was the same. Will was theirs. *Their* son. He smiled. He, Thomas Berrington, had a son. And then the smile faded. He might have another, one he had never seen, one snatched away from him when he was a bare seventeen years of age. He had given no more than a passing thought to Eleanor in over two years. He knew she likely still lived, and lived a good life. But the man who stole her from him, the Duque d'Arreu, would be gone. He had not been a young man when his soldiers left Thomas for dead on the side of a French roadway. But the child Eleanor had been carrying, he, or she, would have near thirty years by now, in the prime of life for a member of the nobility. And he laughed suddenly at the notion that he could join such ranks.

But instead of doing as Lubna suggested and write his thoughts down again, he scribbled a short message, pulled on his robe and went to the long courtyard where soldiers were practicing their sword work. He hesitated a moment, observing those who were skilled and those who were not, finding none who could match the standard he had seen when Olaf trained Moorish soldiers. But there were more of the Spanish, and they had invested in artillery. However good a swordsman might be, however skilled a horseman, an iron ball fired faster than a man could see was a mighty leveller.

Beyond the gate the streets and squares were busy and Thomas overheard talk of more people taken by the Inquisition. He wanted to return to the house of Quys al-Amrhan. Perhaps the man had returned by now, and if not Thomas would try to gain entry. He still remembered the skill of breaking locks Jorge had taught him.

The house lay north and west, set in a huddle of narrow houses, as if they wanted to be hidden from the view of passing strangers. A few old men sat on stoops, and here and there the scent of hashish and opium sweetened the air.

Al-Amrhan's house was indistinguishable from any of the others. Thomas had questioned Belia on why a skilled physician would live in such a modest place, her answer no surprise. Al-Amrhan was a Moor in a city of Spaniards and Jews. The Jews might use his services, but they also had skilled physicians of their own. The Spanish would rather seek out the worst of their own before using such a man. There were a few Moorish exiles who might call on him, but not enough to make a man rich. Or even raise him beyond sleeping cheek by jowl with the city wall.

The house huddled in shadow at the end of a row, the light of lamp or candle absent. Thomas shaded his eyes and leaned close to a poorly fitted window, rippled glass distorting his view. Nothing showed. The closest light came from a lamp burning at the far end of the alley. Thomas looked around before kneeling in front of the door and reaching inside his robe. A simple selection of the right tool, a twist, and the cheap lock gave way. Thomas pushed at the door and entered.

He found candles in the single room that was all the house consisted of, and lit one, doubting there would be any passerby to wonder who was inside. The only windows were either side of the door. The rear wall was solid brick. The room was no more than six paces deep, the same wide. A blackened stove was set in the far corner, the stone above dark with soot. A narrow table and even narrower bed showed where al-Amrhan ate and slept. A wooden dresser held a few plates and an ornament of some kind. Thomas took the candle closer and was surprised to discover a non-working model of the elephant clock that marked off the hours inside the palace of al-Hamra. It made him think al-Amrhan might have some connection to Gharnatah as well as Malaka, but even if he did the information was irrelevant.

Thomas set the guttering candle on the table and pulled out drawers to reveal worn clothing, an assortment of knives more likely used for eating than protection, and then in the bottom he found what he had suspected would be present.

He took out the leather case and unwrapped it on the table, the contents no surprise. He pulled up a chair, sat and leaned close after drawing the candle closer. Too close as it singed his hair, and he pushed it away before trying again.

Familiar instruments, nothing he did not own himself. Clean. Well cared for, as were those inside his robe. There was little use for medical instruments unless they were clean, though he knew many Spanish physicians saw no need.

Thomas withdrew each and turned it close to the candle flame, not exactly sure what he was looking for. A trace of blood? And if he found some what would it prove? But there was none. The instruments might have been purchased only that morning and cleaned since.

He straightened, twisting his spine. It had been a long day and Lubna would be waiting for him. The thought brought a smile to his face, which was instantly wiped away as he caught sight of something coming at him fast. He was too late to stop the blow entirely but managed to bring an arm up to stop a rock splitting his skull open. As he staggered away and fell into the corner beside the stove he glimpsed a robed figure, hood raised. The man snatched at the instruments, turned and ran. Thomas clutched his arm to his chest, fearing it broken, but when he managed to make a fist without the pain worsening he staggered to his feet and set off in pursuit.

CHAPTER TWENTY-SIX

By the time Thomas reached the alley al-Amrhan had disappeared. No ordinary surgeon would have been capable of
such speed. Thomas stopped, slowing his breathing as he
continued to rub at his arm. He heard the strike of boot heels
on cobbles and ran to the end of the alley but still the man
was out of sight. He listened again, trying to place the direction of the rapidly fading footsteps. He was going to lose him
if he didn't do something, so he took a chance, turned right
and ran as fast as he could, which was not as fast as he was
once capable of, but fast enough. Two streets further on he
saw his quarry. There were more people now as they
approached the centre of the city, impeding both of them,
but the closer al-Amrhan came to the Cathedral the thicker
the crowds grew, and Thomas was both taller and stronger.
He pushed his way through, closing the distance between
them. Men pushed back, a few uttering oaths, a few striking
out, but Thomas ignored their blows.

A hundred paces on and a woman carrying a basket of
bread stepped in front of him and he bowled her over, not
even looking back at her wailing cry. A hundred more paces

and he cursed and pushed those impeding him out of the way. The crowd had gathered to watch a line of victims the Inquisition had selected being led toward the bridge and the dungeons beyond, a score of men and women surrounded by red-robed priests, a man at the head holding a gilded cross.

The line blocked al-Amrhan and he turned back, eyes scanning the crowd, passing directly over Thomas, who knew the man had had little chance to see him in the house. He circled to the side as al-Amrhan began to walk in a new direction, moving at a more sedate pace. Thomas's long legs ate up the ground more quickly and he was on the man before he knew it. He reached out and grabbed his arm, fingers closing to prevent escape.

Al-Amrhan swung around, one of the instruments gripped in his hand. He slashed at Thomas's face, who swayed back, came forward again and smashed his forehead into the man's nose. Al-Amrhan's went to his knees. Thomas gripped him beneath his arms and dragged his dead weight along, not that there was much weight. Beneath his robe al-Amrhan was skin and bone and little else, and Thomas wondered why he insisted in staying in Sevilla when Moorish cities needed men of science and would welcome his skill. Unless the killings were his reason.

Thomas dragged al-Amrhan to the side of the square and leaned him against the wall as he started to come around from his stupor. His eyes focused, went away again, came back.

"Who sent you to kill me?" said al-Amrhan, his words slurred by the blood flowing from his broken nose.

"I'm not here to kill you. Why did you run?"

Al-Amrhan touched his nose, winced. "Why do you think I ran? I value my life, such as it is."

"Don't worry, I'll fix it for you," Thomas said. He glanced around, knowing he couldn't take the man to the palace but needed somewhere to question him. There was only one place he could think of. Unless he dragged al-Amrhan to al-Haquim's house and left him to the tender mercies of Abbot Mandana. But no, he could not do that to someone however many he might have killed. Instead he untied the rope holding the robe at his waist and knotted one end around al-Amrhan's wrists, the other wrapped several times through his own. He tugged.

"Follow me, and do not cry out or I will tell them you escaped from the line of prisoners over there." He nodded at the group being led away. He didn't expect al-Amrhan to believe the lie but he followed meekly as if all resistance had drained from him.

Belia was alone in the wide ground floor room when Thomas arrived. He sat al-Amrhan in a chair and used the rope to tie him to it. His head turned, eyes finally falling on Belia who had watched proceedings from the balcony and only now come inside.

"What are you doing here?" he said. "This is not your house. Save me from this madman, send for the guard. You know me, Belia, I do not want to die."

"You won't die," Thomas said, "not unless you have done what I suspect, and it will not be me who condemns you. The courts will do that."

"Then I am truly dead. What am I meant to have done?" He tried to blow the clotting blood from his nose, his eyes watering.

Thomas stepped behind him and reached around. Before al-Amrhan could react he snapped the nose back into place. It would bruise even more, but at least it would set reasonably straight. For however long the man might live, which might be only a matter of days, and Thomas wondered why he had bothered.

"Did you hit him?" asked Belia. She brought a bowl of

water and a cloth and began to clean al-Amrhan's face, dabbing gently at the dried blood.

Thomas pulled a chair close and sat, his knees almost touching those of the other man. He glanced at Belia. "Where is Jorge?"

"He went out. Said he has some things to do." Belia smiled. "I assume you can guess what, that you know what they have been plotting all day?"

Thomas shook his head, but in frustration rather than negation. He tapped al-Amrhan on the chest.

"Why are you killing them?" he said. "And why two together?"

"I don't know what you are talking about. Killing who? You are a madman, sir, and will pay for this unprovoked attack on an innocent man."

"As you would claim, of course." Thomas sat back. "What did you have against Deacon Tabado?"

"Who?"

"Filipe Tabado, Archdeacon to the Archbishop of Sevilla. Did you kill him because of his religion, or something else? Tell me and you might die without too much pain. You might avoid the fires."

From outside a rising wash of sound had grown, the calling of many voices, each raised to overcome those around them. The prisoners were being led across the swaying bridge to the castle beyond. Belia finished cleaning al-Amrhan's face as best she could and went to close the tall windows, shutting out most of the noise.

When she returned al-Amrhan looked toward her. "Tell this madman who I am. I have purchased your herbs many times. We have sat and talked of cures these Spanish have no knowledge of. And this one is as deluded as all the rest."

"Tell him what you have done," said Belia, taking a seat across the table and staring without any hint of sympathy.

"I have done nothing!"

"Then prove it," Thomas said.

"How can I prove something I have not done? I don't even know what it is I am accused of."

"Murder," said Thomas. "Murder going back months, longer. Murder carried out on a pair of victims together." He leaned close. "Why is that? What is the meaning of the two killed at once, side by side? And why display only one?" Something nagged at him, some wisp of meaning he could not grasp.

Al-Amrhan shook his head once more. "Nonsense, you speak only nonsense. Tell him, Belia, tell him I am an innocent man."

She continued to look on without expression.

"Help me!" said al-Amrhan.

"Help yourself," said Belia. "Tell Thomas what he wants to know. Tell him the truth and it will go easier for you." She glanced at Thomas, perhaps to check if he agreed, but he showing nothing, could promise nothing.

"I know no truth!" Al-Amrhan began to weep, tears flowing along his cheeks. "I know no churchmen, no Archdeacons. I scrape what little living I can and keep my own counsel. It is not easy for a Moor in Spain, not these days, and it will only get worse." He shook his head hard, spraying tears. "If I knew what truth you seek I would give it you, but I do not. Ask me what you will and I will answer true, but ask me sense, not nonsense."

It was a good show, Thomas had to give the man that. It was almost convincing.

"Did Jorge say when he would be back?" he asked Belia.

"When does Jorge ever give out information such as that? He asked me to stay up for him, which means he may be late or not. Why?"

"I would like him here. He sees people better than I do.

He would recognise any truth this man spoke. My head spins with too many thoughts and I cannot see clearly anymore."

"Have you eaten?" asked Belia.

"No, not since… not since this morning."

She rose and began to put out bread, meat and cheese. Al-Amrhan watched as if they had both lost their wits.

"What about me?"

"I will help you eat if you are hungry," said Belia.

"I mean what is to become of me. You will simply abandon me here while you stuff your faces? But yes, I have hunger. Free my hands and I will feed myself."

Thomas laughed.

"Tie my wrist to the stove then, I am sure I cannot drag it after me."

"Belia will feed you," Thomas said as he reached for the bread and tore a corner from the cheese. He glanced up. "Won't you?"

Her lips tightened, a flicker of annoyance, but she wrapped bread around a piece of meat and held it for al-Amrhan to bite. He winced as he did so, but hunger overcame discomfort. Thomas saw Belia grow tired of her role as handmaid. She laid food in front of al-Amrhan and let him snuffle at it like an animal. Thomas rose, opened the window and stepped into the night. Smoke gusted across the ships pulled up at the docks. Someone had lit a bonfire and the sound of the mob was a babble of hate. Thomas wanted to go home. This city was not his, and it did not welcome his presence.

When he sensed someone behind him he turned to find Belia had come to join him. He glanced beyond her to check on al-Amrhan, saw he continued to push food around the table with his chin.

"You should come with Jorge when we return to Garnatah," he said.

"He has already asked, and I gave him my answer."

"Which was?" Thomas leaned across the balustrade, trying to see along the waterfront. From beyond the corner of the city wall came a glow, but the crowd seemed to be thinning now the prisoners had disappeared inside the castle. "We should go inside," he said, but made no move.

"Not yet. And my answer is for Jorge's ears, not yours." She smiled and touched his arm, a brush of fingertips, then mirrored his stance, but it was the ships she studied, avoiding what was going on further along the river bank. "If you truly want to know, ask him. I suspect he will tell you anything you wish. You know he loves you."

Thomas scowled. "So he keeps telling me."

Belia laughed. "Yes, he has a surfeit of love. Of words, too. What are you going to do with him?"

Thomas knew who she spoke of, and it wasn't Jorge. "Do you think he could be the man we seek?"

Belia shook her head. "I do not. And you?"

"He could be. He has the skill, and the tools are his. But no, I don't think he is who I seek. I would still like Jorge's opinion."

"Then stay. He will return at some time. Quys is not going anywhere. Go and sleep, Thomas, you are exhausted."

He thought of lying on the bed this woman had shared with Jorge and something must have shown on his face because Belia laughed. "We have three rooms and three beds now. It is a wonder what can be found when money is shown, and Jorge appears to have an inexhaustible supply. Why is that? How does a palace eunuch become a rich man?"

"It is a long story."

"And we have all night, unless he returns soon."

"And if I tell it you may no longer feel the same about him."

"Did he kill someone for it?"

"No."

"Then I will feel the same as I do now. But it is your story to tell or not as you wish."

Thomas pushed hair back from his face, rubbed a hand across his cheeks as if the act could brush away the veil of exhaustion separating him from the world.

"What is he doing out alone at this time of night?"

"He said something about the Cathedral."

"Ah, yes. That. He told you what they have been plotting?"

"You sound as if you do not wish to marry."

"No, I do. But it has been snatched from my control, and I have no idea what they plan."

"You do not like losing control, do you?"

"Do you see everything? Are you like Jorge, who misses nothing?"

"I watch without judging," said Belia. "So yes, I am like him. He asked if I would apply henna to Lubna and I said of course. It will be my pleasure. Yours too, Thomas."

He did not want a reminder of the plot against him and turned to go inside, ready to tell Belia the story of how Jorge had become a rich man, but when he did it was to see the chair al-Amrhan had been tied to tipped over and no sign of him. Thomas cursed and ran outside, but the street was empty. He went to the end and looked across the small square that lay there but it was filled with the crowd returning from the bridge. Al-Amrhan had fled. If he had any sense, Thomas thought, he would keep running until Sevilla lay far behind.

CHAPTER TWENTY-SEVEN

The door to al-Amrhan's house remained unlocked. It swung open to Thomas's touch, but he knew if the man had returned he had already come and gone. He entered in any case, always wanting to be sure he had covered all possibilities. The single room had indeed been emptied, but ransacked. Some passing stranger had seen the door open and entered to steal whatever was worth stealing. Thomas doubted the thief had been much pleased with his haul. He turned, leaving the door open, and ran to the south and the palace, hoping Samuel would be there. Thomas had lost patience with the man, all semblance of friendship draining away. The killing involved a man who possessed the skills of a surgeon, and Samuel had to know more than he had said so far.

Frustration at a lack of progress made Thomas more forceful than he intended because Samuel cried out when he was held against the wall, his feet twitching as they sought the floor. Thomas sighed and put him down.

"What are you doing?"

"Answer my question, Samuel. I am tired and, as you have discovered, in a foul mood."

Samuel sought the narrow chair, pulled it from beneath the table and sat. Thomas stayed where he was, leaning against the stone wall.

"Yes, I know Quys, he is a good physician but struggles to find patients willing to pay him. He's a Moor, like you."

"Not quite like me," Thomas said. "Might he have become desperate enough to accept money for murder?"

"We save lives, not take them. Even you should know that."

Even me? Thomas had no idea what he meant.

"If he wanted to hide where would be go?"

"I cannot help. He has no friends that I know of," said Samuel.

"Other than you."

"I am not a friend. I have used him now and then when I could. I feel sorry for him. It is not his fault people object to his religion. He had enough work before the Inquisition came, but these days it has made everyone suspect their neighbour."

"Might it have turned his mind?"

"You are persistent, aren't you? I do not know him well, as I have already told you, but well enough to judge him incapable of cold blooded murder. And these deaths are nothing if not cold blooded. You will need to direct your suspicions elsewhere."

"Yes, I will."

Thomas turned to leave, tiredness making his head spin for a moment and he reached out to lean against the wall. When he moved again his foot kicked at something set on the floor in an alcove and he glanced, incurious, then stopped.

"What is this?" He tapped the bottle with his toe.

"You know what it is. It is your mixture, is it not?"

"How do you come to have it? I left none after I treated Juan."

Samuel smiled. "Once a thing is known it can be copied, you know that as well as I. Theresa told me of the magical liquor you brought with you. She described it, not well, but well enough. I have a friend, far more skilled than me, and between us we managed to create something close." Samuel frowned, something troubling him, but rather than speak it he went on. "It is not as effective as yours, I know, but I use it to help alleviate the suffering of those who are about to burn."

Lubna was awake when Thomas reached their rooms, Will too, though dressed like some gilded popinjay.

Thomas held his arms out and Will ran at him, launched himself from some distance but managed to clear the gap. His solid little body knocked Thomas onto the bed and he held his son up in his hands, letting love drive out the coldness that had entered his heart.

"Hey *babbaga!*" he said, laughing, using the Arabic word because Will would not understand the Spanish, let alone the English. "Who has dressed you up like a girl?"

"Not girl," said Will, kneeling and leaning on Thomas's chest as he put him down. He wrapped his arms around his neck and squeezed, making Thomas laugh again and to tickle him in order to allow a breath.

"What are you then?"

"Prince Will," he said. "Isbel call me Prince Will."

"The Queen calls you a Prince?"

"No! Prin...princess Isbel. And Hana is funny." Will struggled over princess, too many sibilants in the word for him.

"Hana?" Thomas frowned. "Who is this Hana?"

"He can't say Joanna," said Lubna, lying the other side of Will and wrapping her arms about his round belly. "She is funny, or mad, or something. One moment she is a serious little thing and the next she is even wilder than this one."

"Isabel is good at birthing girls," Thomas said. "Everyone would be happy if this one is a son."

"Too late to change that now," said Lubna. She placed a hand on the swell of her own belly. "What do you think our child is? It does not kick so much of late, so I think a girl."

"Don't believe what the crones tell you."

"Crones have more knowledge than you credit them with." She leaned over Will to offer Thomas a kiss, and the boy giggled and wriggled as he was trapped between them.

"What would you like, boy or girl?" Thomas asked, lying on his back, hands behind his head. His body was starting to relax and he felt as if he was melting into the feather stuffed mattress. Lubna's presence did that for him, just one more reason he loved her as much as he did.

"What about one of each?"

He laughed. "No, there's only one in there."

"I mean later, after this one. I think we should have at least five children, perhaps more. I like carrying a child, it makes me feel I have fulfilled my potential as a woman."

"I want to talk to you about that."

"Oh, Thomas, not in front of Will!" She laughed, covering the boy's ears.

He shook his head, smiling. "Well, that too later, if you wish it. I meant you and your skill. I would have you learn all you are capable of."

A smile and a touch of her hand against his face. "Not so much, then."

"A great deal, and don't make a pretence otherwise. I have been thinking of Malaka."

"Well, I suppose you have to think of something. Better than murder, at least."

"We could live in Malaka for a few years while you attend the infirmary there."

"I'm a woman," said Lubna.

"Really? I hadn't noticed."

"Oh, I think you may have, once or twice. I will not be accepted because of my sex."

"You will if I ask it," Thomas said.

"You have that much influence?"

"It depends – if the people I know are still there, which they may not be, I may have influence. And if not I am known. Am I not surgeon to the Sultan of Gharnatah and his family? Surely my reputation carries some weight. I will have you accepted." He turned his head. "If it is what you wish. I will not force it on you."

"How many years?" asked Lubna. She stroked Will's brow, the boy's eyes closed, his breathing slow.

"One or two. There is a great deal to learn."

"Can you not teach me?"

"Not as well. And there are advances I do not know of, and the depth of knowledge there is as the abyss of the ocean. You will learn more than with me alone."

"But you will come too? I won't go without you. You and Will and whoever I carry, we will all go, yes?"

"We will all go," Thomas said. "Jorge too, and Belia if she wishes it." He lifted Will and carried him through to his bed in the next room, removed the ridiculous clothing and tucked him beneath a cotton sheet. The window above the bed was open and he drew it shut in case Will woke and tried to climb out. The boy would climb anything, oblivious to all danger. A reflection of his grandfather's lineage no doubt, though Thomas was aware of the same wildness inside himself, a wildness he fought to keep in check and sometimes failed. Did that mean Will was his son? He could still not tell. There was much of Helena in the boy as well, her beauty, her hair, in the shadow of the handsome man he would become.

Thomas kissed his son's brow and went back to Lubna, who was already in bed and waiting for him.

CHAPTER TWENTY-EIGHT

Isabel was in a flirtatious mood that did not suit her. Only later would Thomas discover the reason why. While Theresa examined her and Thomas stood behind a screen the Queen maintained a string of conversation that bordered on the immodest. She remarked on Theresa's beauty before fortunately moving on to Will.

"He looked so handsome yesterday when my daughters dressed him," she said. "Just like this father."

Indeed, Thomas thought, *whoever that might be*, but of course he dare say nothing of such a matter.

"Jorge is coming again today," said Isabel, uncaring if Thomas spoke or not for she had enough words for both of them this morning. "I need him to tell me exactly how a Moorish wedding is arranged."

Thomas knew she was waiting for him to answer. "I thought we were marrying in the Cathedral, in a side Chapel that is already Moorish."

"You are, and there will be a Christian ceremony, but there must be a flavour of the Moorish, too. Your culture is so rich, Thomas. Misguided, but rich. Jorge tells me Lubna will have her skin painted with henna. I have never seen such done and have asked if I might observe. And you must visit the chapel we have chosen so you can approve it, though I am sure you will. Lubna and I have had long conversations about the truth of God, both our Gods, but perhaps only one God just the same. She is intelligent, your wife to be, is she not?"

"She is, your grace. How is the Queen, Theresa?"

"Fully recovered."

"Am I?"

"So far as I can tell, your grace," said Theresa.

"Am I well enough to travel, Thomas? And you can come from behind that silly screen now for I am quite modest."

"Where do you want to travel to, your grace?"

Theresa carried a bowl of water and cloths from the room, closing the door behind her. It was against protocol for Thomas to be alone with the Queen, but he had done so often enough in the past he thought nothing of it. He glanced around to find a chair and drew it closer, sat.

"I have decided my child should be born in Alcala de Henares."

"Where is that?" Thomas stretched his legs out, a lethargy settling deep in his bones. The night had been tumultuous and he had not yet managed to make sense of any of the information he had managed to glean, if indeed he had obtained any at all.

"It lies almost exactly in the centre of Spain," said Isabel. "Appropriate for the birth of my second son, no?"

Thomas smiled. "Or fourth daughter."

Isabel made a face and Thomas laughed.

"Tell me, do you think the God of Islam could be the same God you and I worship, or is he the Devil incarnate as some of my advisors would have me believe? Lubna is an intelligent woman, but she claims her God is as forgiving and

214

loving as mine." Isabel leaned forward, eyes bright. "We have discussed the possibility our God is one and the same, only the manner of worship different."

"And what have your spiritual advisors said on the matter? What does Talavera say?"

"I have made no mention of this this to the Friar. Not yet."

"Will you?"

"Lubna and I will discuss the matter further before I sound him out. I need to be sure of the ground I stand on, for he can be a stern tutor, but that is what I need, for there are times my mind moves too fast. He has told me so on several occasions."

"You mean you are curious? That is no sin."

"Not to you, perhaps. Are the English a curious race?"

Thomas laughed. "Oh, they are indeed curious, but not in the manner you mean. Lubna has said nothing of this to me."

"You have had your mind on other matters, she tells me. Despite my disapproval."

"Do I need to follow every command you issue?"

"I am the Queen of Castile and Aragon, the Queen of Spain. I think obedience is expected, is it not?" The twinkle continued to spark in her eyes.

"Even from an Englishman?"

"Ah, yes, you have me there. Do you make progress?"

"In the matter I am not meant to discuss with you?"

"Yes, that one. I have been briefed on the issue, and if anyone can stop the deaths it is you. You have done so before and you will do so again. I hear Abbot Mandana is not involved this time."

"Not directly, no." Thomas didn't want to talk of the killings.

"And that you are also suspicious of Samuel. Was I wrong to return him to the palace?"

"I no longer suspect him of anything, if I ever did, but I

think he might know something he is not even aware of himself yet."

"Are you suspicious of me, Thomas?"

He smiled. "Should I be? Do I need to interrogate you?"

Isabel clapped her hands together. "Oh, you are so clever." She stood, her old self again, sturdy rather than lithe, a rock acting as a beacon to her people. "Come walk with me, there is someone you must meet."

Thomas offered his arm and Isabel laid her hand over it as they walked through the palace and into the sun-shattered heat of the morning, and he saw who she had been speaking of. A man less tall than himself, broad shouldered, firm on wide spread feet. He was looking the other way but turned at the sound of their approach on the flagstone path and grinned.

"Thomas! I hoped you would still be here. I came as soon as I could when I heard my wife was unwell." He clasped his arm to Thomas's, gripping tight, and Thomas returned a matching pressure, a silly game between men but he knew Fernando approved. "Is your friend with you, the one lacking balls?"

"Mind your language," said Isabel, but her expression showed only indulgence. Her husband had returned from war – at least for a while, for war was a constant in this land.

"And your wife? Though I hear not wife yet. If I was a Moor not a Christian I would be tempted to take her as another wife myself. You are a fortunate man, Thomas, a fortunate man indeed."

"But you are a Christian," said Isabel to her husband.

"And want of no woman but you, my love."

Thomas wanted to flee but knew it impossible.

From the side of the gardens came the squeal of children and Will appeared, decked this time as a Roman soldier, a wooden shield in one hand, a tiny sword in the other. He saw

Thomas and ran toward him at the same time as Lubna called out for him not to rush.

"Juan want teach," Will said.

"He's too big for you," Thomas said.

"No. Morfar say big man fall harder."

"Well, he would know." Thomas glanced at Fernando. "Do you approve of your son training mine?"

"They have men with them. Juan asked if it was possible and I said he would need to ask you first, but your son appears to have done so already. We can watch, if you wish." Fernando laughed. "Do you remember when we fought in that town... what was it called?"

"Al-Khala."

"Yes, that was it. Where you were chasing another killer, as I recall. I don't know, you call yourself a physician yet death follows wherever you go." They walked along a path, the edge neatly maintained. Isabel was left behind, already deep in conversation with Lubna, and Fernando stopped and looked back. He sighed. "You are indeed a fortunate man. She is a beauty, is she not? And with child too if my eyes do not deceive me."

Thomas noticed Lubna's belly did indeed show now. The change had been so gradual, and her robes so loose flowing, it had been barely noticeable before.

"She is, your grace."

Fernando punched him on the shoulder. "No more your grace, Thomas, or I will fight you again. It was a draw, as I recall."

"Indeed it was. Fernando."

"We will both be fathers again before long, Thomas. Fortunate men indeed." Another punch which Thomas ignored. "Let us go see our sons fight and discover who is the better."

"And then I have business to attend to," Thomas said.

"So I have been informed. And you will keep me informed in turn." It was not a request, but an order.

Thomas and Jorge waited around the corner from al-Haquim's house, eventually rewarded when Abbot Mandana appeared at the ornate door, looked around and strode away. It was almost noon and Thomas had checked that a religious court was in session. He knew Samuel remained in the palace, skulking when he caught sight of Thomas, no doubt never to forgive him, but it was of no concern. He had liked the man and considered they could be friends, but other needs had overridden any chance of friendship. Thomas had never been one who valued friends, and often wondered what had gone wrong for Jorge to become one. He turned to the man now and nodded for them to follow.

"I don't like him," said Jorge.

"Neither do I. You are not meant to like him, but you have been too concerned with arranging my marriage and I need your skills now. I could have done with them last night."

"So Belia tell me, but you managed, didn't you?"

"The man escaped, remember?" Thomas shook his head and started across the square. The guard who had previously nodded him through stepped to block the half open door.

"I have been told to admit no visitors."

"You remember us from the other night. We are old friends of the Governor." The title slipped free before Thomas was aware of it, but he saw the guard recognised it and wondered if he had accompanied his master from Ronda. "Our business will take a moment, no more, if you can send a message."

The guard stood his ground. Thomas believed he could disarm him but wished the man no harm, and he would need, at the least, to knock him unconscious. It was not an act to carry out lightly. He had seen men lose their wits from a single blow and never recover.

"I owe your master money," said Jorge, stepping closer, too close as always and the guard shifted back a step. Jorge shuffled three gold coins through long and delicate fingers. "In payment for his courtesy when we stayed in Ronda."

Thomas saw the guard knew of what Jorge spoke.

"There is more than what I have in my hand," Jorge said. "Take this for your trouble and go tell him we are here." He held out his hand, waiting.

The guard looked down to where the three coins lay on Jorge's palm. Three gold coins, more than he might earn in half a year.

"I am not–"

"Of course you are not," said Jorge, his voice soft. There was something captivating about him at such times. Thomas considered it one of Jorge's unique skills. He could bend people to his will even as they thought it was they who were doing the favour. It was a seduction of a kind, little different to what he did with women and, Thomas had no doubt, men too.

He waited, and when the man raised his own hand Jorge tipped the coins into it.

"Now go tell him, and be quick."

"How do you do that?" Thomas asked when they were alone. "How can you persuade people so easily?"

"It was the gold did the persuasion," said Jorge, "I was merely the channel to pass it to him." He smiled and stepped through the door, not waiting for the guard to return, and Thomas followed. "He will come with a refusal, of course, so I think it best we avoid such unpleasantness. Besides, the man is still richer than he was, so everyone benefits."

"Other than al-Haquim," Thomas said.

"Ah, well, he is a butcher and a maniac, so I feel no compassion for him. Will you hit him, Thomas? Torture him?"

"I will ask questions, no more."

Jorge smiled. "Then best you tell me what they are so I may ask them on your behalf. You can stand close and glower menacingly. You are good at that."

CHAPTER TWENTY-NINE

They watched the guard stride across the marbled entrance to the doorway and step outside. He was gone only a moment before returning and looking around. Concealed within shade beneath an archway Thomas and Jorge watched, sure they could not be seen. The guard came inside, turned a full circle, then back the other way. It appeared he was satisfied they had gone because he returned to the door, shut and bolted it and disappeared into a niche out of the sun where a chair waited. Still they stayed where they were, sweat trickling down their skin, until the guard's head began to nod. A little longer then Thomas rose and picked up the boots he had removed earlier and moved barefoot in the direction the guard had come from. He did not expect al-Haquim to be in the scented courtyard where the three of them met, but he was, sitting reading a stack of papers. Thomas put his boots gently on the ground and gestured to Jorge, who crept away toward the arch from the entrance to keep watch. Thomas looked around until he settled on a stout door which led into a room dark with shadow. Then he moved fast, falling on al-Haquim before the man could react. Thomas flung one arm around the man's waist, the other clapping a hand to his mouth. He dragged him by his heels toward the door and inside, Jorge following almost immediately, closing the door and throwing the bolt. Thomas flung al-Haquim into a chair and put his foot on his chest to hold him there.

"Hmm, even better than glowering," said Jorge.

Al-Haquim opened his mouth to call out. Thomas moved closer and put a finger to his lips.

"We have questions and you will answer them, every one. This can go easy or it can go hard. Which way is entirely up to you. Do you understand?"

Al-Haquim's face had turned dark red and Thomas could see him trying to hold his anger in check. The man had never been able to moderate himself, reacting too fast and too stupidly to every situation. The loss of Ronda had been made harder by his lack of restraint.

"When Mandana hears of this you are a dead man, Thomas Berrington. You too, you creature."

Jorge smiled and looked around. He found a gilded chair and pulled it across, nodded at Thomas to use it, then went for another.

"It's a shame we cannot send for wine and some of those tiny cakes you told me of."

Despite Jorge's plan Thomas knew al-Haquim would respond better to threats than soft words. He drew a dagger from his belt.

"You tried to have me killed in Ronda," he said, leaning forward, the dagger loose in his hand. "I have executed men for less. Now will you take the sensible course and answer my questions?"

"I will have you dragged screaming to the fires!" Al-Haquim's voice shook. "You will wish you never came to

Sevilla. Even your Queen will not be able to save you from the Abbot."

"He is as powerful as that, is he? Interesting. Or has he only managed to persuade you of such? Now tell me what it is you three are plotting inside these walls. You are not natural bedfellows, but something is going on and I will know what it is." Thomas leaned closer still. "Why are you killing people in pairs? Is that Mandana's doing or yours?"

Al-Haquim tried to push himself back, but the chair was hard and possessed no give. "I have no idea what you are talking of. You are a madman."

"And is Samuel your weapon? I do not believe he would kill on his own behalf, but you have some hold over him, don't you? What is it, money, family, a threat to expose a secret? You will tell me what I want to know and you will hold nothing back." Thomas's hand flicked out and the tip of his knife sliced a narrow line along al-Haquim's cheek. Blood beaded and ran into his beard. The cut barely broke the surface and would heal almost at once, but al-Haquim did not know that and the pain would make him think his face had been laid open.

"Sufan!" al-Haquim yelled, his voice a scream.

Jorge rose and went to the window that looked onto the courtyard. After a while he shook his head.

"Stupid," Thomas said, and cut the other cheek. This time al-Haquim remained silent. "I know you are a coward, so believe me when I say this, Abraham, I will cut you piece by piece until your skin is flayed and falls from your flesh. I recommend the next time you speak you tell me what I want to know." Thomas considered tying the man to the chair. He had brought a length of rope for just such a purpose, but believed it was not necessary. Al-Haquim had quieted, his body stilling, the only movement a tremble of his hand as it pressed to his cheek.

"Ask your questions then, dead man."

Thomas smiled. When he saw the effect of it in al-Haquim's eyes he allowed the smile to grow. A coldness filled him, a coldness that made him capable of killing the man if need be, and al-Haquim saw the same. The pretence was over and Thomas slid the knife back into the scabbard at his belt.

"What are you plotting, the three of you?"

"Not the deaths of men," said al-Haquim.

"I didn't ask what you were *not* doing."

Jorge came and retook his chair. He examined the nails of one hand then drew his own knife. Watching al-Haquim Thomas saw the moment of acceptance. For a brave man it might never come, for a coward it was almost instant.

"The Abbot came to me not long after I arrived in the city with a proposal."

"Why you?"

"I am not without influence, and I brought many followers with me from Ronda."

"What did he propose?"

"He hates the Inquisition. He believes their ideas are wrong. It is not Jews or conversos who are the enemy of Spain but the Moors." His eyes sparked with a fire as they met Thomas's. "Your people. He would wipe you from the face of the earth."

"Yet he works with the Inquisition, he sits in judgement for them."

"To steer them in the wrong direction, he says. And Samuel helps. He knows everyone in this district. He identifies a few to Mandana who are innocent of any crime and Mandana selects them for questioning. The more innocent people who are accused and found to be without guilt the less power the Inquisition will have. Eventually word reach the Queen – from Samuel himself if no-one else tells her, but a stranger would be better – and she will put an end to their evil work. She is a devout woman who hates those who lie about their religion, but she is also just."

Thomas tried to work his mind around what al-Haquim had just told him. It matched some of what Samuel had said, but not all, and he wondered how much Samuel truly knew of Mandana's motives.

"So innocent men and women are put to torture to further Mandana's ambitions?"

Al-Haquim nodded. "In pursuit of a greater good. There are always casualties of war, and this is a war the Abbot fights, a war against the powers of ignorance."

"It is not enough," Thomas said. "He wants more, does he not? As do you."

"He says he will settle for an Archbishopric. Somewhere in Andalucia when it falls." A smile touched al-Haquim's lips. "He has mentioned Granada, which would be a sweet victory for him."

"Why Archbishop?"

"It comes with great power and the means to gather money to the title."

Thomas grunted, not sure he believed Mandana's motives, but reasonably sure al-Haquim did.

"And you? What do you want?"

"Power. I tasted it in Ronda and I would like to sip of its sweetness again. Mandana says he can find me a position in the new lands. There will be much confusion, but those who are prepared will reap the rewards. I do not want Granada, but Malaga perhaps, or Almaria would suit. Yes, somewhere along the coast where the summer heat is tempered by the ocean."

Thomas drew his knife again and turned it in his fingers. He could scarce believe what he was hearing, but recognised the truth. Al-Haquim was proud of their plan. Soon he might come to believe it had been his idea all along.

He examined al-Haquim's chest, looking for a place to strike, coldness welling inside, ice water filling his body.

"No," said Jorge, a single word, but enough to break the spell.

Thomas glanced at him. "Why not?"

"Because you will regret it if you do."

"I am not sure I will. Does he not deserve punishment?"

"He does, but not from you. There will be another way."

Al-Haquim laughed. "What, do you think you can stop us? Mandana is too strong."

"And I am physician to Isabel, Queen of Castile and Spain. I can walk into her chamber and tell her everything you have told me and I will be believed."

"And if you do a friend will be tossed to the crowd." Al-Haquim looked from Thomas to Jorge. "Your friend perhaps, eunuch. Stay silent for a few short weeks and no-one need be harmed, man, woman or child." A faint emphasis on the final word as al-Haquim's gaze returned to Thomas.

Who stood fast, knife rising, but Jorge placed himself between Thomas and al-Haquim. "We must find if he speaks the truth before we kill him."

"We?" Thomas said. He placed his hand on Jorge's chest, felt the heart beating hard within, his own matching it. He had come close to ending al-Haquim's life in this room. He wondered if had Jorge not stepped between would he have struck or not?

He pushed Jorge aside, who suddenly turned and walked to the door, shot the bolts and stepped outside. When Thomas turned back to al-Haquim the man was grinning and Thomas almost did kill him then, his hand twitching in anticipation. He took a breath and held it, leaned close to al-Haquim.

"You can never hide from me, believe that, neither of you can hide. I will come for you when you least expect it and take your miserable excuse for a life. And if anything, *anything* happens to those close to us, if anyone touches them, then both your deaths will be long and painful."

And then he went after Jorge.

"Get off me!" Belia's fists stuck Jorge's chest but he continued to hold her against him as if she might disappear if he let go. She looked toward Thomas. "Tell him to let me go. Or better still, kick him. Jorge, stop it!"

"He thought something had happened to you," Thomas said. He pulled out a chair and sat, a weakness flooding through him as relief came. He reached for a cup and poured wine from the jug waiting on the table.

"Taken? Who would take me? And where?"

Finally, Jorge released her, but his hands continued to stroke her hair, her face, her arms.

"Has anyone been here?" he asked.

"Only that priest, the old one. He said he was a friend of yours."

"What did he want? Did he ask you to go with him?"

"He said he had a message from you." Belia frowned. "Or for you. He mumbled, so I can't be sure which. No, it must have been from you because he wanted me to go to the palace where you both were. I thought the Queen had been taken ill again so I went."

"And Mandana?"

"Came part of the way with me. Then as we approached the Barcas bridge a man approached and spoke with him. He came to me and said there was news, and I was no longer needed. It was all very strange. Did you not send him, either of you?"

"There was no news," Thomas said. "He's letting us know

he could have taken you, could take any of those we love, whenever he wants. I am sure he has access to the palace. I have to warn Lubna." He turned for the door.

"We need to move from here," said Jorge.

"What are you talking about?" said Belia. "We have only just found his house, and it is perfect. I am not moving again."

"It will make no difference," Thomas said, pausing at the door. "If Mandana wants to find us he will. Be vigilant, that is all we can do."

"Or act before he comes again."

"He may not act at all. It was a warning, a show of strength. He was letting us know what could happen. I'm going to the palace. Once I've seen Lubna and Will, I'll find Samuel and see what he has to say, though he is a pawn in this game, nothing more, and no doubt disposable."

Thomas sat Will on his lap, arms wrapped around the small body, holding onto him tightly as Jorge had held Belia. Will was soft against him with the coming of sleep. Thomas could feel the growing muscle in his son's shoulders, had seen how he held himself when he and Juan fought. He could scarce believe the event had only been that morning. It had been a day too filled with information he still needed to digest. He had gone in search of Samuel, wanting to know if he was friend to al-Amrhan, but he was missing from his small room and nobody had seen him.

Thomas kissed the top of Will's hair. "You do know you were meant to let him win, don't you?" he said, referring to Juan. The prince had been sure of victory, but Olaf had trained his grandson well. Perhaps too well.

"Why?"

"Because one day Juan will be King of Spain and you might need a friend."

"Morfar say no mercy," Will said.

"Olaf has no mercy, certainly, but he is a general and you are my son."

"You fight King?"

"Juan is not King yet."

"No. The now King. Fedando."

"Fernando," Thomas corrected.

"What I say. Someone say you fight Fedando. Who win?"

"Nobody won," Thomas said.

"So you lose."

"No, neither of us won. It was a draw."

"Morfar say draw same as lose."

"Morfar says too much," Thomas said.

"No. Not much. Morfar not talk much." Will grinned and clenched his fist, arm across his chest as though holding a battle shield. "Morfar *fight*."

"Indeed he does." But Thomas wondered for how much longer. Olaf Torvaldsson was not young anymore, and despite his strength and size, however great a fighter he was some battles could never be won by strength alone. It was a lesson Thomas knew he should learn himself if he was to protect his family and friends. And still someone in the city was stealing away two people at a time and though he now knew who, he did not know why, or where al-Amrhan might strike next.

CHAPTER THIRTY

Thomas had been in this situation before and his feelings then were the same as now. Nervous. Uncertain he was making the right decision even though he knew he was. And frustrated, but not at the present situation. He had done his duty for the Queen, had spent time with her children and his son, eaten with Jorge and Belia, and between times when he could he had pursued an investigation he feared was beginning to grow stale. In two weeks there had been no more deaths, or none that he had heard of. Abbot Mandana did not request his presence anymore, which was a mercy at least, and Samuel was cool toward him. There had been no repercussion from his threats to al-Haquim, and he suspected the man had shown his usual cowardice and made no mention of it in order to save face. What result the plotting of the three men accomplished Thomas did not know. Jorge was a help, and between them they had tracked down the families of a number of the victims, but if there was any link between them it was beyond their wits to find it. But now, today, he and Lubna would finally wed. Not where either of them wanted, but it was a marker, a proof of their love.

Lubna had been spirited away by Belia, the Queen her co-conspirator, for her second henna night. By now she would be bathed, perfumed and decorated with dark lines of dye. A new set of clothes had been commissioned, Jorge deeply involved in their selection and preparation. Thomas had not been allowed to view them or provide any input. When he asked why Jorge simply looked him up and down and said nothing.

Thomas sat on the wide balcony and stared across the palace gardens. Two men were planting a new tree, an operation involving much conversation and little action. He thought of the information he had discovered and wondered if it had been worth the effort. Nothing he had found offered a clue to why the victims were selected or what the relationship between them was. Jew and Christian, Moor and Hindu, men from distant Africa whose religions defied explanation. All different. All dead. All cut in a variety of ways that showed no logic. The city Hermandos had been informed about al-Amrhan. They said he would be sought out and captured, but there was no sign of him yet. Thomas was sure the man had fled, perhaps to continue his work elsewhere.

He was growing tired of making no progress. When he had been involved in such matters before there had always been a thread to follow, one he could gradually unwind to the heart of the mystery. But not this time. He knew if al-Amrhan remained in Seville he would seek new victims, fresh bodies, and if he did there was a good chance of him being caught. Thomas also knew in hoping for this he was wishing someone dead.

Footsteps sounded and he turned to see Jorge enter the room. Thomas raised a hand, tiredness, or something, making the movement an effort.

"It is time," said Jorge.

"How does she look?"

A smile. "You will see for yourself shortly."

"Who came? Anyone?" Isabel and Fernando had signed a temporary decree of safe passage for anyone who wanted to attend the service, the decree lasting six days. Messages had been sent to Gharnatah but Thomas had heard nothing in response.

"You will discover that as well. Why would I want to spoil a surprise?"

"Nobody, then. Ah well." Thomas forced himself to rise. "Let's get this done."

"I am pleased to see you so enthusiastic. Lubna will be relieved." Jorge was dressed to impress, in flowing silks of multiple colours. It was the first time Thomas had seen them, and was glad he had not been involved in their selection, for he would have tried to stop his friend. But now, seeing them, as vibrant as any courtesan's robes, they enhanced Jorge's sense of difference. At least people would see them coming.

As for Thomas, he was dressed in fine jacket and trousers, boots polished, hair cut shorter and beard shaved. When he had looked in a mirror he hardly recognised the man staring back, but had to admit he looked ten years younger. He would ask Lubna which Thomas she preferred, but half feared for her answer.

It was an hour shy of noon when he and Jorge strode from the palace gates and took the short walk to the Cathedral. The square was busy with people going about their business or simply taking time out from whatever their day might involve. Traders had set up tables and stalls selling a variety of foods, clothing, and finely crafted leather goods. More than a few of those passing turned to look at them as they crossed toward the shaded entrance door which stood open to admit them, but Thomas knew who had attracted their attention. Jorge in turn straightened to his full impressive height and moved in such a way that his robes rippled and swayed, multiple colours alternately revealed and masked. Thomas smiled that he had made an effort.

The air cooled as they entered the Cathedral and walked along the wide nave toward the main altar. Half way along Thomas stopped and dropped to one knee and crossed himself. Jorge remained standing.

As they started up again he said, "Why did you do that? You are no more a believer than am I."

"I do not know who is watching, and the Queen believes me devout. I would have her continue in her misconception."

Two priests approached waving censers, the pungent incense rising to the high vaulted roof. They nodded at the pair as they passed and tried not to stare at Jorge, who led the way as they approached, holding a hand out to ensure Thomas did not try to pass him and enter first.

He is revelling in this moment, Thomas thought, and smiled, finally relaxing. It was like when as a boy he had jumped from a high rock into a deep pool of the Lugge. Fear at first, and then the fall when he could do nothing, the die already cast. Followed by exultation and joy for still being alive at the end of it all.

He heard a murmur of voices, the intonation of a priest speaking Latin, the scent of the incense stronger here, the clack, clack of the censers providing an offbeat accompaniment to the words.

Jorge stopped and looked back. He said nothing as he stared into Thomas's eyes, who was surprised to see a damp glitter in those of his friend. His best friend, he realised. Jorge belonged here, leading him into the side chapel that was built around part of the mosque that had once stood in this place. Lubna would have not allowed the ceremony otherwise.

And then Thomas's skin prickled as the priest stopped chanting and a new voice began to sing the Islamic call to prayer, a high voice rising to the ceiling. He glanced at Jorge, who raised a shoulder.

"The Queen said she would allow it this once, in honour of you both." He smiled. "I think she likes Lubna almost as much as she likes you. I can understand why."

The *adhan* came to an end and Jorge nodded, leading the way. Thomas suppressed a gasp as he entered the small side chapel. What he saw was not possible, but it was there. His eyes did not deceive him.

The tall bulk of Olaf Torvaldsson stood beside Lubna. The figure to her right had no need to turn for Thomas recognised the ice white hair of Helena, who had come with her father to witness the marriage of her sister.

"What–" Thomas began, but Jorge stopped him with a finger against his lips.

"A message was sent. What else did you expect him to do?"

"It is safe?"

"A promise has been made. Fernando still believes in chivalry."

Then Thomas saw Lubna as she moved from where she had been hidden behind her father, and he thought his heart might still in that moment, and he would have been content had it done so, because he could never dream his life could ever be better than this.

She was tiny beside Olaf. Dressed in a pale blue robe that fell to the ground, one sandalled foot showing, the skin curling with patterns. A silk hijab in the same colour covered her hair. She faced straight ahead even though she must have known from the stilling of conversation that Thomas had entered the chapel.

To the left, next to Fernando, sat Isabel, her children also present.

Now and never again, thought Thomas, *in this one instant, al-Andalus and Spain gathered together, at peace.*

Martin de Alarcón sat close by, the only man wearing a weapon, there to act as protector to King and Queen. Also, perhaps, Thomas hoped, as a friend. Beside him was Theresa, a handful of other guests scattered through the small chapel. He took his place beside Lubna, wanting to take her hand but knowing he could not.

The service began, the priest mouthing words in Latin that Thomas understood a little of, knowing Lubna would not, but there was nothing to be done about it and the words were oddly soothing. His mind drifted, the incense, Lubna's presence, the utter strangeness of their situation drawing him out of his normal rationality into some other realm. When he glanced at Lubna she too seemed affected, even though the words meant nothing to her. It was the rhythm, the clank of the censer, the smoke. He saw her lips moving softly and knew she was intoning her own words in Arabic. When he glanced toward the Queen he saw she also watched Lubna, a strange expression on her face. As time passed a sense of unreality settled over Thomas and he felt something he had not done since he became a man. The presence of God. A God he did not believe in, a God he did not trust. But there was something here, in this place, something not of this world. He tried to dismiss the sensation and could not. Is this how Lubna feels when she prays, he wondered? This belonging, this stillness. He was used to his mind always working, always teasing at the next problem, but now it was emptied of all thought and he drifted, those around him growing distant. There was only him, and Lubna, and God. Then Jorge nudged him hard in the ribs.

"The rings," he said.

It had been a matter for discussion. An exchange of rings was not usual in an Islamic wedding, but Lubna knew it meant something to Thomas. So two rings, not one. Thomas did not want Lubna to be marked as his possession if he was not marked as hers. The decision had been made long ago in Gharnatah, and Jorge had brought them with him as if he knew this moment would come before they returned.

Thomas took the ring from Jorge's palm and slid it onto Lubna's finger, then she took the ring from her father's calloused hand and slipped it onto his. It felt strange. Thomas was not one for ornament, and he wondered would he grow used to it or not.

Suddenly people were milling around them. The Queen kissed Lubna's cheek. Fernando followed suit before grasping Thomas's arm and muttering about him being a lucky man, a lucky man indeed. Helena came and kissed him softly on the mouth, a reminder of what had once passed between them, then she moved on, heading for Martin de Alarcón, the second most handsome man in the room. But Helena had no interest in Jorge, and Martin was close to the Spanish King and Queen. When al-Andalus fell, having a friend in those circles would pay dividends.

Jorge laughed at something Olaf said, then Olaf was hugging Thomas, almost breaking his ribs, and he wondered at the stupidity of what he had thought about this man when he had sat with Will on his lap. Olaf was made of oak. He would never weaken. Thomas could imagine Olaf striding the earth a thousand years hence, immortal, invulnerable.

And then it was done. Isabel and Fernando moved into the main nave, Martin close behind. Jorge found Belia, who had been hidden at the back, and Theresa went to join them. Finally Thomas reached out and took Lubna's hand inside his, bent and kissed the mouth that had grown familiar, and felt her lips curl in a smile against his.

"Well," she said, "I'm glad *that* is over. Can we go and consummate the wedding now?"

Thomas laughed. "I think Jorge has something planned."

"So do I, and it does not involve Jorge."

"Marriage is good for you, obviously."

They walked into the nave and on a whim Thomas tugged Lubna in the opposite direction to where the rest had gone. There was a gate at the rear of the Cathedral that led to the remnant of a Moorish garden left after the Spanish sacked the city and, by some miracle – though whose God the miracle came from he could not say – still remained.

They passed through an arch into a walled courtyard dotted with orange trees, fruit hanging heavy from their boughs but not yet ready to harvest, if they ever would in this shade. It seemed they were not the only ones to have come this way because he saw Theresa on the far side talking with a dark-robed man. At first Thomas took him for Samuel, then saw his mistake when the man grabbed Theresa and tried to drag her into a doorway. Theresa slapped the man's face but he continued to grip her arm.

"Hey!" Thomas started forward, breaking into a run. As the man looked up Thomas saw a face he recognised, but could not recall from where. One of the physicians he and Belia had questioned? It was possible. Then the man was running fast, skidding into the Cathedral square. By the time Thomas followed he had disappeared among the throng.

He turned back and went to Theresa, who was rubbing at her arm.

"What was that about? Do you know that man?"

"I have never seen him. He said he had something to show me, something important, but I did not like his face or his tone. There was only one thing he would want from me and he was not getting that."

Lubna arrived and laid her hand on Theresa's shoulder.

"Where was he taking you?" Thomas asked.

Theresa waved a hand. "I don't know. Somewhere that way."

Thomas turned to see a narrow doorway set cornerwise to a pillar, which clearly offered access to the hidden corridors of the Cathedral, those places that provided access to workmen and others. He had started toward the door when Lubna called out to him.

"We are expected," she said, glaring.

"I know, I know, I will be a moment and no longer. Go with Theresa to Jorge's house and I will run. I may even be there before you."

Lubna looked as if she was not going to give way, but before she could object Thomas disappeared through the doorway, because it came to him where he had seen the man before. He had been the cart driver who had almost dismounted him on his arrival into the city. The cart that had contained victims of the plague, but also at least one body that had met its end by other means, and he wondered if al-Amrhan was not the man he sought after all.

CHAPTER THIRTY-ONE

The only light came from small windows set high in the walls. Almost immediately ahead a rough wooden staircase rose steeply, the treads narrow. It was possible to squeeze past on one side where the corridor continued on into shadow. Thomas looked up, looked past the stairs. If the man had managed to abduct Theresa, if indeed that had been his plan, which way would he have taken her? Theresa was slight, but strong. Would he have known this? He must have known she would fight, so which direction? To continue on would require them to go in single file. Thomas imagined her kicking out and breaking free. He turned away, ascended the stairs.

The upper corridor, like the lower, was a means of access, nothing more, squeezed into the space between the rough stone of the outer wall and the finery of within. It reminded Thomas of another narrow passageway he had pursued a different killer through. A girl he had grown to like a great deal had died for him there. He didn't want that to ever happen again.

Here and there on the inner wall were small shelves

holding unlit candles, and Thomas took the time to light every third one. As he moved forward he examined the floor for any sign someone had been this way but saw nothing. An alcove opened to the right, but when he glanced in there was only a tumble of cleaning instruments and some old stools with broken legs. He took a moment to take one of the legs to carry in his hand. He thought of going back and finding someone to accompany him, Olaf perhaps, before smiling at the thought of the man trying to fit into this space.

The corridor curved ahead, any destination constantly hidden until Thomas saw a brighter light from where a room was set to the left. He tried to picture where he was from his knowledge of the outer wall. The room must project from the main cathedral but there were many small obtrusions along its circumference.

As Thomas approached he heard a voice call out, high pitched with fear and panic and he ran, skidding into the room to discover a man tied to a wide table with torn bedsheets, arms and legs splayed wide. The man screamed at the sight of Thomas.

"No, no, I am come to save you."

The man shook his head, eyes wild. He looked behind Thomas, who spun around, but there was no-one there. He went to the table and put his hand to the man's chest, could feel his heart beating hard.

"What is your name?"

For a moment he thought the man would refuse to answer, then he must have recognised something in Thomas and shook his head. His chest deflated. The heartbeat slowed.

"Cañate, Nicolas de Cañate."

"How did you end up here?" Thomas pulled at the knots, not well tied and soon loosened. Cañate raised one arm to rub at his wrist, but the flesh was unmarked and it was more for show than relief.

"I do not know. I was at home going about my daily business when there was a knock at the door. I expected my servant to answer, but the knock came again. When I opened the door a man rushed inside. He pressed something to my face and when I woke I was tied to this table. I thank you, sir. I know not what would have become of me. What did my attacker want, do you think, money?"

"It is possible," Thomas said, though he knew money was no motive here. Whoever had taken Cañate had not wanted money. But something in the man's tale sparked a memory and he leaned close and sniffed. Cañate moved back quickly, Thomas's presence too close for comfort, but he had already recognised the scent. A chemical smell which was unique, and which as far as he knew only a handful of people were familiar with.

Are you a Spaniard?" Thomas asked, and when Cañate nodded added, "And a Christian?"

Another nod. "I am Christian now."

"Now? You converted?"

A third nod. "Years since. And I am not like those devils they burn. I changed my name and embraced the one true God with all my heart."

"But you were not born so."

"It does not matter how a man is born, only how he acts now, and what he believes. Why your questions, sir?"

Cañate was right, there were more pressing matters to ask.

"The man, did you recognise him, see anything of his face?"

Cañate sat up, dropped his legs to the floor and stood, unsteady. He held to the edge of the table. "He said nothing, and he wore a hood, a tall hood as the plague carriers wear. When I saw him, I was sure he had mistaken my house for somewhere else, but then he was on me and the world swam away. What was it he used? I have never heard of such."

"Do you have knowledge of medicines or herbs?"

"Some. It is part of my work to make up tinctures for local physicians. If you ask you will discover the name of Nicolas de Cañate is well respected in Sevilla."

"But you did not know your attacker?"

"I have told you already. Now if you will let me go I intend to report this kidnapping to the Hermandos."

"They will ask the same questions as I am," Thomas said. "What about his clothing?"

"I have already said, he was dressed as a plague carrier. It could be no-one I know for I do not mix in such circles."

"Do you know a woman by the name of Belia?"

"Yes, I do, though I do not approve of what she does. Is she involved? It would not surprise me, not surprise me at all."

"Where do you live?"

"What business is that of yours?"

"Answer me, or I have a mind to tie you back to the table and let that man finish what he had planned for you. Just as soon as he finds a second subject."

"You could try, sir, but I am not without resources now my strength is returning."

Thomas only smiled, his mind spinning theories one after the other, dismissing each as ridiculous only to conjure another ever wilder. This man was taken, and an attempt made on Theresa. A man and a woman? It was rare among the instances, but Mandana had mentioned it had happened before on rare occasions. Which meant this time carried no significance, unless the taking of Theresa, someone known to be close to the Queen, was the significance.

"Where is your house?" Thomas said again, his voice cold.

He planned on visiting Cañate again once this day was over and he could return to less frivolous matters.

Cañate hesitated, but when Thomas took a pace forward he detailed the location and Thomas nodded. He knew the street, if not the house, and could find it. He would go there tomorrow with Jorge. More than likely after noon, for tonight would be a time of drinking and debauchery. At least he was sure that was what Jorge had planned. Cañate started for the corridor, but Thomas was not finished with him yet.

"Wait. At what time were you taken?"

"Time? Does it matter?"

"It may."

"I had broken my fast and started work, so I would say at least two hours before noon."

"Did your captor say anything to you when you woke?"

"He was not here. I was already tied to the table."

"And he did not return?"

Cañate shook his head. "Can I go now?"

Thomas tried to think what else he wanted from the man but knew his mind was spinning with too many other thoughts. He listened to Cañate's footsteps follow the corridor, then stop and return. For a moment Thomas thought he might have remembered something that would be of use, but he had merely gone in the wrong direction. He walked past Thomas and disappeared around the curving wall.

Thomas went along the corridor in the direction Cañate had first taken, curious to know how the man had known it was the wrong way, and discovered the reason almost at once. The corridor came to an abrupt end against a wall of stone, small alcoves providing stands for religious statuary and miniature wooden crosses. It was not quite a dead end, but Thomas saw why Cañate would know he could not have been brought in this way. A set of ledges were set into the vertical wall, every few stones offset to provide a confident man the means of climbing to a higher level.

He went back to the room and paced it, searching for what should be there and was not. One ledge held symbols of religion, on another a collection of rounded stones as would be found in a riverbed, but there were no instruments. Thomas lit another candle and held it over the surface of the table. There were stains etched deep into the wood telling him this place had been used before, and for the same purpose that had been planned on this occasion. He wondered why here, why the killer had changed location from the original plague house.

Was this the new killing ground, the place where others had been subjected to a lunatic's experiment? If so it pointed to someone who knew this room existed. It was not somewhere to be stumbled upon by accident, which meant the killer was familiar with the byways of the cathedral. A religious man? A priest? Is that why Tabado was killed – because he knew who his killer was? Which made it even more important to investigate the man's background.

Thomas sighed. The investigation grew more complex, and exactly what part did Mandana play, if any? It seemed scarcely believable the Abbot knew nothing of the matter, not if the killer was also a man of God. But it was impossible to question Mandana again, not after what had happened between them. Ixbilya was becoming a more dangerous place to be by the day, and for the first time in his life Thomas considered walking away from what was happening here. This was not his city, not his land, and these were not his people. What he could do was take his people away from pestilence and danger.

The heat of the afternoon had driven people indoors, but a few sailors continued to unload cargo along the river bank, their movement slow. A score of ships were drawn up, rigging hanging limp in the still air. Thomas drew glances, making him realise he was too well dressed to be walking this area. He wished for a blade, but his own wedding had hardly been the place to carry one. He glanced along the eastern bank to where Jorge's house lay hidden beyond the curve of the city wall. Ahead the wooden planks of the Puente de Barcas offered access to the far bank where the stone bulk of Castillo de Triana sat. Within those walls men and women were tortured until they admitted to a lie so the pain would stop. On the nearer bank stood the stakes where their souls would be seared from their bodies by flame. With a last look to the west, toward those who were expecting him, Thomas stepped onto the bridge. Half way across a woman accosted him, displaying her breasts and thighs, offering her body in exchange for a coin. Thomas kept walking, but stopped before reaching the far side. Violent tides of duty flowed through him, so strong he swayed and grasped at a wooden upright. The whore shouted at him, words that spilled past without meaning. The river ran deep beneath his feet and he wished it could carry away the violence of this place, but knew it was impossible. What happened on the far side of the river was the Queen's doing, whether it was what she intended or not, and it was only she could bring it to an end. The man Thomas sought might be within the castle walls that housed the barbarity of the Inquisition.

He washed a hand across his face and turned to see a cart emerge from the city gate and rattle toward the bridge. Sitting atop the front beside the driver was Abbot Mandana. Behind him Samuel clung to the wooden side. A dozen men and women were crushed into the back, heads lowered as if

245

they did not want to view the ramparts they were being taken towards.

As the cart moved on to the bridge the whore darted into an alcove built for the purpose. She opened her shirt more in hope than likelihood. Those at the front of the cart ignored her, staring ahead, those behind looking only at their feet. As the cart came close Thomas walked a few paces and followed the whore's lead to step into a recess. He thought Mandana was going to ignore him, but at the last moment the Abbot turned, his face expressionless. Pale grey eyes bored into Thomas's with a hatred that had always simmered beneath the surface and was now let loose. The man had not changed. The man would never change.

Thomas turned to watch the cart as it reached the far bank to disappear through the gates of the castle. Then he turned and walked back to where his wife waited. As he passed he tossed the whore a coin and heard her scrabble on the boards before it could fall through a gap and be lost. Tomorrow. Everything would have to wait until tomorrow. He had a party to attend, and scowled at the thought.

CHAPTER THIRTY-TWO

Jorge was drunk. Very drunk indeed. Thomas had seen him this way before on only a few occasions, but knew he was an amusing drunk, not prone to violence. The windows to the terrace were thrown wide and people Thomas did not know filled the room. The sweet scent of hashish and poppy mixed with the subtler scents worn by the women. Olaf was dressed uncharacteristically in a white blouse and dark pants, his feet encased in elegant shoes which must have been hand-made to fit him. Will sat on his shoulders, grasping Olaf's long hair in his fists and grinning. He caught sight of Thomas and yelled, waved, and pulled harder at Olaf's hair, wanting to be put down. Olaf reached up and swung his grandson wildly through the air and Will screamed in delight before running across the room into Thomas arms. He lifted him and set him on his own shoulders, only wincing slightly as Will's hands twisted his hair.

Lubna was talking with Theresa. When she looked his way he put two fingers to his lips, kissed them and tossed the message in the direction of his wife. She turned away, expressionless, and Thomas knew he was not forgiven. The promise of his wedding night might have to be postponed.

Jorge lounged on a stack of silk cushions, Belia beside him, their limbs intertwined, but they each spoke to others who came to them as if they held court.

Martin de Alarcón stood with a wine glass in his hand talking with Helena, whose entire attention was on him. Thomas knew what magic that attention could wreathe when she chose to use it, and smiled as he thought what secrets Martin might be introduced to as night fell. Thomas tried to recall if Martin was married. It was not the kind of conversation they had ever had, their talk leaning more toward weapons and tactics, or the best way to kill a man without being killed in turn.

Will tugged at his hair and yelled, "Down!" and Thomas deposited him on the floor and went in search of something to drink. A table had been set up, barely able to contain the quantity of food, wine and ale weighing it down. Sticky nuggets of the finest hashish resin sat on a plate together with a pair of silver tongs to avoid fingers becoming stained. Thomas reached for one and popped it onto his tongue, the familiar sweet-tart taste flooding his mouth. He swallowed, seeking oblivion. He poured a cup of wine and drank it down before refilling it. When he turned Queen Isabel stood behind him, as if she had been waiting there for some time.

"Thomas." She smiled and touched his arm with her fingertips. He wondered had she been partaking of the wine too, but doubted it. Her eyes were clear, her skin unflushed. It was the party, he realised, the atmosphere in the house sparking a magic in almost everyone. Conversation. Laughter. Children running around chasing each other. The stern face of the Queen's eldest daughter who stood to one side observing and not joining in. Juan lying on his back laughing while Will sat astride him.

Thomas nodded, wanting to reach out to her as the wine and hashish sang in his blood, their tendrils already driving away his worries and inhibitions.

"Where is Fernando?"

Isabel withdrew her hand and waved it. "Oh, somewhere. He is flirting with your courtesans, but he thinks I don't notice." She laughed, delighted at the world.

"Not *my* courtesans. I believe Jorge considers them his."

Another laugh. "Is he as drunk as he looks?"

"He may be, but he can be the drunkest man in the room and instantly sober if he wishes."

Isabel stepped closer, too close, but Thomas had stopped caring and so, it seemed, had she.

"He is a eunuch."

Thomas nodded.

"But women love him. All women, it seems, young or old, beautiful or ugly."

"Because he loves them in turn. He claims love is as infinite as the great western ocean that lunatic Columb wants to sail across."

"What does he mean by that?"

For a moment Thomas was confused. He wondered if he should have eaten only half the nugget of hashish, but it was too late now. Besides, this was his wedding night, and he had to admit the worries that had plagued him were beginning to slip from his mind.

"Jorge? He tried to explain it to me once, and I almost understood. He believes it his duty to love women. And I have to admit he was born for the job, despite what I did to him."

"What you did?"

Thomas realised he had never spoken to the Queen of how Jorge's unmanning had been at his hand.

"I made him what he is." He smiled as he saw the expression on the Queen's face. She stepped back half a pace and he was tempted to close the gap, his inhibitions eroded by the drug and wine sizzling through his veins. "He was lucky it was me, Isabel. I had created a method of making him what he is without more pain than necessary, and with a good chance of survival. I would not subject you to how the process was done before my method became common. I have performed many others since. Yes, it is cruel, but it is the culture of the Moors and it would happen with or without me."

"As would the pursuit of heretics in Spain." The gap had closed again, but who had closed it Thomas could not recall. Isabel's fingers once more lay against his wrist. He glanced to where Lubna continued to talk with her sister, ignoring him, deliberately or not he could not tell, but suspected deliberate. "Without a strong hand there are those who would inflict even greater suffering on the innocent and guilty alike. My court employs many Jews. Without them Spain would not flourish as she does. We all do things we might regret under other circumstances, but those circumstances do not exist, do they?"

Thomas knew his hand should not be resting on the waist of the Queen of Spain but it had found itself there without conscious volition. Isabel looked up at him, the moment full of a strange potential until a loud voice broke the spell.

"Unhand her, rogue. Only I am allowed to molest the Queen!" It was Fernando, laughing like a madman. He punched Thomas on the shoulder, making him stagger. "Isabel, why do we not have parties like this?"

"We have a position to uphold, my dear." Her attention switched instantly to her husband, and Thomas felt like a fish released from a hook. He looked around, seeking escape, but it was Isabel who moved away toward Lubna and Helena.

Fernando's eyes followed, then rose to appreciate Helena's pale hair that fell almost to her waist. She was dressed in a loose silk robe which accentuated the curves that lay beneath.

"Ah," said Fernando, "if only I were not married."

"In that case she would not want you."

"The King of Spain? Why ever not?"

"If you were not married, would you still be King of Spain?"

Another laugh. Another punch. Thomas was tempted to respond but managed to restrain himself. "In that case I would be King of Aragon, which is a not inconsiderable title."

Thomas leaned close. "Shall I ask on your behalf, your grace?"

For a moment it looked as if Fernando might say yes, then he shook his head. "A man's mind wanders at times, does it not? Even the great Thomas Berrington's, I am sure. Have you upset your wife in some way? I notice she avoids you."

"You know how it is, as a man, I am sure," Thomas said, and Fernando smiled.

"Sometimes I look forward to battle as a respite from royal life." He glanced at Thomas. "But I never said that to you."

"And I will never repeat it. Have you spoken with Olaf?"

"The giant? I am tempted, but unsure how an approach would be greeted. I hear he has no Spanish, and I no Arabic."

"Swedish, perhaps?"

Fernando laughed. "No, no Swedish either. Where is Sweden?"

"Far to the north. Cold. You would not want to go there."

"You have been?"

Thomas shook his head. "Neither have I been to the

moon, but I know I would not like to go there either. Do you want me to act as go-between? I speak both Spanish and Arabic."

"But your Spanish is not good, Thomas."

"Good enough for men of war, I expect. Olaf is a man of few words, and those few contain even less syllables" He started across the room, the floor under his feet pulsing like waves on sand. Olaf's head turned to watch their approach, a grin slowly spreading on his face. He embraced Fernando as one warrior to another, no words required. The unprecedented act of chivalry exhibited by Fernando that allowed Olaf and his party to travel deep into the Spanish hinterland would not go without appreciation. Thomas expected their conversation to be long and include matters that would not normally be spoken of between a King and the general who opposed him. Thomas saw Martin de Alarcón hovering and waved him across, knowing the man could act as interpreter as well as he.

He detoured past Jorge and knelt. "I will need you tomorrow." He held a hand up as Jorge began to object. "Give it no thought tonight, but tomorrow, before noon, I will come for you. I will explain everything then." He moved away before Jorge could respond, but he had looked into the man's eyes and knew his pretence at inebriation was only that. Jorge rarely if ever lost control, and Thomas wondered why he had chosen to do so himself tonight. He returned to the table and swallowed down a flagon of wine, picked up a second, smaller nugget of hashish and placed it on his tongue. Tonight, he sought oblivion.

And then he walked as straight as he could toward Lubna.

She must have seen him coming but made no acknowledgement, continuing to talk with Helena, who did turn her head to smile in greeting. She touched his chest, then kissed him, mouth against mouth as they had once done. When the embrace was over Lubna stared up at him, a mixture of anger and fear in her eyes.

"What is father doing with the King?" asked Helena.

"Not ending the war, unfortunately. Talking of exploits past and future, no doubt."

"I like your friend Martin," she said. "He is what a real man should be."

Thomas smiled, the barb failing to catch in him this time.

"He is unmarried, I think," he said.

"I do not seek a husband. But he is handsome, and I have never had a Spaniard. Are they good in bed?"

"Ask Jorge."

"He has had a Spaniard?"

"He *is* a Spaniard," Thomas said.

"Ah, yes, I always forget that. But Jorge is different."

"Indeed. Why do you not go talk with your father and include him in the conversation? You will understand half of it, and Martin is acting as translator so you may understand it all."

"What interest do I have in the words of men of war?"

Thomas smiled. "I was thinking not of the words, but of a particular man of war. You two were deep in conversation before I called him away."

"Lubna was, less so myself. But perhaps I will." She touched Thomas's face, kissed him again and was gone, leaving only a swirl of perfume behind.

"You can go to her if you want," said Lubna. "You have my permission. A wife must be modest and obey, I understand that. And a good Moor may have many wives."

"I don't want many wives."

"She is more beautiful than me, and more skilled I expect, but you will know about that, won't you."

"I do not want her skill or her beauty. Besides, you are beautiful, more beautiful than you know. Are we friends again, as well as man and wife?"

Lubna's eyes examined the floor. "Why did you abandon me outside the cathedral?"

Thomas raised her chin with a finger. "Do not think on it tonight. I will explain in the morning, but tonight is for you and me and no-one and nothing else. Tonight is our wedding night."

"I have not forgiven you yet," said Lubna.

"But you are my wife now, you have admitted as much. I can order you to forgive me, can I not?"

"You can try." Her eyes rose, a spark in them now. "But you will have to hold me down to make me obey."

"I can do that."

"And kiss my body. After you have undressed me, of course."

"I can do that, too. I am a man of many talents. You have told me so yourself, I believe, on more than one occasion."

"I forget. Once, perhaps. You will need to remind me."

Thomas looked around, a contentment settling through him even as his arousal grew, and the hashish had made his entire being almost uncomfortably sensitive. These people were his friends. All of them. Even those he did not know well. Even the strangers. He saw Will curled into sleep beside Juan on a cushion near the open window. Jorge embraced Belia in full view, and soon they would need to retire to privacy. Olaf and Fernando leaned toward each other, Olaf a foot the taller, exchanging words almost too fast for Martin to translate. Helena clung to his arm, her fingers twisting through his hair. On the far side of the room Theresa was in conversation with a man Thomas did not know, the two of them exchanging touches of promise.

He took Lubna's hand and led her away. "Come, my love, and show me how far the henna strays across your limbs."

She smiled and leaned against his arm. "Oh, it goes everywhere, Thomas. Absolutely everywhere. And you will have to work hard, very hard, to earn my forgiveness for abandoning me as you did."

CHAPTER THIRTY-THREE

The room was pitch dark when Thomas came awake. Lubna leaned over him, but he could only tell by the touch of her hand against his chest.

"There is someone outside," she whispered.

He shook his head. "We are in a house full of people, of course there is someone outside. Go back to sleep."

"No, they are creeping. I heard them."

"Creeping," he said.

"Yes. There – do you hear it?"

And he did. A creak of a stair tread, he knew the exact one, four steps from the top.

"It will be Jorge gone for a piss." Thomas tried to pull Lubna down beside him, then stopped because he heard something else. Unmistakeable, the soft sound of a sword drawn from a scabbard, steel against leather. And a whisper, so more than one person.

He rolled from the bed which was nothing more than a scatter of cushions on the floor, though he barely noticed the discomfort when they came to this room, his mind elsewhere. He patted along the floor until he found the wall, then along the wall until he found his clothing and cursed. No weapon. Of course there was no weapon. He pulled on the too refined trousers Lubna had helped him remove and went to the door, pressed his ear to the wood.

Definitely more than one man, perhaps even three. They had stopped directly outside, though exactly how he knew he could not say, only that he was sure. Then a whisper of a voice and the creak of a board as they moved on. They were looking for someone in particular.

Thomas crept back to the tangle of bedclothes.

"Did Isabel stay, or Fernando?"

"How would I know? You saw them last when I did."

"They will have returned to the palace, they must have. Stay here. Lock the door behind me when I go."

"Stay, Thomas. It is not you they seek."

"Our friends are in these rooms." He rose and crept to the door, opened it a crack and peered out. Candles burned out here, their light making him squint after the utter darkness of the room. He glanced back and pointed to the heavy key sitting in the inner lock, and Lubna nodded, her face set. She ought to know me well enough by now, Thomas thought, then dismissed her from his mind as he sought the cold of killing he knew too well.

He had been right. Three men stood along the corridor, heads together as they whispered. One pointed to a door and another shook his head. Then Thomas ran at them, near silent on bare feet. One of the men looked up at the last moment and uttered a cry which would, with luck, be enough to rouse the others. Thomas turned so his shoulder took the man under the chin. His head snapped back against the wall and Thomas took the sword from his hand and slid it into his chest as the man slumped to the floor. By which time the other two were ready for him. He saw they were experienced, coming at him in an instant, no hint of hesitation. These were men who knew that victory went to those who attacked first and fast.

Blades clashed as Thomas deflected the first man, but he was forced to step back under the onslaught. Under normal circumstances he knew he could beat these two, sure of his own ability. But these were not normal circumstances. Cobwebs of intoxication still clung to his mind and his body felt clumsy. Even so he was sure he would prevail, until another five men came running up the stairs, all pretence at silence gone. Whoever was behind the attack it had been well planned.

Thomas deflected another blade, turned to the side in an attempt to keep both groups of men in sight, but already he knew his death was close and wished he had thought to kiss Lubna one last time before rushing out here.

Then the door at the end of the hallway crashed open and a naked Olaf Torvaldsson stepped out, sword in one hand, axe in the other. He came steadily, almost filling the width of the hallway, and when one of the attackers turned and slashed at him with a sword Olaf swung and removed the man's arm at the elbow. Thomas turned to the three who were now within feet of him and deflected the first blow. He ducked under the second and lifted his sword into a man's guts, who went down screaming, feet scrabbling in his own blood.

"Keep one alive," Thomas called to Olaf, "I need questions answered. You can kill the rest."

Olaf nodded, frowning over whether to merely disable the man in front of him or take his head off. He made a decision and swung, perhaps hoping the man whose arm he had removed would not bleed to death.

Seeing the odds rapidly diminishing the pair in front of Thomas turned and ran. Too late Thomas saw Lubna step from the doorway of their room just as the first man reached her. He slammed into her and she flew sideways, landing awkwardly. The man ignored her only to be met on the stairs by Martin de Alarcón, who took him in the throat before slipping on the spray of blood. The remaining men leaped over him and, though Martin reached up, he could do no more than leave a gash in the leg of one.

Thomas turned and ran along the corridor as Will appeared in the doorway where he had been sleeping with his grandfather. Lubna lay on her front, dazed. She was trying to get to her knees and failing. Thomas dropped the sword he held and lifted her, carrying her through to the room she had foolishly left.

"What were you doing?"

"Trying to help." Tears sparked in her eyes, tears of pain and fear. "My belly hurts," she said.

Thomas laid her on the cushions and drew her legs apart, used his hand to check for any bleeding, satisfied when he found none.

"Stay here," he said. "Do not move. Do not come out again. Hear me?"

Lubna nodded, a grimace on her face as she held the small swell of her belly in both hands.

Thomas went outside, picked up the sword he had dropped and made his way to the end of the gallery where the man Olaf had taken the arm from sat. He leaned against the wall, eyes closed, face pale. Blood pumped from the stump of his arm and Thomas called for a cloth. A hand touched his shoulder and he looked back to find Helena with a torn sheet. He took it and wrapped it tight above the arm. He smashed the hilt of his stolen sword into the wall until wood broke, then levered a piece out and tied it into the cloth, turned to cut off the spray of blood which slowed, then stopped.

Thomas felt the man's neck, cursing until he found a faint pulse.

"Carry him inside," he said to a now trousered Olaf, who bent, grabbed the attacker under his shoulders and dragged him into the room.

"Helena, take Will downstairs. Gather the others, get them to check the doors in case they return with reinforcements."

He followed Olaf into the room where the disabled soldier lay flat on the bed. Olaf lit candles then closed the door. Thomas took a jar of water from the floor and emptied it across the man. He spluttered and rocked his head, but his eyes remained closed.

"Have I killed him?" asked Olaf, only curiosity in his voice. He was a man used to killing and never doubted its purpose. The gift of death was his to offer anyone who tried to take his life, or that of his friends.

"Maybe. If you have we might never find out who sent them, or who they were after."

"You, surely? The rest of us are strangers here, and the King offered us safety."

"This is not Fernando's doing."

"No. We talked. He is an honest man. A chivalrous man. It will make me sad one day to have to kill him on the field of battle." Olaf grinned. "He said the same to me."

Thomas checked the man's pulse again, finding it a little stronger.

"Help me sit him up, and put pillows behind him."

The man groaned as they lifted him and this time his eyes opened, darting around the room as if still under attack. His gaze fell on Olaf and a cry came from his lips.

Thomas gripped the man's chin and turned his face to his own. "It's not him you should fear. Who sent you? And who were you after?"

The man spat in his face.

Thomas reached down and gripped the bloodied stump, squeezed. The man screamed, his legs making motions as he tried to back away, but there was nowhere to go.

"Who did you come for?"

The man shook his head, sweat beading his brow. "If I tell you I am dead."

Thomas smiled, watching what the expression did in the soldier's eyes. "Then you are a dead man either way, because if you do not tell me what I want to know I will kill you. And I will do it slowly. It might even take until dawn before you draw your last breath." He squeezed on the stump again, less violently, but still the man screamed.

Thomas waited until the pain had ebbed then squeezed again. Some small part of him observed his actions and hated what he saw, but that part of his humanity had been set aside until an answer came. It would return, it always did, but there were times he wondered if it did not take a little of the real man with it each time it left.

He leaned close to the man, smelling rank breath and unwashed leather. "As far as I see it, you have two choices, because you are not leaving here until you tell me what I want to know, or you die where you lie, after many hours of agony. He reached again for the stump and the man yelled in anticipation.

"The Alarcón! We were sent to kill Martin de Alarcón."

"On whose orders?"

"I cannot – no, no, don't! Abbot Mandana!"

"Why?"

"You think I know that? I'm a soldier, I do as I'm asked." He glanced at Olaf, back to Thomas, and then his gaze went to the doorway. When Thomas turned he saw Martin standing there, rubbing at his arm where he had knocked it during the brief fight.

"Why would Mandana want you dead, Martin?"

Martin shook his head. "I have no idea. None at all. If Fernando found out such a thing the man would be gone from Sevilla in a moment. Or burned on one of those damnable fires." He looked to the man. "Do you recognise me?"

The soldier nodded.

"Am I the man you came to kill?"

Another nod.

"You can do it, if you wish," Thomas said.

Martin glanced at him, shook his head. "I could not."

"Give me your knife, then," Thomas said.

Martin stepped away, turned and left the room.

Thomas shrugged and looked to Olaf, who in turn looked around for what he knew he had brought to the room but not to the fight. He found a blade, honed to a wicked sharpness, and tossed it hilt first to Thomas. Who snatched it from the air and in the same movement thrust it between the soldier's ribs to pierce his heart.

"By Odin, Thomas, I heard tell you were a cold bastard, but did not believe the tales until now."

"Only when I need be. He said he was dead in any case. I have at least spared him the pain of his master's questioning."

Olaf shook his head. "I hope I never cross you."

Thomas laughed. "The feeling is mutual, Fa." He wiped the blade on the bedclothes and handed it to Olaf. "Good knife, by the way, but you'll need clean sheets."

He found Martin sitting downstairs nursing a mug of wine. Thomas pulled a chair close and sat.

"Why does Mandana want you dead?"

"Did you kill him, the man upstairs? How can you do that, in cold blood?"

"He would have done the same to you, to all of us given the chance."

"I can understand in the heat of battle, but to do it as you did? No."

"Why did Mandana send men to kill you?"

"And it was kill, was it? Not capture, but kill?"

"That's what he said."

"He didn't know why?"

Thomas shook his head.

"I can think of no reason. I don't like the Abbot, and my feelings have been made clear to him, but many do not like him, most far more than me. It's not a reason, otherwise half of Sevilla would be in danger."

"It will be something you know."

Martin gave a grunt. "I know many things, no doubt some of them a danger to me, but I know no secrets about the man that are not also known to Fernando."

"Who makes use of him," Thomas said.

"Against my advice. You cannot hold a serpent to your breast and expect it not to bite you, but he does not listen to all of my counsel. Was the fact they came tonight of significance or not?"

"They knew you would be here, and more vulnerable than in the palace. I don't think they expected to encounter anyone who would fight back, and certainly not someone like Olaf."

Martin barked a laugh. "Gods, I hope I never have to face him in battle. He's an army in his own right."

"And well loved by his men. It would be better not to face him. Tell Fernando the same. You translated between them, what did they have to say?"

"Sounding each other out, and then…" Martin smiled,

sipped at his wine. "And then they spoke of family, their home lands, and their love of this land we all share. It was... strange... and rather beautiful. There was respect between them."

"And soon Olaf and the others must leave."

"It was a generous offer Fernando made, and it is only you he would have made it for. I can think of no other."

Thomas scowled. "I still want to know why Mandana wants you dead."

"So do I." Martin looked across the room. "Do you want me?"

Thomas turned to see Helena wrapped in nothing more than a silk sheet. She smiled – something he was still getting used to.

"Theresa wanted to know if you were coming back to bed now we are all woken."

"I'll be there soon," Martin said. "We have finished here, haven't we?" A glance at Thomas, who nodded.

He watched as Helena turned and ascended the stairs. She had to know the bed sheet covered only the front of her body, but she was nothing if not flagrant in the display of herself, as he well knew. He looked at Martin, who also watched with eyes wide. Thomas wanted to warn him, but knew the man would ignore any words he offered, and he couldn't blame him. Better to let him find out himself what Helena was like. He had to acknowledge she had changed over the last year, but his suspicious nature wondered if the change was genuine or not.

When Martin had gone Thomas drank a cup of wine and refilled it. Beyond the windows the night was a curtain of darkness pricked only by lamps hanging from ships tied to the dock. Someone came clumping down the stairs and Olaf emerged, a man under each arm.

"We need to get rid of these bodies. The river?"

"I have a better idea," Thomas said, rising. "Let me put on more suitable clothes and I'll take one from you."

"I can manage both."

"I know you can, but there is no need. Besides, there are another two up there. And a lot of blood on the stairs. We should try to clean it before the rest of the household wakes."

CHAPTER THIRTY-FOUR

Thomas pulled a cart that stank of disease down the street toward Jorge's house. The night was still dark, the moon hanging close to the horizon, its light peering between roofs and around buildings. He had found the cart on the river bank ready to be used the following day, together with a dozen others. Of the men whose task it would be to fill them there was no sign, and he realised how simple it would have been for the killer to take one to disguise his purpose.

Olaf had brought all four dead soldiers down and stacked them inside the door.

"I think I've cleaned most of the blood away. Lubna came to help."

"She is supposed to be resting after that blow," Thomas said as he lifted one of the men onto his shoulder. He would need to wash thoroughly later, but Jorge had already installed a tub in one of the upstairs rooms.

"She is my daughter, and there was work needed doing," said Olaf.

"Not all your daughters are the same though, are they."

"They each possess their own skills, and all love their father." Olaf tossed a body in the bed of the cart and went back for another. "What are you planning to do with these? I still think the river is good enough for them."

"They will be discovered eventually and questions asked. I know a place they will never be found."

"I could do with somewhere like that," said Olaf, and Thomas laughed, knowing he was not entirely joking.

"Here, put this on." Thomas handed across a dirty grey cloak and tall pointed hat that covered the entire face, before pulling the same onto his own head.

He let Olaf pull the cart because it made sense, and Thomas was still tired. At least the influence of the hashish had faded and his mind was as clear as the star-painted sky. There was barely anyone on the streets, and those few they did encounter suddenly remembered they had forgotten something in the other direction. None came close enough to see the men they carried in the cart had not died of the pestilence. It was one more confirmation to Thomas that this was how the killer he sought must have moved his victims. No wonder he was called the Ghost – a ghost people deliberately looked away from.

The wheels of the cart rumbled loud on the planks of the Barcas bridge.

"What is the big place?" Olaf said as they passed alongside the towering walls of Castillo de Triana.

"It's where the Inquisition holds its prisoners, and where all the records are kept."

"What records?"

"The Spanish are keen on keeping records." He pointed to a side street that led between a shuttered inn and the riverbank.

"They are like you, then," said Olaf.

"Yes, like me. Over there." He indicated a pit dug in the ground. Ashes and streaks of pale quicklime marked the ground around it, and the stench of rotting bodies made the air almost unbreathable, but Olaf barely appeared to notice. Thomas lifted a body onto his shoulder. Olaf did the same with two others, and they carried them to the edge of the pit.

"It will be better if they are well into the middle."

Olaf nodded and dropped his burden, took the shoulders of Thomas's corpse. They counted down in Arabic and threw the body as hard as they could. It sailed through the air before coming down with a soft, damp thud, the sound almost worse than the stink.

Once the others had been similarly dealt with Thomas returned the cart and clothing to where he had found them and led the way back through streets just beginning to turn grey with the coming of dawn.

"Tell me something, Olaf, what does Muhammed do with himself these days?"

"You know as well as me. He sits in his mother's house on the Albayzin and plots his return to power, or he wanders the east of al-Andalus where people still think he possesses power."

"I have been gone a number of weeks, I wondered if anything had changed."

"Abu al-Hasan is fading fast. When he dies, and it will not be long, Muhammed will make a move."

"And you? Where will your loyalty lie?"

"You know where. To whoever rules on the hill. I am the Sultan's man, whoever the Sultan is. I served Muhammed before and will do so again if that is what is required."

"Al-Zagal has no plan to return? He would make a good Sultan."

"He would. But he has made his home in Malaka. He is reinforcing the defences because he knows the Spanish will come, likely next year when the fighting season starts. Take Malaka and you cut Gharnatah off from the sea."

"Gharnatah will not starve," Thomas said.

"No. But it would also cut off our supply of weapons and reinforcements. Gharnatah will need those more than food soon."

"What will you do?"

"Me? I will fight. It is what I am good at."

"I meant when we lose," Thomas said.

"Ah, well, if we lose that means I will no doubt not have to worry about what to do, for I will be dead."

"Try not to be," Thomas said. "I have grown fond of you."

Olaf laughed. "And I you, despite what I used to think of you."

Thomas walked on a moment, the question refusing to be ignored. "What did you used to think of me?"

Olaf slapped Thomas on the back, almost sending him to his knees. "I have seen you fight and seen you heal men, and you are married to my daughter, so what I used to think is of no matter, no matter at all."

"You have no need to sacrifice yourself," Thomas said. "Muhammed is not worthy of such loyalty."

"I have nowhere else to go. I will make my final stand in al-Andalus. As I know you will, but I hope you stay alive for Lubna's sake, and the sake of the child she carries, not to mention Will."

Thomas smiled, and then, in a moment of insight he knew who wanted Martin dead, and it was not Mandana. He had only been doing the bidding of another.

"If Muhammed comes to power, Olaf, I want you to kill him."

Olaf stopped in the middle of the street, his pale skin almost glowing in the rising light.

"You know I cannot do such. I serve the Sultan."

"Do not serve this one. He is the one wants Martin dead. He will have sent money, or made some promise to Mandana in exchange for Martin's head."

"Why would this Mandana do that? He has to live here afterward."

"Because the men he sent were meant to succeed. Meant to kill us all, more than likely. And dead men tell no tales. Martin has power over Muhammed and he wants him dead. For Mandana this was a convenience, and no doubt brought some funds or favour in return."

Olaf shook his head, not seeing it, but Thomas tapped his own skull. "In here, in his head, Muhammed is still the captive of Martin, who had him for almost a year. I saw how they were, how they still are. When Martin is in his presence Muhammed turns into a cringing coward. I do not know how it was done, only that it was. Martin owns that man heart and soul, and Muhammed wants an end to it if he is to be Sultan. And he does want to be Sultan. I believe Fernando wants him to be Sultan, too. Which is why you have to kill him."

Olaf let his breath out in a rush. "You ask a lot of a simple soldier, Thomas."

"I know, but you also know I speak the truth. Muhammed is not his own man. He belongs to Spain. That is what they did to him, turned him against his own people. Not that Muhammed ever had any love for his people, unlike his father. He will be their pawn in al-Hamra, and he will give up al-Andalus whenever they ask it."

A crash came from along the street where a trader dropped the shutters as he opened his store, and the scent of fresh baking reached them, sparking saliva in Thomas's mouth.

"At least consider what I say. Watch him closely, see

whether I am right or not. Then make your own decision. I trust your judgement." He turned and walked along the street, leaving Olaf staring after him.

Thomas was glad for the weight of the sword hanging from his belt as he approached the cathedral square. As soon as they had disposed of the bodies his mind had turned to the events of the day before, and he knew he had been remiss in his duty. He understood the reasons why but they sat uneasy with him, hence his short journey across the city before it came fully awake. Before Lubna came fully awake if she had managed to find sleep again, which was unlikely. He worried at the thought of her sitting in Jorge's house waiting for him, worried for the baby she carried. He was abandoning her again, he knew, but this had to be done. Thomas needed to be sure he had covered every eventuality, had missed no clue.

The narrow doorway was locked for the night, but not to Thomas. It did offer information he filed away for later consideration. At what hour was the door locked, and who would have a key for it?

The corridor beyond was dim, no lamps lit. Who came to light them, and why? What purpose did this curving passageway serve, and what purpose the small chamber where Cañate had been held? His eyes tracked the walls ahead as he climbed the staircase. There was only the one open chamber here, he knew from the day before, but not its purpose. As he approached his feet slowed as he caught a familiar scent. He stopped, listening, but heard nothing. Still he waited. If the man he sought was in the room he did not want to lose him again, but as moments passed no sound came to him and he knew there was no-one alive there.

Whoever the killer was, he had been interrupted the day before, but had not finished. He had found two more victims, and it was their blood that Thomas could smell.

He started forward, the sight that greeted him no surprise, only the sex of one figure causing a moment's confusion. One man, one woman. So the attempt to take Theresa had been deliberate. Both were naked. Both cut, but not in the same way as before.

Thomas went to the man first and leaned across him, as yet not touching the flesh. There was no hint of corruption, and he knew whoever the pair were they had been walking the streets of Sevilla the evening before. Even without that knowledge Thomas's trained eye could see the freshness of the wounds. Blood had barely had time to thicken.

This time the dissections were low on the chest where the ribs came to an end. Skin had been peeled back, layers of muscle cut and examined, the flesh held open by rounded stones. The same kind of stones he had seen at other killing sites.

Thomas pictured the killer using his fingers, feeling for something, but what? That is what the sight reminded him of. He had done as much himself when searching for a tumour in the vain hope of cutting it away, the careful slicing, the slow act of discovery. But what was being searched for? And why cut so precisely? Different victims cut in different places meant the killer had not yet found what he was looking for. So why not cut his victims everywhere? Unless... Thomas fought the resistance of ignorance, forcing his way past... unless what the killer sought could only be found in a body while it was alive?

He moved to the woman, but the sight of a lamp in an alcove made him step aside. He cupped his hand to the glass, which still held a trace of heat, and when he sniffed he smelled soot as well as oil. These two must have died even as he and Olaf were disposing of the soldiers. Had Thomas come here first he would have caught the man in the act, and this would all be over. He would know what reason lay behind the killings, and the man handed over to the authorities.

The woman had been handsome in life, her skin darker than the man's, her hair black, and when Thomas lifted an eyelid the cornea that stared out was also dark. He stepped back and studied her, emotionless. Yesterday she had lived and laughed and loved, but now she was a puzzle to be solved, and Thomas trusted himself to do so. She was not a Moor, and certainly not of Africa, but not Spanish either. Sicilian perhaps, or from further east. He thought of Belia and the tint of her skin, which was close to what he now stared at.

He approached her body and examined the wound, peeling back the layers as he had for the man. His eyes flicked from one to the other. Whoever had cut them was skilled, there could be no doubt of that. As skilled as himself, he wondered? He admitted they might be. Which was good, for there could be few with such attributes in the city, and they would be known. Not one of the physicians Belia had taken him to, so someone else. A stranger, like he was? And if so how would he discover them? He had no doubt he would, with the help of Jorge and Belia and Lubna. Thomas's blood quickened. This could be the moment everything turned in his favour.

The room was still cool, but it would warm once sunlight fell on the cathedral walls. The bodies would start to putrefy. Flies would gather, but they would not have had these two. One of them would have been disposed of, the other displayed.

Thomas sat in the corner, propped up by the meeting of two walls, and pulled his knees to his chest. He waited for whoever had done this to return to dispose of the bodies, for return they would, and then he would have them, whoever they were. He gave no thought to going for help, confident in his own abilities. He rested his head against the corner and closed his eyes, the better to allow himself to think.

CHAPTER THIRTY-FIVE

When Thomas woke from a deep sleep a hand was on him and he drew his sword without thinking and struck out. When his eyes focussed he found Jorge standing before him, arms wide. The tip of Thomas's sword was at his throat but had not drawn blood.

"Remind me never to sleep beside you," said Jorge. "How does Lubna cope? Are you this grumpy every time you wake?"

Thomas lowered his sword, sheathed it. "What are you doing here?"

"Lubna remembered where the man who attacked Theresa went when you followed him, so she sent me to find you, of course."

"Of course. But how did you know I would be here?"

Jorge shook his head. "Oh, Thomas, you are not near as mysterious as you believe. Lubna has the measure of you. She said you would come back because you had unfinished business. Not this, I admit, but you would want to see the location again."

"There has been no more trouble?"

"None that has bothered us. The soldiers will be missed, though, no doubt about it. Mandana will expect them back and when they fail to appear he will know they have failed. You should have killed them all."

"One more black mark against us, but he already wants us dead. What can he do, kill us twice?"

"Just the once would be bad enough." Jorge gave a shiver, but it was for effect only.

"When–" Thomas cut off abruptly as a sound reached him. Boots on stone, coming this way. He held a finger to his lips and motioned Jorge to crouch down, went to join him behind the table. It offered little cover but there was nowhere else. The boots sounded on wooden boards now, approaching at a steady pace. Not a big man, Thomas thought, as they grew louder, but he saw he was wrong when a figure appeared in the entrance. A tall man, cadaverous, dressed in dirty robes that had once been grey, and a tall peaked hood. The clothing of those who disposed of plague bodies. No doubt a cart would be waiting outside.

As the man entered the room Thomas rose, immediately knowing it was too soon. The man closed the gap between him and the table and heaved, tipping the bodies on top of them.

Thomas pushed at the table, but only managed to move it off them when Jorge added his strength. By the time they we free the sound of the killer's flight had faded.

Outside Thomas was surprised at how busy the cathedral square had become while he slept, knowing he was fortunate Jorge had woken him. Had the killer found him lying on the floor he would no doubt have never woken at all.

He climbed onto the lip of a buttress and shaded his eyes, looking over the heads of the crowd, but as he scanned the throng he knew they had lost him. He cursed and jumped down, about to suggest to Jorge they spread out and ask if anyone had seen a fleeing man, when Jorge raised a hand.

"There, Thomas."

Thomas stretched, saw what Jorge was pointing at. The man would have been invisible if not for the robes he wore, which caused the crowd to move away from him so he walked in an empty space.

Jorge yelled, his voice loud. The man glanced back, started to run. He crashed into a seller of roast almonds on the far side of the square, sending man and hot coals crashing to the ground. Thomas began to run as fast as he could, knowing Jorge would be right behind. By the time they reached the cursing tradesman their quarry had fled, but Thomas had seen the alley he had disappeared into and skidded around the turn into it and slowed.

The alley was busy, which was to his advantage. By standing tall he could see over most heads. He caught sight of the man at the far end, his pointed cap discarded so he was less noticeable. Thomas started forward, using his strength and glare to make progress. At the corner he turned left, the same way he had seen the man take. He was no longer in sight, and bundled into a corner was the plague robe. Several narrower alleys led off to the right and there were fewer people now, the sun excluded by high buildings on either side. Thomas trotted along, glancing into each alley, but after two hundred paces he slowed. They had lost him again. He stood next to an open window where an old woman selling some kind of pie stared out at him, her chin on her hand. She raised a pie more in hope than expectation. Thomas ignored her, but Jorge came up beside him and took the pie in exchange for a small coin. He bit into it and made a noise of approval, reached for another and handed it to Thomas.

"Did a man run this way?" Thomas asked the woman.

"Other than you two?"

"Yes, other than us two."

"Only Friar Ramon."

"Who?"

"Friar Ramon Braso. He lives in a shack beyond the city wall east of here. Not a place for men such as yourselves."

"He is a priest?"

The woman was warming to the conversation, barely acknowledging another customer who dropped a small coin on the ledge and took one of her pies. "A Friar. You know the difference, don't you? Ramon prefers to spend his time with people rather than other monks. He is well respected, and many go to him when they are sick."

"Why?" The pie was cooling in his hand and Thomas made to toss it aside.

"Don't waste that if you don't want it," said Jorge, reaching out, seeming to ignore the conversation going on. Thomas handed the pie across.

"Because of what he used to be before he took the cloth, of course," said the woman. "He was a physician. A surgeon. Some say the best in Spain until something happened. Some scandal, but I have not heard what it was."

But you would love to know, wouldn't you, Thomas thought. This Friar Ramon could be no other than the one he had spent weeks in pursuit of, but he had been looking in the wrong place, distracted by his hatred of Abbot Mandana when it was a religious man of another kind he sought.

He glanced along the alley. At the far end two men were arguing over some matter, their voices echoing from the buildings.

"Where is this shack you say he lives?"

"You don't want to go there."

"I am more able than I look," Thomas said. "As is my friend."

"Oh, he looks able enough, and ten years ago I might have invited him inside." The woman cackled. "But San Bernardo is no place for the likes of you."

"San Bernardo?" Thomas said. "Where the Jews bury their dead?"

"Close by, yes." She narrowed eyes already narrow with age. "You are determined to go?"

"I am."

She leaned across the narrow counter and looked at the crumbs from the pie crust Jorge had dropped as he ate. She held another out toward Thomas. "Take it, free. You look like you need feeding up."

Thomas ignored the offered gift and, it seemed, even Jorge had decided he had eaten enough.

"Go straight for a quarter mile," the woman said, putting the pie back on the counter, "then bear right until you reach the city wall and you will be close to the Santa Maria gate. And may God walk with you. It is no place for honest men such as yourselves."

Thomas was already walking away with Jorge at his side when he heard her proposition another customer. The pie had smelled good and he regretted not eating it now. He passed the men still arguing and judged fists would soon fly. After a quarter mile they took an alley to the right and wound their way through increasingly poorer neighbourhoods until they reached the high stone city wall and followed it to an unguarded gate. Beyond it Thomas saw a cluster of houses and shacks. Had this Friar Ramon returned to his lair, or was he somewhere else? If he was not here they might have lost him altogether, and if the man had any sense he would flee Sevilla as fast as he could. It was not the result

Thomas wanted, but if it meant an end to the killings it was one he would accept.

"Not much of a place to live," said Jorge.

To the right a stretch of abandoned ground separated the ruinous district from the Jewish cemetery. There were a cluster of headstones like tangled teeth at its centre with large, more ornate mausoleums toward the edge. Money had been spent here, outside of the city boundary, sitting alongside what had to be one of the poorest of neighbourhoods. Thomas saw what the woman meant. This was not a place to offer a welcome to strangers, but they had to continue their search, and he had a name now. There would be a record of Friar Ramon Braso and it was only a matter of time before he was captured. Even if he tried to flee the name would spread throughout Spain, together with a litany of his crimes.

As they approached the first shacks a broad-shouldered man rose from where he had been sitting in the shade. He spread his legs and crossed his arms. He was tall, strong, but Thomas wished him no harm.

"Did Friar Ramon pass this way?" He tried to conjure a friendly expression on his face but still the man's eyes narrowed, watching only Thomas, seeing no threat in Jorge.

"Who's asking?"

"I am a physician working at the royal palace. I was sent to ask his advice."

The man twitched his head to one side and back. "The royal palace."

"Yes. I heard he has knowledge known to nobody else."

"Don't they employ real physicians anymore?"

Thomas took a step closer and lowered his voice. "It is a matter of some delicacy. I cannot say more, but his services will be well rewarded."

"Ramon cares not for reward. His reward lies not in this world."

"Is your Queen also not head of the Church? Does she not deserve his attention?"

"Men, women, we are all sinners." The man almost smiled. "Particularly here. But yes, Ramon passed not long since. He had been running, I could tell. And if you offer him money he will distribute it here. So go ask, but do not be surprised when he turns you down. You will find him… No, you won't find him, but for a coin I will show you where he lives."

The man stared at Thomas, waiting. Thomas reached beneath his robe, fingers feeling through the coins in his purse, hoping to pull something appropriate out. He was unused to the coinage of Spain and did not want to over-reward the man for his services. He placed a small round of copper on the man's palm, who lifted it to turn in his fingers.

"Aye, enough I expect. Do you have more where this comes from?"

"Not much, no."

"Well, we'll see. Follow me." He turned and strode between the shacks. There were no streets or alleys, just a tumble of wooden walls and torn sailcloth stretched to provide shade. Here and there someone had built in stone, and Thomas saw where a rough garden had been carved from the dry soil. Behind them the city wall rose, excluding those who made their homes here. Beyond the shacks a tributary of the Guadalquivir wound through low hills devoid of grass or crops, only the occasional stunted bush showing that life could find a foothold almost anywhere. Dead on one side, near-desert on the other, it was a place where only the desperate ended up.

"Do you have plague here?" Thomas asked, and the man turned his head.

"Is that what you want of Ramon? Yes, we have plague. Doesn't the entire world? But not as much as within the city. The air is less tainted here, less people to breath it. But if it is because of the plague you want Ramon you will be disappointed. He cannot offer a cure."

"It is not pestilence," Thomas said, "but another matter I would question him on. He is respected here?"

"More than any other. Not merely as a man of God, but because of what he does. He keeps nothing for himself, as you will see. Everything he obtains is shared equally. There are men, women and children here who would not be alive but for him."

The shacks around them grew ever more makeshift until they came to a small clearing almost at the centre of the township.

"This is where we gather, where Ramon preaches each evening, without fail." The man pointed. "He lives there."

It was barely a house, barely even a collection of wooden planks leaning every way but upright. A torn strip of canvas was stretched over part of the interior to provide minimal cover, but the rest was open to the elements. There was no sign of anyone inside, but shade cast dark pools in the corners.

"Thank you, sir," Thomas said and handed the man a second coin. He expected him to return to his observation post, but he remained where he was, once more with legs spread and arms crossed, and Thomas knew they would have a witness to whatever might occur here.

"It might be wise to return another day," said Jorge, leaning close, "with a score of soldiers."

"If we do he will have fled. We do this now or never. We are too close to abandon the chase."

"I see nobody in there."

"He came this way. If he is not in his shack he will be

somewhere nearby." Thomas started across the dusty clearing and ducked beneath the canvas. His hand went to the hilt of his sword, but the interior was empty. There was a blanket laid directly on the bare ground, nowhere to cook, nowhere to eat. No furniture at all other than a low shelf containing some papers and books. Thomas knelt to examine them, found religious tracts, a bible, a few medical texts, recognising one as the same he had in his own library. He picked it up and let it open of its own accord, nodding at what he saw.

"He's learning how to dissect the human body," Thomas said, glancing at Jorge, who remained outside, head uncovered to the sun. Beyond him he saw a few more inhabitants had gathered and were talking with the man who had brought them here.

"People are amused by strange things," said Jorge. "I thought he was already meant to be a great surgeon?"

"So am I, but I still possess books and read them." Thomas put the al-Zahrawi back and leafed through some of the pamphlets, but they were nothing but the wild ravings of zealots.

"Thomas, we are drawing a crowd," said Jorge.

"I noticed. Turn and stare at them. You are big and ugly enough to keep them off for a while until I finish here. I would like to wait and see if Ramon returns."

"How will you know? You have never seen his face. Should I draw my sword?"

"Best not, they might take it badly. And if he returns here we will know it is him."

"You do bring me to some interesting places."

"No thanks are necessary." Thomas took one last look around and rose to his feet. There was nothing to identify the man they sought, no clue to why he was doing what he did. Unless he believed the bile the pamphlets spouted. "I think you are right," he said, "we return with soldiers and tear this entire place apart until we find who is sheltering him."

"There will be trouble," Jorge said.

"Nothing we cannot deal with."

"No, I mean now. There is going to be trouble. Look."

Thomas came out, squinting against the sun. The handful who had gathered earlier had grown to over forty, more drifting into the clearing as he watched. The tall guardian turned toward them, a smile on his lips.

"They are unarmed," Thomas said.

"And we are only two," said Jorge. He too watched the man who had brought them, some kind of leader here.

"Stick a few of them and they'll soon lose interest."

"There are times I fail to understand what Lubna sees in you."

"I don't mean kill them. A slice here, a puncture there. They might think they are dying but I know how to be careful."

"And I do not," said Jorge. "Here they come. I'm going to draw my sword now, if that is all right with you?"

"Not yet."

The crowd formed a solid semi-circle in front of the shack. Thomas glanced behind, wondering if they could flee that way, but saw others had gathered behind as well. He drew his own sword and stood beside Jorge.

"How many times now is this you have tried to get me killed? I am starting to believe you do not love me after all."

"Prick one or two and you'll see them run," Thomas said. "When they do go as fast as you can, straight out and head for the gate."

"With you behind me."

"Of course."

Which is when the crowd parted and a tall man appeared,

dressed in the darned and faded grey robes of a monk. The hood of his robe was thrown back to expose a face that would have been handsome had it not consisted almost entirely of sharp edged bones. A face Thomas had seen twice before. The first time as the man drew a cart of dead where one body had not suffered the plague. A second time in the Cathedral square when he had tried to abduct Theresa.

"I believe you are looking for me, Thomas Berrington."

CHAPTER THIRTY-SIX

"You have the advantage of me, sir." Thomas studied the crowd that had flowed together to close the gap Friar Ramon had passed through.

"Yes, I do appear to have, do I not? But you know my name." A smile came and went, and Thomas experienced the same unease he knew he could spark in others.

"If you accompany us there will be no need for violence," Thomas said.

"I wish you none in return, certainly, for I am a man of God, but sometimes God demands vengeance and justice."

"As do I. You must answer for your actions."

"Not to you, nor your mistress. I answer only to the ultimate power, and I take no heed of the words of the infidel. For that is what you are, is it not? An infidel? One who is without a soul?"

Friar Ramon turned and faced the crowd. He threw his skeletal arms into the air, the sleeves of his robe falling back to display blue marks of self-inflicted tattoos, the sign of the cross repeated again and again, and Thomas wondered how much of the man's body they covered, and what the cost in pain had been.

"I think we are in for some trouble," said Jorge.

"It will come to nothing. These people will not commit murder at his whim. A touch of steel will soon dissuade them."

"There is but one God," Friar Ramon called out, his voice deep, and the gathered assembly, growing as the moment passed, responded to echo his words.

"One God. One leader."

"All others are not to be tolerated. Not Jews, not Moriscos, not the teeming tribes beyond the great desert, not those of the east nor any other man who turns his back on the truth. I seek proof we are the truly anointed children of God, and no man can stop me. Certainly not these two." Ramon turned back, his eyes tracking across Thomas and Jorge, apparently finding nothing to fear there. "What do we do to interlopers and unbelievers?"

"Kill them!" called the crowd.

The response was so instant Thomas knew this situation had been played out before. Whatever hold Ramon had over these people, be it religious zeal, his skill as a physician, or money, they were his, heart and soul. No wonder the man felt safe in his preserve. But Thomas would not submit without taking at least some of them with him, and some might be enough. He drew his sword, the blade scattering shards of sunlight into the eyes of the watchers, some of whom turned away. Beside him Thomas heard the whisper of steel as Jorge followed his example. Then the man who had brought them stepped forward. He carried an axe, the head dark with stains which spoke of its purpose. Thomas wished he had brought Olaf with him rather than Jorge. They might have stood a chance had he done so.

"When I attack, turn and run. There are fewer behind us

and a swing or two will discourage them. Find a way clear and go to the Queen, tell he what we have found, and send troops."

"You will be dead by then," said Jorge.

"And you will not. Now go." Thomas pushed at his friend, who staggered a few paces away before stopping. "Go, damn you, before I stick you myself."

"Kill them!" shouted Friar Ramon. And then, "No, keep the short one alive. He interrupted my work so he will become my next subject. All I will need then is a Christian."

The big man stepped closer and raised his axe, the weight handled easily in his grip.

Jorge turned and ran, swinging his sword, more skilled than he had once been but still lacking the instinct to kill that made him vulnerable. But those he swung at did not know of this shortfall and they stepped back, tripping over each other and falling to the dirt in their hurry to escape his blade.

Thomas sensed the big man coming at him and turned, almost lazy. He ducked beneath the killing blow, hearing the sound it made as it passed over his head and then, when it thudded into the ground he flicked his wrist and took the man behind the knee. His leg buckled and he fell into the dust. Thomas raised the point of his sword and placed it against the man's neck, applying just enough pressure to prick skin and draw blood.

"I have done you a favour today, but there is no need to thank me." With his foot he kicked the axe away, keeping it in his peripheral vision in case someone tried to retrieve it, but he doubted anyone else was strong enough to wield the weapon. Starvation and sickness held sway here. When the man pulled his head back, dragging himself on his knuckles away from the blade, Thomas bent and picked up the axe, grunting from the effort.

"Do not allow him to live!" Ramon's voice was a scream. "He cannot end my work!"

And the others came. Men, women, children, a wave of them. Too many to kill, too many to stop. Thomas's eyes flickered across faces as they came toward him. He saw no weapons, but the weight of bodies alone would be enough to overwhelm him. He could submit or fight, but he had never been willing to submit to anyone. Sheathing his sword Thomas gripped the axe in two hands and swung it around his head. He yelled as he ran toward the front ranks.

They parted, as he knew they would, and he saw Friar Ramon directly ahead, legs planted wide. He held his arms out to the sides as if the power of God alone might stop Thomas. God could not, but logic did. Kill the Friar and the mob would descend on him despite their fear. Already he saw figures closing the gap he had made.

Thomas edged to one side, away from Ramon, opening a new avenue of faces which he ran between, but as fast as he went there was only ever the space around him which instantly closed behind. All it would take was one determined fool to get their head caved in, then the others would fall on him. Sweat stung his eyes, dust rose from pounding feet, and still he could not see a way out from the maze of shacks, and the denizens of the township grew ever bolder, lunging at him, always just out of reach. Thomas knew he could kill several, but was reluctant. These people were not his enemy, they were not who he was after. He had lost sight of Friar Ramon, but imagined him somewhere behind, urging the others on.

He skidded around a turn into a gap between wooden boards and came to a halt, almost losing his footing, which would have been the end, but he managed to stay on his feet. He turned fast, because the way ahead was blocked by the city wall.

A dozen feet away bodies shifted. Women drifted backward as men made their way to the front. Children were dragged away. Now Thomas saw weapons, of a sort. Kitchen knives, lengths of rope with nails knotted into them, anything that was hard or sharp and could be wielded. He swung the axe one way, the other, and the men stepped back, but not in panic as they had at the start of the chase. Their confidence had grown, bolstered by numbers and circumstance.

"Shit," Thomas muttered under his breath. He turned aside and smashed the axe into the wall of one of the shacks, stepped through, still swinging. Wood crashed, canvas fell to impede the four men who lunged at him, and a final swing opened the back wall to sunlight and he darted through. Ahead lay the city wall, the gate two hundred paces to his right, but already bodies were streaming from between the shacks and Thomas began to run, legs heavy, unsure if he could reach safety before they fell on him. He threw the axe aside, not wanting to have to use it and gaining a little speed for its lack.

He was still a hundred paces away when a hand grabbed his cloak and he skidded to one knee. Bodies swarmed over him. There came a blow to his head, a prick of something against his arm, and he tried to stand, bodies clinging to him like ants to honey. And then, all at once, they were gone, running hard to the safety of their township.

Thomas turned, rubbing at a cut on his hand, to discover Jorge approaching, a dozen armed soldiers behind.

"I found them lounging around with nothing better to do, so I thought to bring them with me," he said. "I would of course have come and rescued you without them, but it seemed such a waste not to use their talents." He looked Thomas up and down. "Are you hurt?"

Thomas shook his head. "But I thought that might be the end of me. Thank you."

Jorge laughed. "Are you sure you haven't taken a blow to the head?"

Thomas looked around. There was not a soul in sight. Someone had taken the discarded axe and the ground was churned by the hundred feet that had pursued him, but the township could be deserted. A shiver ran through him despite the heat of the sun. This had been close, the closest he had come to death in many a year, the closest since he had been left for dead beside a French roadway.

He clapped Jorge on the back and embraced him.

"Come on, we haven't finished yet today."

"What do I do with these?" Jorge indicated the soldiers, who had started to gossip, no doubt glad of another tale to tell and embellish. Thomas considered sending them into the township to find Friar Ramon, but knew the man would have fled by now. But not, he thought, out of the city. There was unfinished work for him here, but now Thomas had a face and name, for what they were worth.

CHAPTER THIRTY-SEVEN

They went first to the cathedral but discovered the bodies gone. At Jorge's house Olaf told them he had used the cart to dispose of them, as Thomas had shown him during the night. He believed he had done the right thing, so Thomas did not disabuse him of the notion. The bodies could have provided evidence when they caught Friar Ramon, but the man's confession would be enough.

Belia was kneading dough on the wooden table and Thomas sat and watched for a moment, his mind blank, exhaustion clinging to him, making his limbs slack.

"Where is Lubna?"

"She went to the palace with Will," said Belia. "He wanted to play, and there was a message brought for her."

"From Isabel?"

"The Queen? I don't know, I didn't see the note, only the woman who brought it."

"Theresa?"

"You are full of questions today, aren't you?" Her forearms flexed as she leaned into the dough, her fists buried inside. "Not Theresa. She was the one stayed over last night, wasn't she? Red haired – slept with Martin and Helena."

"I didn't know that."

Belia seemed satisfied with the dough and shaped it into a round, cut a cross on the top before sliding it into the oven. She sat, pushing hair from her face with the back of her hands. "So, there *is* something you don't know. It is almost a blessing." She glanced toward Jorge, something in her eyes changing, her mouth softening.

"What will you do when we leave?" Thomas asked.

"More questions. I don't know. It depends on whether he asks me or not."

"Asks you what?"

"To go with him."

"And if he does?"

"Not all questions have an answer, Thomas." She reached out and touched his hand, smearing it with flour. "Not yet."

"He has a house in Gharnatah. Not as fine as this one, but fine enough." And a harem of sorts, Thomas thought, but made no mention of that. "And there is a garden where you could grow your herbs. Your skills would be of more use there than here."

"Why? Doesn't Sevilla deserve me?"

"Of course. I only meant that Gharnatah appreciates the manner of knowledge you possess. I suspect not everyone here does. You have trouble now and again, do you not?"

"People come to me, or they leave me alone, but no trouble. I think some are afraid of my difference."

Thomas stared at Belia, his eyes tracking her face, trying to see her difference and failing. Yes, she was different in many way, he could tell, but *a* difference? He thought not.

When Jorge sat close and wrapped his arms around her like an octopus she laughed.

Thomas rose and left them to their pleasures. He debated whether to invite Olaf to accompany him to the palace but thought that would be pressing Fernando's chivalry too far. He and Helena, and a few others who had made the journey, were due to set out for Gharnatah within days. Olaf was already growing nervous at being in a Spanish city. He said it smelled strange, and people looked at him oddly. Thomas thought it better not to point out that most people looked at him oddly. Few had seen such a giant of a man.

Thomas took the steps down to the riverfront rather than the door to the street and walked alongside the caravels drawn up there. He saw a familiar face for the second time and called up to Columb, who came to the rail and peered down.

"Is that Thomas Berrington? Come up, come up, I have some fine wine from Portugal and sweetmeats from North Africa."

"I cannot, I am on my way somewhere."

Still Columb did not give up. "I would speak with you, Thomas. Are you still in the employ of the King and Queen?"

Was I ever? Thomas thought, but called back, "I am on my way to the palace now, which is why I cannot take up your offer of hospitality."

"Then wait for me to come down, I will walk a way with you."

Thomas sighed, but waited all the same until Columb clambered down a swaying ladder. He fell into step beside Thomas as he started up once more, beginning to regret he had chosen to come this way. He had wanted to look on Castillo de Triana once more even though he knew its walls were barred to him. He wondered how far Mandana would take this new enmity, or would he be too afraid of what Fernando might do if harm befell Thomas?

"Have you sailed far?" Thomas asked, more out of politeness than interest.

"Not far. Lisboa, the coast of Africa. A short trip for a mariner. We sail for Sicilia in the morn."

"What is it you want to talk to me about?" Thomas was in no mood for small talk, but he saw Columb was uneasy that he was asked to state his business so soon without any preamble. "I have much on my mind," Thomas said, as if in apology for his shortness.

"Does the Queen ever mention me?" asked Columb. "I speak with her advisors, her priests, and they say they pass on my requests, but I am not sure she hears them."

"What requests?"

"To forge a new route to the Indies, of course. You must recall we spoke of it in Ronda. You showed me a map that was claimed to be of the coast of China drawn by some northmen. Was that not proof enough of my ideas?"

"I will mention your name," Thomas said. It was little concern of his if this man wanted to kill himself and his crew in a pointless expedition. The world was more than big enough as it was without someone setting out to discover new lands.

"I would be grateful. Here, take this as thanks." Columb held out a dark bottle to Thomas. "The finest wine of Portugal. Sweet and warming."

"I drink little," Thomas said.

"Then a gift for the Queen, perhaps? When you mention my name to her."

Thomas took the bottle, hoping to get rid of the man, but Columb stayed at his side all the way to the palace gates, regaling Thomas with non-stop chatter relating to his lunatic theories. He only stopped when they reached the wide wooden entrance and Thomas kept going without looking back.

Thomas went first to his rooms. They were clean, fresh smelling, with newly cut flowers decorating the window sills. He half expected to find Lubna recovering there after being hurt, but there was no sense of her presence, no hint of the scent she always carried with her that was not scent but the essence of her. Thomas left the bottle of Portuguese wine on the table and went in search of Samuel. Lubna would be with Isabel, Will with Juan and his sisters, a new plaything for them who would be forgotten the instant they left the city.

Samuel was not in his room, but Thomas found him sitting with Theresa in a side room close to the royal chambers. He glanced up as Thomas entered, only a momentary surprise showing. Their heads had been close together until he disturbed them, and Thomas wondered what was so interesting in their discussion. He considered embarrassing Theresa by asking where she had slept last night, but decided it would be unnecessarily cruel and serve no purpose.

Samuel rose. "I will leave you to your business." He stopped when he reached Thomas. "The Queen continues in good health." He leaned close and whispered, "No thanks to you."

"It is you I would speak with," Thomas said.

"I have been told to talk only of essential matters with you. I will reveal nothing else."

Theresa watched them, a frown creasing her normally placid features. She had bathed and dressed since leaving Jorge's house, but there was a dusting of tiredness beneath her eyes and her lips looked fuller, as if lightly bruised.

"I know the name of the killer I seek," Thomas said, "and want to ask what you know of the man."

"I know no killer," Samuel said.

"Friar Ramon Braso. He trained as a physician I was told, a fine one, too. Trained in Malaka, as did you."

"Ramon? A killer? I refuse to believe it." Samuel shook his

296

head and Thomas watched him carefully, trying to judge whether his show of surprise was an act or not. He knew he should have brought Jorge with him, but it would have been difficult to gain him access to these rooms so close to the royal presence. "I don't believe what you are saying. It is true Ramon and I trained together in Malaga, and at the same time. Yes, he was a fine physician. A skilled surgeon. Better even than you." Samuel took obvious pleasure in the statement.

"If he is so skilled why are you the Queen's physician and not he?"

"It is not always a matter of skill. Ramon's interests lay elsewhere. With the poor, with those in need. And such appointments are a matter of who you know rather than what you know."

"And you know Mandana, who is Fernando's man."

"Do not make it seem such an accusation. Have you never grasped an opportunity when it came your way? Ramon, for all his skill, would have refused such a position. I would have been a fool to do the same."

"When last did you see him?" Thomas asked.

"Not for some time. A year, perhaps a little more, not since he helped me distil your liquor. He was strange even then, but still clever. I heard he had been touched by our Lord and turned into some kind of zealot."

"Of sorts. He lives among the poor outside the city walls."

"Why?"

"Perhaps you should ask him next time you meet."

Samuel sighed, shook his head. "I have told you, I wasn't aware he still lived in Sevilla. If you had told me he was a member of the Inquisition I would have believed you, but this? Ramon was a man of culture. He appreciated the fine things in life. What could change a man so much?"

"You know him, you tell me," Thomas said. "Or perhaps I should ask Abbot Mandana."

"Not if you value your life."

"Are you still working with him and al-Haquim? And are you ready to tell me what you are really doing, the three of you?"

"I believe our purpose has been explained. Now let me leave, I have work to do." Samuel stamped off, making his annoyance known.

Thomas walked to Theresa and touched her shoulder, surprising himself.

"Is Isabel truly well?"

Theresa nodded and laid her hand over his before rising and stepping away. "She is. No thanks to Samuel, but yes, she is well." A smile "I think your wife pleases her. They discuss matters I barely comprehend and try not to listen to. She will be pleased to see you, Thomas, she asked where you were." Another smile. "Catching a murderer, it seems. Well, you are getting a reputation for such, aren't you."

Thomas heard Will's squeal of delight, and then Isabel's soft tones, the voice she used when alone with friends, not the royal voice of command. When he entered the room he saw Isabel and Lubna sitting close together on a bench, and Thomas noticed Lubna had her arms wrapped about her waist. As he approached, before they had seen him, Lubna suddenly pitched forward onto her face and Isabel screamed. A pool of blood spread around Lubna's prone body, her legs moving as if she was trying to walk.

Thomas ran to her and knelt, turning her over.

"The baby," Lubna gasped. "I am losing our baby, Thomas."

Isabel looked down on them, her mouth open. Then she stood and screamed, but the scream was one of pure fear.

"Get her out! Now! Get her away from me!" She turned

and ran past Lubna's prone body just as Will ran up and slid along the floor to them both.

Thomas turned, panicked, to see Theresa standing in the doorway, a hand to her mouth.

"Fetch Samuel," Thomas ordered. "And find someone to take Will away. He cannot see this."

CHAPTER THIRTY-EIGHT

Thomas sat on the edge of the wide bed and held Lubna's hand, staring at the dried blood which still stained his own. She continued to sleep, kept unconscious by a mixture of poppy and herbs Belia had made up.

"I have to offer you an apology," said Samuel. He stood at a table beneath the window, washing his hands in a bowl of water. Only the three of them remained. Theresa had been here but had left to take care of Will, who must be in fear his mother was dead. It had been a close call.

"You need offer me nothing," Thomas said without moving his gaze from Lubna. "She would not have made it without your help."

"That is not true, and you know it. I told you, Ramon was the better surgeon, but you have demonstrated my words a lie today. I know of nobody who could have done what you did."

"I could not save my child," Thomas said, hearing the catch in his voice and not caring. His soul was rasped raw with grief. The child had been a girl. A tiny, perfect girl.

"You had a choice. It was one or the other. And you chose right. Lubna can give you more children, God willing."

"Perhaps, perhaps not. There was damage, and I am sure I inflicted more when I stemmed the bleeding. We won't know, not for a while."

"Women lose babies all the time," said Samuel. "And it was not so far along."

"She *lived*," Thomas said. "For a while my daughter lived!"

"You know it was impossible," said Samuel. He stood at the table, awkward, and Thomas knew the man wanted to leave but could find no excuse to do so. "You saved Lubna's life today. Hold that close and carry it forward. Her life continues. Cherish her soul."

"I do. You can go if you want, she is out of danger now."

"Send for me if you need anything, anything at all."

Thomas heard Samuel's footsteps fade. He leaned over and kissed Lubna's brow, her lips. He wanted to wash his hands but dare not release her for fear she would slip away if he did. He wondered if he could ever release her, and knew he did not want to.

"Wife," he whispered, his forehead against hers.

"Husband," she replied, her voice a breath against his cheek, so light he wondered had he heard right. And then footsteps approached and he had to let go, knowing what was to come. He steeled himself to show no weakness.

A paige entered the room, his eyes avoiding the woman on the bed, skittering away from the tiny linen wrapped bundle set in a corner. "I have a message from the Queen." He held out a parchment, a red wax seal on one side and Thomas walked to him and took it. The paige turned and scuttled away as rapidly as he could without losing face.

Thomas broke the seal and opened the parchment, wondering how Isabel would frame it. He read the words then tossed the letter to one side and returned to Lubna. The letter said nothing he had not expected. He knew as soon as Isabel screamed to get Lubna away from her. Isabel carried a child of her own, a future prince or princess, and she feared being tainted by the child Lubna had lost. It was foolish superstition, but Thomas had seen it before. The rearing of children was considered a matter of God and luck, but mostly luck. Anything that tainted that luck was to be shunned. As he and Lubna were to be shunned.

When more steps sounded he wiped tears away from where they had fallen on Lubna's face, rose and firmed his shoulders. But it was no party of soldiers arriving to escort him from the palace. Instead it was all the people he loved most in the world come for him and Lubna, and his chest hitched as Jorge embraced him. Despite the letter it was the Queen, he knew, who had allowed this, who had sent for them all.

"Where is she?" said Olaf, and at first Thomas thought he meant Lubna, who lay in plain sight, then it came to him and he nodded at the linen-wrapped bundle in the corner.

Olaf went across, hesitated. "Is she…?"

"She is beautiful," Thomas said, and Olaf nodded, as if that was only to be expected.

Olaf knelt and unwrapped the linen, stared for a long time at what it contained. Theresa, Thomas knew, had washed the tiny infant before wrapping her.

"A girl," Olaf said. "I would have liked to be *morfar* to a girl. She looks like Lubna."

"Yes," Thomas said, "she does."

"Did you give her a name?"

"No."

"You must. Wherever her soul is bound she will need a name to be called by."

"Then Lubna must name her."

"She must be named now," said Olaf, "you know she must.

302

She cannot be left like this. She will need to be..." He frowned.

"In the way of Islam," Thomas said. "I have no God, but Lubna does. We will take her outside the city and make a pyre for her. You and I, Olaf, for it should be us."

"And me," said Jorge.

"And me," said Belia.

Thomas nodded. It was as he expected. "And I will think of a name, a Moorish name. Now we have to leave, for I am banned from the palace." He glanced at Jorge. "I assume not from your house?"

"What do you think?"

Olaf re-wrapped the still, tiny infant in the linen and picked her up. He brought the burden to Thomas and held it out.

"I will carry Lubna," Thomas said.

"Don't be a fool. Take your daughter and let us get out of this place."

Thomas took the bundle. Olaf leaned over and picked up his own daughter as though she weighed nothing at all.

"Will you ever return to the palace?"

Thomas glanced at Jorge as he sipped at the Portuguese wine, sweet in his mouth. Columb had been right, it was delicious.

"If she needs me, yes, but Isabel is recovered now. She is no fool though, she knows who is the best physician in Spain."

"And failing his presence she will send for you?"

Thomas pulled a face and glanced to where Lubna slept on a makeshift bed in the wide terrace room because he could not bear to think of her alone upstairs. And he needed company, a reminder life would continue for those remaining. They had walked together through the city to the Macarena gate and beyond, paying a boatman to carry them across to the far bank. Thomas chose the spot, and Lubna, carried by her father because she could not be left behind even if she dozed for most of the journey, nodded her assent.

They settled on a small clearing in a stand of mixed pine and oak. Olaf laid Lubna on the ground so she could lean against a tree, her dead daughter beside her on one side, Belia on the other, while the men went to gather wood.

Afterward, when it was done, they waited while the ashes cooled, then scraped them together into a leather sack. Part way across the river Thomas tipped the contents into the Guadalquivir, ignoring the protests of the boatman.

"Goodbye, Bahja," he said. It was a good name, a name chosen by Lubna, to mean beauty. Thomas kissed his fingers and dipped them into the water. Lubna had fallen into a doze again, cradled against Olaf's broad chest, but he woke her so she could watch the final journey of their daughter who would now never be, never grow to giggle in her father's arms or fall in love or raise children of her own. An entire future, gone.

"Bye bye," said Will, cradled by Jorge, as much a father to him as Thomas.

Now the day beyond the terrace was fading, lamps being lit on ships' rigging. One of the caravels slipped its moorings and set a small sail, men pushing it out from the dock with long poles until the relentless current of the river caught and carried the ship south to the sea. Thomas wondered if it was Columb, but was not curious enough to follow the thought or rise and shade his eyes from the setting sun to see.

"Go to her." A faint voice. Lubna. And this time Thomas did care.

He rose and went to kneel beside her, took her hand in

his. Her eyes were closed but as he waited they opened, the effort almost too much. "Go to Isabel and tell her I will stay away. Explain to her what you know and ask for help. Ask Fernando if she will not, for he will offer it. Finish this thing, Thomas. I am not going to die, but I will be of no help for some time, so go, do what you are good at and find that man. For me. For Bahja. I want no more death and you are the only man who can stop it." Her eyes closed, the speech exhausting her, and within moments she had fallen asleep.

Thomas stayed where he was, unwilling to release her, but he knew she was right. He could not brood around the house for a week or more while she recovered. Life had to go on. Work too. And this was another kind of work he was good at. He had been reluctant to accept such when four years before the Sultan had asked him to find another killer, but as time passed Thomas came to recognise an ability within himself. Only when he accepted it could he learn the skills needed. He would never stop learning, he knew, and that was just and proper, but he could end this thing if he set his mind to it. That he also knew.

He rose and returned to the table, pushed the remaining half bottle of wine across to Jorge, who pushed it back.

"When do we start?" he asked.

"Today."

CHAPTER THIRTY-NINE

Isabel would not see them, which came as no surprise. The sight of Fernando striding from the palace was. A half dozen soldiers accompanied him, but he waved them back and walked to where Thomas and Jorge stood in the soft dark of evening.

"She will come around," he said. "She fears for the child she carries. It is superstition, I know, but I will not go against her wishes, Thomas."

"I understand. Has she spoken to you of the other matter I pursue?"

"The deaths? Yes." Fernando gave a tight smile. "It seems to me that death is your constant companion," and then, aware of what he had said held up a hand. "I apologise. I did not mean it to sound as it does. Forgive me, Thomas." He stepped close and embraced him, the King of Spain standing in a cobbled square with his subjects passing by, unaware of what was happening within feet of them, and as he returned the embrace Thomas knew that both Isabel and Fernando were as Gods to the population, who saw only the pomp and glory but not the person hidden behind it. Now, here, dressed as a common soldier, Fernando went unnoticed.

"There is nothing to forgive, your grace."

Fernando scowled. "Not here, Thomas. Not now." He clapped Jorge on the back. "Does your big friend know of somewhere we can get food and wine, preferably with pretty women to serve it?"

"I am sure he does."

"You know me so well," said Jorge, leading the way across the square, but not far. Even Jorge knew he could not take Fernando to some of the places they had visited.

"So," said Fernando, once they were settled with cups of wine and food on its way, "what would you have discussed with my wife?" He took a swallow of the wine and made a face.

"It gets better with practice," said Jorge, sampling his own and also finding it lacking.

"First, I want your generosity to my friends extended until Lubna recovers. She needs her father beside her, and I give my word on Olaf's good behaviour."

Fernando smiled. "I like the big man. I may have to kill him one day but I will do so with regret."

"He said the same about you," Thomas said.

"It is agreed," said Fernando. "He has safe passage in Spain for as long as he needs. The others who came with him, too. I hear Martin has grown besotted with one of them."

"People do," Thomas said.

"That was too easy. What else?"

"The killings." Thomas leaned over the table, then had to sit back as a serving girl put bowls of meat, rice and sauce on the table. "I have discovered the name of the culprit. He is protected from me for the moment, but not from you. Two dozen good men will flush him out and we can all get on with our lives."

"Two dozen? Are you sure he is the one you seek?"

"He admitted as much."

"Why is he doing it?" asked Fernando as he reached for a slice of pork. He dipped it into the spiced sauce and popped it into his mouth.

"That I don't know, not yet. He cuts the bodies with care, not anger. I suspect he is looking for something, but what it is I have no idea. No two cuttings are the same."

"Has Samuel seen the bodies?"

"He has not. Would it help if he did?"

Fernando shook his head. "I don't know, but he is a good physician and may have an opinion."

"Then it is a pity the bodies are gone," Thomas said.

"You lost them?"

"Olaf disposed of them while we were chasing the suspect. He did not know. It was–" Thomas broke off. He had been about to mention the attack on the house, but was sure Fernando knew nothing of it, and it might only cause more trouble if he did.

"That was foolish of him," said Fernando, his fingers trying to decide between a piece of lamb and a tiny songbird steeped in wine. "Yes, I can give you soldiers. Three dozen might be better than two, but why so many? Do you have a name for the man?"

"We do. Friar Ramon Braso. He lives in the heart of a district of shacks beyond the eastern wall. Jorge and I followed him there. We barely escaped with our lives. Yes, three dozen will do it. My thanks." When Thomas looked up from selecting a chunk of beef Fernando was staring at him.

"Friar Ramon?"

Thomas nodded. Beside him Jorge had fallen into conversation with the serving girl.

"I know him. Are you sure he is your killer? Samuel recommended him to us as a second physician for the palace and I met the man. It was over a year ago now, but there was something unsettling about him I didn't like. Even so he did not strike me as someone who would kill in cold blood."

"You have heard the city talk of the Ghost, have you not?"

"I have. Are you saying Friar Ramon is this mythic Ghost?"

Thomas pushed down the frustration that threatened to spill from him. Fernando led a life detached from his people however much he tried to make it appear otherwise. He had not experienced the terror on the streets at the mention of that word, a terror even greater than that wrought by the plague.

"Not mythic, and he has as good as admitted the acts to us."

"Then you should speak with Isabel's confessor. He and Ramon were close at one time and for all I know may still be."

"When we have captured him he will tell us his true purpose," Thomas said. "If not I will talk with Talavera then. That is who you mean, is it not? We have exchanged words before."

"My wife consults him on all religious matters. I'll arrange it for tomorrow evening if you do not catch your man."

"We will catch him," Thomas said, "with the help of your soldiers. This time he will not escape justice."

"So, what now?" Jorge stood beside Thomas on the edge of the city as Fernando's soldiers passed them, some muttering about a waste of time, others grinning because they had managed to ferment a little trouble. "Has he fled the city?"

"His work here is not concluded," Thomas said. "But he'll be more careful now."

"Then we've lost him. I may go back to Gharnatah with Olaf and Helena. This town stinks, and every day I wake healthy and sane comes as a surprise."

"If Lubna is sufficiently healed I will send her with you. Fernando has left his invitation open-ended for now. Stay, help me catch the man, and we can all go home together. I'll even ask Columb if we can sail with him to Malaka, it's only half the distance to travel from there, and the scenery is better. We will be in al-Andalus the entire way."

"I'll think on it."

"Has Belia told you her decision yet?"

"No, but she will come."

"I tried to offer her some encouragement," Thomas said.

"And despite that I still think she will come."

"What will you do with the Nubians?"

"Belia is open minded," said Jorge.

"Do you fuck them all?" Thomas asked.

"Not at the same time, but yes, I have fucked them all." He glanced at Thomas. "Is there anything wrong with that? I do not force myself on them, they come to me willingly, but I would give them all up if Belia asks."

"You fall in love too easily."

"You say that as if it is a bad thing, Thomas. What do we do now?"

"You go back to the house. I come with you to check on Lubna. Then I visit Isabel's confessor. If he is still in contact with Ramon then he might know where the man has gone to ground."

"Will he tell you if he does? I suspect they share a common fanaticism."

They turned and entered the city gate. Ahead the soldiers

maintained their discipline as they headed toward the barracks.

At Jorge's house Lubna was sitting up sipping at a bowl of broth. When she had taken enough Thomas carried her to another room and examined her. The bleeding had stopped, and the weals from Thomas's application of hot iron were healing. Lubna was young, her body capable of miracles. Whether she could carry another child was something they would have to wait and see about, but she was already talking of wanting to try again. "Just not for a week or two," she said with a smile, and Thomas knew she truly was getting better.

"Where is Belia?" he asked, taking her weight on his arm. She had insisted on walking back to the large room.

"She said she needed to go to her house. She wants to make up some tinctures to speed my recovery. She also said she must visit the market now all these people are in the house."

"And Olaf eats enough for three men," Thomas said.

"I am pleased he came, even if he did have to witness our loss."

"His too," Thomas said. "Will loves his *morfar* a great deal, but I fear Olaf will turn him into a berserker yet."

"No, he is his father's son, too," said Lubna, and Thomas wondered whether she spoke the truth or not, still uncertain. There were times when he watched Will and saw a gesture that could have been made by him, others when he seemed a stranger. But Thomas gave little thought anymore to whether he was Will's true father or not. The boy was his son.

"Will you be all right here if I go to the palace?"

"Will you see her?"

"Isabel? No. It's her priest I want to talk with."

"Then go, but do not take long. We need to discuss what

we do once I have recovered enough to travel. Whether we all go, or only some of us. Father grows anxious, and bored. He likes the luxury of this house well enough, but he never has been one to choose luxury over excitement."

Thomas led her toward the makeshift bed, but Lubna shook her head. She wanted to sit at the table. Helena had returned from wherever she had been, and Thomas wondered if she had been visiting Martin de Alarcón, and if so exactly what that meant. But he knew, for Helena, sex often meant little at all. It was a means to an end, to gain influence and power. Also, she liked mischief. She might have bedded Martin just to annoy Thomas. Then he berated himself. Not everything she did was about him, more than likely very little at all. But he acknowledged she had changed over the past year, perhaps even before then. The bitterness that once tainted her was fading, but he could not yet tell what might replace it.

He forgot about Helena as he strode toward the palace, working through what he wanted to ask Talavera. The priest had admitted he and Ramon were close at one time, almost father and son. He might be reluctant to give up someone so close, but Thomas could be persuasive.

CHAPTER FORTY

Thomas sent a message and Friar Hernando de Talavera sent another in return. He would not admit Thomas to the palace but would meet him at the Cathedral, in the same chapel where only two days before he and Lubna had married. In the eyes of a Christian God, at least. There would have to be another ceremony when they returned home, if only to ease the feelings of those who had missed out on the celebrations. It would also give Jorge another chance to arrange a party.

Thomas detoured via the killing chamber, but it lay empty, the table taken away, no sign that anything untoward had ever taken place here. Recalling a thought from when he first discovered the place Thomas descended the stone steps and squeezed past them, curious where the lower passageway led. It curved around as the upper did, but did not end in the same place. Instead it continued on. Narrow alcoves marked his progress, some with dust covered statuary, others containing wooden chests with stout locks. A curtained opening appeared on the inner side and Thomas peered through, found himself at the back of the huge nave.

There was no barrier here and anyone who knew of this entrance would be able to enter and leave at will.

Ahead candles burned. Thomas watched as an old woman shuffled forward to light another. The air smelled of incense, and from somewhere out of sight a voice intoned words in Latin. Thomas waited for the woman to say her prayers and leave, then slipped into the main body of the Cathedral. He found the old Moorish remnant where he and Lubna had been married and sat. He stared into space, and anyone watching would believe he was a fool with an empty head, but he was tracing the skeins of connection and logic, following trails that made more sense now, even if not quite sense enough.

He looked up at the sound of soft footsteps to see Friar Talavera enter the chapel. The man dropped to one knee and crossed himself before rising and turning to Thomas, who remained seated, then thought better of it and rose to his feet.

"Thank you for coming."

"It is only because the Queen asked it of me. I have no love of infidels."

"I am an Englishman," Thomas said.

"No, you are an infidel. You married an infidel, and in God's eyes that makes you no better than her. But I am here, and will answer your questions if I can." He indicated one of the seats with a hand. "My bones ache less if I sit."

Thomas waited for him to be comfortable before sitting close and leaning forward.

"You are a friend to Ramon Braso, I understand. How long have you known him?"

Talavera's mouth tightened and for a moment Thomas thought he was going to refuse to answer, but then his eyes sought a corner of the chapel and he said, "Since he was a boy of little more than eight years. He came to our monastery with no mention of who his parents might be or where he had come from. It was obvious he was in need, and that at some point in his recent past had been badly beaten. We mended him, both physically and spiritually, and when he expressed an interest in becoming a healer himself he was sent to learn."

"Sent to Malaka," Thomas said. "Why there?"

"Why not? I might dislike the heathen but I recognise the skills you possess, skills we in Spain can use to our advantage. If you are fool enough to admit an enemy and train him why should we not go?"

"And Samuel was there as well?" Thomas continued to pull at one of the threads in his mind, not sure if it was attached to anything or not.

"So I understand. I did not know it at the time, but when Samuel became a physician to the palace we talked a little. It pleased me that the two had studied side by side, two Spaniards in a foreign land. They would have been a comfort to each other."

"I trained at Malaka," Thomas said, not sure why he was telling the man. "But it was a long time ago. It is a good school."

"So Ramon said." Talavera leaned closer. "I cannot believe the claims you make, Thomas Berrington. They have no connection to the man I know, who is pious and humble. He does much good work among the poor. I tried to fashion a position for him in the palace but my influence only stretches so far. And now you come here with your accusations."

"I have witnessed the result of his acts with my own eyes, and he confessed them in front of me."

Talavera straightened. An old man but with the questioning mind of a younger one. Thomas knew he was Isabel's closest spiritual advisor, never allowing her to accept easy doctrine. Despite being unbending in his devotion it was also rumoured that it was Talavera who drew the sting from the worst excesses of the Inquisition, though Thomas could barely comprehend what worse punishment could be inflicted.

"He might have..." Talavera started, stopped. He stared ahead toward a statue of Christ in agony.

All of Christianity seemed to consist of agony in one form or another, Thomas thought. He recalled the sense of otherness that had overtaken him during the wedding ceremony, that sense of something larger than himself, something gazing down, judging but not partaking in human life. Had that been God? Did He actually exist? And if so was Lubna's God simply another prophet's interpretation of the same being? Thomas didn't know if he wanted to believe or not, knew it would require proof, not simply faith. For Lubna, for Talavera and Isabel, faith was enough, more than enough. Thomas was not made that way.

"He might have what?"

Talavera shook his head, wiped a hand across his face. "He is my friend. More than a friend. Ramon is like a son to me, and a father cannot give up a son no matter what he might have done."

"Even to save more innocent lives?"

"We would sit in front of the fire on winter nights and discuss theology long after dark. A glass of wine, a little food – plain of course, nothing rich. Ramon would not accept even a hint of luxury. One of the topics we came back to again and again was how to separate those who truly believed from those who did not, those who only pretended to belief." He glanced at Thomas. "It was, you see, the Inquisition we spoke of. The Inquisition and its crude methods."

"Did Ramon approve?" Thomas was willing to allow

Talavera to tell his story, assuming it had a point. If not it was only time and he would get what he wanted eventually.

"He approved of the end but not the means. He was convinced there had to be a better way to judge a man than torture. All torture achieves is to make a man confess to something he has not done to bring it to an end. You say he – no, we talk only of the man you seek, Ramon's guilt is not proven yet – you say he has cut bodies?"

"With great skill."

"Ramon is skilled, certainly." Talavera wiped a hand across his face, his eyes seeking the suffering of Christ. For a long time Thomas thought the man would say no more, but a sense of rightness won out in the end. "He was a good child. A good man. But after he returned from Malaga something had changed in him. He had acquired a zeal that was not been present before. Oh, he was a good Christian, as good as any man I ever knew, but this was different. Bordering on... obsession."

"He came to you?"

Talavera nodded, his eyes locked on the figure of Christ, arms spread, hands and feet nailed. Thomas had heard tales of such statues bleeding. Was that what Ramon saw when he looked at such a figure, creating pain in his imagination?

"He told me he had become convinced only true Christians possess a soul," said Talavera. "That non-believers, heathens, infidels, all the great mass of misguided humanity who live beyond God's divine light do not possess a soul. That a new born baby does not possess a soul. That the act of baptism allows God's glory to flood into a body and nestle within." Talavera sighed. He had convinced himself, Thomas knew. It was the reason for what Ramon did. "He told me, over and over, that if he could find the seat of the human soul, God's gift to righteous men, then the torture, the maiming, even the burnings would come to an end."

"Why would they end?" Thomas said. "Do you expect unbelievers to convert simply to avail themselves of this mythical soul? The Inquisition's work would continue with even more zeal."

"Not if Ramon could prove who was a true believer and who was not. Inquisitors seek the truth in a man's heart. Ramon would be able to reveal that directly."

"And kill the subject as a result."

"He claimed not. He claimed once found it would be a simple matter to show whether someone possessed a soul or not."

"He is mad," Thomas said, and Talavera turned sharply.

"Mad? Do you not believe you possess a soul? Does God not inhabit your very being? He is within me every moment of every day, and will be until I draw my final breath. These places you saw the bodies, were they dark?"

"They had no windows. Without lamps, yes, they would be dark. But Ramon could not cut the bodies without light."

"No. But at the end he would extinguish them, so he could look for the spark of life as it left the body, to discover where it had lodged. Where did he cut?"

Thomas touched his chest, to the left, to the centre. "These places I have seen, but there were others, many others. As if he needed to search everywhere he could."

Talavera nodded. "We discussed the seat of the soul. Ramon was sure it lay next to the heart. I argued it resides here, in our mind," he tapped his skull, "and it is not a physical thing. How can it be when it is God's gift?"

"Where would he go?" Thomas asked. "Where would he feel safe?"

"I–"

"The Queen will want him taken."

"Yes, she will. I know she will. But it is hard, Thomas Berrington, to give up someone you love."

"Is there anyone else I can ask?"

A shake of the head. "No. Ramon knows many people, thousands, but I am the only one truly close to him. Samuel too, perhaps, but not in the same way, and they are not as close as when they were in Malaga together." Talavera rose and walked to the small altar where Thomas had stood with Lubna only days before. He knelt and crossed himself, muttered words, asking for forgiveness perhaps. More genuflections, then he rose once more and turned, spoke to a point beyond Thomas's shoulder. "He will have gone to Castillo de Triana. There will be people there who regard his ideas with sympathy. And if he truly is guilty of the crimes you accuse him of," Talavera's voice caught, "you must know Ramon does not turn aside from a task, however hard it is."

CHAPTER FORTY-ONE

Thomas did not know what to do so went to talk with Jorge, who could often offer no advice at all but the simple act of talking would clarify his thoughts. Except Jorge wasn't at the house.

"He's gone looking for Belia," said Helena. She sat cross-legged on the floor, playing with Will and seeming to enjoy the experience.

"Why, where is Belia?"

Helena looked up, a scowl on her face, and Thomas was almost relieved at the return of her usual bad temper. "That's why they've gone looking. Because she didn't come back."

"Who is they?"

"*Fa* went too."

"How long has she been missing? She might have been distracted, a patient come calling."

"Since noon, and now it's—" She frowned, shook her head, "—now it's late." Helena did not hold with too clear a notion of time. She pushed a wooden block toward Will, who scooped it up and added it to the wall of the structure he was building, and Helena smiled, a rare softness enhancing her beauty.

"Will you stay and look after Will if I go after them?" Thomas said.

"I will have to, will I not?"

"Is Lubna sleeping?"

"Upstairs. Belia gave her something before she left this morning. There is more I can give if she wakes, but she is better, much better." She looked up at him again. "There will be more children, Thomas. Lubna is strong, and she loves you."

Thomas's thoughts were still reeling at the change in Helena as he ascended the stairs and knelt beside the bed Lubna lay on. Her eyes opened and she smiled.

Thomas took her hand. "Do you want another draft of whatever it is Belia has made for you?"

Lubna shook her head. "No, I will sleep without."

"How are you?"

"I feel like a horse has galloped over me. But better than I was, and my head is clearing." A tear gathered in her left eye but refused to be released. "We will try again, Thomas, and if nothing happens then Will is more than enough."

He kissed her lips and stayed as long as he dared, but eventually duty dug its insidious claws into him and he rose and left on tiptoe. He walked fast through busy streets to where Belia's house lay, knowing he should have asked when Jorge and Olaf left, for this was where they would also come, and if Belia was not in residence the pair would have started looking elsewhere by now. But he had not asked, and it was the obvious starting point, so Thomas kept going. The door to Belia's house was closed but unlocked. No light showed inside. Still, Thomas entered and checked every room before leaving.

He stood on the edge of the square, trying to think where

Jorge and Olaf would be, but had no need to try hard because they entered the far side of the square and saw him. Jorge ran across, his normally benign features creased with concern.

"Is she back?"

Thomas shook his head. "Where have you been?"

"Everywhere. We went to the riverside and asked at all the ships drawn up, but nobody has seen her or even knew who we spoke of. The Cathedral next. I tried the house of al-Haquim but there was nobody there other than the guards and servants. I even tried the palace. Theresa came out to talk with us, but she has not seen her either. She could be lying dead or dying in some alley and we cannot help!" Jorge swayed and Thomas reached out to steady him, turned to look at Olaf, who shook his head to show he knew no more but was also worried, about Jorge as well as Belia.

"Have you questioned the houses here in the square?" Thomas asked.

"No. Should we?" Jorge moved away and Thomas reached out to stop him.

"Wait, you need to know what to ask. The hour grows late, people will be suspicious of strangers."

"We will ask have they seen her, won't we?" said Jorge.

"We also ask have they seen any strangers. Other than us, of course." Thomas caught Olaf's nod of agreement. "If we split up we can cover the houses more quickly. Olaf will go with you. He has no Spanish but his presence alone might loosen tongues."

"Who will loosen tongues for you?" asked Jorge, starting to pull away, impatient to start, and Thomas merely smiled.

He started to the left, rapping on doors and waiting, moving on if there was no answer. He was hoping one of the houses close to Belia's would know something, but he had reached the far side before he heard anything of use.

At a narrow house of three stories the door opened

almost as soon as he knocked, and he knew the inhabitants of this small part of Sevilla had been watching through their windows as strangers questioned their neighbours. The man who answered was as elongated as his house, having to duck to exit the doorway.

"We are looking for Belia Orovita, sir. I take it you know her?"

A nod.

"She has gone missing, and I would ask have you seen anything unusual today, likely early after noon."

"Only the plague carrier," said the man. "I had not heard of a death in the square, but there is death everywhere these days. He went toward Belia's house but was no doubt mistaken, for I saw her enter it myself not an hour before."

Thomas tried to quell a rising tide of panic. "Did they argue?"

"Who?"

"Belia and the plague carrier!"

"I did not see them talking, and next time I looked the man had gone, his cart too. As I said, he must have come to the wrong house."

Thomas ran to where Jorge was talking with a woman, two children clinging to her skirts.

"She saw something," said Jorge as he heard Thomas's arrival. "Belia talking to a man in grey robes."

Thomas started to speak, stopped himself. How could he tell Jorge that Belia had been taken by Ramon? It would destroy him. But how could he not tell him if they were to have any chance of rescuing her?

"You know something, don't you." Jorge stepped close until his chest was almost touching Thomas's.

Thomas forced himself to meet Jorge's glare. "He has taken her. Ramon has taken her." He spoke Arabic so as to include Olaf.

"Beyond the city walls?" said Jorge.

"Not there. Talavera told me where Ramon still has friends. He believes he has gone to Triana."

"Aai! Then she is lost to us!" Jorge gripped Thomas's arms to keep himself from collapsing.

"Not yet. I need to find Samuel, he has access and might be able to get us inside."

"Yes, Samuel, a good idea, he will help," said Jorge. "Let's go." He started across the square, and this time Thomas let him go.

"This is not good," said Olaf as they followed, his voice low, showing none of the panic Jorge had.

"No, it is not. But if she has been taken it was not long since, so there is a chance we can find her before Ramon starts his work." He started across the square after Jorge, who knocked against a man as he entered an alley, ignoring the cries of protest.

"Why take her? As some kind of punishment on you both?"

"It is possible. But he also needs a subject who is not a Christian. Belia is known to him and meets that condition. But yes, it is more likely to show us that he can take anyone he wants, at any time. He can slip between the shadows of this city like the Ghost that gave him a name."

"Then we are fortunate it was not Lubna," said Olaf. "Or Helena. Or, by all the Gods in Valhalla, Will. This Samuel will help?"

"I think so. He is a friend to Belia too."

"Like Jorge is a friend?" asked Olaf.

"No, not like Jorge, but not for want of wishing it I suspect. You two had better wait outside. Jorge they may admit, but I want you to stop him doing anything foolish. He has already lost one woman he loves to Mandana, a second might break him."

"He is stronger than he appears," said Olaf. "Which is a good thing, for he looks soft."

"Not as soft as he once was," Thomas said. "And you have been training him with the sword, as you have me."

"But he is not naturally skilled like you. Still, he shows some improvement."

At the palace Thomas was once more admitted with no more than a nod. He had sent Olaf to take Jorge to an inn near the waterfront but not allow him to drink.

A paige informed Thomas that Samuel was with the Queen so he started toward the man's modest room then stopped and turned back. He didn't know if he would be able to get close to the Queen, but if he managed to do so he could ask her help.

It was not as difficult as he imagined, and thinking back he recognised it never had been. Guards were posted at the entrances to the palace but here, in the inner sanctum with the gardens protected by high walls, only servants moved through the hallways, eyes downcast as they passed. No doubt a call would bring dozens of men, but Thomas did not expect anyone to call out at his presence. He heard voices while still two doorways from Isabel's chambers, all of them familiar. The Queen herself, Theresa, Samuel, and also the King. Good, he would be even more sympathetic.

He approached quietly, stood for a moment in full view. A discussion was going on, Samuel a part of it. Thomas was pleased to see Theresa wiping the Queen's hands with a cloth. It had taken him a long time to persuade anyone here that keeping the body clean was an aid to good health.

Before he could decipher the matter under discussion Isabel looked up, a sixth sense alerting her to his presence. She looked startled for a moment before smoothing her features. She fluttered Theresa aside, who turned as she carried the water bowl away, her eyes meeting Thomas's without surprise.

Fernando strode across the room. "You know you are banned from these chambers."

"I am aware of that, but I must speak with you both, Samuel in particular." He almost asked what their discussion had concerned, but knew it was most likely to do with household matters rather than conspiracy.

"Why should we listen to you? You are tainted. My wife wants nothing to do with you anymore." His words a show for Isabel.

Thomas tamped down a rising anger, cutting off a response before it could spill from his tongue. "Isabel is an intelligent woman, she will recognise her mistake soon. But I need assistance tonight, Fernando."

"Your grace," he said.

"Forgive me, your grace. But I need help now. Ramon has taken Belia, Jorge's friend. You met her after the wedding. I believe you were much taken with her beauty."

"The Jewess? What do you mean Ramon has taken her?"

"If you are not going to expel Thomas, my dear, bring him close so we may all hear what he has to say."

See, Thomas thought, *already rationality is driving out suspicion.*

Fernando glanced back, his eyes returning to Thomas, who saw that he had won this first small encounter. He followed the King of Aragon and Castile into the room, where Fernando took up a protective stance beside his wife.

"What is going on, Thomas, why have you invaded this place when you know you are no longer welcome?"

"A life is at stake."

"Whose?"

"Jorge's woman, Belia." He knew Isabel had spent time at the house talking with both Belia and Lubna, her curiosity continuing to be pricked at how such diverse religions might be reconciled, and what they had in common.

"She is ill? Why have you come here if the pestilence has taken her?"

"A pestilence, yes, but the pestilence of a single man." He glanced at Fernando, who knew a little more of what he spoke. "She has been taken to the Inquisitor's prison beyond the river."

"Why?"

Thomas almost laughed. Did Isabel not know there was no *why* to who was chosen? It could be no more than a whim, a wrong glance, a word spoken out of place, the whisper of a neighbour, or nothing at all that chose those who lived from those who died. There was no rationality anymore, only hate, suspicion, and retribution. Except in this instance the why was easy.

"She is taken because of me. Ramon took her to show he could. To show that no-one, and nowhere, is safe."

"What do you expect us to do?" said Isabel. "It is a matter for the Inquisitors now."

"Not Inquisitors. Ramon must know them, must have access to Triana, but he is not a part of that organisation. He has taken Belia there to kill her. To search for her soul, or lack of it. I thought..." Thomas realised he had not thought. He had come here in expectation of a miracle. That the King and Queen would tear down the walls of Castillo de Triana and free all those inside. "I thought if I could borrow the same number of soldiers we took outside the walls this morning I could find her."

"We cannot," said Isabel, her face set, all emotion held in check.

Does she want to help or not, Thomas wondered? He could not tell.

"Three dozen men, your grace. That is all I ask."

"It is not possible!" She rose and walked away, her face turned toward the window. She went onto the terrace, her body rigid with either anger or shame.

"Isabel!" Thomas called out, and saw her shoulders twitch, but her gaze remained resolutely turned away.

Fernando gripped Thomas's arm and drew him away. He could break free, they both knew he could, but to do so would change their relationship forever. Broken as it was now Thomas expected time to heal the wounds.

"Take him from here," said Fernando to Samuel. "Make sure you escort him through the gate and inform the guards he is not to be admitted again."

Samuel did not take Thomas's arm, but he had no need to. Though it seemed he did have a need to explain, or excuse the behaviour of Isabel and Fernando.

"Who rules in Gharnatah?" he asked, using the Arabic pronunciation he would have learned while training in Malaka.

"The Sultan rules," Thomas said, frowning.

"And if the Sultan decreed that Allah did not exist, that his priests on earth were powerless, what would happen?"

"He would be Sultan no more," Thomas said, beginning to see the point of the conversation.

"And in Spain the ultimate power does not reside with either of the people in there, and they know it better than anyone in this land. Their marriage was only allowed by Papal decree. They rule with the permission of a Pope in Rome who could withdraw his support at any time. He will not, because they fight for Christendom against the infidel you side with. What goes on inside the walls of Triana is done in the name of God but, more importantly, in the name of the Pope. Neither King nor Queen will defy that power."

Thomas stopped walking. "Then she is lost. By morning his work will be done and she will be dead. Cut open."

"Not yet," said Samuel. "I am allowed access." A brief smile, tinged with bitterness. "They still need someone skilled on occasion. I will try to find her, try to find Ramon and reason with him. We were close friends once, that might still count for something."

Yes, Thomas thought, *and I might have misjudged you.*

"I am sorry," he said, but Samuel only frowned, not privy to the thoughts inside Thomas's head. Which was good, he considered, for those thoughts were dark with retribution, fire, and blood.

CHAPTER FORTY-TWO

It took both Olaf and Thomas to restrain Jorge, to stop him running across the bridge to Castillo de Triana. For a moment Thomas was sure he would break free and they would have to follow unprepared, but in the end Jorge saw sense and they returned to the house beside the river. Will had been placed upstairs in bed beside Lubna, and Thomas stood in the door and watched them both without entering. Better to let them sleep so they would know nothing of what was about to happen. He closed the door and crept down the stairs on bare feet.

Olaf sat at the table cleaning his sword even though it required no cleaning. Jorge paced like one of the lions caged behind the palace of al-Hamra. He carried a sword in each hand and held one out to Thomas, who took it, slicing the air to gauge the feel.

"It's a good sword," he said.

"It should be. It's one of Daniel's," said Jorge. "See," he held his own blade out, "it has his mark. The O and D intertwined here."

Thomas lifted his own blade and saw the same mark. "Where did it come from?"

"I bought them, of course. My brother's skill with metal has spread far and wide since Fernando appointed him smith to the royal court. He continues to live in Qurtuba, but his weapons travel far and wide."

"I don't recall a blade with a finer balance," Thomas said. "It must have cost a good sum."

"I am nothing if not a rich man," said Jorge. "And would give it all up for Belia's safe return." He looked into Thomas's eyes. "Samuel should have returned by now with news."

"The castle is a big place and Ramon might be anywhere inside. We must give him more time. Besides, our business, if we have to conduct it, will benefit from being done in the small hours of the morning."

"And if she is dead by then?"

"The victims I have seen are all been killed close to dawn, in the small hours before the first rays of the sun. It is what he does, it seems, and he will not change his method now."

Olaf held a hand out and Jorge passed him his own sword before turning away, his shoulders hunched. The big general rose, swung the blade, held it out to Jorge who did not take it. "It is too light for me. I'll stick to what I know." Olaf laid the sword on the table and went back to cleaning his own blade, a heavy, triangular sword favoured by men of the north. Thomas had tried it once and could barely lift it high enough to strike a blow.

"Do we fight our way in?" asked Olaf, his tone suggesting it was the option he favoured.

"It would be impossible," Thomas said. "There are hundreds within the castle walls, at least a quarter of them soldiers. We would be cut down before we got a dozen paces.

"Not without loss on their side," said Olaf. "And the Spanish are cowards. Kill one or two and the others will flee."

"You forget they fight for their God. It is not an option we should choose, even if it is the only one left to us."

"So how do we get in?" asked Jorge. He continued to pace, unable to rest, though rest is what they all needed because Thomas had an inkling of a plan.

"We wait for Samuel to return. There is still time. And then in the dead hours of night we go, if we must, when everyone is tired and bored. We will try to look as if we belong and simply walk inside."

"And if you are challenged?" asked Olaf.

"There will be few on the outer gate at that time of night. We kill them and gain access. But only if it is necessary. Stealth will be our friend tonight, not the clash of steel."

"That is a shame," said Olaf.

Jorge stopped pacing and put his fists on the table. "We must go now. It is late enough and it will give us more time to search for her."

"If she is there I believe I know where she will be held," Thomas said. "We go directly there, free her and get out as fast as we can. With luck there will be no bloodshed, either theirs or ours."

"You make it sound as if bloodshed is a bad thing," said Olaf. "These are Spaniards. I was born to kill Spaniards."

"You were born a long way from here," Thomas reminded him.

"But I was young when I travelled south."

"Kill Spaniards tonight and Fernando will withdraw his offer of safe passage. You die too."

Olaf grinned. "But I will take many with me."

"Father," said Helena, who had sat the entire time listening without comment, and Olaf turned his head as though surprised to discover the presence of his most beautiful daughter. "Listen to Thomas. Your wife needs you. Lubna needs you, and so do I." She reached across the table and covered his knuckled hand with the elegance of her own. "Al-Andalus needs you. Thomas has prevailed in such situations before. He came to rescue me, remember. Trust him. I know it is hard for a man such as you who is more used to leading, but this matter requires subtlety."

"I can be subtle," said Olaf.

"Yes. Subtle enough to decide whether to strike at a man's head or belly. Listen to Thomas. Follow him, if only for tonight. Listen to him for the sake of Belia and Jorge and the rest of us who want to see you all return alive." Helena's eyes flickered toward Thomas, and he saw something in them he had never done before, not even when she had shared his bed, and it worried him, but he dismissed the idea as being brought on by the strain of the night.

"When?" Olaf said, turning to Thomas.

"Two or three hours yet. We should try to sleep."

"Sleep?" Jorge's voice rose. "How can we sleep?"

"Yes," said Olaf, "sleep is good before battle. It stills the mind."

"I cannot sleep!" Jorge started for the terrace, stopped, looked at the door as if planning to leave immediately.

Helena rose and brought a jug of wine and four cups to the table. She poured for each of them and Thomas watched her drop something into one of the cups. When he looked up, catching her eye, she offered a faint smile and passed the cups around, ensuring Jorge was handed the one she had drugged.

Olaf drained his in a single gulp. Thomas sipped. Jorge looked at the cup as if it was something foreign, a tremble in the hand holding it.

"Fill them again," Thomas said, holding his cup out. Once Helena had done so he held the cup in the air. "To our endeavours this night! May success walk with us." He knocked his cup against Helena's and Olaf's, waited for Jorge to come to the table, which in the end he did, dragging his feet like a chastised boy. He returned the salutation and when Thomas raised the wine to his mouth Jorge did the same.

"How much?" Thomas asked of Helena a while later as Jorge lay with his head on the table, a glisten of drool hanging from the corner of his mouth.

"He will wake in time, and with a clear head," she said. "It is the residue of what Belia prepared for Lubna." She walked to the terrace and leaned on the rail. The ships were quiet, swinging lamps the only movement. After a while Thomas rose and joined her.

"If we do not return—"

Helena put her hand on his chest, stopping him. "You will return."

"If we do not you are to take Lubna and Will home."

Helena shook her head, ice-white hair exposing and masking her face in turn. The scar she had once used the hair to hide was barely visible anymore. "Do not talk of it, for it cannot happen. You are Thomas Berrington. Death is your friend. He will not take you yet, it is not your time."

"None of us know when is our time."

"Tonight is not yours. I know it." Helena took a step, and before Thomas was aware of what was happening her lips were against his and he cursed his body's reaction. She could still affect him even as he saw the mischief in her. A mischief that had been lacking of late.

He put his hands on her waist and pushed her away, saw a smile of satisfaction to know she had sparked confusion in his mind. Thomas released her as if her body burned. Then he dropped over the railing to the riverside below and began to run toward the palace, one more task to complete before Jorge woke and the rest of tonight's work could begin.

On the Barcas bridge they passed two carts of plague victims on their way to the lime pits, but neither cart master so much as glanced in their direction, three men dressed for battle, heavily armed, leather jerkins protecting their torsos. Olaf had pulled on a helmet which barely fitted, his eyes blazing like coals from a brazier. The planks of the bridge shook under their heels and Thomas feared the sound was loud enough to wake the entire population of Castillo de Triana. He glanced toward Jorge, whose face was as set as Olaf's.

Jorge had woken as Helena promised, clear headed and calm. Not his usual self, for that would only come with the freeing of Belia, but controllable. Olaf might be a different matter. The big general revelled in mayhem, and their work tonight required more subtle endeavours.

A single guard dozed at the main gate, there for show rather than vigilance, for people avoided this place unless they worked within. The man sat up, then rose at their approach. His eyes took on a wary look as he saw their manner of dress, and he stepped to block their way.

"You gentlemen appear to be lost. The whorehouse is that way, but it will be closed at this time of night."

Thomas saw Olaf tense, and stepped forward, fumbling into his pocket for what he had gone to Samuel's room to fetch. It had taken some time to find it, but eventually he discovered the small bottle of liquor hidden in a compartment beneath a loose floorboard. Now he emptied a little onto a muslin cloth and stepped close to the man as he started to draw his sword.

"There is no need for violence," Thomas said, and held the cloth to the man's face. He gripped him with his other arm until the body slackened.

"I must get some of that," said Olaf.

"Find somewhere to hide him. He'll sleep an hour at least. There has been enough killing done."

Thomas handed him his burden then entered the outer corridor. He waited, listening, but the only sounds were distant and came from prisoners moaning or crying out.

"Where?" said Jorge.

Thomas pointed rather than speaking, and put a finger to his lips to remind the others, before leading the way deep into the heart of the enemy stronghold.

The cries of the prisoners grew louder as they descended to the lower level, the stink of the river tainting the air here. Locked doors appeared to either side and they split up, each looking inside before moving on. Chains rattled as those held within tried to reason, believing them their captors.

"How many rooms are there?" asked Jorge, glancing into the next and moving on.

"No more than three score."

"And all these will die?" said Olaf with a scowl.

"Not all. Some will be released, though not unharmed. Their bodies will be broken, sometimes beyond repair. And then–" He stopped as a lone gaoler turned the corner ahead of them, tying the cord at the waist of his trousers. He came to a halt, then turned to flee.

Olaf sprinted, faster than a big man had any right to. He caught the gaoler just as he started to call out and grasped his head. Thomas expected to hear a snap, but then he saw Olaf was waiting. He crossed the distance and used the liquor again.

"I am surprised we have not seen more," he said as Olaf dragged the man away.

"They do not expect casual visitors at this time of night."

"Which is good for us. I think we need to look along the way he came from, in case there are others."

Thomas nodded.

They discovered Belia crouched on the floor of a chamber no more than fifty paces away. It was not the place Mandana had shown Thomas all those weeks before. Not the killing room. The door was locked, but Thomas allowed Jorge to pick the lock, knowing he was the more skilled of them.

Belia looked up from where she was crouched in a corner, her arms wrapped tight around, as though if she could make herself small enough her captors would not be able to see her. Jorge went to his knees and clutched her to his chest, stroking the hair from her face, whispering words meant only for the two of them.

"That was disappointingly easy," said Olaf, and Thomas cuffed him on the back of the head, ducking as the big man tried to return the compliment before asking, "Do we go out the way we came in?"

"If we can. But I've a mind to wait around and see if Ramon is somewhere here. If Belia was his first victim he may have gone in search of the second." He glanced at Belia. There were questions he wanted to ask but even he knew now was not the time. And he knew the safety of his companions overrode his wish to capture Ramon.

"With luck we will meet a dozen men. A dozen would be a good number, don't you think?"

"I would prefer none. Now be quiet." Thomas checked that Jorge and Belia were ready, then started forward.

They were a third of the way to freedom when they came to a crossing of corridors running in four directions. Thomas knew they should take the left-hand turn, but there was something wrong. Not wrong, not exactly, but there was something different that had not been there when they came this way before. He heard a voice, rational but arguing with itself. It came from the opposite direction, and he wanted to follow its siren call.

He glanced at the others, made a decision.

"Go, you know the way. There is something I must do here."

"We do not leave you," said Olaf.

"I will be right behind. I brought us in, I can find my way out. Take Belia as fast as you can and trust me to follow."

Olaf hesitated, then nodded. If Thomas insisted on this madness it made sense the rest of them should not also put themselves in danger. Olaf took one of Belia's arms and moved away fast, dragging her between him and Jorge as they disappeared around a turn.

Thomas stood, listening as the voice gathered in pace, slackened. He knew exactly what it was, and who spoke the words. Friar Ramon Braso had started his work.

CHAPTER FORTY-THREE

"No, no, wrong... it must be here... or here... this has to be the one, a true convert, but does that mean his soul is as strong as a child born into Christ? Does not our saviour say a man brought to God is better than one who has always known God? He does, yes, I am sure he does... so where is it? Not here, not here at all. I need... I need a better subject, one I can be sure of. The Archdeacon, yes, he should have been the one and was not. He was weak, like all men... yes, yes, like all men..."

Thomas peered around an open doorway into a small chamber. A lamp hung from a chain, swinging gently. Ramon stood beside a table where a single body lay stripped and tied down. Only one body, which offered a clue to how Ramon undertook his task. Was this man a Christian then, with Belia being kept for later? And this the way each pair of deaths occurred – one body dissected while the other was kept apart? It made sense, for the second victim would cry out, would scream at the fate awaiting them. Only when he was finished with this subject would Ramon go for Belia.

When the man tied to the table rolled his head and

opened his eyes Thomas almost cried out, and then when a figure moved in a shadowed corner he could not help himself. From the darkness where he had been hidden Samuel stepped out, a finger held to his lips. Ramon's back was to him, his concentration focused entirely on the man he was killing.

Some sense made Ramon glance up, not toward Thomas but to where Samuel had taken another step, a dozen feet still separating them. His hand snapped up, a glitter of lamp-light against the blade.

"Why did you bring him here?"

Samuel moved more quickly, stopping suddenly as Ramon slashed at him. While he was distracted Thomas moved fast, throwing his arms around Ramon, twisting his wrist so the blade clattered to the floor. Then Samuel was there, a linen rag in his hand, and the acrid stink of Thomas's liquor filled the air as he pressed it across Ramon's face. Within moments Ramon's body passed from rigid to slack. Thomas waited a moment then released his grip, letting the man fall to crack his head on the stone floor. Samuel stepped close and kicked Ramon in the face, over and over until Thomas pulled him away.

"What are you doing? You will kill him."

"No more than he deserves. I came looking for Belia. I haven't found her yet, but I did find him." He glanced at the figure lying on the table, who had gone still.

Thomas leaned over and placed a hand on the blood-slicked chest, but whatever life the man had clung hard to was gone. For a moment he studied the cuts, seeing that Ramon had started to look in a fresh location.

"Jorge has Belia," Thomas said. "With luck they will be outside the castle by now." A quick glance to Ramon, but he remained comatose, blood dripping from a ruined nose. "What do we do with him now?"

"If it was up to me we would kill him here," said Samuel. "But it is not. We will hand him over to the Hermandos."

Thomas looked around, found what he had hoped was there. The heavy wooden door had a key inserted on the inside and he went to retrieve it.

"Or we lock him in here with his handiwork and bring them to him. There can be no doubt of his guilt then."

"What if he takes his own life?" said Samuel. "He will wake sooner or later and realise he is trapped." He stared at Ramon. "He was my friend once. A good friend. Loyal. Brave. I would not have him commit such a sin."

Thomas shook his head, failing to understand Samuel. A moment before he had been ready to kick Ramon into oblivion, now he was worried about his soul. He took the blade Ramon had dropped and cut through the knots tying his solitary victim to the table. He rolled Ramon onto his front and tied his hands behind him, lifted his feet and tied them too, then drew a rope between them so he would be unable to stand. He glanced up at Samuel to find him staring at him.

"Satisfied? Good enough?"

Samuel offered a nod.

"Then let's lock him in and leave this place before we are found."

"What has happened to Belia?" asked Samuel.

"I told you, we found her. She'll be beyond the bridge by now, safe."

"Not safe. None of you are safe. Not even me anymore. I went to Mandana. He is the only man who could set her free, and I pled her case. He made me argue. It was not easy, but the argument was a ploy. Had he given in too easily he knew I would have been suspicious"

"Who is the man on the table?"

"I know not. Some unfortunate."

"Mandana wants me dead," Thomas said. "Jorge too for

341

what we did against him all those years ago. That is why he would not help you, knowing we would mount some foolish raid to save her."

Samuel finally moved, dropping the linen cloth to the floor and striding to the door. He swung it hard in anger, and Thomas placed his hand against it to prevent himself being locked in as well.

"Take care!"

Samuel shook his head, as if his mind had been elsewhere. "I am sorry. I wanted to ensure he could not escape. I apologise."

Thomas stepped through the door then allowed Samuel to close and lock it. He held his hand out for the key, but Samuel smiled and slid it into a pocket of his robe. "Would you allow me to take a little credit for my work this night, Thomas? Or do you want it all for yourself?"

Thomas had no care if the man wanted to garner the honours. "How did you find him?"

"The same way I suspect you did," Samuel said as they started along the corridor. He smiled. "Ramon always maintained a commentary as he worked, for as long as I have known him. At one time the physicians in Malaga would come to watch him, to listen and learn. He made sense then."

"You showed bravery to come here." And then, because the question had to be asked. "Mandana and al-Haquim, the plotting you were part of, were you convinced of the rightness of their cause?"

"I believe they wanted to stop the Inquisition. Or if not stop it then change the direction. But now I am convinced I was lied to. As was al-Haquim. I half believe Mandana might have encouraged Ramon, for he knew the man, I think I even introduced them over a year ago."

"It would not surprise me," Thomas said. "Mandana is as mad as he has always been."

"Mad? You think me mad?"

Thomas stopped abruptly. He had been too involved in their conversation, searching for more truth, as if truth might make a difference. He knew he should have learned better long since.

When he raised his head Abbot Mandana stood in the corridor, more than a dozen armed men blocking their route to escape. An escape that was so close. Beyond, Thomas could see the heavy wooden gate, the first misted grey light of dawn washing across the road behind.

Mandana glanced at Samuel. "I will make it quick for you." Turned toward Thomas. "As for you…"

Thomas spat on the ground between them.

"As I would expect." He looked past Thomas. "What did you do with Ramon? He is dead, I assume?"

"Living when I left him, but there is always hope."

"Except for you." Mandana turned aside and spoke to one of the soldiers. "Take another man and go fetch him. You know the chamber he works in."

The soldier nodded to another and they trotted along the corridor without even a glance at Thomas.

Only thirteen men now, Thomas thought, as if it might make a difference. Thirteen men plus Mandana, a man who could never be underestimated.

"How many?" Thomas said. "How many has he taken at your command, how many has he killed in his fruitless search?"

Mandana lifted a shoulder, as if it was no matter to him. "Not at my command, Berrington. He was a zealot. I admit he came to me thinking I might sympathise with his aims, and perhaps I did, but you can never trust a madman."

"As you would well know." Thomas slipped the long blade Ramon had been using into Samuel's hand.

Then he drew his own sword and kept it loose at his side,

letting his body and mind still, shedding all thought. The odds were poor, but he had fought worse odds in the past and come out the victor.

Thomas took a step forward, saw a flicker of something in Mandana's eyes, but what he could not tell. Amusement, perhaps. "You care not for man or God or anyone but yourself and your own insane ideas. Fernando knows not what he has allowed back into the nest."

"Oh, he knows full well what he has done," said Mandana.

Thomas looked beyond the men to the gate, a hunger for freedom threatening to distract him from what must be done, and saw something that gave him hope. Emerging from the mist that had risen from the river stepped a man, tall and broad of shoulder. In one hand he carried a heavy axe, in the other a sword.

"I wish you had not come here," said Mandana, "for now I am uncertain what to do with you." He stepped to one side where a passage offered some protection. "Do not allow them to leave," he said to his men. "If he tries you can kill him if you must, but I would rather him captured." He glanced at Thomas, his expression cold.

From the edge of his vision Thomas saw Samuel fall back, take a pace and then another, distancing himself as he slid into a narrow corridor. Mandana made no move to stop him, knowing Samuel had nowhere to go. The only exit from Triana lay ahead.

Thomas forgot him almost at once. There was nothing to be done if the man was a coward, nothing at all, and he had a fight to win. He rolled his shoulders, raised his sword and took a step toward the men in the front rank. Beyond he saw Olaf approach from the rear and held up a hand to stop him. The liquor would do him no good here, but talk might. He was tired of killing.

"Look behind you," he said. "Look and see that I am not

alone. Look and see the nature of the man opposing you." He saw some of the men turn their heads and knew the sight of Olaf would weaken their knees. "Mandana told you not to kill me. Well, I would prefer that as well, but not if it means I cannot walk out of this place now." He took a step, another. "We can fight, or you can pretend I used some trick to make my escape." Another glance across faces which no longer showed certainty. Thomas held his arms out to his sides, moving slowly along the front rank of men, expecting an attack but still nothing came, and he knew that was Olaf's doing.

Thomas was half way to freedom when a man on the left made a move. He raised his sword and ran at Thomas, but too slow. Olaf took him with a vicious blow that almost severed his head. Thomas tensed, waiting for the others to attack, but they only looked at their fallen comrade and then away. Thomas made a motion with his fingers. Go. And they did, slowly at first then all at once together.

Thomas shook his head and turned to look into the dim tunnel where Samuel had disappeared. Was he still working with Mandana? Had they escaped together to continue plotting against the King and Queen? Was that what Mandana had meant all that time ago at their first meeting, when he said Samuel was his spy in the palace?

He wanted to pursue them both, extract a justice of some kind even if it meant the justice a sword brought. But Olaf tapped him on the shoulder, a tap that would have felled most men.

"Come on, let's get out of here before the bastards come back with reinforcements."

CHAPTER FORTY-FOUR

"Finish it now" said Olaf as he crossed the Barcas bridge beside Thomas. "Leave him alive and he will come for you again."

"He came for Martin, not me," Thomas said.

"No, he came for you. That man wanted you dead back there, whatever he said." Olaf glanced at Thomas, the bridge swaying beneath the weight of him. "And if I had not come you would be lying in a pool of your own blood. Oh, you would have taken several with you, but one man against a dozen? Not even you could have prevailed, and I know how fast and skilled you are."

"Not even me?" Thomas smiled. "And you?"

"Oh, of course I would have killed them all, with or without your help."

"I'm sure you would."

As they emerged from the bridge onto the dockside Thomas slowed, thinking of what Olaf has said, not sure if Mandana did want him dead. He looked north, but Jorge's house was hidden beyond the curve of the city wall, and he knew it was not where he was headed, not yet.

"You can go back to the house," he said.

"Not if you intend to do what I think," said Olaf. "What if you meet another dozen soldiers?"

"This is not your battle."

"You are married to my daughter. Of course this is my battle."

Thomas knew it was pointless arguing with Olaf so led the way into the city, following streets grown familiar, until they stood outside al-Haquim's house. The double door was thrown wide and the expected guard was not to be seen.

"Have they fled?" asked Olaf.

"Why would they? Mandana is not afraid of me."

"Perhaps he should be."

Thomas stepped into the courtyard. When he turned toward the inner rooms he saw why the guard was not at the gate. He sprawled half in the small pool, his head beneath the surface, the water coloured with blood.

"He's tying up loose ends," Thomas said, ignoring the dead man and going to the courtyard where Mandana, al-Haquim and Samuel spent their time. He expected to find it empty, to find the entire house empty of anyone still alive, and in that last he was correct.

Al-Haquim reclined on gilded cushions. A low table held a plate of the small cakes that were too sweet, and a pot of coffee. When Thomas touched the pot it was still hot. Al-Haquim too was warm to the touch, but all life had fled. Thomas knelt and examined his wounds. One to the throat, deep, exposing cartilage and muscle, several more to his chest and flanks, but they had come after the killing strike. He reached out and closed the man's eyes, rose slowly, suddenly tired. Tired of death. Tired of intrigue. Wondering what secrets al-Haquim had held that meant he could not continue living. Thomas had detested the man, found nothing of humanity within him, but men could change however little chance there appeared they would do so.

He looked around but al-Haquim was the only occupant. Even so Thomas prowled the rooms in search of Samuel, expecting to discover his body too.

"We should go before someone else comes and thinks we did this," said Olaf.

Thomas nodded, distracted. Did Mandana believe himself so above the law he could kill at will?

"Yes, we should go." He glanced at Olaf, glad the man had insisted on coming even if he had not been needed. "You to Jorge's house and me to the palace. You should prepare some carts and pack trunks for leaving as soon as possible."

Olaf nodded, knowing the reason. If Mandana had done this, had ordered them killed in Triana, there would be nowhere safe in Ixbilya for either of them, nor their friends.

"No," said Isabel. "I forbid you to leave."

Thomas bit back a retort before it could escape his lips. Only days before this woman had banned him from her presence and now, when he requested to be allowed to go, she was denying him that, too. Exactly what *did* she want? Isabel was pale, dark shadows beneath her eyes, and Thomas felt a moment's guilt at not attending her more closely. He wondered if he should find Samuel and ask him to examine the Queen.

He turned to Fernando. "I need to talk with you about Mandana." He glanced toward the door. "We could walk the garden together."

Fernando shook his head. "You are obsessed with that man. He has changed, I tell you."

"We cannot discuss him here," Thomas said, aware of

Isabel's presence. There was news to impart to Fernando but he did not want his wife to hear it. She was still delicate and he would protect her from what must be done. A glance at Isabel and Thomas started for the door, made his way to the terrace where stacked arches were constructed of small clay bricks. The early morning sun still lay below the surrounding walls, but its rays caught the upper balconies and painted them red. In the distance a man sat on a stone bench, turned away as if in contemplation of the beauty of the trees.

Fernando was a long time arriving but eventually he came, as Thomas knew he would.

"She wanted to come too," he said, stopping beside Thomas, a scowl on his face. "She was insistent, and I had to be so in return. This had best be important."

"Mandana tried to kill me this morning."

Fernando turned to him. "He…" He stopped, frowning. He glanced away toward the lone figure still sitting on the bench and Thomas all at once knew who the man was.

"He came to you, didn't he? What was his excuse?" And then Thomas saw it. "He told you I was dead and wanted to break the news. What was his reason?"

"He told me you lived," said Fernando. "And that the attack on you was not of his doing."

"Al-Haquim is dead," Thomas said.

"Who is al-Haquim?"

"The Governor of Ronda." And when Fernando frowned. "The ex-Governor of Ronda."

"Ah, the old Jew. He had many years."

"He was murdered. By Mandana." Thomas nodded at the still figure.

"Impossible. Mandana came here directly from Triana. He had me woken so he could bring the news without delay. He told me you had captured the killer, this Ghost, is that what they call him? That you had captured and lost him."

"Lost him? He was not lost when last I saw him."

"Did you really take that Moorish General into Triana, Thomas? What did you think you were trying to achieve? All he knows is how to kill."

"Then it was lucky I took him, wasn't it."

Fernando sighed and washed a hand across his face. "I am in a sour mood. Too little sleep and too much incident. Sometimes I think life would be easier if I had never known you, God help me." He crossed himself, as his wife frequently did, but for him it was a gesture with little meaning. "Mandana wants to talk to you, to explain what you think you saw."

"I didn't *think* I saw anything, I d*id* see it. He wanted me captured. If Olaf had not been there I would be locked in a dungeon and you and Isabel would never know what happened to me."

"If you were that might make my life simpler." Fernando waved a hand. "No, I didn't mean that, forgive me." He glanced up, his eyes on the distant figure. "He wants to talk to you. Alone. The two of you, without my presence. For which, to be honest, I am glad."

"We have nothing to talk of."

"Then I must take his word for everything that has happened. You know the big Swede must leave today, and all those who came with him. I would send you away too, but Isabel insists she needs you."

"Samuel is a good physician."

"I believe it if you tell me, but she wants you with us. Samuel will come as insurance, but what insurance you need is beyond me for you appear to be impossible to kill." He punched Thomas on the shoulder. "Now go talk with Mandana, then tell your friends to leave the city. If they are discovered here beyond sunset I will send the Inquisition for them, sins or not."

The sun had reached the corner of the garden by the time Thomas reached the bench. Mandana did not look up, but he did pat the stone beside him. Thomas looked at the hand, old, mottled, and wondered how many more days the man had left to him. He chose not to sit.

"You have caused me a great deal of trouble, Thomas Berrington," Mandana said. "And a considerable loss of income."

"How much was Muhammed going to pay you for Martin's head?"

"His heart, actually. As proof of the deed."

"How would he know it was Martin's heart?"

"He must trust me."

Thomas laughed. He closed his eyes and turned his face up to the sun, orange light flooding his senses before he turned away and looked at Mandana.

"A scarce few hours since you would have seen me tossed to the Inquisition or worse? Was it you killed al-Haquim?"

Mandana turned sharply. "Abraham is dead?"

"Murdered. His guard and most likely that boy who shared his bed, too."

"It is a shame. We had work unfinished. You had help to escape, I assume. The big man?"

"Yes, the big man."

"I would have preferred it had he not killed one of my men. Keeping the deaths quiet will cause me aggravation."

"Why would you want it kept quiet?"

"Because if I tell Fernando that giant killed one of his

soldiers he might take your heads, and I do not want to see that happen."

"I thought that is exactly what you would want," Thomas said. "Besides, it appears Fernando knows what happened."

Mandana shook his head as if disappointed in one of his monks. "I bear you no ill will, Thomas Berrington, not anymore. Once, perhaps. For this." He held up the stump of his left arm. The sleeve of his robe fell back to reveal red flesh pitted with weeping sores.

Thomas stared at it for a long moment before saying anything, and when he did the words came hard. "You are in danger of losing more than a hand without treatment."

"It aches, nothing more. Samuel has done what he can, he says. Ointments and oils and washing. As if washing helped anything, but I do as he asks because I have work unfinished."

"Can I?" Thomas reached out a hand but waited.

"You can do better, I suppose," said Mandana, the smile on his lips almost hidden beneath his beard.

"Better than Samuel, certainly."

"Look then, if it pleases you."

Thomas cupped the stump. The skin was warm, damp with perspiration. He squeezed once, watched as Mandana winced.

"It pains you."

"I told you, a little, no more."

"There is infection."

"Can you do anything for that? I think not. Samuel says it must be suffered. The body will heal itself... or not."

"I know someone who makes better salves than Samuel." He released the stump and looked into Mandana's eyes. "But why should I help you?"

"And why should I trust you?" Mandana sighed and covered his arm, held it across his chest as if the examination had seated a hurt deep in the bone. "We have a history, do we not? But it is old history. Three years is a long time to hold hatred close, and I have let mine go. You should do the same. What is the alternative, if you refuse to help me?"

"I am not refusing to help. Neither am I offering it. But you may be right about it being time to let what lies between us go. If you can be trusted. And the alternative if you ignore the infection will be to remove your arm at the elbow. Higher if you continue to pretend it is nothing. And removing it is not without its own dangers."

Mandana reached awkwardly across himself and patted the bench with his right hand.

"Sit, Thomas. I am getting an ache in my neck staring up at you."

"Why should I believe your words? I have heard other things you have said, harsh words."

"Sometimes what a man says is meant only for the audience he speaks to. Like the words I spoke with Abraham. But there are other words in a man's heart that hold the truth. Believe me when I say I am a changed man. I do not plot against the King and Queen, but for them against this Inquisition which threatens to tear Spain apart." He sighed. "Yes, I hated you, but I have seen how they both admire you, and I see how you protect them. Isabel from what ails her. Fernando from his own ignorance. You and I share a common ambition."

"No." Thomas shook his head, remaining on his feet. "Your ambition is the destruction of al-Andalus."

"The destruction of the Moorish caliphate, not the land. That fool Boabdil is no leader. You cannot put your trust in him."

"There are others," Thomas said.

"If you mean the Sultan and his brother, they are old men tainted by their own corruption. Spain could wait for al-

Andalus to fall apart on its own, which it will, but that would take time, and Isabel and Fernando want see Spain reunited in their lifetimes."

"So we do not share the same ambition, for I would see al-Andalus continue."

"Al-Andalus is a land, not a ruler, surely you can see that. The land will remain. Man cannot tear down the mountains nor block the mighty rivers. Under Spain al-Andalus will thrive. Under a different God, that is all."

"And the people?"

"If the people bend the knee to Spain they will be accepted, can remain in their homes and farm their lands."

Thomas walked away, needing space to think. Mandana's argument carried a logic he had not heard from the man before, and it worried him because he was tempted to believe he had changed. And yet... past experience would indicate otherwise, that Mandana was evil to the core. But men did change. Thomas was aware he had changed himself, was not as rigid as he had once been, and he thanked Lubna for that, for unlocking the chains he had wrapped around his heart. What might have changed Mandana? What chains did he carry? He turned back, stared at the man on the bench, saw him for what he was - old and sick. Yes, such things could change a man.

"What were you plotting in that house?" Thomas said.

"Not plotting. Protecting." He patted the bench again, the same awkward gesture, and this time Thomas walked to it and sat. "This man you pursue," a smile, "this Ghost. Can you accept a truth if I tell it?" He waited until Thomas offered a brief nod. "Good. That truth is Abraham knew him and believed in his madness, that the human soul can be uncovered, displayed for all to see."

"Samuel too?" Though Thomas was not sure whether to believe the words yet.

"No, not Samuel. At least I do not think so. Though it was Samuel who introduced the two of them to each other. Abraham was more circumspect with him, but I think he believed I would share his obsession."

Thomas leaned forward, arms across his knees. It would explain why al-Haquim lay dead. Ramon had gone back for him after his escape from Triana. He was removing anyone who could betray him. Did that put Samuel in danger as well?

"We left Ramon unconscious and locked in a dungeon. Was it you who freed him?"

"Why would I do such a thing?"

"You knew where he worked, you showed me that chamber yourself. Is this no more than a twisted tale you are spinning me? Is it you who is behind what Ramon does? It is convenient al-Haquim is dead and cannot defend himself."

"The guards in Triana know Ramon," said Mandana. "He is familiar to them all. One of them will have heard his cries. They would have no reason to keep him captive."

"Do they know what he does?"

"They believe he does God's work, as they believe all who work within those walls do. Abraham was a bitter man. Some of that was your doing, he told me. He wanted you killed when he knew you were in Sevilla and I told him you were to be left unharmed, but I believe he talked with Ramon about you."

"I still don't see it. Al-Haquim had too much to lose."

"No, you are wrong. He had much to gain if Ramon's mad theories were right. Suppose he *is* right, Thomas? That a man's soul can be uncovered and proven? Abraham wanted it to be the truth because then, he was convinced, Jews could be seen to possess a soul as well as Moors, everyone in the world, and this madness would cease."

"It is not religion that drives it," Thomas said.

"Perhaps not. But it would be a strong argument, would it not?"

Thomas straightened, shook his head. "Except Ramon is mad. I have cut into bodies more than anyone, bodies both living and dead, and if the soul nestled some place within, however obscure, I would have found it by now. If man possesses a soul it is not physical."

"I would agree, for is that not what the Bible tells us? But Abraham was not a reader of the Bible."

"He always looked for the simple solution, the one that meant less effort for him, and it got him killed in the end. Ramon went there and cut the ties that bound them together. He is out there now, a free man. A free madman killing whatever friends he had." Thomas stared into space as connections formed. He stood, started away walking. When Mandana called after him he came to a halt and turned back. "If Ramon is killing his friends, does he regard you as one?"

Mandana shook his head. "I never met him."

"But Samuel did," Thomas said. "According to him they were the best of friends. And then there is Talavera – a man who claims to be like a father to him."

CHAPTER FORTY-FIVE

Thomas was uneasy as he walked through the streets from the palace to Jorge's house, his route too easy to predict. But if Ramon had laid a trap for him it was not to be sprung today. He had found Samuel and warned him to take care, then left a message to be passed to Talavera, but whether the priest would take any notice was a question Thomas could not answer.

At the house two carts were drawn up outside, four mules tethered between the harnesses, and Olaf was carrying trunks and bundles of clothing to stack in the back. He stopped when he saw Thomas and stretched, showing the first sign of weakness Thomas had ever seen.

"Are you sure Lubna is well enough to travel?" asked Olaf.

"She heals fast, and Belia will be with you as well as Helena. They will ensure nothing ill befalls her. As will you."

"And you cannot come with us?" Olaf looked around at the now busy street. "Come away with us, Thomas, leave this place of evil and return to where you belong."

Thomas smiled. "If only I could, but I must keep in good favour with the Queen. We will need her before long, all of us. That man is not yet caught and events have changed. I think he has passed some tipping point and I expect more deaths."

"Forget him. What he does here is not your business. Do what you have to and stay within the palace walls where you are safe. Ignore everything else. For my daughter, Thomas, and my grandson. Stay alive and come back to them."

"I am not dead yet."

"No, you are a hard man to kill, I will give you that." He turned as Jorge came from the house, staggering beneath the weight of a trunk. Will followed behind with a small box of little weight, but he copied Jorge's effort.

"I told you I would bring that," said Olaf. "It is too heavy for you."

"It is mine," said Jorge, as if that was explanation enough. He glanced at Thomas. "You are staying, I take it?"

"She wants my decision tonight."

"But you have already made it, haven't you?"

Olaf went inside to fetch more supplies. Helena came and stood in the doorway, one hand on the stone. She watched Thomas and Jorge without expression.

"I'm thinking it over."

"Damn you, Thomas Berrington. I want to leave with Belia, but you know I cannot if you insist on this foolishness."

"Go. I don't need you." He saw the words hurt Jorge but did not attempt to soften them, even though he would have welcomed the man at his side. There was something about the two of them together that added to more than the natural sum, but he couldn't allow Jorge to abandon Belia, and he wanted him beside Lubna and Will on the journey, almost trusting him more than Olaf.

"You must leave by the San Roque gate," he said. "It will take you an hour longer, but better than crossing the river and passing Triana. Bear a little south once you're beyond the city wall. There is a tributary, but you can wade it if you can't find a bridge. There is one, somewhere, we crossed it when I arrived." The thought of coming into the city seemed strange to Thomas, as if the memory belonged to someone else, no more than a tale overheard.

"You will come with us that far, won't you?" said Olaf. "Unless you have something more important than your friends and your wife?"

"I… no, nothing more important. But I must be back by nightfall."

"If she decides she doesn't want you, catch us up, we will not be going fast, not with all of this to carry. Helena has purchased many clothes in the Spanish fashion. She says they will prove useful."

"Not for many years, I hope," Thomas said.

"We shall see. Come in, we are about to share a meal before leaving. Lubna was asking where you were."

"How is Belia? Is there any permanent damage, do you know?"

"You ask me? I take it you are *not* going to eat with us, then?"

"I have something to do. I'll be back before you leave."

"At least go to see Lubna," said Olaf, his tone cold. "Your *wife*, Lubna, in case it has slipped your mind."

"I will–" Thomas was about to make another excuse, but knew it would be one too far even for himself to accept. He nodded and walked inside, his arm brushing Helena, who refused to move out of the way.

In the wide ground floor room the scent of fine spices filled the air. Belia was at the fire and Thomas went to her first, touched her shoulder so she started before recognising him.

"Sorry, I didn't think," he said.

A smile. "It is all right. It will take time, but I know these things I feel now will fade eventually. You are staying to eat, aren't you?"

Thomas shook his head. "I wanted to know how you were."

"I am well." Her eyes flickered away from his.

"Did they…" He sighed, wondering why this could be so hard when he had had the same conversation a thousand times before. "Did they hurt you?"

"Yes."

"Badly?"

"Yes."

"When you feel up to it, and she too, you must ask Lubna to examine you."

"She has already done so, and applied some salve. She says I am bruised, and there is some bleeding, but it will pass. It is not my body that will remember what they did."

"And Jorge?"

She touched Thomas's face with the palm of her hand, smiled. "Jorge loves me still. Did you think he might not?"

"No, not for a moment."

Belia lifted on her toes and kissed Thomas on the cheek. "Join us soon. He is not complete without you, nor you without him."

Thomas nodded and turned to find Jorge staring at them.

"If you have quite finished kissing my woman, you have your own trying to descend the stairs."

Thomas moved quickly, catching Lubna at the top step as she tried to decide on the best approach. He avoided her having to make a decision by scooping her up and descending with her giggling against his chest. He carried her all the way into the big room and set her on her preferred cushions, kneeling beside her.

"You are not coming, are you," she said.

"I cannot. Not yet."

She touched his face. "I understand. You must do what you have to. Catch this man and finish it for good."

"The Queen demands my presence," Thomas said.

"Then use that as your excuse. I will wait for you in our home, and by the time you return my body will be healed and we can try again." She leaned her forehead against his. "I await that day with much impatience, for I am feeling stronger every day, and I miss your touch on me."

"As do I."

"Really? You like touching me? Where?"

Thomas kissed her and rose to help the others.

Thomas sat on the edge of the lead cart beside Lubna, her hand in his. Olaf urged the mules through crowds which had thickened. Jorge sat on the cart behind with Belia beside him. Helena, as scented and perfect as ever, sat with Will on her lap, the two of them talking softly together, the sight of them stirring something both tender and worrying within Thomas.

He sat beside Olaf, his eyes scanning every face that came toward them, but Ramon was not among them. No doubt he would be selecting his next set of victims after being interrupted.

Eventually the San Roque gate appeared and they passed through to a near empty roadway that snaked away northeast. Thomas was tempted to stay where he was on the cart but knew such a dream impossible. When the carts reached a ford across the river Guadaria he touched Lubna's cheek and jumped to the ground, his feet sinking into mud hidden by long grass. He moved to a higher tump and watched as the carts rocked through the crossing, waiting as they climbed the shallow slope beyond. Only when he could see them no more did he turn and re-enter the city.

Noon had come and gone, but sunset was several hours away yet, and Thomas wanted to walk the streets in search of Friar Ramon Braso. Not that he expected to stumble across him. Sevilla was a large city and the crowds were dense that afternoon, the stink of them tainting the air. The only respite came when a plague cart trundled along causing everyone to draw back into side streets.

There were more carts now, and had been for several days. The plague had peaked in the Spring and then waned, but never left completely. There was always the danger it would return, and it had. Thomas considered demanding every cart man remove his peaked hood so he could ensure Ramon did not hide beneath, but a lethargy filled him and he began to wonder if he cared anymore. Unless it was that he was alone again, as he had been when he arrived. Every moment took his friends further away. Every moment stretched into an empty future before he would see them again. He smiled at Lubna's returning sense of fun, smiled at himself for not seeing it when she first came to his house. She had been an assistant then, a servant to her sister Helena, who still shared his roof and his bed. It had been so long ago, with so many deaths between then and now, it might have been someone else's life.

Thomas slapped his own face, drawing looks from the people flowing along the main thoroughfare, and firmed his shoulders. There would be time for rest later, after Ramon was caught. Which it did not appear would be today.

In the palace courtyard carts were drawn up on two sides, their beds being loaded with provisions. An enclosed carriage sat ready for horses to be hitched and men moved around, each with a job to do. Thomas started along the corridor, intending to speak with Samuel if he could find him, but a passing servant stopped and told him the Queen wanted him. The Queen wanted him now.

Thomas had been hoping to catch up on some sleep before he was called for, but knew the request could not be ignored. In the royal quarters more servants carried trunks through the rooms, no doubt destined for one of the carts outside.

Fernando stared out of a window toward the gardens. When Thomas went to his side he saw three peacocks displaying.

"There must be a lesson in those birds," said Fernando. "All that beauty and they make such terrible eating. I would prefer a more modest appearance and a tastier meat." He glanced at Thomas. "What have you done with your day? Did you speak with Mandana? When he asked for you he did not sound angry. Have the pair of you made your peace? It would please us both, for we are becoming used to your presence."

"I should have visited Isabel by now."

"She is expecting you in the next room. A servant came to say you were on your way."

Thomas turned, surprised when Fernando stayed where he was.

Isabel sat at a desk reading papers, but set them aside when she saw Thomas and rose to her feet. She came and stood before him, looking up, her eyes tracking his face. Thomas reached out and touched her neck, feeling the strong, slow beat of her heart.

"What is all the loading of carts?" He asked. "Are you leaving?"

"We are all leaving, Thomas. Events have changed. The

pestilence grows more gruesome by the day and Fernando insists we leave Sevilla for somewhere safer."

"There is no escaping the plague."

"You have."

"As have you. And I did not escape it. I fell ill as a boy but recovered. I believe it is that which protects me now. And keeping myself clean. Plague is spread by dirt, I am sure."

"Then I will also keep myself clean."

"And away from your subjects."

"That I cannot promise."

"Where do you go?"

"North, where it is cooler."

"It will be cooler in Sevilla in a few months."

"Where we feel safer, then. You have an answer for me?"

Thomas looked toward the window, wanting to say one thing, knowing he must say another. "You will have me until your child is delivered safe."

Isabel smiled. "So, the rest of the year?"

"Yes. You can have the balance of the year. Then I must return to my family."

"Or they to you."

Thomas frowned. "Lubna is banned from your presence, and it is she I will be with more than anyone else."

"I may have been hasty, Thomas. I apologise. My reaction was... intemperate, and foolish. I have sought advice and been assured the loss of a child in one woman cannot be transmitted to another. Is she still in the city?"

"They left this morning," Thomas said.

"But could be caught up with?"

The idea was tempting, but Thomas wanted Lubna away from Sevilla and this Catholic King and Queen as much as the Queen wanted to leave Sevilla behind. Three months. He could manage three months alone. And he still had unfinished business.

"When does your party depart?"

"In the morning."

"A man continues to walk these streets, and I would see him behind bars before I leave."

"You have tonight then, Thomas, for when we go you come with us, whether he is caught or not. I have sent a note telling Mandana the man is to be captured if he shows his face in the castle. I can do no more."

"My thanks, your grace." It was not enough, but Thomas knew he could not say so.

Isabel made a moue of distaste but let his use of formality pass on this occasion.

I walk on egg shells, Thomas thought, one moment best friend to this couple, the next a vassal to be ordered at their whim. It was the way of power, he knew, glad he had never had such bestowed upon him.

CHAPTER FORTY-SIX

Had Thomas ridden alone he could have gone north from the city and reached their destination of Alcala de Henares within a week, but of course he could not. Instead he travelled in the company of a train of carts and coaches which would take a circuitous route so that the population of towns and cities might witness the glory of their rulers.

For the first two days Thomas roamed several miles in advance, following the ridges and high ground, his head turned south to where the mighty Guadalquivir was a constant companion. His eyes tracked the undulating land beyond the river in search of another party of travellers. There had been a time or two he thought he could make something out, but there was no certainty. Plumes of dust marked where horses rode, but distance made individuals impossible to see. The only evidence was the dust hanging in the air, drifting east in a steady wind. By the third day he knew Lubna and the others would be half way to their destination and fell back to ride among the others, Martin de Alarcón and Fernando, at least a hundred soldiers and half that number of priests, many regaled in red robes. Thomas had hoped to leave the Inquisition behind, but it appeared at least a goodly portion of the Inquisition had decided to travel with them, no doubt sure that wickedness existed throughout Spain. Each evening he ate in the tent erected for Isabel and Fernando, ensuring that the rigours of the journey were not too much for her, before unrolling his own bedsheet and staring up at the sky until sleep came as a blessed relief from his misery. Samuel accompanied the party but was rarely seen, there only as insurance should something befall Thomas.

On the fourth night, half a day from Qurtuba where they would stay a week, Theresa came to him. She drew back his blanket and slipped beneath. When Thomas startled awake with her hands already on him he pushed her away, discovered her nakedness and recoiled.

"Get out!"

"I know you want me."

"Go to Martin, he is a man who might welcome your advances, for I do not."

"I do not love Martin."

"You do not love me. God's teeth, you will be with your husband tomorrow."

"Which is why I am here tonight. I may never have the chance again. Once, Thomas, once is all I ask." Her hands grew busy again, tugging at the ties on his clothing, and he rolled away and stalked into the darkness. In the morning she glanced at him from within her coach, a knowing smile on her face.

On the third night after their arrival in Qurtuba, as he slept in the room assigned him in the palace, she came to him again, but this time she had no designs on his body.

"There is something you have to see," she said, leaning over him, fully dressed this time.

"What hour is it?"

"It will soon be dawn, but this cannot wait."

Thomas washed hands across his face. "Turn your back, then."

Theresa laughed but did as requested. Thomas dressed quickly, and it was only as he pulled on his boots he saw the darkened glass of the window created a perfect mirror where Theresa had been able to watch the entire proceedings.

"Is it far?"

"It is within the cathedral."

So not far then. The city was familiar to Thomas from his visit three years before, and it was a matter of moments to cross to the cathedral that was a mosque in all but name. Theresa said nothing as she walked beside him, which was unusual enough in itself to draw his notice. Not that conversation was easy. The cacophony of the wooden water mills straddling the rapids of the Guadalquivir was loud in the growing light of the coming dawn. They would normally be stilled overnight if the Queen was in residence, but on this occasion she had not been expected.

"Along here," said Theresa, as they entered the vast space, stone columns rising to form a confusion of perspective. She led the way to a small side chapel, brighter than the rest of the interior, and Thomas saw why he had been called for and cursed, punching his fist against the wall. He should have known when he was called in the small hours, for that was the time Ramon struck.

"It is him, isn't it?" said Theresa.

"It can be no other." He went to the table – no, not table, an altar that had been dragged in here – and leaned over the pair of bodies. The faint scent of the liquor used to steal their wits still hung above their faces. This time the victims were both female, the first he had seen Ramon take. Was that a sign he had less knowledge of this city, or was he growing more desperate? And how had he obtained a fresh supply of the liquor so soon, or had he always had it hidden away somewhere, ready to be called on?

Thomas touched the neck of one to find it still warm, blood draining from an opening in her flank, but when he felt for a pulse he found none. He checked the other body, expecting nothing different, and was not disappointed.

"I have already checked for signs of life," said Theresa. "I was sent for first, in case they still lived."

"Who came for you?"

"A priest. He acts as night watchman."

"Did he not think to find Samuel? He could confirm the death as surely as me."

"I think he went to him first, but he was away from his room, so then he came to me, and I to you. It is you would be called in any case if this is the work of the Ghost."

"Where is this night watchman?"

"In the sacristy at the far end of the cathedral."

Thomas went into the main chamber, looked around.

"That way," said Theresa, pointing. "I assume you want me to take care of the bodies before anyone finds them? Unless you need to study them further?"

"No, I am finished. I know who does this now and their wounds tell us nothing. But see if you can discover who they are, it might offer a clue to where Ramon is hiding."

"Oh, I know who they are. The night watchman recognised both."

Thomas started away through the echoing space, his boot heels loud. The priest was expecting him and came out to meet him part way, a short, plump man with a bald head revealed by a cowl which was thrown back.

"Have you been here all night?" Thomas asked.

"Since midnight mass, yes."

"Did you hear anything?"

The man shook his head. "Nothing. But I may have dozed once or twice."

Thomas pictured Ramon cutting the women, their screams piercing the air. Nobody would be able to doze through that.

"And you are sure you did not leave at any time?"

"I walked to the bridge to stretch my legs. It was quiet and it helps with the boredom."

"You are here in the Cathedral every night?"

A nod. "It is work I can do. I am not a good priest, I have been told, but this task allows me to maintain the cloth. And I help elsewhere."

"Do you walk to the bridge every night?"

"Unless it is raining."

Thomas almost laughed, stifling the sound into a cough. "And when did it last rain? Two, three months since?"

"Something like that."

Three nights, Thomas thought, was the time they had been in Qurtuba. Had Ramon followed their party from Sevilla? Not a difficult task, for their number ensured passage was slow, that same number making them hard to miss. But if he had, Thomas wanted to know why. The man had made his escape and was free to kill anywhere he liked. Why follow the man who knew most about him, who most wanted him captured? And was three nights long enough for Ramon to observe, to choose his victims, to learn when the cathedral would lie abandoned?

"Do you go to the bridge always at the same time?" Thomas said to the night watchman.

"An hour after mass," said the priest. "It is when my eyes begin to grow heavy so I take myself into the fresh air."

"How long were you away?"

"Not long. I walked to the other side of the river, sat on

the stones and listened to the water and those damnable creaking wheels, then walked back. Less than an hour."

More than long enough. And the timing fitted with the evidence.

And that evidence pointed to the certainty Ramon had followed them to Qurtuba. Thomas wondered if one of those dust plumes he observed had been raised by the man's horse. Staying at a distance, watching them as he had been watched in turn.

Which meant any business he had in Sevilla was abandoned, or Sevilla had not been where his business lay. The thought raised a curl of anxiety within Thomas.

He thanked the priest and returned to the small chapel. Theresa had brought soldiers and they were carrying the bodies away.

"Dress them first," Thomas ordered.

"With what?"

Thomas glanced at Theresa. "Anything You can surely find something. They have been violated enough, I will not see them violated further."

The soldiers slunk off with Theresa. Thomas took the time before they returned to examine the bodies one more time. The location of the wounds had changed from those he had seen before, which meant Ramon still sought the location of the soul. How long would he continue the search if left at large? Forever, because he would never discover what he sought. Or would he? Thomas made a promise to talk with Talavera again, to ask if he believed the human soul was a physical object, with a physical location. He was sure the man had said not, but there had been discussions between the two of them. What had Ramon said during those conversations?

Thomas went to the side door and breathed deep of the misted air. A few early risers passed by. They ignored him, but he examined each of their faces, searching for the one he sought, knowing it would not be there. Ramon must know by now Thomas had discovered the bodies. Likely he might even be hidden, watching his handiwork being discovered. Thomas was sure that was how it would be, the man wanting to see the results of his endeavours. Then he would slink away to hide and choose his next victims. A matching pair. One Christian, one not. This time they were both female, and that fact triggered a connection in Thomas's mind. Ramon sought the human soul, which must be assumed to be present in both male and female. But did he believe the soul resided in Christians only? Or both Christian and heathen alike? What was it he searched for, what difference? And if it was a difference why not take a single victim only, not two? Thomas was missing something – the significance of two bodies. They meant something to Ramon, but what? And the logic, if he sought the soul, raised a new notion, that the soul of the highest power in the land might be the strongest soul of all. One more easily identified.

Thomas walked fast across the steep roadway to a small paved area and crossed it, the palace coming into view, tendrils of mist curling around its facade. As he approached a man waiting at the door turned and saw him at the same moment Thomas recognised the man. Friar Ramon Braso, dressed in ordinary clothing, which is why Thomas had ignored him at first. He called out and began to run.

Ramon turned and sprinted toward the river, and Thomas grinned. To cross it Ramon would have to double back to the bridge or flee west along the bank, and Thomas saw he was already gaining. But instead of doing either of these Ramon simply threw himself into the rapids. Thomas reached the bank and skidded to a halt.

Ramon's head appeared, sank again as the fast water carried him toward the thrashing boards of a waterwheel.

Ramon tried to look back to see if he had been followed, but there was no time, the boards almost on him, and he sank beneath the water once again.

Thomas moved along the river bank, running until he was downriver of the waterwheel. He scanned the churning surface, looking for a sign, but none showed. He moved upriver, staring at the boards of the water-wheel as they emerged from a thrashing spume, expecting to see Ramon's broken body delivered up, but in that he was disappointed. Where was the man? Should he fetch guards and have them search the riverbank? Was there any point? And how far would they need to go? The water here was fast. If Ramon had escaped with his life he might be half a mile downstream by now. Thomas turned away, frustrated, and made his way back to the palace.

"That man who was here, what did he want?"

Thomas saw the guard knew at once who he meant. "Didn't like the look of him. Wouldn't show his face, but someone had given him a sound beating. His eyes were all that showed, and they were black."

"Yes, they would be. What did he want?"

"He had a message for the Queen, but I wouldn't take it, not at first. I wasn't going to leave my post, not with the likes of him about." The guard looked Thomas up and down, unsure of what he saw but a hint of recognition must have come. "Do you know who he was, sir?"

"I do. What happened to the letter?"

"When I wouldn't take it he lost his temper. Tried to force his way past me. Me! I don't let anyone pass me."

"Good man. The note?"

The guard shook his head. "I told you, I wouldn't take it. The Queen has many petitioners, but they must go through the right channels, not come calling to the gate at dawn."

Thomas clapped the man on the shoulder, for a moment making him flinch. "Which way did he go when he left you?"

"That way." A raised hand. "Around the side of the palace toward the river. He'll be across the bridge by now, long gone."

"Gone, anyway," Thomas said. He thanked the guard and walked slowly along the path Ramon would have taken, head down, eyes searching. It was likely he had taken the note with him to his death, but Thomas had learned never to make assumptions based on what he believed to be true. He had been wrong too many times in the past. As he was this time.

The letter fluttered in a grating, a rising breeze holding it there, but not so strong as to press it through the metal rails. Ramon must have fled with it clutched in his hand and lost hold of it in his haste. Thomas went to one knee and retrieved it, broke the seal, which was no more than an unmarked daub of white wax from a tallow candle.

The writing inside has been made rapidly, scrawled letters almost falling off the page, but their message was clear enough.

Your grace, forgive me for contacting you in such a way, but I have grave news of a danger to yourself. The man known as Samuel Ibrahim has been conducting wicked experiments on your subjects and I fear he plans to make you his next victim. Meet me at the cathedral entrance in an hour and I will provide clear proof.

There was no signature, and in places the ink had been smeared, almost making some words indecipherable. But there was no need for every one to be clear. This was the work of a madman even to think it would be taken seriously. A madman who was now almost certainly dead.

CHAPTER FORTY-SEVEN

"I don't understand," said Isabel, when she eventually returned from the Cathedral, her devotions taking precedence over everything else. At least she had allowed Thomas the comfort of taking extra guards as she walked the short distance. Until a body was found he would remain alert. Men had been sent along the river bank to look for Ramon. They had been gone two hours without sending any message, which he considered a bad sign.

Isabel and Fernando sat at a table, platters of fruit, cheeses and meat laid out. The children were somewhere close but had been despatched when Thomas said he needed to discuss a serious matter.

"I believe Ramon truly thought you would respond to his request." Thomas sat when Isabel waved a hand in invitation, adjusting his thoughts to accommodate what appeared to be one of their informal meetings.

"He must be dead," said Fernando around a mouthful of pigeon, its juices staining his beard. "We need worry about him no more."

"I won't believe it until I see his body with my own eyes," Thomas said. "He is strong and insane, a combination that keeps men alive who should not be. I am more interested in why he wants Isabel." Thomas watched carefully to ensure he had read the signals right and the use of the Queen's name was allowed.

"Does he intend to plead for mercy?" Isabel laughed, a pretty sound. Her fingers hovered over the plates before selecting a fig. She examined it, returned the fruit and selected something else. "He must know there is no mercy after what he has done. Unless he is even more mad than you say and truly thinks I might believe his wild claims about Samuel. Eat, Thomas, there is more than enough for three."

Indeed there was. Enough for six, and he was ravenous. He tore a piece from a shank of lamb and tried not to wolf it down too fast.

"We should send for Samuel and see what he has to say about the accusation. Ramon is mad enough, it's true, but this is too simple a ruse unless his mind has descended into an even deeper lunacy. But a kernel of logic remains. He is searching for the physical location of the human soul, and I believe it likely Samuel knows something of where his obsession came from."

Isabel waved a hand. "Yes, you might need to question Samuel, I agree, but we do not want him with us here spoiling our meal. Find him later if you must. I spoke with Talavera on the matter. He said you had also discussed it with him. He is of a mind the soul cannot be found in one place. It is of the spirit, not the flesh, and departs on death to rise to heaven or sink to hell. This Ramon was a friend to him at one time, was he not? Why would he not share the same belief?"

"Do all Christians share a common orthodoxy?" Thomas

said. "And this matter is not one that can be decided by the reading of a passage of the Bible."

"You know your Bible so well, do you, Thomas?" A smile from Isabel.

"As a child I could have quoted any passage." Ignoring the fact he was no longer a child and had not so much as glanced at the book in over thirty years. He recalled the struggle to learn the Latin words in the heavy book that sat on a lectern in Lemster Priory, the book that Brother Bernard had insisted he study in exchange for other knowledge, access to knowledge of more interest to Thomas than the words of a God even then he was starting to lose faith in. A God that had abandoned him when he was accused of murder.

"Talavera is my spiritual advisor," said Isabel. "Which is why I seek his advice in matters he is better suited to know about. His beliefs are based on what is written by God's hand. There is no other truth than what is writ there, as we all of us know."

"And Talavera claims there is no physical soul in the body," Thomas said, which was also his true opinion, but he felt no need to mention he did not believe in any soul at all. "But what matters most is what Ramon believes. He is convinced the soul is an object he can uncover. Talavera told me Ramon looks on him as a father. That they would sit at night by a fire and discuss matters of theology, including that of the soul." Thomas stared into space for a moment before glancing at Isabel. "Talavera may not be telling you every-thing, have you considered that? If Ramon looks on him as a father I am sure Talavera looks on Ramon as a son. Can a father betray the trust of his son, even when he knows he is misguided?"

"This is more than misguided, Thomas. And Talavera would not keep such a secret from me, his Queen."

"If you are sure." Thomas knew he could force the matter only so far, his relationship with this woman one of shifting tides and sands, never knowing from one moment to the next how she would react, how much leeway he was allowed. "I will find Samuel and talk to him. He studied in Malaka alongside Samuel and may know of something there that formed the kernel for his obsession?"

"I have not seen Samuel since we left Sevilla," said Fernando. "Are you sure he accompanied us?"

"He is with our party, yes, but has had no call to deal with Isabel. But you will see enough of him once the child is born and I leave." Thomas did not want to say that Samuel was deliberately ignoring him.

He saw Isabel open her mouth to speak, then saw too the effort of will she made to remain silent. It was an argument they would have at a later time, he knew, one that would come as sure as night followed day.

"Then ask him," said Fernando. "If Ramon showed signs then Samuel would have seen them. I do not know him well, but have been told he is a skilled physician, and not a stupid man."

"Neither is Ramon. I worry he has evaded us and is still intent on harming the Queen."

"You work too hard and worry too much, Thomas," said Isabel. "I have soldiers around me constantly. The man will not be allowed near even if he does live."

"He does not want to come to you, Isabel, he wants you to go to him."

"Then he is a fool. How could he possibly think I would do such a thing?" She wiped her hands in a damp linen cloth and laid it on the table.

"Why not me?" said Fernando, almost sulky. "Am I not also God's representative on earth?"

"Do you claim the greater devotion?" Thomas said. "I do not doubt your belief, but the entire population looks to the Queen for religious example."

"Who would he take alongside me?" asked Isabel, leaning forward, her fingertips together.

"A non-believer, no doubt, as he has in the past. He needs two subjects to prove only true Christians possess a soul. I believe he always starts with the one he considers a believer in the hope he will discover the seat of the soul. The other victim is then only for confirmation. He would search and find nothing."

Isabel steepled her fingers, staring at Thomas over the tips of them. "I spoke long with Talavera in search of the truth, but as in so much about our Lord truth is often in the individual's mind and faith. Perhaps if a man truly believes enough that the human soul is a physical object then, for him, it will be. Others they will never see it."

"And you, Isabel, what do you believe?" Thomas leaned forward in unconscious mirroring of her, Fernando forgotten. It might have been only the two of them in the room.

"I believe we can never know. God's mystery will always remain that, a mystery to us all, to me, to Talavera, even to you, Thomas, who seems able to out tease the truth of a matter where no-one else can." She smiled. "Perhaps he intends you as his second victim." Her lips held a smile but her eyes were sharp as they continued to examine him, and he wondered how much he might have revealed of his true self to this woman who also saw through every subterfuge.

"He would not take Thomas," said Fernando, breaking the spell between the two of them. "Why would he? There are a thousand in this city he would take first."

Isabel sat up, smoothing her dress as if it had been creased. "If Ramon is not dead we will discuss this further, but I do not believe he lives. The river has taken him and will deliver his bones to the sea." She winced and sighed. "I am tired, Thomas, even though I have only recently come from my bedchamber. Talk with Fernando, make plans if you must, for men love to plan. Let me know when they find the man dead. We have only two more days in Cordoba and then we travel north."

By noon soldiers were returning without finding any sign of Ramon. Thomas wanted to walk the banks of the Guadalquivir himself to make sure, but made himself resist the call. He had to trust others to carry out their jobs with skill. He could not do everything himself.

Thomas went in search of Samuel, sure he must have noticed some sign in Ramon when they were in Malaka, for they had been closer than brothers for a time. He failed to find him but did come across Theresa holding one of Isabel's heavily braided dresses against her breast. She looked up at the sound of Thomas's approach, but instead of showing surprise or guilt she smiled as if between conspirators.

"You are making a habit of stealing the Queen's dresses, it seems," Thomas said.

"Not stealing, borrowing. Not even that. You could regard it as keeping them supple." She held the dress out to him. "Here, feel the material, it is stiff with disuse. It needs the warmth of a body to loosen the cloth. Perhaps you can help dress me in her robes, Thomas? I would need to be naked first, of course." Theresa smiled. "Then I can come to you dressed as the Queen. If I come to your room you would not refuse me then, would you? We can pretend I am she. You would enjoy that, would you not, even if you are married to Lubna now? It would be such a grand game."

Thomas shook his head. "Put it away."

"I will do anything you ask, Thomas, you know that."

"Stop it," he said.

"Only one thing can make me stop, and you know what that is. You should give in. You will enjoy the experience, I promise."

Another shake of his head. "Have you not been to your husband? You should take your frustrations out on him, not me."

"He is old," said Theresa.

"So am I."

"Not as old. And you are not old here." She tapped his brow. "Or–" But Thomas caught her hand as it descended and turned away, leaving Theresa to her dreams.

Fernando was in the gardens practicing his sword craft with two of his men, the clash of blades sharp, light splintering from metal. Thomas stood and watched for a while, relieved to be distracted from his thoughts. There was still no sign of Ramon, and he was coming to the conclusion the man must have survived his trip down the river. How was a miracle, but miracles happened even to evil men, it seemed. If he still lived it was only a matter of waiting for a new approach from him. Thomas was convinced he was right. The next target would be Isabel. There was no other way Ramon could prove his theories other than cutting into the highest power in the land. He would see the death of his Queen as a price worth paying for the knowledge it provided.

Fernando paused to catch his breath and saw Thomas, beckoned him over.

"Should we spar again, Thomas, like we did before?"

"When you beat me, your grace?" Formality restored in front of the soldiers.

"As I recall it was a draw."

"Only because you took mercy on me."

Fernando laughed. "What about these men, then? They are too scared of hurting me to try hard, but I am sure they would love to kill you."

"You make it sound most appealing, your grace."

"Come on, amuse me, show me how good you really are, Thomas Berrington." Fernando glanced at the two men. "You will try to kill him?"

"If you ask it, your grace."

Thomas had no wish to fight the men but a thrum of tension ran through him and he thought some hard exercise might purge it.

"You are not allowed to kill them, Thomas, understood?"

"Should I stand on one leg as well? Or would that still make it too easy?" He glanced at the men. "Are they any good?"

"That you will find out." Fernando held his sword out. It was a fine weapon, and as Thomas took it he saw the sign of Daniel Olmos on the blade.

"If they do kill me, will you send news to my family?"

Fernando laughed. "Of course. I might even make you a Duque to honour your memory."

"That makes it almost worth the losing, your grace."

Thomas turned and moved fast, sending the sword of one soldier spinning out of his hand before blocking a panicked blow from the other. He stepped back and pointed to the sword lying on the grass, waiting until the man retrieved it, waiting until they were ready this time, then grinned as they came at him side by side. Too obvious.

He disarmed both then waited once more.

"Try," Fernando ordered his men. "You make it too easy for him. I will not punish you if you kill him."

Thomas shook his head, deflecting a sudden blow from

the right. This time they spread out, coming from either side so he had to parry and thrust in opposite directions. They were also trying harder, perhaps not hard enough to kill him, but more than before. Thomas knew he could take them both any time he wanted, but had no wish to harm either man.

As he fought everything else faded from his mind, as he had hoped. There was only combat, the clash of steel, the flash of blades and the eyes of the men pitted against him. Surety flooded his body, filling him with a cold fire, bringing a harsh arousal with it and he was grateful Theresa was not waiting for him because he knew he might be unable to restrain himself if she were.

Sweat stung his eyes and he shook it away.

His arm began to ache, but he knew the men were tiring also, and faster than him, just as he knew he could end this at any time, but the joy of battle was on him and he did not want it to stop. He recalled the first time he had discovered this gift, for gift it was, one that had kept him alive a hundred times or more. It was not something he deserved or worked to obtain, merely something given him at birth. The first time he had fought and killed a man Thomas had been thirteen years old and his own life had almost been forfeit. The man had wanted his boots. His father's boots. They were too big for Thomas but he wore them anyway, and the man had demanded them. He had been a soldier too, wandering France after the Battle of Castillon which had brought defeat to the English and death to John Berrington. The battle that had orphaned Thomas. The soldier had companions, but no more than a half dozen. They sat and watched the fight, calling out encouragement to their man, then a huge cry when Thomas's blade took him through the belly. The man sank to his knees, hands trying to stem the blood that pulsed from the wound to pool on the ground. It wasn't the first time Thomas had experienced the cold fire that took over his body, but it was the first time he had killed a man. He glanced at the companions, preparing to kill them all if he had to, but they made no move.

"Finish him," one said. "He'll last a day in agony if you don't."

Thomas looked at the soldier, who tried to shuffle backwards, and knew it was the truth, so he pushed his sword down through the man's shoulder to pierce his heart. That was when he had joined the small company of men. He thought they took him in as some kind of mascot, little knowing that within a year he would be their leader, and their number would have grown to a score, and that their band would ravage the land south of the Garonne river.

A glint of sunlight on steel brought Thomas back to the present and he realised he had been fighting without thought, thrusting and parrying in a dream. The memory, almost as real as the day he experienced it, disgusted him. He had tried over the years to leave the Thomas Berrington of that time behind, to expunge his memory entirely, and all it took was a stupid fight to bring it rushing back. He had done things no man could be proud of. The only pride he took was that he had turned his back on that life and chosen a better path.

Anger at himself filled him and he attacked hard, disarming both men and throwing their swords as far as he could.

As the killing lust drained from him he heard clapping and turned to see Isabel and Theresa standing side by side on the balcony. Fernando too was applauding.

"Huzzah, Thomas. Damn me, if I had a hundred like you I could end this war tomorrow."

Thomas smiled as he handed the sword back to Fernando. "You forget I fight for the other side, your grace."

Fernando let out an enormous laugh and clapped Thomas on the back, laid his arm over his shoulder.

"But afterward, Thomas, you and I will rule the world. Alongside our wives, of course."

"Of course."

CHAPTER FORTY-EIGHT

The palace was as silent as it ever grew when the King and Queen were present, a distant background hum of work carried out in kitchens and workrooms, the occasional footsteps of a servant. Thomas passed an occasional guard as he made his way through the corridors. He had finally found Samuel in his rooms and asked his questions only for Samuel to shake his head.

"He showed nothing, Thomas. I have already told you, he was the best surgeon I have ever seen. Better than me, better even than you. He was as rational as any man I have ever known. He picked up knowledge like an urchin picks up a spilled coin, without thought or effort. If there was any sign of insanity I did not see it. Or there was none then."

Thomas had pressed, searching for some tiny clue, but Samuel was adamant. If Ramon was mad, his madness had developed much later.

"Besides," Samuel had said, "he is dead, isn't he?"

"Not yet. Or not yet that I know. And until I know it he is not dead."

He had left Samuel to his studies, but instead of returning

to his own room in the eastern wing of the palace his feet took him as though of their own accord toward Isabel's chambers. Except he knew Isabel was only an excuse.

He did not understand the emotion roiling through him. Did not want to understand it. He had been in almost this exact same situation before and only an attack by Mandana had stopped what would have felt like betrayal. And if that had been betrayal what would it be now? Except... even as his legs carried him he shook his head, trying to believe the excuses he conjured.

He needed to ask Theresa if the Queen was well, concerned about her condition.

He needed to berate Theresa for her constant teasing when she knew nothing could come of it.

He needed to see Theresa.

Dressed as the Queen.

He tried to think of those he loved, of where Jorge, Olaf and Lubna would be by now. Home, no doubt, Lubna and Will returned to the house on the Albayzin with its view of al-Hamra. Olaf in his spartan rooms alongside the barracks, Fatima pleased at his return. And Helena would be in the house on the Alkazaba that had been gifted to Thomas but in which he had spent only a single night. A night burned in his memory with guilt and joy, for Will had been the result of his weakness. At least Lubna had not yet shared his bed then, but it barely mattered, for Thomas knew he had sinned in his mind. He knew he was a man of many imperfections and weakness, and there were times he wondered exactly what Lubna found to love in him.

Nothing. Not tonight. Perhaps not ever again.

He stopped at the end of a corridor and leaned on the stone cill of a window, breathing hard of the cool night air that drifted in. A tremor ran through him, of fear, of lust, of shame.

When he looked up a cry escaped his lips. Across the dark courtyard another window offered a view into a candlelit chamber. At first he thought he was looking at Isabel, except Isabel would never dress herself, and the body that was slowly being hidden beneath a gold-threaded gown showed no sign of carrying a child, and he knew it was Theresa who stood there, half revealed as she drew the dress to her shoulders and reached back to tie the tiny clips to close it. Her hair was piled atop her head in copy of the Queen. They were the same height, the same build, and it was only because he had seen her with the dress earlier he could be sure who he watched. The thought of what would happen if he continued made his legs weak.

Then he saw a figure appear. At first he took it for Fernando and it struck him that it was not beyond the King to take Theresa dressed as his wife. But this figure was too tall and all at once Thomas knew who it was as the man raised a grey hood and slipped it over Theresa's head.

Thomas ran, careening through corridors too fast for safety.

When he reached the chamber it was empty, but the acrid-sweet scent of the liquor hung heavy in the air. His flight had alerted guards, and the guards in turn had alerted Fernando, who came crashing into the room with a sword in his hand.

"Jesu's scars, Thomas, what are you doing? I thought he had returned."

"He has, and taken Theresa in mistake for Isabel."

"How could he? They are nothing alike."

"They are when Theresa is wearing one of Isabel's robes." He turned and started away, but Fernando grasped his arm.

"Don't walk away from me."

Thomas jerked himself free. "Then come with me. He is out there with Theresa and will have somewhere safe to take her. Are you willing for him to kill another victim? Someone you know?"

Outside he turned and surveyed the dark city. The river lay at the foot of the slope. Two inns in a small square were pulling down their shutters.

"How can he have escaped us?" said Fernando. "How, Thomas? He is meant to be dead!"

"Be quiet, I am thinking."

Fernando grabbed his arm again and turned Thomas around. "Thinking? Thinking? There's been too much fucking thinking and not enough action. *Where is he!*"

Thomas ignored the King of Castile, Aragon and Spain, and once more turned away.

He closed his eyes.

Was Ramon a friend of Abbot Mandana after all?

Qurtuba had been Mandana's base when he started to kill three years before, and Thomas had tracked his deeds through the city, learning the alleys and roadways as well as he knew those of Gharnatah.

Ramon would have a place. A safe place prepared, ready with a table and instruments and ties for his victims. The first would already be waiting there. Theresa might also be there now, being stripped and tied down. It might be too late. Except Ramon had started on the other woman first last time, the unbeliever, rushed, true, but keeping the main prize until last. He would do the same again. Thomas prayed he would do the same again.

He closed his eyes, drawing alleys in his mind.

Where?

And then it came to him, the only possibility, and he wondered if the keys to the Church of San Bartolomu still hung in the same place in the house Lawrence had once lived in, perhaps even lived in again. It was the place where Mandana had taken his victims after they had been prepared.

The place where Jorge and his lover Esperanza had been held before the final parade of Semana Santa.

Thomas opened his eyes and looked at Fernando. "I think I know where he has taken her.

The house where Lawrence had once lived lay abandoned, as did other houses around the small square, just as they did in Ixbilya. The ravening pestilence was no respecter of position or godliness. Thomas found the keys where they had always hung and took them to the carved door. When he unlocked it and pushed nothing happened. The door had been barred from the inside.

Fernando had come and he called up his men and they began to hammer at the door, but Thomas knew it would take hours to break it down. There was another way, though, one Lawrence had shown him years ago, and he went back to the house and along a narrow corridor to what had once been a library but was now a bare room.

A narrow door was set at the far end, offering an alternative entrance to the Church. This door too was locked, but there was a key for it hanging from a hook where it had always been. Thomas turned it, making no effort to keep the noise down. He could hear the sound of hammering from where Fernando's soldiers continued to batter at the main door, and whoever lay inside would not hear the small sound he made

Thomas pushed, relieved that the killer had not known of this other entrance.

He stepped through, at first believing he was wrong, that this was not the place, as total darkness greeted him. The sound of the soldiers hammering on the door filled the narrow space, making thought almost impossible. Then a light flared and a lamp was drawn up to swing on the end of a cord. By the faint illumination Thomas made out a hunched figure, two more showing pale in the swaying light. Both women. Both naked. One paler than the other. Both still alive. The killer had not started his work yet, only now completing preparations. Thomas watched him check the knots on makeshift ties torn from a length of cloth.

He started forward, going faster when he saw the tall figure unroll instruments and select a narrow blade. The man hovered over the darker skinned woman, then moved, his impatience for an answer driving him to start with Theresa. As he laid one hand against the side of her breast to judge the first cut Thomas sprinted.

He hit Ramon hard, grabbed his hair and smashed his face down onto the table. Not making the same mistake as before Thomas pulled at the bindings holding Theresa and wrapped them around Ramon's hands while he still clutched them to his face. He tried to fight back but Thomas was stronger and got both hands cinched tight in front before taking more cloth and binding his feet. Only then did he return to the table to free Theresa.

She sat up, arms covering her breasts. Thomas smiled at the show of modesty after the number of times she had offered herself to him, but even he saw the situation was different now.

"Where did he put your clothes?"

Theresa nodded, still too shocked to talk. Thomas found the ornate robes and brought them back, turned away as she dressed. He worked on the bindings of the other woman and helped her sit. She made no effort to cover herself and Thomas experienced a sudden recognition. He had seen the woman before, three years earlier, in a brothel when he was searching for a missing girl. He tried to summon up the name. It evaded him, but he was sure it was the same girl.

He went to her discarded clothing and returned with a pale robe.

"I know you," she said, still uncovered, making no effort to hide herself.

"And I know you. When did he take you?"

"A few hours since. He came and offered twice my usual rate and like a fool I took him upstairs. I should have known there was something wrong by how fast he finished. He must have given me something because I woke up tied to this table. What did he want with us?" She glanced at Theresa, her modesty restored.

"Nothing you want to hear about."

Thomas went to the main doors and worked the thick oak bars free, stepped back fast as they flew inward followed by half a dozen men and Fernando, who showed puzzlement at first but recovered quickly.

"Where is he?"

"Over there," Thomas said, not bothering to turn, not wanting to look at the man again.

"Where?"

"There!" Now Thomas did turn. He knew the interior of the church was dim, but was Fernando a fool? Which is when he discovered it was he who was the fool. Ramon had been left in a corner, hands and feet bound, but a single length of cloth lay on the stone floor.

"He can't have escaped," said Fernando. "There is nowhere to go."

"I came in by another door," Thomas said, moving fast to where it remained open. He passed through, out of the small house and into the courtyard. When he reached the square soldiers continued to mill about. "Did he come this way?"

"Did who come this way?" One of the soldiers, his tunic marking him as an officer of some kind.

"Ramon! Did he come this way?"

"It is the middle of the night. We haven't seen a soul."

Thomas turned. He had to still be inside somewhere. He started back toward the church, making for the main doors this time, when a shout brought him to a halt. Men were pointing at the domed roof of the church, and Thomas craned his neck to follow their hands.

A tall figure stood on the edge of the roof where a lead gutter offered scant footing. He had freed his legs and hands and walked with arms extended. Thomas tracked the edge of the roof and saw that if he managed to get to the corner it might be possible to leap to the roof of the adjoining house, and from there attempt an escape.

"I want men over there," he shouted, pulling at the soldier nearest him.

"Who are you to give us orders?"

Thomas cursed, but was saved by Fernando who strode from the church and turned to look up as Ramon almost lost his footing. He was over half way to where he could attempt the leap.

"Do as he says," said Fernando. "His orders are as good as mine." He came to stand beside Thomas. "He can't get away this time, can he?"

"Not unless he has wings under that robe and can fly."

"Maybe he has. He's escaped us enough times before. Not that I blame you. Madmen have a subtle logic that allows them to confound mere mortals." Fernando looked up to where the figure was edging along the gutter. No more than a dozen paces now. "I don't suppose there's any point in sending someone up after him?"

"And lose one of our own? No, I think not." Thomas tried to judge the distance the man would have to leap. Too far or not? He had the advantage of height, but that meant he would be falling, too. Did that make the feat easier or more difficult? Thomas could not tell.

"He has to decide now," said Fernando. Around him his men had fallen silent, transfixed by the man who now stood on the meeting of two roofs. He looked down at them as if seeking an alternative way, but there was none short of him descending the way he had come up, and that was no option. But neither was the leap. There were men surrounding all escape routes now.

"We have him," said Fernando, slapping Thomas on the back.

A voice called out and boots sounded loud on the cobbles as a soldier ran across to them and stopped in front of the King.

"Your grace, we have found the man you seek."

Fernando grasped the man's shoulders. "What are you talking about? The man we seek is up there. Look, you can see him for yourself!"

The soldier frowned. "The man you asked us to search for is over a mile downstream of here, your grace. The body is broken but we are sure it is him."

Fernando frowned. "Make sense man, that is impossible."

"The priest, your grace. Ramon Braso. His body is discovered."

Thomas turned away, some new certainty settling through him. He stared up at the figure on the precipice. Tall, like Ramon, skeletal, like Ramon, but the description fitted another man equally as well. A swell of dread rose in him as recognition came, at the thought of the danger Isabel had been placed in. Thomas filled his lungs ready to call out, which was the moment the figure steeled himself and threw his body into empty space, trusting his God to perform a miracle.

He might have made it had his robe not snagged on the gutter and pulled him up short a few scant feet from the roof he was attempting to reach. He yelled, a curse more than a scream, and then he fell.

Thomas didn't see him land, but he heard it, a wet sound that augured bad news. Or good news, more like.

He discovered Samuel lying on his back. Blood ran from beneath his skull like an opened tap, but he was still alive. His eyes scanned the dark night sky as if searching for something and failing to find it.

Thomas knelt beside him, surprised when Samuel clutched at his robe and pulled him close. His other hand rose and there was a flash of light against sharp steel. Thomas reared back, falling on his side as the blade slashed through the air where a moment before his neck had been. Samuel was like a bug it was impossible to kill, however hard you stamped on it. Except, this time there could be no escape. His life was draining from him as Thomas regained his knees and reached for the wrist. He twisted the blade free, then checked for other weapons before leaning over Samuel again.

"Was it Mandana put you up to it?" he said, but Samuel only chuckled, a smile on his lips.

"Oh no, this was all my own idea. A visionary works alone."

Thomas didn't believe him. He considered lifting the man, shaking him until he obtained a confession, but there was not enough time. And then Samuel spoke for the last time.

"Look, I see it now! My soul ascends to heaven. Can you see it, Thomas Berrington? It is a thread of silver." His hand rose, clutching at something, and for a moment Thomas believed he saw it too, exactly as Samuel said, a thread of light rising from the centre of his body. Then it was gone, if it had ever been there, and his body stilled. Thomas checked for a pulse but knew he would find none.

He reached out to close the man's eyes but Fernando said, "No. Let him see the fires of hell burn for ever."

Thomas withdrew, tension draining from his body to be replaced by exhaustion.

"So it ends," said Fernando, helping Thomas to his feet.

"Does it? Was Samuel the architect of this or only a tool?"

"You fear without cause, Thomas. You see the hand of Mandana behind everything. Why? What would it gain him? He has been taken back inside the fold and would not dare risk his position a second time. Come, we must tell Isabel the good news." Another slap on the back. "And you and I deserve wine, rich wine to drown our aches and pains. You in particular, for you have run down another killer of men." Fernando shook his head. "Truly, you are death itself, Thomas Berrington, there is no escape from you. Remind me to never cross you."

But Thomas was thinking of Samuel's last moments. Of that thread of silver, and the more he thought of it the more he believed perhaps there *had* been some truth behind the man's madness after all. And if there was a grain of truth then all men of all religions and races possessed that soul, for Samuel had only worn the religion of Spain as a mantle over his true self.

Thomas wanted wine, but took a bottle to his own room, seeking solitude. He needed to know what he had missed, and how. Had Samuel been so clever, or he so stupid? He realised it must have started in Malaka when the two men attended the infirmary together. Perhaps Ramon had spoken of his conversations with Talavera, their talk of the soul and whether it existed or not. Had Samuel started the work long before, or only recently? Thomas knew he would discover the answer if he chose to return to Ixbilya, but knew he would not do so. It did not matter now. The man was dead. He had corrupted Ramon, not the other way around, and used the man's mental fragility to draw him into his own obsession.

Samuel's access to Triana made sense now. It would be he, not Ramon who could go anywhere he wished. And that night when they freed Belia, Samuel had been encouraging Ramon, not watching him. And it had been Samuel who had freed Ramon from the dungeon. Had they both gone to al-Haquim's house to remove all trace of evidence, or had Samuel done so alone?

Thomas poured the last of the wine into a goblet and drank it down in a single swallow. He had been misled the entire time because he had liked Samuel, had trusted him. He started to mutter a vow never to trust anyone again, then stopped. Living life that way was impossible.

As sleep drew him into its embrace he thought of what Fernando and others had said. Was death truly his companion? His friend? Thomas shivered, and then darkness engulfed him.

CHAPTER FORTY-NINE

Theresa emerged from the room where Isabel lay in labour. "She bleeds again, and the child is not coming. I fear we will lose one or the other, if not both."

"I cannot," Thomas said. "You know I cannot. It is not seemly for me to attend the Queen."

"Oh, it is all well and good in your fabled al-Andalus but not here? You told me how you helped women of the harem during childbirth. Help your Queen now!"

Thomas considered it wise not to point out that Isabel was not his Queen. The depth of winter had arrived and with it came flurries of snow on the courtyard outside. This castle in the heart of Spain reminded Thomas of why he had no longing to return to England. The days were short and the air too cold for bones accustomed to the south. As the months had passed Isabel had grown heavier, and Fernando had found frequent excuses to go hunting. Thomas sat with Isabel and they talked, of Spain and England, and what the future might hold for all of them. And now there might be no future for Isabel if Thomas did nothing.

"Cover her, then," he said, "so she cannot see me, nor I

her." He turned aside and ran to his room to fetch instruments, praying they would not be needed, but better to have them than not. If it came to cutting at least one life would be lost. When he returned he went directly into the room, the copper scent of blood in the air.

"Is that Thomas?"

He glanced at Theresa, but she merely lifted her shoulder and shook her head. Not my doing.

"It is, your grace."

A chuckle that changed to a groan. "I believe we may be passed beyond formality here, Thomas. Do your worst, or best, but I have a request of you."

He moved so he could see Isabel. Her face was pale, sweat standing out on it. He had heard she was stoic during childbirth, but this was not normal. The infant she carried that Thomas had saved once now stood on the brink of another precipice.

"I know it is bad," said Isabel. "I sense it. If it comes to a choice between myself and my child, you are to save me, Thomas. Do you understand?"

He nodded. The request came as no surprise. To another the instruction might appear selfish, but he saw it for what it was. For a mother to choose herself over her child was a hard decision, but Spain needed a strong Queen more than it needed another prince or princess.

"I will do all I can."

"I know you will." A grimace as fresh pain lanced through her. "I am glad it is you who is here." For a moment she clutched at his hand. "Now do your work and we will never mention your presence at my bedside again."

Thomas moved to where Isabel could not see him. He glanced at Theresa, the other women in the room almost invisible to him. They fussed with water and rags. One held Isabel's hand on one side when she bore down, another on the other side. A third wiped her brow with a cloth wrapped around chunks of ice hacked from the courtyard outside.

"Tell me what to do," said Theresa.

"Clean her as best you can. Let me see the damage, if any." He stared at what he was not allowed to see, but his personal feelings had shut down and this was professional, nothing more. He let his breath go in a rush. "It might not be possible to save both."

"Then get the baby out fast. Don't think about saving it."

"You heard what she said?" Thomas said.

"And she is right. Spain needs a strong Queen, now more than ever." Her eyes sought his, a challenge in them. "Unless you would rather see her die."

Thomas rose and went to the narrow table laid beneath the window. An array of instruments of birthing lay there, as fearsome as the torture irons in Castillo de Triana. His hand hovered over one, another, settled on a third. He saw Theresa's eyes follow the device as he sat on a low stool and decided how to start.

The baby's head showed, already distorted from passing through the birth channel, but that was nothing unusual.

"Good, at least it's the right way around," Thomas said.

"It is, but too large. She is a delicate woman."

"She has had difficulties before?"

"She has, but she is brave, and pain means nothing to her, even now."

The woman he was trying to save had made hardly any noise the entire time, and Thomas offered a sharp nod.

"Take care when I start. If the bleeding worsens I may have to stop, but I intend this to be fast, and it will not be pretty. Be ready with the cloths. We have one chance only."

He turned his wrist, easing the leather hook alongside the baby's head. He closed his eyes, projecting all sensation along his fingers and into the hook. He turned it, drew back.

Cursed and tried again, this time catching the hook between the child's legs. This was, he knew, more than likely the single hope of saving both of them. He had other instruments but they were destructive, and the child would die.

"Use your hand beneath the skull to protect it," he said to Theresa.

"Do we warn her?"

"Say nothing. On the next contraction I will apply force. There will be one chance only, so be ready."

Thomas waited, closing his eyes again. He felt a movement and sensed Isabel tense.

"Now!"

He pulled, harder than someone watching would believe possible, and as Isabel bore down Theresa used her hands to cradle the baby's head. Thomas put a foot against the bed and pulled even harder and in a shower of fluid and blood the baby came in a rush. Theresa cradled the infant while Thomas cut the cord, then she wrapped it in linen and carried it to the side.

"Give it to one of the others," Thomas barked. "I need you here."

Theresa handed the child across and returned.

"Wet cloths, clean her up. I think I'm going to have to stitch some of this and cauterise. She's losing too much blood. As fast as you can."

Thomas went to a small brazier he had hoped not to use. It already contained grey charcoal and an iron rod rested in it. Thomas blew, bringing the rod to red heat, then held one end in a leather glove and returned. Theresa had done a good job of cleaning Isabel, and Thomas leaned against her shoulder, the two of them working in concert as he drew back muscle and dabbed at the worst flow of blood with the rod. Isabel jerked and breath hissed between her teeth, but still she did not cry out. Thomas continued, and after a while he knew Isabel had fainted away and worked faster still before she came around.

It took little time, but a time that stretched to infinity, before he sat back and dropped the rod to the floor where a remnant of heat burned a mark in the wood.

"It is done?" said Theresa.

"It is done," Thomas said. "She will recover or not, but I have done all I can, and I believe she will recover. The child?"

"It lives. Did you not hear it bawling?"

Thomas smiled and shook his head. "A boy, as you predicted?"

"Another girl. The Queen is good at carrying girls."

"This is more than likely the last child she will carry." Thomas drew away, stood, his head spinning for a moment, then he looked down on the Queen of Castile, her face pale but all strain gone for the moment. "There will be pain when she wakes. I will give you a list of herbs. Find what you can and I will show you how to make a salve, and a pill to ease her." He glanced at the table where his instruments were laid out. "Have someone clean those well. Make sure they are thorough."

Thomas walked out into the courtyard where snow had been cleared into piles around the edges, walked through to a small practice yard where the sound of metal on metal told him the way. Already he was thinking of the journey south, once Isabel was fully recovered. Thinking of his family. Of Gharnatah. Of the scant few remaining years of peace before his world was dashed away by this man and woman who had made him their friend. And he wondered, now that Samuel was dead, would she let him go?

Fernando saw him at once but finished his practice before stopping and coming across.

"A girl," Thomas said.

Fernando nodded. "A shame, but I like girls well enough. And Isabel?"

"It was a difficult birth, but she will recover."

"God willing," said Fernando, and Thomas nodded.

"Yes. God willing. Do you have a name yet?"

Fernando smiled. "Isabel had a name for each, whether it be boy or girl. She will be called Catherine after her grandmother."

"My mother was named Catherine," Thomas said. "But I only ever heard my father call her Cat."

"Is she alive?" asked Fernando.

"Taken by the pestilence before I left England."

"It is the scourge of this earth. You are the man to ask, Thomas, can nothing be done against it? Nothing at all?"

"There is less in al-Andalus, so my recommendation is to wash more often, your grace." He flinched when Fernando punched him on the shoulder, but the King was grinning, and without warning pulled Thomas into an embrace.

"Thank you, Thomas Berrington, for what you have done for Spain this day." He released him, but only after embracing him far longer than was seemly. "Do you not want to know what Isabel would have chosen if it had been a boy?"

"But it was not. Catherine is a good name. A strong name." He looked up and saw Fernando grinning, shook his head. "Then it's lucky it is a girl, isn't it? That would have been a stupid name for a Prince."

HISTORICAL NOTE

I have taken some liberties with the timing of events during the year 1485 when *The Inquisitor* is set, mainly to include the city of Sevilla as a setting, but also because some events overlap with the previous book. It was in Sevilla that the Inquisition reached its more barbarous heights, and here that the exquisite palace of the Real Alcazar can be found. In my telling of events Isabel and Fernando return to Sevilla after the defeat of Ronda, which was told in *The Incubus*.

In reality they left Sevilla in March 1485 because of an outbreak of the Plague, which was less prevalent in Spain than northern latitudes, but still to be greatly feared.

My telling of the story and the facts begin to coincide once more with the Queen's journey to Jaen to continue planning the war against the Moors, and of course from there north to Alcala de Real where Katherine of Aragon was born on the 15th or 16th of December 1485. Katherine was indeed the last child Isabel bore, but certainly not for the reasons I have given in the book.

The Moorish name for Sevilla was Ixbilya, which looks strange until you write it phonetically: Isbilya, and remember that a v in Spanish is generally pronounced the same as a b in English.

The home of the Inquisition in Sevilla was the Castello de San Jorge, but a few centuries before it was also known as Castello de Triana, and the Triana neighbourhood still exists to this day south of the Guadalquivir. Although I considered using the more modern name of the Inquisition's home, Jorge would not allow me. He wanted no connection to such a place, even if it was only the sharing of a name.

As is usual in the chronicles of Thomas Berrington I have taken liberties with facts where they are not concisely documented. Perhaps the biggest liberty this time is for Thomas to assist at the birth of Katherine. It is unthinkable that a man would be allowed access to the birthing chamber in those days, but as always Thomas infiltrates himself into many places he should not be.

At several points in the text I use the Swedish word *Morfar*, which translates as grandfather, but more literally mother's father, which is who Olaf Torvaldsson is to William Berrington. For those who are curious, the father's father is *Farfar*. My thanks to our Swedish neighbour and her sons for teaching me this when talking to the boys' grandmother and grandfather on their visits to the UK.

As before I offer thanks to the Viking Sisters Gee and Trish who regaled me with information about how Viking warriors were trained from a young age in the use of shield and axe. I only hope I have done them justice. If not, I suspect I am in trouble at our next meeting in Harrogate.

The decoration Lubna undergoes prior to her wedding, her henna night, goes back to early Islamic times and is a common ritual in that religion. It involves the decoration of hands, feet and other parts of the body using intricate designs etched with henna dye. Although there is no direct link, some casual references indicate this may be the source of our current "hen night" in the UK.

The Inquisitor brings us to the half way point in the story of Thomas Berrington. In Book 6, *The Fortunate Dead*, set in 1487, Thomas and Lubna move to Malaga to continue her education. But, as always, nothing is ever simple.

Expect *The Fortunate Dead* to appear in late 2018, with book 7, *A Darkness Fallen*, to follow soon after.

REFERENCES

There is much confusion and misunderstanding about the Spanish Inquisition, not all of it the fault of Monty Python's Flying Circus. While traditionally the Inquisition has been seen as a ruthless and cruel operation in the main it was in fact a force for order. However, when my book is set it is shortly after new individuals came to the fore, among them Tomas de Torquemada, appointed chief Inquisitor by Queen Isabel herself. For a period of around ten years the Inquisition did become a force of evil, but primarily caused by greed rather than religious zeal. The period 1482-92 was a turmoil in Spain. Al-Andalus was slowly being eroded, and Spain was stretching the muscles it would use to conquer swathes of South America as well as large areas to the West of North America too. One only has to look at the names of many towns and cities in California to realise this. Los Angeles, San Fransisco, San Louis Obispo - open up Google maps of the western United States and you will see who originally conquered these lands.

The Spanish Inquisition, a Historical Revision, Henry Kamen. Yale University Press, 4th Edition, 2014. ISBN: 9780300180510.

Dogs of God, Columbus, the Inquisition and the Defeat of the Moors, James Reston Jr. Doubleday, 2005. ISBN: 0385505484.

ABOUT THE AUTHOR

David Penny published 4 novels in the 1970's before being seduced by a steady salary. He has now returned to his true love of writing with the first 5 books in a planned 10 book series of historical mysteries set in Moorish Spain at the end of the 15ᵗʰ Century. He is currently working on the sixth book in the series.

Find out more about David Penny
www.davidpennywriting.com

Lightning Source UK Ltd.
Milton Keynes UK
UKHW010652170520
363344UK00003B/970